Eugene Aram, Complete

by Baron Edward Bulwer Lytton

Copyright © 9/8/2015
Jefferson Publication

ISBN-13: 978-1517266516

Printed in the United States of America

All rights reserved. No part of this book may be reprinted or reproduced or utilized in any form or by any electronic, mechanical, or other means, now known or hereafter invented, including photocopying and recording, or in any form of storage or retrieval system, without prior permission in writing from the publisher.'

Contents

- BOOK I. 4
  - CHAPTER I. 4
  - CHAPTER II. 6
  - CHAPTER III. 10
  - CHAPTER IV. 14
  - CHAPTER V. 15
  - CHAPTER VI. 18
  - CHAPTER VII. 21
  - CHAPTER VIII. 26
  - CHAPTER IX. 27
  - CHAPTER X. 30
  - CHAPTER XI. 33
  - CHAPTER XII. 38
- BOOK II. 41
  - CHAPTER I. 41
  - CHAPTER II. 42
  - CHAPTER III. 43
  - CHAPTER IV. 45
  - CHAPTER V. 49
  - CHAPTER VI. 52
  - CHAPTER VII. 54
  - CHAPTER VIII. 57
- BOOK III. 61
  - CHAPTER I. 61
  - CHAPTER II. 63
  - CHAPTER III. 66
  - CHAPTER IV. 70
  - CHAPTER V. 71
  - CHAPTER VI. 74
  - CHAPTER VII. 76
- BOOK IV. 81
  - CHAPTER I. 81
  - CHAPTER II. 84
  - CHAPTER III. 87
  - CHAPTER IV. 90
  - CHAPTER V. 94
  - CHAPTER VI. 96
  - CHAPTER VII. 98
  - CHAPTER VIII. 99
  - CHAPTER IX. 101
  - CHAPTER X. 104

CHAPTER XI.	109
BOOK V.	113
CHAPTER I.	113
CHAPTER II.	115
CHAPTER III.	119
CHAPTER IV.	124
CHAPTER V.	127
CHAPTER VI.	131
CHAPTER VII.	133
CHAPTER VIII.	139

BOOK I.

CHAPTER I.

```
THE VILLAGE.—ITS INHABITANTS.—AN OLD MANORHOUSE: AND AN ENGLISH
   FAMILY; THEIR HISTORY, INVOLVING A MYSTERIOUS EVENT.
```

"Protected by the divinity they adored, supported by the earth which they cultivated, and at peace with themselves, they enjoyed the sweets of life, without dreading or desiring dissolution." Numa Pompilius.

In the country of—there is a sequestered hamlet, which I have often sought occasion to pass, and which I have never left without a certain reluctance and regret. It is not only (though this has a remarkable spell over my imagination) that it is the sanctuary, as it were, of a story which appears to me of a singular and fearful interest; but the scene itself is one which requires no legend to arrest the traveller's attention. I know not in any part of the world, which it has been my lot to visit, a landscape so entirely lovely and picturesque, as that which on every side of the village I speak of, you may survey. The hamlet to which I shall here give the name of Grassdale, is situated in a valley, which for about the length of a mile winds among gardens and orchards, laden with fruit, between two chains of gentle and fertile hills.

Here, singly or in pairs, are scattered cottages, which bespeak a comfort and a rural luxury, less often than our poets have described the characteristics of the English peasantry. It has been observed, and there is a world of homely, ay, and of legislative knowledge in the observation, that wherever you see a flower in a cottage garden, or a bird-cage at the window, you may feel sure that the cottagers are better and wiser than their neighbours; and such humble tokens of attention to something beyond the sterile labour of life, were (we must now revert to the past,) to be remarked in almost every one of the lowly abodes at Grassdale. The jasmine here, there the vine clustered over the threshold, not so wildly as to testify negligence; but rather to sweeten the air than to exclude it from the inmates. Each of the cottages possessed at its rear its plot of ground, apportioned to the more useful and nutritious product of nature; while the greater part of them fenced also from the unfrequented road a little spot for the lupin, the sweet pea, or the many tribes of the English rose. And it is not unworthy of remark, that the bees came in greater clusters to Grassdale than to any other part of that rich and cultivated district. A small piece of waste land, which was intersected by a brook, fringed with ozier and dwarf and fantastic pollards, afforded pasture for a few cows, and the only carrier's solitary horse. The stream itself was of no ignoble repute among the gentle craft of the Angle, the brotherhood whom our associations defend in the spite of our mercy; and this repute drew welcome and periodical itinerants to the village, who furnished it with its scanty news of the great world without, and maintained in a decorous custom the little and single hostelry of the place. Not that Peter Dealtry, the proprietor of the "Spotted Dog," was altogether contented to subsist upon the gains of his hospitable profession; he joined thereto the light cares of a small farm, held under a wealthy and an easy landlord; and being moreover honoured with the dignity of clerk to the parish, he was deemed by his neighbours a person of no small accomplishment, and no insignificant distinction. He was a little, dry, thin man, of a turn rather sentimental than jocose; a memory well stored with fag-ends of psalms, and hymns which, being less familiar than the psalms to the ears of the villagers, were more than suspected to be his own composition; often gave a poetic and semi-religious colouring to his conversation, which accorded rather with his dignity in the church, than his post at the Spotted Dog. Yet he disliked not his joke, though it was subtle and delicate of nature; nor did he disdain to bear companionship over his own liquor, with guests less gifted and refined.

In the centre of the village you chanced upon a cottage which had been lately white-washed, where a certain preciseness in the owner might be detected in the clipped hedge, and the exact and newly mended style by which you approached the habitation; herein dwelt the beau and bachelor of the village, somewhat antiquated it is true, but still an object of great attention and some hope to the elder damsels in the vicinity, and of a respectful popularity, that did not however prohibit a joke, to the younger part of the sisterhood. Jacob Bunting, so was this gentleman called, had been for many years in the king's service, in which he had risen to the rank of corporal, and had saved and pinched together a certain small independence upon which he now rented his cottage and enjoyed his leisure. He had seen a good deal of the world, and profited in shrewdness by his experience; he had rubbed off, however, all superfluous devotion as he rubbed off his prejudices, and though he drank more often than any one else with the landlord of the Spotted Dog, he also quarrelled with him the oftenest, and testified the least forbearance at the publican's segments of psalmody. Jacob was a tall, comely, and perpendicular personage; his threadbare coat was scrupulously brushed, and his hair punctiliously plastered at the sides into two stiff obstinate-looking curls, and at the top into what he was pleased to call a feather, though it was much more like a tile. His conversation had in it something peculiar; generally it assumed a quick, short, abrupt turn, that, retrenching all superfluities of pronoun and conjunction, and marching at once upon the meaning of the sentence, had in it a military and Spartan significance, which betrayed how difficult it often is for a man to forget that he has been a corporal. Occasionally indeed, for where but in farces is the phraseology of the humorist always the same? he escaped into a more enlarged and christianlike method of dealing with the king's English, but that was chiefly noticeable, when from conversation he launched himself into lecture, a luxury the worthy soldier loved greatly to indulge, for much had he seen and somewhat had he reflected; and valuing himself, which was odd in a corporal, more on his knowledge of the world than his knowledge even of war, he rarely missed any occasion of edifying a patient listener with the result of his observations.

After you had sauntered by the veteran's door, beside which you generally, if the evening were fine, or he was not drinking with neighbour Dealtry—or taking his tea with gossip this or master that—or teaching some emulous urchins the broadsword exercise—or snaring trout in the stream—or, in short, otherwise engaged; beside which, I say, you not unfrequently beheld him sitting on a rude bench, and enjoying with half-shut eyes, crossed legs, but still unindulgently erect posture, the luxury of his pipe; you ventured over a little wooden bridge; beneath which, clear and shallow, ran the rivulet we have before honorably mentioned; and a walk of a few minutes brought you to a moderately sized and old-fashioned mansion—the manor-house of the parish. It stood at the very foot of the hill; behind, a rich, ancient, and hanging wood, brought into relief—the exceeding freshness and verdure of the patch of green meadow immediately in front. On one side, the garden was bounded by the village churchyard, with its simple mounds, and its few scattered and humble tombs. The church was of great antiquity; and it was only in one point of view that you caught more than a glimpse of its grey tower and graceful spire, so thickly and so darkly grouped the yew tree and the larch around the edifice. Opposite the gate by which you gained the house, the view was not extended, but rich with wood and pasture, backed by a hill, which; less verdant than its fellows, was covered with sheep: while you saw hard by the rivulet darkening and stealing away; till your sight, though not your ear, lost it among the woodland.

Trained up the embrowned paling on either side of the gate, were bushes of rustic fruit, and fruit and flowers (through plots of which green and winding alleys had been cut with no untasteful hand) testified by their thriving and healthful looks, the care bestowed upon them. The main boasts of the garden were, on one side, a huge horse-chesnut tree—the largest in the village; and on the other, an arbour covered without with honeysuckles, and tapestried within by moss. The house, a grey and quaint building of the time of James I. with stone copings and gable roof, could scarcely in these days have been deemed a fitting residence for the lord of the manor. Nearly the whole of the centre was occupied by the hall, in which the meals of the family were commonly held—only two other sitting-rooms of very moderate dimensions had been reserved by the architect for the convenience or ostentation of the proprietor. An ample porch jutted from the main building, and this was covered with ivy, as the windows were with jasmine and honeysuckle; while seats were ranged inside the porch covered with many a rude initial and long-past date.

The owner of this mansion bore the name of Rowland Lester. His forefathers, without pretending to high antiquity of family, had held the dignity of squires of Grassdale for some two centuries; and Rowland Lester was perhaps the first of the race who had stirred above fifty miles from the house in which each successive lord had received his birth, or the green churchyard in which was yet chronicled his death. The present proprietor was a man of cultivated tastes; and abilities, naturally not much above mediocrity, had been improved by travel as well as study. Himself and one younger brother had been early left masters of their fate and their several portions. The younger, Geoffrey, testified a roving and dissipated turn. Bold, licentious, extravagant, unprincipled,—his career soon outstripped the slender fortunes of a cadet in the family of a country squire. He was early thrown into difficulties, but, by some means or other they never seemed to overwhelm him; an unexpected turn—a lucky adventure—presented itself at the very moment when Fortune appeared the most utterly to have deserted him.

Among these more propitious fluctuations in the tide of affairs, was, at about the age of forty, a sudden marriage with a young lady of what might be termed (for Geoffrey Lester's rank of life, and the rational expenses of that day) a very competent and respectable fortune. Unhappily, however, the lady was neither handsome in feature nor gentle in temper; and, after a few years of quarrel and contest, the faithless husband, one bright morning, having collected in his proper person whatever remained of their fortune, absconded from the conjugal hearth without either warning or farewell. He left nothing to his wife but his house, his debts, and his only child, a son. From that time to the present little had been known, though much had been conjectured, concerning the deserter. For the first few years they traced, however, so far of his fate as to learn that he had been seen once in India; and that previously he had been met in England by a relation, under the disguise of assumed names: a proof that whatever his occupations, they could scarcely be very respectable. But, of late, nothing whatsoever relating to the wanderer had transpired. By some he was imagined dead; by most he was forgotten. Those more immediately connected with him—his brother in especial, cherished a secret belief, that wherever Geoffrey Lester should chance to alight, the manner of alighting would (to use the significant and homely metaphor) be always on his legs; and coupling the wonted luck of the scapegrace with the fact of his having been seen in India, Rowland, in his heart, not only hoped, but fully expected, that the lost one would, some day or other, return home laden with the spoils of the East, and eager to shower upon his relatives, in recompense of long desertion,

"With richest hand... barbaric pearl and gold."

But we must return to the forsaken spouse.—Left in this abrupt destitution and distress, Mrs. Lester had only the resource of applying to her brother-in-law, whom indeed the fugitive had before seized many opportunities of not leaving wholly unprepared for such an application. Rowland promptly and generously obeyed the summons: he took the child and the wife to his own home,—he freed the latter from the persecution of all legal claimants,—and, after selling such effects as remained, he devoted the whole proceeds to the forsaken family, without regarding his own expenses on their behalf, ill as he was able to afford the luxury of that self-neglect. The wife did not long need the asylum of his hearth,—she, poor lady, died of a slow fever produced by irritation and disappointment, a few months after Geoffrey's desertion. She had no need to recommend her children to their kindhearted uncle's care. And now we must glance over the elder brother's domestic fortunes.

In Rowland, the wild dispositions of his brother were so far tamed, that they assumed only the character of a buoyant temper and a gay spirit. He had strong principles as well as warm feelings, and a fine and resolute sense of honour utterly impervious to attack. It was impossible to be in his company an hour and not see that he was a man to be respected. It was equally impossible to live with him a week and not see that he was a man to be beloved. He also had married, and about a year after that era in the life of his brother, but not for the same advantage of fortune. He had formed an attachment to the portionlesss daughter of a man in his own neighbourhood and of his own rank. He wooed and won her, and for a few years he enjoyed that greatest happiness which the world is capable of bestowing—the society and the love of one in whom we could wish for no change, and beyond whom we have no desire. But what Evil cannot corrupt Fate seldom spares. A few months after the birth of a second daughter the young wife of Rowland Lester died. It was to a widowed hearth that the wife and child of his brother came for shelter. Rowland was a man of an affectionate and warm heart: if the blow did not crush, at least it changed him. Naturally of a cheerful and ardent disposition, his mood now became soberized and sedate. He shrunk from the rural gaieties and companionship he had before courted and enlivened, and, for the first time in his life, the mourner felt the holiness of solitude. As his nephew and his motherless daughters grew up, they gave an object to his seclusion and a relief to his reflections. He found a pure and unfailing delight in watching the growth of their young minds, and guiding their differing dispositions; and, as time at length enabled the to return his affection, and appreciate his cares, he became once more sensible that he had a HOME.

The elder of his daughters, Madeline, at the time our story opens, had attained the age of eighteen. She was the beauty and the boast of the whole country. Above the ordinary height, her figure was richly and exquisitely formed. So translucently pure and soft was her complexion, that it might have seemed the token of delicate health, but for the dewy and exceeding redness of her lips, and the freshness of teeth whiter than pearls. Her eyes of a deep blue, wore a thoughtful and serene expression, and her forehead, higher and broader than it usually is in women, gave promise of a certain nobleness of intellect, and added dignity, but a feminine dignity, to the more tender characteristics of her beauty. And indeed, the peculiar tone of Madeline's mind fulfilled the indication of her features, and was eminently thoughtful and high-wrought. She had early testified a remarkable love for study, and not only a desire for knowledge, but a veneration for those who possessed it. The remote corner of the county in which they lived, and the rarely broken seclusion which Lester habitually preserved from the intercourse of their few and scattered neighbours, had naturally cast each member of the little circle upon his or her own resources. An accident, some five years ago, had confined Madeline for several weeks or rather months to the house; and as the old hall possessed a very respectable share of books, she had then matured and confirmed that love to reading and reflection, which she had at a yet earlier period prematurely evinced. The woman's tendency to romance naturally tinctured her meditations, and thus, while they dignified, they also softened her mind. Her sister Ellinor, younger by two years, was of a character equally gentle, but less elevated. She looked up to her sister as a superior being. She felt pride without a shadow of envy, at her superior and surpassing beauty; and was unconsciously guided in her pursuits and predilections, by a mind she cheerfully acknowledged to be loftier than her own. And yet Ellinor had also her pretensions to personal loveliness, and pretensions perhaps that would be less reluctantly acknowledged by her own sex than those of her sister. The sunlight of a happy and innocent heart sparkled on her face, and gave a beam it gladdened you to behold, to her quick hazel eye, and a smile that broke out from a thousand dimples. She did not possess the height of Madeline, and though not so slender as to be curtailed of the roundness and feminine luxuriance of beauty, her shape was slighter, feebler, and less rich in its symmetry than her sister's. And this the tendency of the physical frame to require elsewhere support, nor to feel secure of strength, influenced perhaps her mind, and made love, and the dependence of love, more necessary to her than to the thoughtful and lofty Madeline. The latter might pass through life, and never see the one to whom her heart could give itself away. But every village might possess a hero whom the imagination of Ellinor could clothe with unreal graces, and to whom the lovingness of her disposition might bias her affections. Both, however, eminently possessed that earnestness and purity of heart, which would have made them, perhaps in an equal degree, constant and devoted to the object of an attachment, once formed, in defiance of change and to the brink of death.

Their cousin Walter, Geoffrey Lester's son, was now in his twenty-first year; tall and strong of person, and with a face, if not regularly handsome, striking enough to be generally deemed so. High-spirited, bold, fiery, impatient; jealous of the affections of those he loved; cheerful to outward seeming, but restless, fond of change, and subject to the melancholy and pining mood common to young and ardent minds: such was the character of Walter Lester. The estates of Lester were settled in the male line, and devolved therefore upon him. Yet there were moments when he keenly felt his orphan and deserted situation; and sighed to think, that while his father perhaps yet lived, he was a dependent for affection, if not for maintenance, on the kindness of others. This reflection sometimes gave an air of sullenness or petulance to his character, that did not really belong to it. For what in the world makes a man of just pride appear so unamiable as the sense of dependence?

CHAPTER II.

A PUBLICAN, A SINNER, AND A STRANGER

"Ah, Don Alphonso, is it you? Agreeable accident! Chance presents you to my eyes where you were least expected." Gil Blas.

It was an evening in the beginning of summer, and Peter Dealtry and the ci-devant Corporal sate beneath the sign of The Spotted Dog (as it hung motionless from the bough of a friendly elm), quaffing a cup of boon companionship. The reader will imagine the two men very different from each other in form and aspect; the one short, dry, fragile, and betraying a love of ease in his unbuttoned vest, and a certain lolling, see-sawing method of balancing his body upon his chair; the other, erect and solemn, and as steady on his seat as if he were nailed to it. It was a fine, tranquil balmy evening; the sun had just set, and the clouds still retained the rosy tints which they had caught from his parting ray. Here and there, at scattered intervals, you might see the cottages peeping from the trees around them; or mark the smoke that rose from their roofs—roofs green with mosses and house-leek,—in graceful and spiral curls against the clear soft air. It was an English scene, and the two men, the dog at their feet, (for Peter Dealtry favoured a wirey stone-coloured cur, which he called a terrier,) and just at the door of the little inn, two old gossips, loitering on the threshold in familiar chat with the landlady, in cap and kerchief,—all together made a groupe equally English, and somewhat picturesque, though homely enough, in effect.

"Well, now," said Peter Dealtry, as he pushed the brown jug towards the Corporal, "this is what I call pleasant; it puts me in mind—"

"Of what?" quoth the Corporal.

"Of those nice lines in the hymn, Master Bunting.

```
'How fair ye are, ye little hills,
  Ye little fields also;
Ye murmuring streams that sweetly run;
  Ye willows in a row!'
```

"There is something very comfortable in sacred verses, Master Bunting; but you're a scoffer."

"Psha, man!" said the Corporal, throwing out his right leg and leaning back, with his eyes half-shut, and his chin protruded, as he took an unusually long inhalation from his pipe; "Psha, man!—send verses to the right-about—fit for girls going to school of a Sunday; full-grown men more up to snuff. I've seen the world, Master Dealtry;—the world, and be damned to you!—augh!"

"Fie, neighbour, fie! What's the good of profaneness, evil speaking and slandering?—

```
'Oaths are the debts your spendthrift soul must pay;
  All scores are chalked against the reckoning day.'
Just wait a bit, neighbour; wait till I light my pipe."
```

"Tell you what," said the Corporal, after he had communicated from his own pipe the friendly flame to his comrade's; "tell you what—talk nonsense; the commander-in-chief's no Martinet—if we're all right in action, he'll wink at a slip word or two. Come, no humbug—hold jaw. D'ye think God would sooner have snivelling fellow like you in his regiment, than a man like me, clean limbed, straight as a dart, six feet one without his shoes!—baugh!"

This notion of the Corporal's, by which he would have likened the dominion of Heaven to the King of Prussia's body-guard, and only admitted the elect on account of their inches, so tickled mine host's fancy, that he leaned back in his chair, and indulged in a long, dry, obstreperous cachinnation. This irreverence mightily displeased the Corporal. He looked at the little man very sourly, and said in his least smooth accentuation:—

"What—devil—cackling at?—always grin, grin, grin—giggle, giggle, giggle—psha!"

"Why really, neighbour," said Peter, composing himself, "you must let a man laugh now and then."

"Man!" said the Corporal; "man's a noble animal! Man's a musquet, primed, loaded, ready to supply a friend or kill a foe—charge not to be wasted on every tom-tit. But you! not a musquet, but a cracker! noisy, harmless,—can't touch you, but off you go, whizz, pop, bang in one's face!—baugh!"

"Well!" said the good-humoured landlord, "I should think Master Aram, the great scholar who lives down the vale yonder, a man quite after your own heart. He is grave enough to suit you. He does not laugh very easily, I fancy."

"After my heart? Stoops like a bow!"

"Indeed he does look on the ground as he walks; when I think, I do the same. But what a marvellous man it is! I hear, that he reads the Psalms in Hebrew. He's very affable and meek-like for such a scholard."

"Tell you what. Seen the world, Master Dealtry, and know a thing or two. Your shy dog is always a deep one. Give me a man who looks me in the face as he would a cannon!"

"Or a lass," said Peter knowingly.

The grim Corporal smiled.

"Talking of lasses," said the soldier, re-filling his pipe, "what creature Miss Lester is! Such eyes!—such nose! Fit for a colonel, by God! ay, or a major-general!"

"For my part, I think Miss Ellinor almost as handsome; not so grand-like, but more lovesome!"

"Nice little thing!" said the Corporal, condescendingly. "But, zooks! whom have we here?"

This last question was applied to a man who was slowly turning from the road towards the inn. The stranger, for such he was, was stout, thick-set, and of middle height. His dress was not without pretension to a rank higher than the lowest; but it was threadbare and worn, and soiled with dust and travel. His appearance was by no means prepossessing; small sunken eyes of a light hazel and a restless and rather fierce expression, a thick flat nose, high cheekbones, a large bony jaw, from which the flesh receded, and a bull throat indicative of great strength, constituted his claims to personal attraction. The stately Corporal, without moving, kept a vigilant and suspicious eye upon the new comer, muttering to Peter,—"Customer for you; rum customer too—by Gad!"

The stranger now reached the little table, and halting short, took up the brown jug, without ceremony or preface, and emptied it at a draught.

The Corporal stared—the Corporal frowned; but before—for he was somewhat slow of speech—he had time to vent his displeasure, the stranger, wiping his mouth across his sleeve, said, in rather a civil and apologetic tone,

"I beg pardon, gentlemen. I have had a long march of it, and very tired I am."

"Humph! march," said the Corporal a little appeased, "Not in his Majesty's service—eh?"

"Not now," answered the Traveller; then, turning round to Dealtry, he said: "Are you landlord here?"

"At your service," said Peter, with the indifference of a man well to do, and not ambitious of halfpence.

"Come, then, quick—budge," said the Traveller, tapping him on the back: "bring more glasses—another jug of the October; and any thing or every thing your larder is able to produce—d'ye hear?"

Peter, by no means pleased with the briskness of this address, eyed the dusty and way-worn pedestrian from head to foot; then, looking over his shoulder towards the door, he said, as he ensconced himself yet more firmly on his seat—

"There's my wife by the door, friend; go, tell her what you want."

"Do you know," said the Traveller, in a slow and measured accent—"Do you know, master Shrivel-face, that I have more than half a mind to break your head for impertinence. You a landlord!—you keep an inn, indeed! Come, Sir, make off, or—"

"Corporal!—Corporal!" cried Peter, retreating hastily from his seat as the brawny Traveller approached menacingly towards him—"You won't see the peace broken. Have a care, friend—have a care I'm clerk to the parish—clerk to the parish, Sir—and I'll indict you for sacrilege."

The wooden features of Bunting relaxed into a sort of grin at the alarm of his friend. He puffed away, without making any reply; meanwhile the Traveller, taking advantage of Peter's hasty abandonment of his cathedrarian accommodation, seized the vacant chair, and drawing it yet closer to the table, flung himself upon it, and placing his hat on the table, wiped his brows with the air of a man about to make himself thoroughly at home.

Peter Dealtry was assuredly a personage of peaceable disposition; but then he had the proper pride of a host and a clerk. His feeling were exceedingly wounded at this cavalier treatment—before the very eyes of his wife too—what an example! He thrust his hands deep into his breeches pockets, and strutting with a ferocious swagger towards the Traveller, he said:—

"Harkye, sirrah! This is not the way folks are treated in this country: and I'd have you to know, that I'm a man what has a brother a constable."

"Well, Sir!"

"Well, Sir, indeed! Well!—Sir, it's not well, by no manner of means; and if you don't pay for the ale you drank, and go quietly about your business, I'll have you put in the stocks for a vagrant."

This, the most menacing speech Peter Dealtry was ever known to deliver, was uttered with so much spirit, that the Corporal, who had hitherto preserved silence—for he was too strict a disciplinarian to thrust himself unnecessarily into brawls,—turned approvingly round, and nodding as well as his stock would suffer him at the indignant Peter, he said: "Well done! 'fegs—you've a soul, man!—a soul fit for the forty-second! augh!—A soul above the inches of five feet two!"

There was something bitter and sneering in the Traveller's aspect as he now, regarding Dealtry, repeated—

"Vagrant—humph! And pray what is a vagrant?"

"What is a vagrant?" echoed Peter, a little puzzled.

"Yes! answer me that."

"Why, a vagrant is a man what wanders, and what has no money."

"Truly," said the stranger smiling, but the smile by no means improved his physiognomy, "an excellent definition, but one which, I will convince you, does not apply to me." So saying, he drew from his pocket a handful of silver coins, and, throwing them on the table, added: "Come, let's have no more of this. You see I can pay for what I order; and now, do recollect that I am a weary and hungry man."

No sooner did Peter behold the money, than a sudden placidity stole over his ruffled spirit:—nay, a certain benevolent commiseration for the fatigue and wants of the Traveller replaced at once, and as by a spell, the angry feelings that had previously roused him.

"Weary and hungry," said he; "why did not you say that before? That would have been quite enough for Peter Dealtry. Thank God! I am a man what can feel for my neighbours. I have bowels—yes, I have bowels. Weary and hungry!—you shall be served in an instant. I may be a little hasty or so, but I'm a good Christian at bottom—ask the Corporal. And what says the Psalmist, Psalm 147?—

```
'By Him, the beasts that loosely range
  With timely food are fed:
He speaks the word—and what He wills
  Is done as soon as said.'"
```

Animating his kindly emotions by this apt quotation, Peter turned to the house. The Corporal now broke silence: the sight of the money had not been without an effect upon him as well as the landlord.

"Warm day, Sir:—your health. Oh! forgot you emptied jug—baugh! You said you were not now in his Majesty's service: beg pardon—were you ever?"

"Why, once I was; many years ago."

"Ah!—and what regiment? I was in the forty-second. Heard of the forty-second? Colonel's name, Dysart; captain's, Trotter; corporal's, Bunting, at your service."

"I am much obliged by your confidence," said the Traveller drily. "I dare say you have seen much service."

"Service! Ah! may well say that;—twenty-three years' hard work: and not the better for it! A man that loves his country is 'titled to a pension—that's my mind!—but the world don't smile upon corporals—augh!"

Here Peter re-appeared with a fresh supply of the October, and an assurance that the cold meat would speedily follow.

"I hope yourself and this gentleman will bear me company," said the Traveller, passing the jug to the Corporal; and in a few moments, so well pleased grew the trio with each other, that the sound of their laughter came loud and frequent to the ears of the good housewife within.

The traveller now seemed to the Corporal and mine host a right jolly, good-humoured fellow. Not, however, that he bore a fair share in the conversation—he rather promoted the hilarity of his new acquaintances than led it. He laughed heartily at Peter's jests, and the Corporal's repartees; and the latter, by degrees, assuming the usual sway he bore in the circle of the village, contrived, before the viands were on the table, to monopolize the whole conversation.

The Traveller found in the repast a new excuse for silence. He ate with a most prodigious and most contagious appetite; and in a few seconds the knife and fork of the Corporal were as busily engaged as if he had only three minutes to spare between a march and a dinner.

"This is a pretty, retired spot," quoth the Traveller, as at length he finished his repast, and threw himself back on his chair—a very pretty spot. Whose neat old-fashioned house was that I passed on the green, with the gable-ends and the flower-plots in front?

"Oh, the Squire's," answered Peter; "Squire Lester's an excellent gentleman."

"A rich man, I should think, for these parts; the best house I have seen for some miles," said the Stranger carelessly.

"Rich—yes, he's well to do; he does not live so as not to have money to lay by."

"Any family?"

"Two daughters and a nephew."

"And the nephew does not ruin him. Happy uncle! Mine was not so lucky," said the Traveller.

"Sad fellows we soldiers in our young days!" observed the Corporal with a wink. "No, Squire Walter's a good young man, a pride to his uncle!"

"So," said the pedestrian, "they are not forced to keep up a large establishment and ruin themselves by a retinue of servants?—Corporal, the jug."

"Nay!" said Peter, "Squire Lester's gate is always open to the poor; but as for shew, he leaves that to my lord at the castle."

"The castle, where's that?"

"About six miles off, you've heard of my Lord—, I'll swear."

"Ah, to be sure, a courtier. But who else lives about here? I mean, who are the principal persons, barring the Corporal and yourself, Mr. Eelpry—I think our friend here calls you."

"Dealtry, Peter Dealtry, Sir, is my name.—Why the most noticeable man, you must know, is a great scholar, a wonderfully learned man; there yonder, you may just catch a glimpse of the tall what-d'ye-call-it he has built out on the top of his house, that he may get nearer to the stars. He has got glasses by which I've heard that you may see the people in the moon walking on their heads; but I can't say as I believe all I hear."

"You are too sensible for that, I'm sure. But this scholar, I suppose, is not very rich; learning does not clothe men now-a-days—eh, Corporal?"

"And why should it? Zounds! can it teach a man how to defend his country? Old England wants soldiers, and be d—d to them! But the man's well enough, I must own, civil, modest—"

"And not by no means a beggar," added Peter; "he gave as much to the poor last winter as the Squire himself."

"Indeed!" said the Stranger, "this scholar is rich then?"

"So, so; neither one nor t'other. But if he were as rich as my lord, he could not be more respected; the greatest folks in the country come in their carriages and four to see him. Lord bless you, there is not a name more talked on in the whole county than Eugene Aram."

"What!" cried the Traveller, his countenance changing as he sprung from his seat; "what!—Aram!—did you say Aram? Great God! how strange!"

Peter, not a little startled by the abruptness and vehemence of his guest, stared at him with open mouth, and even the Corporal took his pipe involuntarily from his lips.

"What!" said the former, "you know him, do you? you've heard of him, eh?"

The Stranger did not reply, he seemed lost in a reverie; he muttered inaudible words between his teeth; now he strode two steps forward, clenching his hands; now smiled grimly; and then returning to his seat, threw himself on it, still in silence. The soldier and the clerk exchanged looks, and now outspake the Corporal.

"Rum tantrums! What the devil, did the man eat your grandmother?"

Roused perhaps by so pertinent and sensible a question, the Stranger lifted his head from his breast, and said with a forced smile, "You have done me, without knowing it, a great kindness, my friend. Eugene Aram was an early and intimate acquaintance of mine: we have not met for many years. I never guessed that he lived in these parts: indeed I did not know where he resided. I am truly glad to think I have lighted upon him thus unexpectedly."

"What! you did not know where he lived? Well! I thought all the world knew that! Why, men from the univarsities have come all the way, merely to look at the spot."

"Very likely," returned the Stranger; "but I am not a learned man myself, and what is celebrity in one set is obscurity in another. Besides, I have never been in this part of the world before!"

Peter was about to reply, when he heard the shrill voice of his wife behind.

"Why don't you rise, Mr. Lazyboots? Where are your eyes? Don't you see the young ladies."

Dealtry's hat was off in an instant,—the stiff Corporal rose like a musquet; the Stranger would have kept his seat, but Dealtry gave him an admonitory tug by the collar; accordingly he rose, muttering a hasty oath, which certainly died on his lips when he saw the cause which had thus constrained him into courtesy.

Through a little gate close by Peter's house Madeline and her sister had just passed on their evening walk, and with the kind familiarity for which they were both noted, they had stopped to salute the landlady of the Spotted Dog, as she now, her labours done, sat by the threshold, within hearing of the convivial group, and plaiting straw. The whole family of Lester were so beloved, that we question whether my Lord himself, as the great nobleman of the place was always called, (as if there were only one lord in the peerage,) would have obtained the same degree of respect that was always lavished upon them.

"Don't let us disturb you, good people," said Ellinor, as they now moved towards the boon companions, when her eye suddenly falling on the Stranger, she stopped short. There was something in his appearance, and especially in the expression of his countenance at that moment, which no one could have marked for the first time without apprehension and distrust: and it was so seldom that, in that retired spot, the young ladies encountered even one unfamiliar face, that the effect the stranger's appearance might have produced on any one, might well be increased for them to a startling and painful degree. The Traveller saw at once the sensation he had created: his brow lowered; and the same unpleasing smile, or rather sneer, that we have noted before, distorted his lip, as he made with affected humility his obeisance.

"How!—a stranger!" said Madeline, sharing, though in a less degree, the feelings of her sister; and then, after a pause, she said, as she glanced over his garb, "not in distress, I hope."

"No, Madam!" said the stranger, "if by distress is meant beggary. I am in all respects perhaps better than I seem."

There was a general titter from the Corporal, my host, and his wife, at the Traveller's semi-jest at his own unprepossessing appearance: but Madeline, a little disconcerted, bowed hastily, and drew her sister away.

"A proud quean!" said the Stranger, as he re-seated himself, and watched the sisters gliding across the green.

All mouths were opened against him immediately. He found it no easy matter to make his peace; and before he had quite done it, he called for his bill, and rose to depart.

"Well!" said he, as he tendered his hand to the Corporal, "we may meet again, and enjoy together some more of your good stories. Meanwhile, which is my way to this—this—this famous scholar's—Ehem?"

"Why," quoth Peter, "you saw the direction in which the young ladies went; you must take the same. Cross the stile you will find at the right—wind along the foot of the hill for about three parts of a mile, and you will then see in the middle of a broad plain, a lonely grey house with a thingumebob at the top; a servatory they call it. That's Master Aram's."

"Thank you."

"And a very pretty walk it is too," said the Dame, "the prettiest hereabouts to my liking, till you get to the house at least; and so the young ladies think, for it's their usual walk every evening!"

"Humph,—then I may meet them."

"Well, and if you do, make yourself look as Christian-like as you can," retorted the hostess.

There was a second grin at the ill-favoured Traveller's expense, amidst which he went his way.

"An odd chap!" said Peter, looking after the sturdy form of the Traveller. "I wonder what he is; he seems well edicated—makes use of good words."

"What sinnifies?" said the Corporal, who felt a sort of fellow-feeling for his new acquaintance's brusquerie of manner;—"what sinnifies what he is. Served his country,—that's enough;—never told me, by the by, his regiment;—set me a talking, and let out nothing himself;— old soldier every inch of him!"

"He can take care of number one," said Peter. "How he emptied the jug; and my stars! what an appetite!"

"Tush," said the Corporal, "hold jaw. Man of the world—man of the world,—that's clear."

CHAPTER III.

A DIALOGUE AND AN ALARM.—A STUDENT'S HOUSE.

"A fellow by the hand of Nature marked,
Quoted, and signed, to do a deed of shame."
—Shakspeare.—King John.

"He is a scholar, if a man may trust
The liberal voice of Fame, in her report.
Myself was once a student, and indeed

```
Fed with the self-same humour he is now."
    —Ben Jonson.—Every Man in his Humour.
```

The two sisters pursued their walk along a scene which might well be favoured by their selection. No sooner had they crossed the stile, than the village seemed vanished into earth; so quiet, so lonely, so far from the evidence of life was the landscape through which they passed. On their right, sloped a green and silent hill, shutting out all view beyond itself, save the deepening and twilight sky; to the left, and immediately along their road lay fragments of stone, covered with moss, or shadowed by wild shrubs, that here and there, gathered into copses, or breaking abruptly away from the rich sod, left frequent spaces through which you caught long vistas of forestland, or the brooklet gliding in a noisy and rocky course, and breaking into a thousand tiny waterfalls, or mimic eddies. So secluded was the scene, and so unwitnessing of cultivation, that you would not have believed that a human habitation could be at hand, and this air of perfect solitude and quiet gave an additional charm to the spot.

"But I assure you," said Ellinor, earnestly continuing a conversation they had begun, "I assure you I was not mistaken, I saw it as plainly as I see you."

"What, in the breast pocket?"

"Yes, as he drew out his handkerchief, I saw the barrel of the pistol quite distinctly."

"Indeed, I think we had better tell my father as soon as we get home; it may be as well to be on our guard, though robbery, I believe, has not been heard of in Grassdale for these twenty years."

"Yet for what purpose, save that of evil, could he in these peaceable times and this peaceable country, carry fire arms about him. And what a countenance! Did you note the shy, and yet ferocious eye, like that of some animal, that longs, yet fears to spring upon you."

"Upon my word, Ellinor," said Madeline, smiling, "you are not very merciful to strangers. After all, the man might have provided himself with the pistol which you saw as a natural precaution; reflect that, as a stranger, he may well not know how safe this district usually is, and he may have come from London, in the neighbourhood of which they say robberies have been frequent of late. As to his looks, they are I own unpardonable; for so much ugliness there can be no excuse. Had the man been as handsome as our cousin Walter, you would not perhaps have been so uncharitable in your fears at the pistol."

"Nonsense, Madeline," said Ellinor, blushing, and turning away her face;—there was a moment's pause, which the younger sister broke.

"We do not seem," said she, "to make much progress in the friendship of our singular neighbour. I never knew my father court any one so much as he has courted Mr. Aram, and yet, you see how seldom he calls upon us; nay, I often think that he seeks to shun us; no great compliment to our attractions, Madeline."

"I regret his want of sociability, for his own sake," said Madeline, "for he seems melancholy as well as thoughtful, and he leads so secluded a life, that I cannot but think my father's conversation and society, if he would but encourage it, might afford some relief to his solitude."

"And he always seems," observed Ellinor, "to take pleasure in my father's conversation, as who would not? how his countenance lights up when he converses! it is a pleasure to watch it. I think him positively handsome when he speaks."

"Oh, more than handsome!" said Madeline, with enthusiasm, "with that high, pale brow, and those deep, unfathomable eyes!"

Ellinor smiled, and it was now Madeline's turn to blush.

"Well," said the former, "there is something about him that fills one with an indescribable interest; and his manner, if cold at times, is yet always so gentle."

"And to hear him converse," said Madeline, "it is like music. His thoughts, his very words, seem so different from the language and ideas of others. What a pity that he should ever be silent!"

"There is one peculiarity about his gloom, it never inspires one with distrust," said Ellinor; "if I had observed him in the same circumstances as that ill-omened traveller, I should have had no apprehension."

"Ah! that traveller still runs in your head. If we were to meet him in this spot."

"Heaven forbid!" cried Ellinor, turning hastily round in alarm—and, lo! as if her sister had been a prophet, she saw the very person in question at some little distance behind them, and walking on with rapid strides.

She uttered a faint shriek of surprise and terror, and Madeline, looking back at the sound, immediately participated in her alarm. The spot looked so desolate and lonely, and the imagination of both had been already so worked upon by Ellinor's fears, and their conjectures respecting the ill-boding weapon she had witnessed, that a thousand apprehensions of outrage and murder crowded at once upon the minds of the two sisters. Without, however, giving vent in words to their alarm, they, as by an involuntary and simultaneous suggestion, quickened their pace, every moment stealing a glance behind, to watch the progress of the suspected robber. They thought that he also seemed to accelerate his movements; and this observation increased their terror, and would appear indeed to give it some more rational ground. At length, as by a sudden turn of the road they lost sight of the dreaded stranger, their alarm suggested to them but one resolution, and they fairly fled on as fast as the fear which actuated, would allow, them. The nearest, and indeed the only house in that direction, was Aram's, but they both imagined if they could come within sight of that, they should be safe. They looked back at every interval; now they did not see their fancied pursuer—now he emerged again into view—now—yes—he also was running.

"Faster, faster, Madeline, for God's sake! he is gaining upon us!" cried Ellinor: the path grew more wild, and the trees more thick and frequent; at every cluster that marked their progress they saw the Stranger closer and closer; at length, a sudden break,—a sudden turn in the landscape;—a broad plain burst upon them, and in the midst of it the Student's solitary abode!

"Thank God, we are safe!" cried Madeline. She turned once more to look for the Stranger; in so doing, her foot struck against a fragment of stone, and she fell with great violence to the ground. She endeavoured to rise, but found herself, at first, unable to stir from the spot. In this state she looked, however, back, and saw the Traveller at some little distance. But he also halted, and after a moment's seeming deliberation, turned aside, and was lost among the bushes.

With great difficulty Ellinor now assisted Madeline to rise; her ancle was violently sprained, and she could not put her foot to the ground; but though she had evinced so much dread at the apparition of the stranger, she now testified an almost equal degree of fortitude in bearing pain.

"I am not much hurt, Ellinor," she said, faintly smiling, to encourage her sister, who supported her in speechless alarm: "but what is to be done? I cannot use this foot; how shall we get home?"

"Thank God, if you are not much hurt!" said poor Ellinor, almost crying, "lean on me—heavier—pray. Only try and reach the house, and we can then stay there till Mr. Aram sends home for the carriage."

"But what will he think? how strange it will seem!" said Madeline, the colour once more visiting her cheek, which a moment since had been blanched as pale as death.

"Is this a time for scruples and ceremony?" said Ellinor. "Come! I entreat you, come; if you linger thus, the man may take courage and attack us yet. There! that's right! Is the pain very great?"

"I do not mind the pain," murmured Madeline; "but if he should think we intrude? His habits are so reserved—so secluded; indeed I fear—"

"Intrude!" interrupted Ellinor. "Do you think so ill of him?—Do you suppose that, hermit as he is, he has lost common humanity? But lean more on me, dearest; you do not know how strong I am!"

Thus alternately chiding, caressing, and encouraging her sister, Ellinor led on the sufferer, till they had crossed the plain, though with slowness and labour, and stood before the porch of the Recluse's house. They had looked back from time to time, but the cause of so much alarm appeared no more. This they deemed a sufficient evidence of the justice of their apprehensions.

Madeline would even now fain have detained her sister's hand from the bell that hung without the porch half imbedded in ivy; but Ellinor, out of patience—as she well might be—with her sister's unseasonable prudence, refused any longer delay. So singularly still and solitary was the plain around the house, that the sound of the bell breaking the silence, had in it something startling, and appeared in its sudden and shrill voice, a profanation to the deep tranquillity of the spot. They did not wait long—a step was heard within—the door was slowly unbarred, and the Student himself stood before them.

He was a man who might, perhaps, have numbered some five and thirty years; but at a hasty glance, he would have seemed considerably younger. He was above the ordinary stature; though a gentle, and not ungraceful bend in the neck rather than the shoulders, somewhat curtailed his proper advantages of height. His frame was thin and slender, but well knit and fair proportioned. Nature had originally cast his form in an athletic mould; but sedentary habits, and the wear of mind, seemed somewhat to have impaired her gifts. His cheek was pale and delicate; yet it was rather the delicacy of thought than of weak health. His hair, which was long, and of a rich and deep brown, was worn back from his face and temples, and left a broad high majestic forehead utterly unrelieved and bare; and on the brow there was not a single wrinkle, it was as smooth as it might have been some fifteen years ago. There was a singular calmness, and, so to speak, profundity, of thought, eloquent upon its clear expanse, which suggested the idea of one who had passed his life rather in contemplation than emotion. It was a face that a physiognomist would have loved to look upon, so much did it speak both of the refinement and the dignity of intellect.

Such was the person—if pictures convey a faithful resemblance—of a man, certainly the most eminent in his day for various and profound learning, and a genius wholly self-taught, yet never contented to repose upon the wonderful stores it had laboriously accumulated.

He now stood before the two girls, silent, and evidently surprised; and it would scarce have been an unworthy subject for a picture—that ivied porch—that still spot—Madeline's reclining and subdued form and downcast eyes—the eager face of Ellinor, about to narrate the nature and cause of their intrusion—and the pale Student himself, thus suddenly aroused from his solitary meditations, and converted into the protector of beauty.

No sooner did Aram gather from Ellinor the outline of their story, and of Madeline's accident, than his countenance and manner testified the liveliest and most eager sympathy. Madeline was inexpressibly touched and surprised at the kindly and respectful earnestness with which this recluse scholar—usually so cold and abstracted in mood—assisted and led her into the house: the sympathy he expressed for her pain—the sincerity of his tone—the compassion of his eyes—and as those dark—and to use her own thought—unfathomable orbs bent admiringly and yet so gently upon her, Madeline, even in spite of her pain, felt an indescribable, a delicious thrill at her heart, which in the presence of no one else had she ever experienced before.

Aram now summoned the only domestic his house possessed, who appeared in the form of an old woman, whom he seemed to have selected from the whole neighbourhood as the person most in keeping with the rigid seclusion he preserved. She was exceedingly deaf, and was a proverb in the village for her extreme taciturnity. Poor old Margaret; she was a widow, and had lost ten children by early deaths. There was a time when her gaiety had been as noticeable as her reserve was now. In spite of her infirmity, she was not slow in comprehending the accident Madeline had met with; and she busied herself with a promptness that shewed her misfortunes had not deadened her natural kindness of disposition, in preparing fomentations and bandages for the wounded foot.

Meanwhile Aram, having no person to send in his stead, undertook to seek the manor-house, and bring back the old family coach, which had dozed inactively in its shelter for the last six months, to convey the sufferer home.

"No, Mr. Aram," said Madeline, colouring; "pray do not go yourself: consider, the man may still be loitering on the road. He is armed—good Heavens, if he should meet you!"

"Fear not, Madam," said Aram, with a faint smile. "I also keep arms, even in this obscure and safe retreat; and to satisfy you, I will not neglect to carry them with me."

"As he spoke, he took from the wainscoat, from which they hung, a brace of large horse pistols, slung them round him by a leather belt, and flinging over his person, to conceal weapons so alarming to any less dangerous passenger he might encounter, the long cloak then usually worn in inclement seasons, as an outer garment, he turned to depart.

"But are they loaded?" asked Ellinor.

Aram answered briefly, in the affirmative. It was somewhat singular, but the sisters did not then remark it, that a man so peaceable in his pursuits, and seemingly possessed of no valuables that could tempt cupidity, should in that spot, where crime was never heard of, use such habitual precaution.

When the door closed upon him, and while the old woman, relieved with a light hand and soothing lotions, which she had shewn some skill in preparing, the anguish of the sprain, Madeline cast glances of interest and curiosity around the apartment into which she had had the rare good fortune to obtain admittance.

The house had belonged to a family of some note, whose heirs had outstripped their fortunes. It had been long deserted and uninhabited; and when Aram settled in those parts, the proprietor was too glad to get rid of the incumbrance of an empty house, at a nominal rent. The solitude of the place had been the main attraction to Aram; and as he possessed what would be considered a very extensive assortment of books, even for a library of these days, he required a larger apartment than he would have been able to obtain in an abode more compact and more suitable to his fortunes and mode of living.

The room in which the sisters now found themselves was the most spacious in the house, and was indeed of considerable dimensions. It contained in front one large window, jutting from the wall. Opposite was an antique and high mantelpiece of black oak. The rest of the room was walled from the floor to the roof with books; volumes of all languages, and it might even be said, without much exaggeration, upon all sciences, were strewed around, on the chairs, the tables, or the floor. By the window stood the Student's desk, and a large old-fashioned chair of oak. A few papers, filled with astronomical calculations, lay on the desk, and these were all the witnesses of the result of study. Indeed Aram does not appear to have been a man much inclined to reproduce the learning he acquired;—what he wrote was in very small proportion to what he had read.

So high and grave was the reputation he had acquired, that the retreat and sanctum of so many learned hours would have been interesting, even to one who could not appreciate learning; but to Madeline, with her peculiar disposition and traits of mind, we may readily conceive that the room presented a powerful and pleasing charm. As the elder sister looked round in silence, Ellinor attempted to draw the old woman into conversation. She would fain have elicited some particulars of the habits and daily life of the recluse; but the deafness of their attendant was so obstinate and hopeless, that she was forced to give up the attempt in despair. "I fear," said she at last, her good-nature so far overcome by impatience as not to forbid a slight yawn; "I fear we shall have a dull time of it till my father arrives. Just consider, the fat black mares, never too fast, can only creep along that broken path,—for road there is none: it will be quite night before the coach arrives."

"I am sorry, dear Ellinor, my awkwardness should occasion you so stupid an evening," answered Madeline.

"Oh," cried Ellinor, throwing her arms around her sister's neck, "it is not for myself I spoke; and indeed I am delighted to think we have got into this wizard's den, and seen the instruments of his art. But I do so trust Mr. Aram will not meet that terrible man."

"Nay," said the prouder Madeline, "he is armed, and it is but one man. I feel too high a respect for him to allow myself much fear."

"But these bookmen are not often heroes," remarked Ellinor, laughing.

"For shame," said Madeline, the colour mounting to her forehead. "Do you not remember how, last summer, Eugene Aram rescued Dame Grenfeld's child from the bull, though at the literal peril of his own life? And who but Eugene Aram, when the floods in the year before swept along the low lands by Fairleigh, went day after day to rescue the persons, or even to save the goods of those poor people; at a time too, when the boldest villagers would not hazard themselves across the waters?—But bless me, Ellinor, what is the matter? you turn pale, you tremble.'

"Hush!" said Ellinor under her breath, and, putting her finger to her mouth, she rose and stole lightly to the window; she had observed the figure of a man pass by, and now, as she gained the window, she saw him halt by the porch, and recognised the formidable Stranger. Presently the bell sounded, and the old woman, familiar with its shrill sound, rose from her kneeling position beside the sufferer to attend to the summons. Ellinor sprang forward and detained her: the poor old woman stared at her in amazement, wholly unable to comprehend her abrupt gestures and her rapid language. It was with considerable difficulty and after repeated efforts, that she at length impressed the dulled sense of the crone with the nature of their alarm, and the expediency of refusing admittance to the Stranger. Meanwhile, the bell had rung again,—again, and the third time with a prolonged violence which testified the impatience of the applicant. As soon as the good dame had satisfied herself as to Ellinor's meaning, she could no longer be accused of unreasonable taciturnity; she wrung her hands and poured forth a volley of lamentations and fears, which effectually relieved Ellinor from the dread of her unheeding the admonition. Satisfied at having done thus much, Ellinor now herself hastened to the door and secured the ingress with an additional bolt, and then, as the thought flashed upon her, returned to the old woman and made her, with an easier effort than before, now that her senses were sharpened by fear, comprehend the necessity of securing the back entrance also; both hastened away to effect this precaution, and Madeline, who herself desired Ellinor to accompany the old woman, was left alone. She kept her eyes fixed on the window with a strange sentiment of dread at being thus left in so helpless a situation; and though a door of no ordinary dimensions and doubly locked interposed between herself and the intruder, she expected in breathless terror, every instant, to see the form of the ruffian burst into the apartment. As she thus sat and looked, she shudderingly saw the man, tired perhaps of repeating a summons so ineffectual, come to the window and look pryingly within: their eyes met; Madeline had not the power to shriek. Would he break through the window? that was her only idea, and it deprived her of words, almost of sense. He gazed upon her evident terror for a moment with a grim smile of contempt; he then knocked at the window, and his voice broke harshly on a silence yet more dreadful than the interruption.

"Ho, ho! so there is some life stirring! I beg pardon, Madam, is Mr. Aram—Eugene Aram, within?"

"No," said Madeline faintly, and then, sensible that her voice did not reach him, she reiterated the answer in a louder tone. The man, as if satisfied, made a rude inclination of his head and withdrew from the window. Ellinor now returned, and with difficulty Madeline found words to explain to her what had passed. It will be conceived that the two young ladies watched the arrival of their father with no lukewarm expectation; the stranger however appeared no more; and in about an hour, to their inexpressible joy, they heard the rumbling sound of the old coach as it rolled towards the house. This time there was no delay in unbarring the door.

CHAPTER IV.

THE SOLILOQUY, AND THE CHARACTER, OF A RECLUSE.—THE INTERRUPTION.

> "Or let my lamp at midnight hour
> Be seen in some high lonely tower,
> Where I may oft outwatch the Bear,
> Or thrice-great Hermes, and unsphere
> The spirit of Plato."
> —Milton.—Il Penseroso.

As Aram assisted the beautiful Madeline into the carriage—as he listened to her sweet voice—as he marked the grateful expression of her soft eyes—as he felt the slight yet warm pressure of her fairy hand, that vague sensation of delight which preludes love, for the first time, in his sterile and solitary life, agitated his breast. Lester held out his hand to him with a frank cordiality which the scholar could not resist.

"Do not let us be strangers, Mr. Aram," said he warmly. "It is not often that I press for companionship out of my own circle; but in your company I should find pleasure as well as instruction. Let us break the ice boldly, and at once. Come and dine with me to-morrow, and Ellinor shall sing to us in the evening."

The excuse died upon Aram's lips. Another glance at Madeline conquered the remains of his reserve: he accepted the invitation, and he could not but mark, with an unfamiliar emotion of the heart, that the eyes of Madeline sparkled as he did so.

With an abstracted air, and arms folded across his breast, he gazed after the carriage till the winding of the valley snatched it from his view. He then, waking from his reverie with a start, turned into the house, and carefully closing and barring the door, mounted with slow steps to the lofty chamber with which, the better to indulge his astronomical researches, he had crested his lonely abode.

It was now night. The Heavens broadened round him in all the loving yet august tranquillity of the season and the hour; the stars bathed the living atmosphere with a solemn light; and above—about—around—

"The holy time was quiet as a nun Breathless with adoration." He looked forth upon the deep and ineffable stillness of the night, and indulged the reflections that it suggested.

"Ye mystic lights," said he soliloquizing: "worlds upon worlds—infinite—incalculable.—Bright defiers of rest and change, rolling for ever above our petty sea of mortality, as, wave after wave, we fret forth our little life, and sink into the black abyss;—can we look upon you, note your appointed order, and your unvarying course, and not feel that we are indeed the poorest puppets of an all-pervading and resistless destiny? Shall we see throughout creation each marvel fulfilling its pre-ordered fate—no wandering from its orbit—no variation in its seasons—and yet imagine that the Arch-ordainer will hold back the tides He has sent from their unseen source, at our miserable bidding? Shall we think that our prayers can avert a doom woven with the skein of events? To change a particle of our fate, might change the destiny of millions! Shall the link forsake the chain, and yet the chain be unbroken? Away, then, with our vague repinings, and our blind demands. All must walk onward to their goal, be he the wisest who looks not one step behind. The colours of our existence were doomed before our birth—our sorrows and our crimes;—millions of ages back, when this hoary earth was peopled by other kinds, yea! ere its atoms had formed one layer of its present soil, the Eternal and the all-seeing Ruler of the universe, Destiny, or God, had here fixed the moment of our birth and the limits of our career. What then is crime?—Fate! What life?—Submission!"

Such were the strange and dark thoughts which, constituting a part indeed of his established creed, broke over Aram's mind. He sought for a fairer subject for meditation, and Madeline Lester rose before him.

Eugene Aram was a man whose whole life seemed to have been one sacrifice to knowledge. What is termed pleasure had no attraction for him. From the mature manhood at which he had arrived, he looked back along his youth, and recognized no youthful folly. Love he had hitherto regarded with a cold though not an incurious eye: intemperance had never lured him to a momentary self-abandonment. Even the innocent relaxations with which the austerest minds relieve their accustomed toils, had had no power to draw him from his beloved researches. The delight monstrari digito; the gratification of triumphant wisdom; the whispers of an elevated vanity; existed not for his self-dependent and solitary heart. He was one of those earnest and high-wrought enthusiasts who now are almost extinct upon earth, and whom Romance has not hitherto attempted to pourtray; men not uncommon in the last century, who were devoted to knowledge, yet disdainful of its fame; who lived for nothing else than to learn. From store to store, from treasure to treasure, they proceeded in exulting labour, and having accumulated all, they bestowed nought; they were the arch-misers of the wealth of letters. Wrapped in obscurity, in some sheltered nook, remote from the great stir of men, they passed a life at once unprofitable and glorious; the least part of what they ransacked would appal the industry of a modern student, yet the most superficial of modern students might effect more for mankind. They lived among oracles, but they gave none forth. And yet, even in this very barrenness, there seems something high; it was a rare and great spectacle—Men, living aloof from the roar and strife of the passions that raged below, devoting themselves to the knowledge which is our purification and our immortality on earth, and yet deaf and blind to the allurements of the vanity which generally accompanies research; refusing the ignorant homage of their kind, making their sublime motive their only meed, adoring Wisdom for her sole sake, and set apart in the populous universe, like stars, luminous with their own light, but too remote from the earth on which they looked, to shed over its inmates the lustre with which they glowed.

From his youth to the present period, Aram had dwelt little in cities though he had visited many, yet he could scarcely be called ignorant of mankind; there seems something intuitive in the science which teaches us the knowledge of our race. Some men emerge from their seclusion, and find, all at once, a power to dart into the minds and drag forth the motives of those they see; it is a sort of second sight, born with them, not acquired. And Aram, it may be, rendered yet more acute by his profound and habitual investigations of our metaphysical frame, never quitted his solitude to mix with others, without penetrating into the broad traits or prevalent infirmities their characters possessed. In this, indeed, he differed from the scholar tribe, and even in abstraction was mechanically vigilant and observant. Much in his nature would, had early circumstances given it a different bias, have fitted him for worldly superiority and command. A resistless energy, an unbroken perseverance, a profound and scheming and subtle thought, a genius fertile in resources, a tongue clothed with eloquence, all, had his ambition so chosen, might have given him the same empire over the physical, that he had now attained over the intellectual world. It could not be said that Aram wanted benevolence, but it was dashed, and mixed with a certain scorn: the benevolence was the offspring of his nature, the scorn seemed the result of his pursuits. He would feed the birds from his window, he would tread aside to avoid the worm on his path; were one of his own tribe in danger, he would save him at the hazard of his life:—yet in his heart he despised men, and believed them beyond amelioration. Unlike the present race of schoolmen, who incline to the consoling hope of human perfectibility, he saw in the gloomy past but a dark prophecy of the future. As Napoleon wept over one wounded soldier in the field of battle, yet ordered without emotion, thousands to a certain death; so Aram would have sacrificed himself for an individual, but would not have sacrificed a momentary gratification for his race. And this sentiment towards men, at once of high disdain and profound despondency, was perhaps the cause why he rioted in indolence upon his extraordinary mental wealth, and could not be persuaded either to dazzle the world or to serve it. But by little and little his fame had broke forth from the limits with which he would have walled it: a man who had taught himself, under singular difficulties, nearly all the languages of the civilized earth; the profound mathematician, the elaborate antiquarian, the abstruse philologist, uniting with his graver lore the more florid accomplishments of science, from the scholastic trifling of heraldry to the gentle learning of herbs and flowers, could scarcely hope for utter obscurity in that day when all intellectual acquirement was held in high honour, and its possessors were drawn together into a sort of brotherhood by the fellowship of their pursuits. And though Aram gave little or nothing to the world himself, he was ever willing to communicate to others any benefit or honour derivable from his researches. On the altar of science he kindled no light, but the fragrant oil in the lamps of his more pious brethren was largely borrowed from his stores. From almost every college in Europe came to his obscure abode letters of acknowledgement or inquiry; and few foreign cultivators of learning visited this country without seeking an interview with Aram. He received them with all the modesty and the courtesy that characterized his demeanour; but it was noticeable that he never allowed these interruptions to be more than temporary. He proffered no hospitality, and shrunk back from all offers of friendship; the interview lasted its hour, and was seldom renewed. Patronage was not less distasteful to him than sociality. Some occasional visits and condescensions of the great, he had received with a stern haughtiness, rather than his wonted and subdued urbanity. The precise amount of his fortune was not known; his wants were so few, that what would have been poverty to others might easily have been competence to him; and the only evidence he manifested of the command of money, was in his extended and various library.

He had now been about two years settled in his present retreat. Unsocial as he was, every one in the neighbourhood loved him; even the reserve of a man so eminent, arising as it was supposed to do from a painful modesty, had in it something winning; and he had been known to evince on great occasions, a charity and a courage in the service of others which removed from the seclusion of his habits the semblance of misanthropy and of avarice. The peasant drew aside with a kindness mingled with his respect, as in his homeward walk he encountered the pale and thoughtful Student, with the folded arms and downcast eyes, which characterised the abstraction of his mood; and the village maiden, as she curtsied by him, stole a glance at his handsome but melancholy countenance; and told her sweetheart she was certain the poor scholar had been crossed in love.

And thus passed the Student's life; perhaps its monotony and dullness required less compassion than they received; no man can judge of the happiness of another. As the Moon plays upon the waves, and seems to our eyes to favour with a peculiar beam one long track amidst the waters, leaving the rest in comparative obscurity; yet all the while, she is no niggard in her lustre—for though the rays that meet not our eyes seem to us as though they were not, yet she with an equal and unfavouring loveliness, mirrors herself on every wave: even so, perhaps, Happiness falls with the same brightness and power over the whole expanse of Life, though to our limited eyes she seems only to rest on those billows from which the ray is reflected back upon our sight.

From his contemplations, of whatsoever nature, Aram was now aroused by a loud summons at the door;—the clock had gone eleven. Who could at that late hour, when the whole village was buried in sleep, demand admittance? He recollected that Madeline had said the Stranger who had so alarmed them had inquired for him, at that recollection his cheek suddenly blanched, but again, that stranger was surely only some poor traveller who had heard of his wonted charity, and had called to solicit relief, for he had not met the Stranger on the road to Lester's house; and he had naturally set down the apprehensions of his fair visitants to a mere female timidity. Who could this be? no humble wayfarer would at that hour crave assistance;—some disaster perhaps in the village. From his lofty chamber he looked forth and saw the stars watch quietly over the scattered cottages and the dark foliage that slept breathlessly around. All was still as death, but it seemed the stillness of innocence and security: again! the bell again! He thought he heard his name shouted without; he strode once or twice irresolutely to and fro the chamber; and then his step grew firm, and his native courage returned. His pistols were still girded round him; he looked to the priming, and muttered some incoherent words; he then descended the stairs, and slowly unbarred the door. Without the porch, the moonlight full upon his harsh features and sturdy frame, stood the ill-omened Traveller.

CHAPTER V.

A DINNER AT THE SQUIRE'S HALL.—A CONVERSATION BETWEEN TWO
RETIRED MEN WITH DIFFERENT OBJECTS IN RETIREMENT.—DISTURBANCE
FIRST INTRODUCED INTO A PEACEFUL FAMILY.

"Can he not be sociable?"
—Troilus and Cressida.

"Subit quippe etiam ipsius inertiae dulcedo;
et invisa primo desidia postremo amatur."
—Tacitus.

"How use doth breed a habit in a man!
This shadowy desert, unfrequented woods,
I better brook than flourishing people towns."
—Winter's Tale.

The next day, faithful to his appointment, Aram arrived at Lester's. The good Squire received him with a warm cordiality, and Madeline with a blush and a smile that ought to have been more grateful to him than acknowledgements. She was still a prisoner to the sofa, but in compliment to Aram, the sofa was wheeled into the hall where they dined, so that she was not absent from the repast. It was a pleasant room, that old hall! Though it was summer—more for cheerfulness than warmth, the log burnt on the spacious hearth: but at the same time the latticed windows were thrown open, and the fresh yet sunny air stole in, rich from the embrace of the woodbine and clematis, which clung around the casement.

A few old pictures were paneled in the oaken wainscot; and here and there the horns of the mighty stag adorned the walls, and united with the cheeriness of comfort associations of that of enterprise. The good old board was crowded with the luxuries meet for a country Squire. The speckled trout, fresh from the stream, and the four-year-old mutton modestly disclaiming its own excellent merits, by affecting the shape and assuming the adjuncts of venison. Then for the confectionery,—it was worthy of Ellinor, to whom that department generally fell; and we should scarcely be surprised to find, though we venture not to affirm, that its delicate fabrication owed more to her than superintendence. Then the ale, and the cyder with rosemary in the bowl, were incomparable potations; and to the gooseberry wine, which would have filled Mrs. Primrose with envy, was added the more generous warmth of port which, in the Squire's younger days, had been the talk of the country, and which had now lost none of its attributes, save "the original brightness" of its colour.

But (the wine excepted) these various dainties met with slight honour from their abstemious guest; and, for though habitually reserved he was rarely gloomy, they remarked that he seemed unusually fitful and sombre in his mood. Something appeared to rest upon his mind, from which, by the excitement of wine and occasional bursts of eloquence more animated than ordinary, he seemed striving to escape; and at length, he apparently succeeded. Naturally enough, the conversation turned upon the curiosities and scenery of the country round; and here Aram shone with a peculiar grace. Vividly alive to the influences of Nature, and minutely acquainted with its varieties, he invested every hill and glade to which remark recurred with the poetry of his descriptions; and from his research he gave even scenes the most familiar, a charm and interest which had been strange to them till then. To this stream some romantic legend had once attached itself, long forgotten and now revived;—that moor, so barren to an ordinary eye, was yet productive of some rare and curious herb, whose properties afforded scope for lively description;—that old mound was yet rife in attraction to one versed in antiquities, and able to explain its origin, and from such explanation deduce a thousand classic or celtic episodes.

No subject was so homely or so trite but the knowledge that had neglected nothing, was able to render it luminous and new. And as he spoke, the scholar's countenance brightened, and his voice, at first hesitating and low, compelled the attention to its earnest and winning music. Lester himself, a man who, in his long retirement, had not forgotten the attractions of intellectual society, nor even neglected a certain cultivation of intellectual pursuits, enjoyed a pleasure that he had not experienced for years. The gay Ellinor was fascinated into admiration; and Madeline, the most silent of the groupe, drank in every word, unconscious of the sweet poison she imbibed. Walter alone seemed not carried away by the eloquence of their guest. He preserved an unadmiring and sullen demeanour, and every now and then regarded Aram with looks of suspicion and dislike. This was more remarkable when the men were left alone; and Lester, in surprise and anger, darted significant and admonitory looks towards his nephew, which at length seemed to rouse him into a more hospitable bearing. As the cool of the evening now came on, Lester proposed to Aram to enjoy it without, previous to returning to the parlour, to which the ladies had retired. Walter excused himself from joining them. The host and the guest accordingly strolled forth alone.

"Your solitude," said Lester, smiling, "is far deeper and less broken than mine: do you never find it irksome?"

"Can Humanity be at all times contented?" said Aram. "No stream, howsoever secret or subterranean, glides on in eternal tranquillity."

"You allow, then, that you feel some occasional desire for a more active and animated life?"

"Nay," answered Aram; "that is scarcely a fair corollary from my remark. I may, at times, feel the weariness of existence—the tedium vitae; but I know well that the cause is not to be remedied by a change from tranquillity to agitation. The objects of the great world are to be pursued only by the excitement of the passions. The passions are at once our masters and our deceivers;—they urge us onward, yet present no limit to our progress. The farther we proceed, the more dim and shadowy grows the goal. It is impossible for a man who leads the life of the world, the life of the passions, ever to experience content. For the life of the passions is that of a perpetual desire; but a state of content is the absence of all desire. Thus philosophy has become another name for mental quietude; and all wisdom points to a life of intellectual indifference, as the happiest which earth can bestow."

"This may be true enough," said Lester, reluctantly; "but—"

"But what?"

"A something at our hearts—a secret voice—an involuntary impulse—rebels against it, and points to action—action, as the true sphere of man."

A slight smile curved the lip of the Student; he avoided, however, the argument, and remarked,

"Yet, if you think so, the world lies before you; why not return to it?"

"Because constant habit is stronger than occasional impulse; and my seclusion, after all, has its sphere of action—has its object."

"All seclusion has."

"All? Scarcely so; for me, I have my object of interest in my children."

"And mine is in my books."

"And engaged in your object, does not the whisper of Fame ever animate you with the desire to go forth into the world, and receive the homage that would await you?"

"Listen to me," replied Aram. "When I was a boy, I went once to a theatre. The tragedy of Hamlet was performed: a play full of the noblest thoughts, the subtlest morality, that exists upon the stage. The audience listened with attention, with admiration, with applause. I said to myself, when the curtain fell, 'It must be a glorious thing to obtain this empire over men's intellects and emotions.' But now an Italian mountebank appeared on the stage,—a man of extraordinary personal strength and slight of hand. He performed a variety of juggling tricks, and distorted his body into a thousand surprising and unnatural postures. The audience were transported beyond themselves: if they had felt delight in Hamlet, they glowed with rapture at the mountebank: they had listened with attention to the lofty thought, but they were snatched from themselves by the marvel of the strange posture. 'Enough,' said I; 'I correct my former notion. Where is the glory of ruling men's minds, and commanding their admiration, when a greater enthusiasm is excited by mere bodily agility, than was kindled by the most wonderful emanations of a genius little less than divine?' I have never forgotten the impression of that evening."

Lester attempted to combat the truth of the illustration, and thus conversing, they passed on through the village green, when the gaunt form of Corporal Bunting arrested their progress.

"Beg pardon, Squire," said he, with a military salute; "beg pardon, your honour," bowing to Aram; "but I wanted to speak to you, Squire, 'bout the rent of the bit cot yonder; times very hard—pay scarce—Michaelmas close at hand—and—"

"You desire a little delay, Bunting, eh?—Well, well, we'll see about it, look up at the Hall to-morrow; Mr. Walter, I know wants to consult you about letting the water from the great pond, and you must give us your opinion of the new brewing."

"Thank your honour, thank you; much obliged I'm sure. I hope your honour liked the trout I sent up. Beg pardon, Master Aram, mayhap you would condescend to accept a few fish now and then; they're very fine in these streams, as you probably know; if you please to let me, I'll send some up by the old 'oman to-morrow, that is if the day's cloudy a bit."

The Scholar thanked the good Bunting, and would have proceeded onward, but the Corporal was in a familiar mood.

"Beg pardon, beg pardon, but strange-looking dog here last evening—asked after you—said you were old friend of his—trotted off in your direction—hope all was right, Master?—augh!"

"All right!" repeated Aram, fixing his eyes on the Corporal, who had concluded his speech with a significant wink, and pausing a full moment before he continued, then as if satisfied with his survey, he added:

"Ay, ay, I know whom you mean; he had known me some years ago. So you saw him! What said he to you of me?"

"Augh! little enough, Master Aram, he seemed to think only of satisfying his own appetite; said he'd been a soldier."

"A soldier, humph!"

"Never told me the regiment, though,—shy—did he ever desert, pray, your honour?"

"I don't know;" answered Aram, turning away. "I know little, very little, about him!" He was going away, but stopped to add: "The man called on me last night for assistance; the lateness of the hour a little alarmed me. I gave him what I could afford, and he has now proceeded on his journey."

"Oh, then, he won't take up his quarters hereabouts, your honour?" said the Corporal, inquiringly.

"No, no; good evening."

"What! this singular stranger, who so frightened my poor girls, is really known to you;" said Lester, in surprise: "pray is he as formidable as he seemed to them?"

"Scarcely," said Aram, with great composure; "he has been a wild roving fellow all his life, but—but there is little real harm in him. He is certainly ill-favoured enough to—" here, interrupting himself, and breaking into a new sentence, Aram added: "but at all events he will frighten your nieces no more—he has proceeded on his journey northward. And now, yonder lies my way home. Good evening." The abruptness of this farewell did indeed take Lester by surprise.

"Why, you will not leave me yet? The young ladies expect your return to them for an hour or so! What will they think of such desertion? No, no, come back, my good friend, and suffer me by and by to walk some part of the way home with you."

"Pardon me," said Aram, "I must leave you now. As to the ladies," he added, with a faint smile, half in melancholy, half in scorn, "I am not one whom they could miss;—forgive me if I seem unceremonious. Adieu."

Lester at first felt a little offended, but when he recalled the peculiar habits of the Scholar, he saw that the only way to hope for a continuance of that society which had so pleased him, was to indulge Aram at first in his unsocial inclinations, rather than annoy him by a troublesome hospitality; he therefore, without further discourse, shook hands with him, and they parted.

When Lester regained the little parlour, he found his nephew sitting, silent and discontented, by the window. Madeline had taken up a book, and Ellinor, in an opposite corner, was plying her needle with an air of earnestness and quiet, very unlike her usual playful and cheerful vivacity. There was evidently a cloud over the groupe; the good Lester regarded them with a searching, yet kindly eye.

"And what has happened?" said he, "something of mighty import, I am sure, or I should have heard my pretty Ellinor's merry laugh long before I crossed the threshold."

Ellinor coloured and sighed, and worked faster than ever. Walter threw open the window, and whistled a favourite air quite out of tune. Lester smiled, and seated himself by his nephew.

"Well, Walter," said he, "I feel, for the first time in these ten years, I have a right to scold you. What on earth could make you so inhospitable to your uncle's guest? You eyed the poor student, as if you wished him among the books of Alexandria!"

"I would he were burnt with them!" answered Walter, sharply. "He seems to have added the black art to his other accomplishments, and bewitched my fair cousins here into a forgetfulness of all but himself."

"Not me!" said Ellinor eagerly, and looking up.

"No, not you, that's true enough; you are too just, too kind;—it is a pity that Madeline is not more like you."

"My dear Walter," said Madeline, "what is the matter? You accuse me of what? being attentive to a man whom it is impossible to hear without attention!"

"There!" cried Walter passionately; "you confess it; and so for a stranger,—a cold, vain, pedantic egotist, you can shut your ears and heart to those who have known and loved you all your life; and—and—"

"Vain!" interrupted Madeline, unheeding the latter part of Walter's address.

"Pedantic!" repeated her father.

"Yes! I say vain, pedantic!" cried Walter, working himself into a passion. What on earth but the love of display could make him monopolize the whole conversation?—What but pedantry could make him bring out those anecdotes and allusions, and descriptions, or whatever you call them, respecting every old wall or stupid plant in the country?

"I never thought you guilty of meanness before," said Lester gravely.

"Meanness!"

"Yes! for is it not mean to be jealous of superior acquirements, instead of admiring them?"

"What has been the use of those acquirements? Has he benefited mankind by them? Shew me the poet—the historian—the orator, and I will yield to none of you; no, not to Madeline herself in homage of their genius: but the mere creature of books—the dry and sterile collector of other men's learning—no—no. What should I admire in such a machine of literature, except a waste of perseverance?—And Madeline calls him handsome too!"

At this sudden turn from declamation to reproach, Lester laughed outright; and his nephew, in high anger, rose and left the room.

"Who could have thought Walter so foolish?" said Madeline.

"Nay," observed Ellinor gently, "it is the folly of a kind heart, after all. He feels sore at our seeming to prefer another—I mean another's conversation—to his!"

Lester turned round in his chair, and regarded with a serious look, the faces of both sisters.

"My dear Ellinor," said he, when he had finished his survey, "you are a kind girl—come and kiss me!"

CHAPTER VI.

THE BEHAVIOUR OF THE STUDENT.—A SUMMER SCENE—ARAM'S
CONVERSATION WITH WALTER, AND SUBSEQUENT COLLOQUY WITH
      HIMSELF.

```
"The soft season, the firmament serene,
The loun illuminate air, and firth amene
The silver-scalit fishes on the grete
O'er-thwart clear streams sprinkillond for the heat,"
    —Gawin Douglas.

    "Ilia subter
Caecum vulnus habes; sed lato balteus auro
Praetegit."
    —Persius.
```

Several days elapsed before the family of the manor-house encountered Aram again. The old woman came once or twice to present the inquiries of her master as to Miss Lester's accident; but Aram himself did not appear. This want to interest certainly offended Madeline, although she still drew upon herself Walter's displeasure, by disputing and resenting the unfavourable strictures on the scholar, in which that young gentleman delighted to indulge. By degrees, however, as the days passed without maturing the acquaintance which Walter had disapproved, the youth relaxed in his attacks, and seemed to yield to the remonstrances of his uncle. Lester had, indeed, conceived an especial inclination towards the recluse. Any man of reflection, who has lived for some time alone, and who suddenly meets with one who calls forth in him, and without labour or contradiction, the thoughts which have sprung up in his solitude, scarcely felt in their growth, will comprehend the new zest, the awakening, as it were, of the mind, which Lester found in the conversation of Eugene Aram. His solitary walk (for his nephew had the separate pursuits of youth) appeared to him more dull than before; and he longed to renew an intercourse which had given to the monotony of his life both variety and relief. He called twice upon Aram, but the student was, or affected to be, from home; and an invitation he sent him, though couched in friendly terms, was, but with great semblance of kindness, refused.

"See, Walter," said Lester, disconcerted, as he finished reading the refusal—"see what your rudeness has effected. I am quite convinced that Aram (evidently a man of susceptible as well as retired mind) observed the coldness of your manner towards him, and that thus you have deprived me of the only society which, in this country of boors and savages, gave me any gratification."

Walter replied apologetically, but his uncle turned away with a greater appearance of anger than his placid features were wont to exhibit; and Walter, cursing the innocent cause of his uncle's displeasure towards him, took up his fishing-rod and went out alone, in no happy or exhilarated mood.

It was waxing towards eve—an hour especially lovely in the month of June, and not without reason favoured by the angler. Walter sauntered across the rich and fragrant fields, and came soon into a sheltered valley, through which the brooklet wound its shadowy way. Along the margin the grass sprung up long and matted, and profuse with a thousand weeds and flowers—the children of the teeming June. Here the ivy-leaved bell-flower, and not far from it the common enchanter's night-shade, the silver weed, and the water-aven; and by the hedges that now and then neared the water, the guelder-rose, and the white briony, overrunning the thicket with its emerald leaves and luxuriant flowers. And here and there, silvering the bushes, the elder offered its snowy tribute to the summer. All the insect youth were abroad, with their bright wings and glancing motion; and from the lower depths of the bushes the blackbird darted across, or higher and unseen the first cuckoo of the eve began its continuous and mellow note. All this cheeriness and gloss of life, which enamour us with the few bright days of the English summer, make the poetry in an angler's life, and convert every idler at heart into a moralist, and not a gloomy one, for the time.

Softened by the quiet beauty and voluptuousness around him, Walter's thoughts assumed a more gentle dye, and he broke out into the old lines:

"Sweet day, so soft, so calm, so bright; The bridal of the earth and sky," as he dipped his line into the current, and drew it across the shadowy hollows beneath the bank. The river-gods were not, however, in a favourable mood, and after waiting in vain for some time, in a spot in which he was usually successful, he proceeded slowly along the margin of the brooklet, crushing the reeds at every step, into that fresh and delicious odour, which furnished Bacon with one of his most beautiful comparisons.

He thought, as he proceeded, that beneath a tree that overhung the waters in the narrowest part of their channel, he heard a voice, and as he approached he recognised it as Aram's; a curve in the stream brought him close by the spot, and he saw the student half reclined beneath the tree, and muttering, but at broken intervals, to himself.

The words were so scattered, that Walter did not trace their clue; but involuntarily he stopped short, within a few feet of the soliloquist: and Aram, suddenly turning round, beheld him. A fierce and abrupt change broke over the scholar's countenance; his cheek grew now pale, now flushed; and his brows knit over his flashing and dark eyes with an intent anger, that was the more withering, from its contrast to the usual calmness of his features. Walter drew back, but Aram stalking directly up to him, gazed into his face, as if he would read his very soul.

"What! eaves-dropping?" said he, with a ghastly smile. "You overheard me, did you? Well, well, what said I?—what said I?" Then pausing, and noting that Walter did not reply, he stamped his foot violently, and grinding his teeth, repeated in a smothered tone "Boy! what said I?"

"Mr. Aram," said Walter, "you forget yourself; I am not one to play the listener, more especially to the learned ravings of a man who can conceal nothing I care to know. Accident brought me hither."

"What! surely—surely I spoke aloud, did I not?—did I not?"

"You did, but so incoherently and indistinctly, that I did not profit by your indiscretion. I cannot plagiarise, I assure you, from any scholastic designs you might have been giving vent to."

Aram looked on him for a moment, and then breathing heavily, turned away.

"Pardon me," he said; "I am a poor half-crazed man; much study has unnerved me; I should never live but with my own thoughts; forgive me, Sir, I pray you."

Touched by the sudden contrition of Aram's manner, Walter forgot, not only his present displeasure, but his general dislike; he stretched forth his hand to the Student, and hastened to assure him of his ready forgiveness. Aram sighed deeply as he pressed the young man's hand, and Walter saw, with surprise and emotion, that his eyes were filled with tears.

"Ah!" said Aram, gently shaking his head, "it is a hard life we bookmen lead. Not for us is the bright face of noon-day or the smile of woman, the gay unbending of the heart, the neighing steed, and the shrill trump; the pride, pomp, and circumstance of life. Our enjoyments are few and calm; our labour constant; but that is it not, Sir?—that is it not? the body avenges its own neglect. We grow old before our time; we wither up; the sap of youth shrinks from our veins; there is no bound in our step. We look about us with dimmed eyes, and our breath grows short and thick, and pains and coughs, and shooting aches come upon us at night; it is a bitter life—a bitter life—a joyless life. I would I had never commenced it. And yet the harsh world scowls upon us: our nerves are broken, and they wonder we are querulous; our blood curdles, and they ask why we are not gay; our brain grows dizzy and indistinct, (as with me just now,) and, shrugging their shoulders, they whisper their neighbours that we are mad. I wish I had worked at the plough, and known sleep, and loved mirth—and—and not been what I am."

As the Student uttered the last sentence, he bowed down his head, and a few tears stole silently down his cheek. Walter was greatly affected—it took him by surprise; nothing in Aram's ordinary demeanour betrayed any facility to emotion; and he conveyed to all the idea of a man, if not proud, at least cold.

"You do not suffer bodily pain, I trust?" asked Walter, soothingly.

"Pain does not conquer me," said Aram, slowly recovering himself. "I am not melted by that which I would fain despise. Young man, I wronged you—you have forgiven me. Well, well, we will say no more on that head; it is past and pardoned. Your father has been kind to me, and I have not returned his advances; you shall tell him why. I have lived thirteen years by myself, and I have contracted strange ways and many humours not common to the world—you have seen an example of this. Judge for yourself if I be fit for the smoothness, and confidence, and ease of social intercourse; I am not fit, I feel it! I am doomed to be alone—tell your father this—tell him to suffer me to live so! I am grateful for his goodness—I know his motives—but have a certain pride of mind; I cannot bear sufferance—I loath indulgence. Nay, interrupt me not, I beseech you. Look round on Nature—behold the only company that humbles me not—except the dead whose souls speak to us from the immortality of books. These herbs at your feet, I know their secrets—I watch the mechanism of their life; the winds—they have taught me their language; the stars—I have unravelled their mysteries; and these, the creatures and ministers of God—these I offend not by my mood—to them I utter my thoughts, and break forth into my dreams, without reserve and without fear. But men disturb me—I have nothing to learn from them—I have no wish to confide in them; they cripple the wild liberty which has become to me a second nature. What its shell is to the tortoise, solitude has become to me—my protection; nay, my life!"

"But," said Walter, "with us, at least, you would not have to dread restraint; you might come when you would; be silent or converse, according to your will."

Aram smiled faintly, but made no immediate reply.

"So, you have been angling!" he said, after a short pause, and as if willing to change the thread of conversation. "Fie! It is a treacherous pursuit; it encourages man's worst propensities—cruelty and deceit."

"I should have thought a lover of Nature would have been more indulgent to a pastime which introduces us to her most quiet retreats."

"And cannot Nature alone tempt you without need of such allurements? What! that crisped and winding stream, with flowers on its very tide—the water-violet and the water-lily—these silent brakes—the cool of the gathering evening—the still and luxuriance of the universal life around you; are not these enough of themselves to tempt you forth? if not, go to—your excuse is hypocrisy."

"I am used to these scenes," replied Walter; "I am weary of the thoughts they produce in me, and long for any diversion or excitement."

"Ay, ay, young man! The mind is restless at your age—have a care. Perhaps you long to visit the world—to quit these obscure haunts which you are fatigued in admiring?"

"It may be so," said Walter, with a slight sigh. "I should at least like to visit our great capital, and note the contrast; I should come back, I imagine, with a greater zest to these scenes."

Aram laughed. "My friend," said he, "when men have once plunged into the great sea of human toil and passion, they soon wash away all love and zest for innocent enjoyments. What once was a soft retirement, will become the most intolerable monotony; the gaming of social existence—the feverish and desperate chances of honour and wealth, upon which the men of cities set their hearts, render all pursuits less exciting, utterly insipid and dull. The brook and the angle—ha!—ha!—these are not occupations for men who have once battled with the world."

"I can forego them, then, without regret;" said Walter, with the sanguineness of his years. Aram looked upon him wistfully; the bright eye, the healthy cheek, and vigorous frame of the youth, suited with his desire to seek the conflict of his kind, and gave a naturalness to his ambition, which was not without interest, even to the recluse.

"Poor boy!" said he, mournfully, "how gallantly the ship leaves the port; how worn and battered it will return!"

When they parted, Walter returned slowly homewards, filled with pity towards the singular man whom he had seen so strangely overpowered; and wondering how suddenly his mind had lost its former rancour to the Student. Yet there mingled even with these kindly feelings, a little displeasure at the superior tone which Aram had unconsciously adopted towards him; and to which, from any one, the high spirit of the young man was not readily willing to submit.

Meanwhile, the Student continued his path along the water side, and as, with his gliding step and musing air, he roamed onward, it was impossible to imagine a form more suited to the deep tranquillity of the scene. Even the wild birds seemed to feel, by a sort of instinct, that in him there was no cause for fear; and did not stir from the turf that neighboured, or the spray that overhung, his path.

"So," said he, soliloquizing, but not without casting frequent and jealous glances round him, and in a murmur so indistinct as would have been inaudible even to a listener—"so, I was not overheard,—well, I must cure myself of this habit; our thoughts, like nuns, ought not to go abroad without a veil. Ay, this tone will not betray me, I will preserve its tenor, for I can scarcely altogether renounce my sole confidant—SELF; and thought seems more clear when uttered even thus. 'Tis a fine youth! full of the impulse and daring of his years; I was never so young at heart. I was—nay, what matters it? Who is answerable for his nature? Who can say, 'I controlled all the circumstances which made me what I am?' Madeline,—Heavens! did I bring on myself this temptation? Have I not fenced it from me throughout all my youth, when my brain did at moments forsake me, and the veins did bound? And now, when the yellow hastens on the green of life; now, for the first time, this emotion—this weakness—and for whom? One I have lived with—known—beneath whose eyes I have passed through all the fine gradations, from liking to love, from love to passion? No;—one, whom I have seen but little; who, it is true, arrested my eye at the first glance it caught of her two years since, but with whom till within the last few weeks I have scarcely spoken! Her voice rings on my ear, her look dwells on my heart; when I sleep, she is with me; when I wake, I am haunted by her image. Strange, strange! Is love then, after all, the sudden passion which in every age poetry has termed it, though till now my reason has disbelieved the notion?... And now, what is the question? To resist, or to yield. Her father invites me, courts me; and I stand aloof! Will this strength, this forbearance, last?—Shall I encourage my mind to this decision?" Here Aram paused abruptly, and then renewed: "It is true! I ought to weave my lot with none. Memory sets me apart and alone in the world; it seems unnatural to me, a thought of dread—to bring another being to my solitude, to set an everlasting watch on my uprisings and my downsittings; to invite eyes to my face when I sleep at nights, and ears to every word that may start unbidden from my lips. But if the watch be the watch of love—away! does love endure for ever? He who trusts to woman, trusts to the type of change. Affection may turn to hatred, fondness to loathing, anxiety to dread; and, at the best, woman is weak, she is the minion to her impulses. Enough, I will steel my soul,—shut up the avenues of sense,—brand with the scathing-iron these yet green and soft emotions of lingering youth,—and freeze and chain and curdle up feeling, and heart, and manhood, into ice and age!"

CHAPTER VII.

THE POWER OF LOVE OVER THE RESOLUTION OF THE STUDENT.—ARAM BECOMES A FREQUENT GUEST AT THE MANOR-HOUSE.—A WALK.—CONVERSATION WITH DAME DARKMANS.—HER HISTORY.—POVERTY AND ITS EFFECTS.

MAD. "Then, as Time won thee frequent to our hearth,

Didst thou not breathe, like dreams, into my soul

Nature's more gentle secrets, the sweet lore

Of the green herb and the bee-worshipp'd flower?

And when deep Night did o'er the nether Earth

Diffuse meek quiet, and the Heart of Heaven

With love grew breathless—didst thou not unrol

The volume of the weird chaldean stars,

And of the winds, the clouds, the invisible air,

Make eloquent discourse, until, methought,

No human lip, but some diviner spirit

Alone, could preach such truths of things divine?

And so—and so—"

ARAM. "From Heaven we turned to Earth,

And Wisdom fathered Passion."

. . . .

ARAM. "Wise men have praised the Peasant's thoughtless lot,

And learned Pride hath envied humble Toil;

If they were right, why let us burn our books,

And sit us down, and play the fool with Time,

Mocking the prophet Wisdom's high decrees,

And walling this trite Present with dark clouds,

'Till Night becomes our Nature; and the ray

Ev'n of the stars, but meteors that withdraw

The wandering spirit from the sluggish rest

Which makes its proper bliss. I will accost

This denizen of toil."

—From Eugene Aram, a MS. Tragedy.

"A wicked hag, and envy's self excelling

In mischiefe, for herself she only vext,

But this same, both herself and others eke perplext."

. . . .

"Who then can strive with strong necessity,

That holds the world in his still changing state,

. . . .

Then do no further go, no further stray,

But here lie down, and to thy rest betake."

—Spenser.

Few men perhaps could boast of so masculine and firm a mind, as, despite his eccentricities, Aram assuredly possessed. His habits of solitude had strengthened its natural hardihood; for, accustomed to make all the sources of happiness flow solely from himself, his thoughts the only companion—his genius the only vivifier—of his retreat; the tone and faculty of his spirit could not but assume that austere and vigorous energy which the habit of self-dependence almost invariably produces; and yet, the reader, if he be young, will scarcely feel surprise that the resolution of the Student, to battle against incipient love, from whatever reasons it might be formed, gradually and reluctantly melted away. It may be noted, that the enthusiasts of learning and reverie have, at one time or another in their lives, been, of all the tribes of men, the most keenly susceptible to love; their solitude feeds their passion; and deprived, as they usually are, of the more hurried and vehement occupations of life, when love is once admitted to their hearts, there is no counter-check to its emotions, and no escape from its excitation. Aram, too, had just arrived at that age when a man usually feels a sort of revulsion in the current of his desires. At that age, those who have hitherto pursued love, begin to grow alive to ambition; those who have been slaves to the pleasures of life, awaken from the dream, and direct their desire to its interests. And in the same proportion, they who till then have wasted the prodigal fervours of youth upon a sterile soil; who have served Ambition, or, like Aram, devoted their hearts to Wisdom; relax from their ardour, look back on the departed years with regret, and commence, in their manhood, the fiery pleasures and delirious follies which are only pardonable in youth. In short, as in every human pursuit there is a certain vanity, and as every acquisition contains within itself the seed of disappointment, so there is a period of life when we pause from the pursuit, and are discontented with the acquisition. We then look around us for something new—again follow—and are again deceived. Few men throughout life are the servants to one desire. When we gain the middle of the bridge of our mortality, different objects from those which attracted us upward almost invariably lure us to the descent. Happy they who exhaust in the former part of the journey all the foibles of existence! But how different is the crude and evanescent love of that age when thought has not given intensity and power to the passions, from the love which is felt, for the first time, in maturer but still youthful years! As the flame burns the brighter in proportion to the resistance which it conquers, this later love is the more glowing in proportion to the length of time in which it has overcome temptation: all the solid and, concentred faculties ripened to their full height, are no longer capable of the infinite distractions, the numberless caprices of youth; the rays of the heart, not rendered weak by diversion, collect into one burning focus;

```
[Love is of the nature of a burning glass, which kept
 still in one place, fireth; changed often it doth nothing!"
```
—Letters by Sir John Suckling.]

the same earnestness and unity of purpose which render what we undertake in manhood so far more successful than what we would effect in youth, are equally visible and equally triumphant, whether directed to interest or to love. But then, as in Aram, the feelings must be fresh as well as matured; they must not have been frittered away by previous indulgence; the love must be the first produce of the soil, not the languid after-growth.

The reader will remark, that the first time in which our narrative has brought Madeline and Aram together, was not the first time they had met; Aram had long noted with admiration a beauty which he had never seen paralleled, and certain vague and unsettled feelings had preluded the deeper emotion that her image now excited within him. But the main cause of his present and growing attachment, had been in the evident sentiment of kindness which he could not but feel Madeline bore towards him. So retiring a nature as his, might never have harboured love, if the love bore the character of presumption; but that one so beautiful beyond his dreams as Madeline Lester, should deign to exercise towards him a tenderness, that might suffer him to hope, was a thought, that when he caught her eye unconsciously fixed upon him, and noted that her voice grew softer and more tremulous when she addressed him, forced itself upon his heart, and woke there a strange and irresistible emotion, which solitude and the brooding reflection that solitude produces—a reflection so much more intense in proportion to the paucity of living images it dwells upon—soon ripened into love. Perhaps even, he would not have resisted the impulse as he now did, had not at this time certain thoughts connected with past events, been more forcibly than of late years obtruded upon him, and thus in some measure divided his heart. By degrees, however, those thoughts receded from their vividness, into the habitual deep, but not oblivious, shade beneath which his commanding mind had formerly driven them to repose; and as they thus receded, Madeline's image grew more undisturbedly present, and his resolution to avoid its power more fluctuating and feeble. Fate seemed bent upon bringing together these two persons, already so attracted towards each other. After the conversation recorded in our last chapter, between Walter and the Student, the former, touched and softened as we have seen, in spite of himself, had cheerfully forborne (what before he had done reluctantly) the expressions of dislike which he had once lavished so profusely upon Aram; and Lester, who, forward as he had seemed, had nevertheless been hitherto a little checked in his advances to his neighbour by the hostility of his son, now felt no scruple to deter him from urging them with a pertinacity that almost forbade refusal. It was Aram's constant habit, in all seasons, to wander abroad at certain times of the day, especially towards the evening; and if Lester failed to win entrance to his house, he was thus enabled to meet the Student in his frequent rambles, and with a seeming freedom from design. Actuated by his great benevolence of character, Lester earnestly desired to win his solitary and unfriended neighbour from a mood and habit which he naturally imagined must engender a growing melancholy of mind; and since Walter had detailed to him the particulars of his meeting with Aram, this desire had been considerably increased. There is not perhaps a stronger feeling in the world than pity, when united with admiration. When one man is resolved to know another, it is almost impossible to prevent him: we see daily the most remarkable instances of perseverance on one side conquering distaste on the other. By degrees, then, Aram relaxed from his insociability; he seemed to surrender himself to a kindness, the sincerity of which he was compelled to acknowledge; if he for a long time refused to accept the hospitality of his neighbour, he did not reject his society when they met, and this intercourse by little and little progressed, until ultimately the recluse yielded to solicitation, and became the guest as well as companion. This, at first accident, grew, though not without many interruptions, into habit; and at length few evenings were passed by the inmates of the Manor-house without the society of the Student. As his reserve wore off, his conversation mingled with its attractions a tender and affectionate tone. He seemed grateful for the pains which had been taken to allure him to a scene in which, at last, he acknowledged he found a happiness that he never experienced before: and those who had hitherto admired him for his genius, admired him now yet more for his susceptibility to the affections.

There was not in Aram any thing that savoured of the harshness of pedantry, or the petty vanities of dogmatism: his voice was soft and low, and his manner always remarkable for its singular gentleness, and a certain dignified humility. His language did indeed, at times, assume a tone of calm and patriarchal command; but it was only the command arising from an intimate persuasion of the truth of what he uttered. Moralizing upon our nature, or mourning over the delusions of the world, a grave and solemn strain breathed throughout his lofty words and the profound melancholy of his wisdom; but it touched, not offended—elevated, not humbled—the lesser intellect of his listeners; and even this air of unconscious superiority vanished when he was invited to teach or explain. That task which so few do gracefully, that an accurate and shrewd thinker has said: "It is always safe to learn, even from our enemies; seldom safe to instruct even our friends," [Note: Lacon.] Aram performed with a meekness and simplicity that charmed the vanity, even while it corrected the ignorance, of the applicant; and so various and minute was the information of this accomplished man, that there scarcely existed any branch even of that knowledge usually called practical, to which he could not impart from his stores something valuable and new. The agriculturist was astonished at the success of his suggestions; and the mechanic was indebted to him for the device which abridged his labour in improving its result.

It happened that the study of botany was not, at that day, so favourite and common a diversion with young ladies as it is now, and Ellinor, captivated by the notion of a science that gave a life and a history to the loveliest of earth's offspring, besought Aram to teach her its principles.

As Madeline, though she did not second the request, could scarcely absent herself from sharing the lesson, this pursuit brought the pair—already lovers—closer and closer together. It associated them not only at home, but in their rambles throughout that enchanting country; and there is a mysterious influence in Nature, which renders us, in her loveliest scenes, the most susceptible to love! Then, too, how often in their occupation their hands and eyes met:—how often, by the shady wood or the soft water-side, they found themselves alone. In all times, how dangerous the connexion, when of different sexes, between the scholar and the teacher! Under how many pretences, in that connexion, the heart finds the opportunity to speak out.

Yet it was not with ease and complacency that Aram delivered himself to the intoxication of his deepening attachment. Sometimes he was studiously cold, or evidently wrestling with the powerful passion that mastered his reason. It was not without many throes, and desperate resistance, that love at length overwhelmed and subdued him; and these alternations of his mood, if they sometimes offended Madeline and sometimes wounded, still rather increased than lessened the spell which bound her to him. The doubt and the fear—the caprice and the change, which agitate the surface, swell also the tides, of passion. Woman, too, whose love is so much the creature of her imagination, always asks something of mystery and conjecture in the object of her affection. It is a luxury to her to perplex herself with a thousand apprehensions; and the more restlessly her lover occupies her mind, the more deeply he enthrals it.

Mingling with her pure and tender attachment to Aram, a high and unswerving veneration, she saw in his fitfulness, and occasional abstraction and contradiction of manner, a confirmation of the modest sentiment that most weighed upon her fears; and imagined that at those times he thought her, as she deemed herself, unworthy of his love. And this was the only struggle which she conceived to pass between the affection he evidently bore her, and the feelings which had as yet restrained him from its open avowal.

One evening, Lester and the two sisters were walking with the Student along the valley that led to the house of the latter, when they saw an old woman engaged in collecting firewood among the bushes, and a little girl holding out her apron to receive the sticks with which the crone's skinny arms unsparingly filled it. The child trembled, and seemed half-crying; while the old woman, in a harsh, grating croak, was muttering forth mingled objurgation and complaint.

There was something in the appearance of the latter at once impressive and displeasing; a dark, withered, furrowed skin was drawn like parchment over harsh and aquiline features; the eyes, through the rheum of age, glittered forth black and malignant; and even her stooping posture did not conceal a height greatly above the common stature, though gaunt and shrivelled with years and poverty. It was a form and face that might have recalled at once the celebrated description of Otway, on a part of which we have already unconsciously encroached, and the remaining part of which we shall wholly borrow.

"—On her crooked shoulders had she wrapped The tattered remnants of an old stript hanging, That served to keep her carcase from the cold, So there was nothing of a piece about her. Her lower weeds were all o'er coarsely patched With different coloured rags, black, red, white, yellow, And seemed to speak variety of wretchedness."

"See," said Lester, "one of the eyesores of our village, (I might say) the only discontented person."

"What! Dame Darkmans!" said Ellinor, quickly. "Ah! let us turn back. I hate to encounter that old woman; there is something so evil and savage in her manner of talk—and look, how she rates that poor girl, whom she has dragged or decoyed to assist her!"

Aram looked curiously on the old hag. "Poverty," said he, "makes some humble, but more malignant; is it not want that grafts the devil on this poor woman's nature? Come, let us accost her—I like conferring with distress."

"It is hard labour this?" said the Student gently.

The old woman looked up askant—the music of the voice that addressed her sounded harsh on her ear.

"Ay, ay!" she answered. "You fine gentlefolks can know what the poor suffer; ye talk and ye talk, but ye never assist."

"Say not so, Dame," said Lester; "did I not send you but yesterday bread and money? and when do you ever look up at the Hall without obtaining relief?"

"But the bread was as dry as a stick," growled the hag: "and the money, what was it? will it last a week? Oh, yes! Ye think as much of your doits and mites, as if ye stripped yourselves of a comfort to give it to us. Did ye have a dish less—a 'tato less, the day ye sent me—your charity I 'spose ye calls it? Och! fie! But the Bible's the poor cretur's comfort."

"I am glad to hear you say that, Dame," said the good-natured Lester; "and I forgive every thing else you have said, on account of that one sentence."

The old woman dropped the sticks she had just gathered, and glowered at the speaker's benevolent countenance with a malicious meaning in her dark eyes.

"An' ye do? Well, I'm glad I please ye there. Och! yes! the Bible's a mighty comfort; for it says as much that the rich man shall not inter the kingdom of Heaven! There's a truth for you, that makes the poor folk's heart chirp like a cricket—ho! ho! I sits by the imbers of a night, and I thinks and thinks as how I shall see you all burning; and ye'll ask me for a drop o' water, and I shall laugh thin from my pleasant seat with the angels. Och—it's a book for the poor that!"

The sisters shuddered. "And you think then that with envy, malice, and all uncharitableness at your heart, you are certain of Heaven? For shame! Pluck the mote from your own eye!"

"What sinnifies praching? Did not the Blessed Saviour come for the poor? Them as has rags and dry bread here will be ixalted in the nixt world; an' if we poor folk have malice as ye calls it, whose fault's that? What do ye tache us? Eh?—answer me that. Ye keeps all the larning an' all the other fine things to yoursel', and then ye scould, and thritten, and hang us, 'cause we are not as wise as you. Och! there is no jistice in the Lamb, if Heaven is not made for us; and the iverlasting Hell, with its brimstone and fire, and its gnawing an' gnashing of teeth, an' its theirst, an' its torture, and its worm that niver dies, for the like o' you."

"Come! come away," said Ellinor, pulling her father's arm.

"And if," said Aram, pausing, "if I were to say to you,—name your want and it shall be fulfilled, would you have no charity for me also?"

"Umph," returned the hag, "ye are the great scolard; and they say ye knows what no one else do. Till me now," and she approached, and familiarly, laid her bony finger on the student's arm; "till me,—have ye iver, among other fine things, known poverty?"

"I have, woman!" said Aram, sternly.

"Och ye have thin! And did ye not sit and gloat, and eat up your oun heart, an' curse the sun that looked so gay, an' the winged things that played so blithe-like, an' scowl at the rich folk that niver wasted a thought on ye? till me now, your honour, till me!"

And the crone curtesied with a mock air of beseeching humility.

"I never forgot, even in want, the love due to my fellow-sufferers; for, woman, we all suffer,—the rich and the poor: there are worse pangs than those of want!"

"Ye think there be, do ye? that's a comfort, umph! Well, I'll till ye now, I feel a rispict for you, that I don't for the rest on 'em; for your face does not insult me with being cheary like their's yonder; an' I have noted ye walk in the dusk with your eyes down and your arms crossed; an' I have said,—that man I do not hate, somehow, for he has something dark at his heart like me!"

"The lot of earth is woe," answered Aram calmly, yet shrinking back from the crone's touch; "judge we charitably, and act we kindly to each other. There—this money is not much, but it will light your hearth and heap your table without toil, for some days at least!"

"Thank your honour: an' what think you I'll do with the money?"

"What?"

"Drink, drink, drink!" cried the hag fiercely; "there's nothing like drink for the poor, for thin we fancy oursels what we wish, and," sinking her voice into a whisper, "I thinks thin that I have my foot on the billies of the rich folks, and my hands twisted about their intrails, and I hear them shriek, and—thin I'm happy!"

"Go home!" said Aram, turning away, "and open the Book of life with other thoughts."

The little party proceeded, and, looking back, Lester saw the old woman gaze after them, till a turn in the winding valley hid her from his sight.

"That is a strange person, Aram; scarcely a favourable specimen of the happy English peasant;" said Lester, smiling.

"Yet they say," added Madeline, "that she was not always the same perverse and hateful creature she is now."

"Ay," said Aram, "and what then is her history?"

"Why," replied Madeline, slightly blushing to find herself made the narrator of a story, "some forty years ago this woman, so gaunt and hideous now, was the beauty of the village. She married an Irish soldier whose regiment passed through Grassdale, and was heard of no more till about ten years back, when she returned to her native place, the discontented, envious, altered being you now see her."

"She is not reserved in regard to her past life," said Lester. "She is too happy to seize the attention of any one to whom she can pour forth her dark and angry confidence. She saw her husband, who was afterwards dismissed the service, a strong, powerful man, a giant of his tribe, pine and waste, inch by inch, from mere physical want, and at last literally die from hunger. It happened that they had settled in the country in which her husband was born, and in that county, those frequent famines which are the scourge of Ireland were for two years especially severe. You may note, that the old woman has a strong vein of coarse eloquence at her command, perhaps acquired in (for it partakes of the natural character of) the country in which she lived so long; and it would literally thrill you with horror to hear her descriptions of the misery and destitution that she witnessed, and amidst which her husband breathed his last. Out of four children, not one survives. One, an infant, died within a week of the father; two sons were executed, one at the age of sixteen, one a year older, for robbery committed under aggravated circumstances; and the fourth, a daughter, died in the hospitals of London. The old woman became a wanderer and a vagrant, and was at length passed to her native parish, where she has since dwelt. These are the misfortunes which have turned her blood to gall; and these are the causes which fill her with so bitter a hatred against those whom wealth has preserved from sharing or witnessing a fate similar to hers."

"Oh!" said Aram, in a low, but deep tone, "when—when will these hideous disparities be banished from the world? How many noble natures—how many glorious hopes—how much of the seraph's intellect, have been crushed into the mire, or blasted into guilt, by the mere force of physical want? What are the temptations of the rich to those of the poor? Yet see how lenient we are to the crimes of the one,—how relentless to those of the other! It is a bad world; it makes a man's heart sick to look around him. The consciousness of how little individual genius can do to relieve the mass, grinds out, as with a stone, all that is generous in ambition; and to aspire from the level of life is but to be more graspingly selfish."

"Can legislators, or the moralists that instruct legislators, do so little, then, towards universal good?" said Lester, doubtingly.

"Why? what can they do but forward civilization? And what is civilization, but an increase of human disparities? The more the luxury of the few, the more startling the wants, and the more galling the sense, of poverty. Even the dreams of the philanthropist only tend towards equality; and where is equality to be found, but in the state of the savage? No; I thought otherwise once; but I now regard the vast lazar-house around us without hope of relief:—Death is the sole Physician!"

"Ah, no!" said the high-souled Madeline, eagerly; "do not take away from us the best feeling and the highest desire we can cherish. How poor, even in this beautiful world, with the warm sun and fresh air about us, that alone are sufficient to make us glad, would be life, if we could not make the happiness of others!"

Aram looked at the beautiful speaker with a soft and half-mournful smile. There is one very peculiar pleasure that we feel as we grow older,—it is to see embodied in another and a more lovely shape the thoughts and sentiments we once nursed ourselves; it is as if we viewed before us the incarnation of our own youth; and it is no wonder that we are warmed towards the object, that thus seems the living apparition of all that was brightest in ourselves! It was with this sentiment that Aram now gazed on Madeline. She felt the gaze, and her heart beat delightedly, but she sunk at once into a silence, which she did not break during the rest of their walk.

"I do not say," said Aram, after a pause, "that we are not able to make the happiness of those immediately around us. I speak only of what we can effect for the mass. And it is a deadening thought to mental ambition, that the circle of happiness we can create is formed more by our moral than our mental qualities. A warm heart, though accompanied but by a mediocre understanding, is even more likely to promote the happiness of those around, than are the absorbed and abstract, though kindly powers of a more elevated genius; but (observing Lester about to interrupt him), let us turn from this topic,—let us turn from man's weakness to the glories of the mother-nature, from which he sprung."

And kindling, as he ever did, the moment he approached a subject so dear to his studies, Aram now spoke of the stars, which began to sparkle forth,—of the vast, illimitable career which recent science had opened to the imagination,—and of the old, bewildering, yet eloquent theories, which from age to age had at once misled and elevated the conjecture of past sages. All this was a theme which his listeners loved to listen to, and Madeline not the least. Youth, beauty, pomp, what are these, in point of attraction, to a woman's heart, when compared to eloquence?—the magic of the tongue is the most dangerous of all spells!

CHAPTER VIII.

THE PRIVILEGE OF GENIUS.—LESTER'S SATISFACTION AT THE ASPECT OF EVENTS.—HIS CONVERSATION WITH WALTER.—A DISCOVERY.

"Alc.—I am for Lidian:
This accident no doubt will draw him from his hermit's life!

"Lis.—Spare my grief, and apprehend
What I should speak."
—Beaumont and Fletcher.—The Lovers' Progress.

In the course of the various conversations our family of Grassdale enjoyed with their singular neighbour, it appeared that his knowledge had not been confined to the closet; at times, he dropped remarks which shewed that he had been much among cities, and travelled with the design, or at least with the vigilance, of the observer; but he did not love to be drawn into any detailed accounts of what he had seen, or whither he had been; an habitual though a gentle reserve, kept watch over the past—not indeed that character of reserve which excites the doubt, but which inspires the interest. His most gloomy moods were rather abrupt and fitful than morose, and his usual bearing was calm, soft, and even tender.

There is a certain charm about great superiority of intellect, that winds into deep affections which a much more constant and even amiability of manners in lesser men, often fails to reach. Genius makes many enemies, but it makes sure friends—friends who forgive much, who endure long, who exact little; they partake of the character of disciples as well as friends. There lingers about the human heart a strong inclination to look upward—to revere: in this inclination lies the source of religion, of loyalty, and also of the worship and immortality which are rendered so cheerfully to the great of old. And in truth, it is a divine pleasure to admire! admiration seems in some measure to appropriate to ourselves the qualities it honours in others. We wed,—we root ourselves to the natures we so love to contemplate, and their life grows a part of our own. Thus, when a great man, who has engrossed our thoughts, our conjectures, our homage, dies, a gap seems suddenly left in the world; a wheel in the mechanism of our own being appears abruptly stilled; a portion of ourselves, and not our worst portion, for how many pure, high, generous sentiments it contains, dies with him! Yes! it is this love, so rare, so exalted, and so denied to all ordinary men, which is the especial privilege of greatness, whether that greatness be shewn in wisdom, in enterprise, in virtue, or even, till the world learns better, in the more daring and lofty order of crime. A Socrates may claim it to-day—a Napoleon to-morrow; nay, a brigand chief, illustrious in the circle in which he lives, may call it forth no less powerfully than the generous failings of a Byron, or the sublime excellence of the greater Milton.

Lester saw with evident complacency the passion growing up between his friend and his daughter; he looked upon it as a tie that would permanently reconcile Aram to the hearth of social and domestic life; a tie that would constitute the happiness of his daughter, and secure to himself a relation in the man he felt most inclined, of all he knew, to honour and esteem. He remarked in the gentleness and calm temper of Aram much that was calculated to ensure domestic peace, and knowing the peculiar disposition of Madeline, he felt that she was exactly the person, not only to bear with the peculiarities of the Student, but to venerate their source. In short, the more he contemplated the idea of this alliance, the more he was charmed with its probability.

Musing on this subject, the good Squire was one day walking in his garden, when he perceived his nephew at some distance, and remarked that Walter, on seeing him, was about, instead of coming forward to meet him, to turn down an alley in an opposite direction.

A little pained at this, and remembering that Walter had of late seemed estranged from himself, and greatly altered from the high and cheerful spirits natural to his temper, Lester called to his nephew; and Walter, reluctantly and slowly changing his purpose of avoidance, advanced and met him.

"Why, Walter!" said the uncle, taking his arm; "this is somewhat unkind, to shun me; are you engaged in any pursuit that requires secrecy or haste?"

"No, indeed, Sir!" said Walter, with some embarrassment; "but I thought you seemed wrapped in reflection, and would naturally dislike being disturbed."

"Hem! as to that, I have no reflections I wish concealed from you, Walter, or which might not be benefited by your advice." The youth pressed his uncle's hand, but made no reply; and Lester, after a pause, continued:—

"You seem, Walter, I am most delighted to think, entirely to have overcome the little unfavourable prepossession which at first you testified towards our excellent neighbour. And for my part, I think he appears to be especially attracted towards yourself, he seeks your company; and to me he always speaks of you in terms, which, coming from such a quarter, give me the most lively gratification."

Walter bowed his head, but not in the delighted vanity with which a young man generally receives the assurance of another's praise.

"I own," renewed Lester, "that I consider our friendship with Aram one of the most fortunate occurrences in my life; at least," added he with a sigh, "of late years. I doubt not but you must have observed the partiality with which our dear Madeline evidently regards him; and yet more, the attachment to her, which breaks forth from Aram, in spite of his habitual reserve and self-control. You have surely noted this, Walter?"

"I have," said Walter, in a low tone, and turning away his head.

"And doubtless you share my satisfaction. It happens fortunately now, that Madeline early contracted that studious and thoughtful turn, which I must own at one time gave me some uneasiness and vexation. It has taught her to appreciate the value of a mind like Aram's. Formerly, my dear boy, I hoped that at one time or another, she and yourself might form a dearer connection than that of cousins. But I was disappointed, and I am now consoled. And indeed I think there is that in Ellinor which might be yet more calculated to render you happy; that is, if the bias of your mind should ever lean that way."

"You are very good," said Walter, bitterly. "I own I am not flattered by your selection; nor do I see why the plainest and least brilliant of the two sisters must necessarily be the fittest for me."

"Nay," replied Lester, piqued, and justly angry, "I do not think, even if Madeline have the advantage of her sister, that you can find any fault with the personal or mental attractions of Ellinor. But indeed this is not a matter in which relations should interfere. I am far from any wish to prevent you from choosing throughout the world any one whom you may prefer. All I hope is, that your future wife will be like Ellinor in kindness of heart and sweetness of temper."

"From choosing throughout the world!" repeated Walter; "and how in this nook am I to see the world?"

"Walter! your voice is reproachful!—do I deserve it?"

Walter was silent.

"I have of late observed," continued Lester, "and with wounded feelings, that you do not give me the same confidence, or meet me with the same affection, that you once delighted me by manifesting towards me. I know of no cause for this change. Do not let us, my son, for I may so call you—do not let us, as we grow older, grow also more apart. Time divides with a sufficient demarcation the young from the old; why deepen the necessary line? You know well, that I have never from your childhood insisted heavily on a guardian's authority. I have always loved to contribute to your enjoyments, and shewn you how devoted I am to your interests, by the very frankness with which I have consulted you on my own. If there be now on your mind any secret grievance, or any secret wish, speak it, Walter:—you are alone with the friend on earth who loves you best!"

Walter was wholly overcome by this address: he pressed his good uncle's hand to his lips, and it was some moments before he mustered self-composure sufficient to reply.

"You have ever, ever been to me all that the kindest parent, the tenderest friend could have been:—believe me, I am not ungrateful. If of late I have been altered, the cause is not in you. Let me speak freely: you encourage me to do so. I am young, my temper is restless; I have a love of enterprise and adventure: is it not natural that I should long to see the world? This is the cause of my late abstraction of mind. I have now told you all: it is for you to decide."

Lester looked wistfully on his nephew's countenance before he replied—

"It is as I gathered," said he, "from various remarks which you have lately let fall. I cannot blame your wish to leave us; it is certainly natural: nor can I oppose it. Go, Walter, when you will!"

The young man turned round with a lighted eye and flushed cheek.

"And why, Walter?" said Lester, interrupting his thanks, "why this surprise? why this long doubt of my affection? Could you believe I should refuse a wish that, at your age, I should have expressed myself? You have wronged me; you might have saved a world of pain to us both by acquainting me with your desire when it was first formed; but, enough. I see Madeline and Aram approach,—let us join them now, and to-morrow we will arrange the time and method of your departure.

"Forgive me, Sir," said Walter, stopping abruptly as the glow faded from his cheek, "I have not yet recovered myself; I am not fit for other society than yours. Excuse my joining my cousin, and—"

"Walter!" said Lester, also stopping short and looking full on his nephew, "a painful thought flashes upon me! Would to heaven I may be wrong!—Have you ever felt for Madeline more tenderly than for her sister?"

Walter literally trembled as he stood. The tears rushed into Lester's eyes:—he grasped his nephew's hand warmly—

"God comfort thee, my poor boy!" said he, with great emotion; "I never dreamt of this."

Walter felt now that he was understood. He gratefully returned the pressure of his uncle's hand, and then, withdrawing his own, darted down one of the intersecting walks, and was almost instantly out of sight.

CHAPTER IX.

THE STATE OF WALTER'S MIND.—AN ANGLER AND A MAN OF THE
WORLD.—A COMPANION FOUND FOR WALTER.

"This great disease for love I dre,
There is no tongue can tell the wo;
I love the love that loves not me,
I may not mend, but mourning mo."
—The Mourning Maiden.

"I in these flowery meads would be,
These crystal streams should solace me,
To whose harmonious bubbling voice

I with my angle would rejoice."
—Izaac Walton.

When Walter left his uncle, he hurried, scarcely conscious of his steps, towards his favourite haunt by the water-side. From a child, he had singled out that scene as the witness of his early sorrows or boyish schemes; and still, the solitude of the place cherished the habit of his boyhood.

Long had he, unknown to himself, nourished an attachment to his beautiful cousin; nor did he awaken to the secret of his heart, until, with an agonizing jealousy, he penetrated the secret at her own. The reader has, doubtless, already perceived that it was this jealousy which at the first occasioned Walter's dislike to Aram: the consolation of that dislike was forbid him now. The gentleness and forbearance of the Student's deportment had taken away all ground of offence; and Walter had sufficient generosity to acknowledge his merits, while tortured by their effect. Silently, till this day, he had gnawed his heart, and found for its despair no confidant and no comfort. The only wish that he cherished was a feverish and gloomy desire to leave the scene which witnessed the triumph of his rival. Every thing around had become hateful to his eyes, and a curse had lighted upon the face of Home. He thought now, with a bitter satisfaction, that his escape was at hand: in a few days he might be rid of the gall and the pang, which every moment of his stay at Grassdale inflicted upon him. The sweet voice of Madeline he should hear no more, subduing its silver sound for his rival's ear:—no more he should watch apart, and himself unheeded, how timidly her glance roved in search of another, or how vividly her cheek flushed when the step of that happier one approached. Many miles would at least shut out this picture from his view; and in absence, was it not possible that he might teach himself to forget? Thus meditating, he arrived at the banks of the little brooklet, and was awakened from his reverie by the sound of his own name. He started, and saw the old Corporal seated on the stump of a tree, and busily employed in fixing to his line the mimic likeness of what anglers, and, for aught we know, the rest of the world, call the "violet fly."

"Ha! master,—at my day's work, you see:—fit for nothing else now. When a musquet's halfworn out, schoolboys buy it—pop it at sparrows. I be like the musket: but never mind—have not seen the world for nothing. We get reconciled to all things: that's my way—augh! Now, Sir, you shall watch me catch the finest trout you have seen this summer: know where he lies—under the bush yonder. Whi—sh! Sir, whi—sh!"

The Corporal now gave his warrior soul up to the due guidance of the violet-fly: now he shipped it lightly on the wave; now he slid it coquettishly along the surface; now it floated, like an unconscious beauty, carelessly with the tide; and now, like an artful prude, it affected to loiter by the way, or to steal into designing obscurity under the shade of some overhanging bank. But none of these manoeuvres captivated the wary old trout on whose acquisition the Corporal had set his heart; and what was especially provoking, the angler could see distinctly the dark outline of the intended victim, as it lay at the bottom,—like some well-regulated bachelor who eyes from afar the charms he has discreetly resolved to neglect.

The Corporal waited till he could no longer blind himself to the displeasing fact, that the violet-fly was wholly inefficacious; he then drew up his line, and replaced the contemned beauty of the violet-fly, with the novel attractions of the yellow-dun.

"Now, Sir!" whispered he, lifting up his finger, and nodding sagaciously to Walter. Softly dropped the yellow-dun upon the water, and swiftly did it glide before the gaze of the latent trout; and now the trout seemed aroused from his apathy, behold he moved forward, balancing himself on his fins; now he slowly ascended towards the surface; you might see all the speckles of his coat;—the Corporal's heart stood still—he is now at a convenient distance from the yellow-dun; lo, he surveys it steadfastly; he ponders, he see-saws himself to and fro. The yellow-dun sails away in affected indifference, that indifference whets the appetite of the hesitating gazer, he darts forward; he is opposite the yellow-dun,—he pushes his nose against it with an eager rudeness,—he—no, he does not bite, he recoils, he gazes again with surprise and suspicion on the little charmer; he fades back slowly into the deeper water, and then suddenly turning his tail towards the disappointed bait, he makes off as fast as he can,—yonder,—yonder, and disappears! No, that's he leaping yonder from the wave; Jupiter! what a noble fellow! What leaps he at?—a real fly—"Damn his eyes!" growled the Corporal.

"You might have caught him with a minnow," said Walter, speaking for the first time.

"Minnow!" repeated the Corporal gruffly, "ask your honour's pardon. Minnow!—I have fished with the yellow-dun these twenty years, and never knew it fail before. Minnow!—baugh! But ask pardon; your honour is very welcome to fish with a minnow if you please it."

"Thank you, Bunting. And pray what sport have you had to-day?"

"Oh,—good, good," quoth the Corporal, snatching up his basket and closing the cover, lest the young Squire should pry into it. No man is more tenacious of his secrets than your true angler. "Sent the best home two hours ago; one weighed three pounds, on the faith of a man; indeed, I'm satisfied now; time to give up;" and the Corporal began to disjoint his rod.

"Ah, Sir!" said he, with a half sigh, "a pretty river this, don't mean to say it is not; but the river Lea for my money. You know the Lea?—not a morning's walk from Lunnun. Mary Gibson, my first sweetheart, lived by the bridge,—caught such a trout there by the by!—had beautiful eyes—black, round as a cherry—five feet eight without shoes—might have listed in the forty-second."

"Who, Bunting!" said Walter smiling, "the lady or the trout?"

"Augh!—baugh!—what? Oh, laughing at me, your honour, you're welcome, Sir. Love's a silly thing—know the world now—have not fallen in love these ten years. I doubt—no offence, Sir, no offence—I doubt whether your honour and Miss Ellinor can say as much."

"I and Miss Ellinor!—you forge yourself strangely, Bunting," said Walter, colouring with anger.

"Beg pardon, Sir, beg pardon—rough soldier—lived away from the world so long, words slipped out of my mouth—absent without leave."

"But why," said Walter, smothering or conquering his vexation,—"why couple me with Miss Ellinor? Did you imagine that we,—we were in love with each other?"

"Indeed, Sir, and if I did, 'tis no more than my neighbours imagine too."

"Humph! your neighbours are very silly, then, and very wrong."

"Beg pardon, Sir, again—always getting askew. Indeed some did say it was Miss Madeline, but I says,—says I,—'No! I'm a man of the world—see through a millstone; Miss Madeline's too easy like; Miss Nelly blushes when he speaks;'scarlet is love's regimentals—it was ours in the forty-second, edged with yellow—pepper and salt pantaloons! For my part I think,—but I've no business to think, howsomever—baugh!"

"Pray what do you think, Mr. Bunting? Why do you hesitate?"

"'Fraid of offence—but I do think that Master Aram—your honour understands—howsomever Squire's daughter too great a match for such as he!"

Walter did not answer; and the garrulous old soldier, who had been the young man's playmate and companion since Walter was a boy; and was therefore accustomed to the familiarity with which he now spoke, continued, mingling with his abrupt prolixity an occasional shrewdness of observation, which shewed that he was no inattentive commentator on the little and quiet world around him.

"Free to confess, Squire Walter, that I don't quite like this larned man, as much as the rest of 'em—something queer about him—can't see to the bottom of him—don't think he's quite so meek and lamb-like as he seems:—once saw a calm dead pool in foren parts—peered down into it—by little and little, my eye got used to it—saw something dark at the bottom—stared and stared—by Jupiter—a great big alligator!—walked off immediately—never liked quiet pools since—augh, no!"

"An argument against quiet pools, perhaps, Bunting; but scarcely against quiet people."

"Don't know as to that, your honour—much of a muchness. I have seen Master Aram, demure as he looks, start, and bite his lip, and change colour, and frown—he has an ugly frown, I can tell ye—when he thought no one nigh. A man who gets in a passion with himself may be soon out of temper with others. Free to confess, I should not like to see him married to that stately beautiful young lady—but they do gossip about it in the village. If it is not true, better put the Squire on his guard—false rumours often beget truths—beg pardon, your honour—no business of mine—baugh! But I'm a lone man, who have seen the world, and I thinks on the things around me, and I turns over the quid—now on this side, now on the other—'tis my way, Sir—and—but I offend your honour."

"Not at all; I know you are an honest man, Bunting, and well affected to our family; at the same time it is neither prudent nor charitable to speak harshly of our neighbours without sufficient cause. And really you seem to me to be a little hasty in your judgment of a man so inoffensive in his habits and so justly and generally esteemed as Mr. Aram."

"May be, Sir—may be,—very right what you say. But I thinks what I thinks all the same; and indeed, it is a thing that puzzles me, how that strange-looking vagabond, as frighted the ladies so, and who, Miss Nelly told me, for she saw them in his pocket, carried pistols about him, as if he had been among cannibals and hottentots, instead of the peaceablest county that man ever set foot in, should boast of his friendship with this larned schollard, and pass a whole night in his house. Birds of a feather flock together—augh!—Sir!"

"A man cannot surely be answerable for the respectability of all his acquaintances, even though he feel obliged to offer them the accommodation of a night's shelter."

"Baugh!" grunted the Corporal. "Seen the world, Sir—seen the world—young gentlemen are always so good-natured; 'tis a pity, that the more one sees the more suspicious one grows. One does not have gumption till one has been properly cheated—one must be made a fool very often in order not to be fooled at last!"

"Well, Corporal, I shall now have opportunities enough of profiting by experience. I am going to leave Grassdale in a few days, and learn suspicion and wisdom in the great world."

"Augh! baugh!—what?" cried the Corporal, starting from the contemplative air which he had hitherto assumed. "The great world?—how?—when?—going away;—who goes with your honour?"

"My honour's self; I have no companion, unless you like to attend me;" said Walter, jestingly—but the Corporal affected, with his natural shrewdness, to take the proposition in earnest.

"I! your honour's too good; and indeed, though I say it, Sir, you might do worse; not but what I should be sorry to leave nice snug home here, and this stream, though the trout have been shy lately,—ah! that was a mistake of yours, Sir, recommending the minnow; and neighbour Dealtry, though his ale's not so good at 'twas last year; and—and—but, in short, I always loved your honour—dandled you on my knees;—You recollect the broadsword exercise?—one, two, three—augh! baugh!—and if your honour really is going, why rather than you should want a proper person who knows the world, to brush your coat, polish your shoes, give you good advice—on the faith of a man, I'll go with you myself!"

This alacrity on the part of the Corporal was far from displeasing to Walter. The proposal he had at first made unthinkingly, he now seriously thought advisable; and at length it was settled that the Corporal should call the next morning at the manor-house, and receive instructions as to the time and method of their departure. Not forgetting, as the sagacious Bunting delicately insinuated, "the wee settlements as to wages, and board wages, more a matter of form, like, than any thing else—augh!"

CHAPTER X.

THE LOVERS.—THE ENCOUNTER AND QUARREL OF THE RIVALS.

```
Two such I saw, what time the laboured ox
In his loose traces from the furrow came.
        —Comus.


Pedro. Now do me noble right.
Rod. I'll satisfy you;
But not by the sword.
    —Beaumont and Fletcher.—The Pilgrim.
```

While Walter and the Corporal enjoyed the above conversation, Madeline and Aram, whom Lester soon left to themselves, were pursuing their walk along the solitary fields. Their love had passed from the eye to the lip, and now found expression in words.

"Observe," said he, as the light touch of one who he felt loved him entirely rested on his arm,—"Observe, as the later summer now begins to breathe a more various and mellow glory into the landscape, how singularly pure and lucid the atmosphere becomes. When, two months ago, in the full flush of June, I walked through these fields, a grey mist hid yon distant hills and the far forest from my view. Now, with what a transparent stillness the whole expanse of scenery spreads itself before us. And such, Madeline, is the change that has come over myself since that time. Then, if I looked beyond the limited present, all was dim and indistinct. Now, the mist had faded away—the broad future extends before me, calm and bright with the hope which is borrowed from your love!"

We will not tax the patience of the reader, who seldom enters with keen interest into the mere dialogue of love, with the blushing Madeline's reply, or with all the soft vows and tender confessions which the rich poetry of Aram's mind made yet more delicious to the ear of his dreaming and devoted mistress.

"There is one circumstance," said Aram, "which casts a momentary shade on the happiness I enjoy—my Madeline probably guesses its nature. I regret to see that the blessing of your love must be purchased by the misery of another, and that other, the nephew of my kind friend. You have doubtless observed the melancholy of Walter Lester, and have long since known its origin."

"Indeed, Eugene," answered Madeline, "it has given me great pain to note what you refer to, for it would be a false delicacy in me to deny that I have observed it. But Walter is young and high-spirited; nor do I think he is of a nature to love long where there is no return!"

"And what," said Aram, sorrowfully,—"what deduction from reason can ever apply to love? Love is a very contradiction of all the elements of our ordinary nature,—it makes the proud man meek,—the cheerful, sad,—the high-spirited, tame; our strongest resolutions, our hardiest energy fail before it. Believe me, you cannot prophesy of its future effect in a man from any knowledge of his past character. I grieve to think that the blow falls upon one in early youth, ere the world's disappointments have blunted the heart, or the world's numerous interests have multiplied its resources. Men's minds have been turned when they have not well sifted the cause themselves, and their fortunes marred, by one stroke on the affections of their youth. So at least have I read, Madeline, and so marked in others. For myself, I knew nothing of love in its reality till I knew you. But who can know you, and not sympathise with him who has lost you?"

"Ah, Eugene! you at least overrate the influence which love produces on men. A little resentment and a little absence will soon cure my cousin of an ill-placed and ill-requited attachment. You do not think how easy it is to forget."

"Forget!" said Aram, stopping abruptly; "Ay, forget—it is a strange truth! we do forget! the summer passes over the furrow, and the corn springs up; the sod forgets the flower of the past year; the battle-field forgets the blood that has been spilt upon its turf; the sky forgets the storm; and the water the noon-day sun that slept upon its bosom. All Nature preaches forgetfulness. Its very order is the progress of oblivion. And I—I—give me your hand, Madeline,—I, ha! ha! I forget too!"

As Aram spoke thus wildly, his countenance worked; but his voice was slow, and scarcely audible; he seemed rather conferring with himself, than addressing Madeline. But when his words ceased, and he felt the soft hand of his betrothed, and turning, saw her anxious and wistful eyes fixed in alarm, yet in all unsuspecting confidence, on his face; his features relaxed into their usual serenity, and kissing the hand he clasped, he continued, in a collected and steady tone,

"Forgive me, my sweetest Madeline. These fitful and strange moods sometimes come upon me yet. I have been so long in the habit of pursuing any train of thought, however wild, that presents itself to my mind, that I cannot easily break it, even in your presence. All studious men—the twilight Eremites of books and closets, contract this ungraceful custom of soliloquy. You know our abstraction is a common jest and proverb: you must laugh me out of it. But stay, dearest!—there is a rare herb at your feet, let me gather it. So, do you note its leaves—this bending and silver flower? Let us rest on this bank, and I will tell you of its qualities. Beautiful as it is, it has a poison."

The place in which the lovers rested, is one which the villagers to this day call "The Lady's-seat;" for Madeline, whose history is fondly preserved in that district, was afterwards wont constantly to repair to that bank (during a short absence of her lover, hereafter to be noted), and subsequent events stamped with interest every spot she was known to have favoured with resort. And when the flower had been duly conned, and the study dismissed, Aram, to whom all the signs of the seasons were familiar, pointed to her the thousand symptoms of the month which are unheeded by less observant eyes; not forgetting, as they thus reclined, their hands clasped together, to couple each remark with some allusion to his love or some deduction which heightened compliment into poetry. He bade her mark the light gossamer as it floated on the air; now soaring high—high into the translucent atmosphere; now suddenly stooping, and sailing away beneath the boughs, which ever and anon it hung with a silken web, that by the next morn, would glitter with a thousand dew drops. "And, so," said he fancifully, "does Love lead forth its numberless creations, making the air its path and empire; ascending aloof at its wild will, hanging its meshes on every bough, and bidding the common grass break into a fairy lustre at the beam of the daily sun!"

He pointed to her the spot, where, in the silent brake, the harebells, now waxing rare and few, yet lingered—or where the mystic ring on the soft turf conjured up the associations of Oberon and his train. That superstition gave licence and play to his full memory and glowing fancy; and Shakspeare—Spenser—Ariosto—the magic of each mighty master of Fairy Realm—he evoked, and poured into her transported ear. It was precisely such arts, which to a gayer and more worldly nature than Madeline's might have seemed but wearisome, that arrested and won her imaginative and high-wrought mind. And thus he, who to another might have proved but the retired and moody Student, became to her the very being of whom her "Maiden meditation" had dreamed—the master and magician of her fate.

Aram did not return to the house with Madeline; he accompanied her to the garden gate, and then taking leave of her, bent his way homeward. He had gained the entrance of the little valley that led to his abode, when he saw Walter cross his path at a short distance. His heart, naturally susceptible to kindly emotion, smote him as he remarked the moody listlessness of the young man's step, and recalled the buoyant lightness it was once wont habitually to wear. He quickened his pace, and joined Walter before the latter was aware of his presence.

"Good evening," said he, mildly; "if you are going my way, give me the benefit of your company."

"My path lies yonder," replied Walter, somewhat sullenly; "I regret that it is different from yours."

"In that case," said Aram, "I can delay my return home, and will, with your leave, intrude my society upon you for some few minutes."

Walter bowed his head in reluctant assent. They walked on for some moments without speaking, the one unwilling, the other seeking an occasion, to break the silence.

"This to my mind," said Aram at length, "is the most pleasing landscape in the whole country; observe the bashful water stealing away among the woodlands. Methinks the wave is endowed with an instinctive wisdom, that it thus shuns the world."

"Rather," said Walter, "with the love for change which exists everywhere in nature, it does not seek the shade until it has passed by 'towered cities,'and 'the busy hum of men.'"

"I admire the shrewdness of your reply," rejoined Aram; "but note how far more pure and lovely are its waters in these retreats, than when washing the walls of the reeking town, receiving into its breast the taint of a thousand pollutions, vexed by the sound, and stench, and unholy perturbation of men's dwelling-place. Now it glasses only what is high or beautiful in nature—the stars or the leafy banks. The wind that ruffles it, is clothed with perfumes; the rivulet that swells it, descends from the everlasting mountains, or is formed by the rains of Heaven. Believe me, it is the type of a life that glides into solitude, from the weariness and fretful turmoil of the world.

'No flattery, hate, or envy lodgeth there, There no suspicion walled in proved steel, Yet fearful of the arms herself doth wear, Pride is not there; no tyrant there we feel!'"

[Phineas Fletcher.]

"I will not cope with you in simile, or in poetry," said Walter, as his lip curved; "it is enough for me to think that life should be spent in action. I hasten to prove if my judgment be erroneous."

"Are you, then, about to leave us?" inquired Aram.

"Yes, within a few days."

"Indeed, I regret to hear it."

The answer sounded jarringly on the irritated nerves of the disappointed rival.

"You do me more honour than I desire," said he, "in interesting yourself, however lightly, in my schemes or fortune!"

"Young man," replied Aram, coldly, "I never see the impetuous and yearning spirit of youth without a certain, and it may be, a painful interest. How feeble is the chance, that its hopes will be fulfilled! Enough, if it lose not all its loftier aspirings, as well as its brighter expectations."

Nothing more aroused the proud and fiery temper of Walter Lester than the tone of superior wisdom and superior age, which his rival assumed towards him. More and more displeased with his present companion, he answered, in no conciliatory tone, "I cannot but consider the warning and the fears of one, neither my relation nor my friend, in the light of a gratuitous affront."

Aram smiled as he answered,

"There is no occasion for resentment. Preserve this hot spirit, and high self-confidence, till you return again to these scenes, and I shall be at once satisfied and corrected."

"Sir," said Walter, colouring, and irritated more by the smile than the words of his rival, "I am not aware by what right or on what ground you assume towards me the superiority, not only of admonition but reproof. My uncle's preference towards you gives you no authority over me. That preference I do not pretend to share."—He paused for a moment, thinking Aram might hasten to reply; but as the Student walked on with his usual calmness of demeanour, he added, stung by the indifference which he attributed, not altogether without truth, to disdain, "And since you have taken upon yourself to caution me, and to forebode my inability to resist the contamination, as you would term it, of the world, I tell you, that it may be happy for you to bear so clear a conscience, so untouched a spirit as that which I now boast, and with which I trust in God and my own soul I shall return to my birth-place. It is not the holy only that love solitude; and men may shun the world from another motive than that of philosophy."

It was now Aram's turn to feel resentment, and this was indeed an insinuation not only unwarrantable in itself, but one which a man of so peaceable and guileless a life, affecting even an extreme and rigid austerity of morals, might well be tempted to repel with scorn and indignation; and Aram, however meek and forbearing in general, testified in this instance that his wonted gentleness arose from no lack of man's natural spirit. He laid his hand commandingly on young Lester's shoulder, and surveyed his countenance with a dark and menacing frown.

"Boy!" said he, "were there meaning in your words, I should (mark me!) avenge the insult;—as it is, I despise it. Go!"

So high and lofty was Aram's manner—so majestic was the sternness of his rebuke, and the dignity of his bearing, as he now waving his hand turned away, that Walter lost his self-possession and stood fixed to the spot, absorbed, and humbled from his late anger. It was not till Aram had moved with a slow step several paces backward towards his home, that the bold and haughty temper of the young man returned to his aid. Ashamed of himself for the momentary weakness he had betrayed, and burning to redeem it, he hastened after the stately form of his rival, and planting himself full in his path, said, in a voice half choked with contending emotions,

"Hold!—you have given me the opportunity I have long desired; you yourself have now broken that peace which existed between us, and which to me was more bitter than wormwood. You have dared,—yes, dared to use threatening language towards me. I call on you to fulfil your threat. I tell you that I meant, I designed, I thirsted to affront you. Now resent my purposed—premeditated affront as you will and can!"

There was something remarkable in the contrasted figures of the rivals, as they now stood fronting each other. The elastic and vigorous form of Walter Lester, his sparkling eyes, his sunburnt and glowing cheek, his clenched hands, and his whole frame, alive and eloquent with the energy, the heat, the hasty courage, and fiery spirit of youth; on the other hand,—the bending frame of the student, gradually rising into the dignity of its full height—his pale cheek, in which the wan hues neither deepened nor waned, his large eye raised to meet Walter's bright, steady, and yet how calm! Nothing weak, nothing irresolute could be traced in that form—or that lofty countenance; yet all resentment had vanished from his aspect. He seemed at once tranquil and prepared.

"You designed to affront me!" said he; "it is well—it is a noble confession;—and wherefore? What do you propose to gain by it?—a man whose whole life is peace, you would provoke to outrage? Would there be triumph in this, or disgrace?—A man whom your uncle honours and loves, you would insult without cause—you would waylay—you would, after watching and creating your opportunity, entrap into defending himself. Is this worthy of that high spirit of which you boasted?—is this worthy a generous anger, or a noble hatred? Away! you malign yourself. I shrink from no quarrel—why should I? I have nothing to fear: my nerves are firm—my heart is faithful to my will; my habits may have diminished my strength, but it is yet equal to that of most men. As to the weapons of the world—they fall not to my use. I might be excused by the most punctilious, for rejecting what becomes neither my station nor my habits of life; but I learnt this much from books long since, 'hold thyself prepared for all things:'—I am so prepared. And as I can command the spirit, I lack not the skill, to defend myself, or return the hostility of another." As Aram thus said, he drew a pistol from his bosom; and pointed it leisurely towards a tree, at the distance of some paces.

"Look," said he, "you note that small discoloured and white stain in the bark—you can but just observe it;—he who can send a bullet through that spot, need not fear to meet the quarrel which he seeks to avoid."

Walter turned mechanically, and indignant, though silent, towards the tree. Aram fired, and the ball penetrated the centre of the stain. He then replaced the pistol in his bosom, and said:—

"Early in life I had many enemies, and I taught myself these arts. From habit, I still bear about me the weapons I trust and pray I may never have occasion to use. But to return.—I have offended you—I have incurred your hatred—why? What are my sins?"

"Do you ask the cause?" said Walter, speaking between his ground teeth. "Have you not traversed my views—blighted my hopes—charmed away from me the affections which were more to me than the world, and driven me to wander from my home with a crushed spirit, and a cheerless heart. Are these no cause for hate?"

"Have I done this?" said Aram, recoiling, and evidently and powerfully affected. "Have I so injured you?—It is true! I know it—I perceive it—I read your heart; and—bear witness Heaven!—I felt for the wound that I, but with no guilty hand, inflict upon you. Yet be just:—ask yourself, have I done aught that you, in my case, would have left undone? Have I been insolent in triumph, or haughty in success? if so, hate me, nay, spurn me now."

Walter turned his head irresolutely away.

"If it please you, that I accuse myself, in that I, a man seared and lone at heart, presumed to come within the pale of human affections;—that I exposed myself to cross another's better and brighter hopes, or dared to soften my fate with the tender and endearing ties that are meet alone for a more genial and youthful nature;—if it please you that I accuse and curse myself for this—that I yielded to it with pain and with self-reproach—that I shall think hereafter of what I unconsciously cost you with remorse—then be consoled!"

"It is enough," said Walter; "let us part. I leave you with more soreness at my late haste than I will acknowledge, let that content you; for myself, I ask for no apology or—."

"But you shall have it amply," interrupted Aram, advancing with a cordial openness of mien not usual to him. "I was all to blame; I should have remembered you were an injured man, and suffered you to have said all you would. Words at best are but a poor vent for a wronged and burning heart. It shall be so in future, speak your will, attack, upbraid, taunt me, I will bear it all. And indeed, even to myself there seems some witchcraft, some glamoury in what has chanced. What! I favoured where you love? Is it possible? It might teach the vainest to forswear vanity. You, the young, the buoyant, the fresh, the beautiful?—And I, who have passed the glory and zest of life between dusty walls; I who—well, well, fate laughs at probabilities!"

Aram now seemed relapsing into one of his more abstracted moods; he ceased to speak aloud, but his lips moved, and his eyes grew fixed in reverie on the ground. Walter gazed at him for some moments with mixed and contending sensations. Once more, resentment and the bitter wrath of jealousy had faded back into the remoter depths of his mind, and a certain interest for his singular rival, despite of himself, crept into his breast. But this mysterious and fitful nature, was it one in which the devoted Madeline would certainly find happiness and repose?—would she never regret her choice? This question obtruded itself upon him, and while he sought to answer it, Aram, regaining his composure, turned abruptly and offered him his hand. Walter did not accept it, he bowed with a cold respect. "I cannot give my hand without my heart," said he; "we were foes just now; we are not friends yet. I am unreasonable in this, I know, but—"

"Be it so," interrupted Aram; "I understand you. I press my good will on you no more. When this pang is forgotten, when this wound is healed, and when you will have learned more of him who is now your rival, we may meet again with other feelings on your side."

Thus they parted, and the solitary lamp which for weeks past had been quenched at the wholesome hour in the Student's home, streamed from the casement throughout the whole of that night; was it a witness of the calm and learned vigil, or of the unresting heart?

CHAPTER XI.

THE FAMILY SUPPER.—THE TWO SISTERS IN THEIR CHAMBER.
—A MISUNDERSTANDING FOLLOWED BY A CONFESSION.—WALTER'S
APPROACHING DEPARTURE AND THE CORPORAL'S BEHAVIOUR THEREON.—
THE CORPORAL'S FAVOURITE INTRODUCED TO THE READER.—THE
CORPORAL PROVES HIMSELF A SUBTLE DIPLOMATIST.

So we grew together
Like to a double cherry, seeming parted,
But yet an union in partition.
—Midsummer Night's Dream.

The Corporal had not taken his measures so badly
in this stroke of artilleryship.—Tristram Shandy.

It was late that evening when Walter returned home, the little family were assembled at the last and lightest meal of the day; Ellinor silently made room for her cousin beside herself, and that little kindness touched Walter. "Why did I not love her?" thought he, and he spoke to her in a tone so affectionate, that it made her heart thrill with delight. Lester was, on the whole, the most pensive of the group, but the old and young man exchanged looks of restored confidence, which, on the part of the former, were softened by a pitying tenderness.

When the cloth was removed, and the servants gone, Lester took it on himself to break to the sisters the intended departure of their cousin. Madeline received the news with painful blushes, and a certain self-reproach; for even where a woman has no cause to blame herself, she, in these cases, feels a sort of remorse at the unhappiness she occasions. But Ellinor rose suddenly and left the room.

"And now," said Lester, "London will, I suppose, be your first destination. I can furnish you with letters to some of my old friends there: merry fellows they were once: you must take care of the prodigality of their wine. There's John Courtland—ah! a seductive dog to drink with. Be sure and let me know how honest John looks, and what he says of me. I recollect him as if it were yesterday; a roguish eye, with a moisture in it; full cheeks; a straight nose; black curled hair; and teeth as even as dies:—honest John shewed his teeth pretty often, too: ha, ha! how the dog loved a laugh. Well, and Peter Hales—Sir Peter now, has his uncle's baronetcy—a generous, open-hearted fellow as ever lived—will ask you very often to dinner—nay, offer you money if you want it: but take care he does not lead you into extravagances: out of debt, out of danger, Walter. It would have been well for poor Peter Hales, had he remembered that maxim. Often and often have I been to see him in the Marshalsea; but he was the heir to good fortunes, though his relations kept him close; so I suppose he is well off now. His estates lie in—shire, on your road to London; so, if he is at his country-seat, you can beat up his quarters, and spend a month or so with him: a most hospitable fellow."

With these little sketches of his cotemporaries, the good Squire endeavoured to while the time; taking, it is true, some pleasure in the youthful reminiscences they excited, but chiefly designing to enliven the melancholy of his nephew. When, however, Madeline had retired, and they were alone, he drew his chair closer to Walter's, and changed the conversation into a more serious and anxious strain. The guardian and the ward sate up late that night; and when Walter retired to rest, it was with a heart more touched by his uncle's kindness, than his own sorrows.

But we are not about to close the day without a glance at the chamber which the two sisters held in common. The night was serene and starlit, and Madeline sate by the open window, leaning her face upon her hand, and gazing on the lone house of her lover, which might be seen afar across the landscape, the trees sleeping around it, and one pale and steady light gleaming from its lofty casement like a star.

"He has broken faith," said Madeline: "I shall chide him for this to-morrow. He promised me the light should be ever quenched before this hour."

"Nay," said Ellinor in a tone somewhat sharpened from its native sweetness, and who now sate up in the bed, the curtain of which was half-drawn aside, and the soft light of the skies rested full upon her rounded neck and youthful countenance—"nay, Madeline, do not loiter there any longer; the air grows sharp and cold, and the clock struck one several minutes since. Come, sister, come!"

"I cannot sleep," replied Madeline, sighing, "and think that yon light streams upon those studies which steal the healthful hues from his cheek, and the very life from his heart."

"You are infatuated—you are bewitched by that man," said Ellinor, peevishly.

"And have I not cause—ample cause?" returned Madeline, with all a girl's beautiful enthusiasm, as the colour mantled her cheek, and gave it the only additional loveliness it could receive. "When he speaks, is it not like music?—or rather, what music so arrests and touches the heart? Methinks it is Heaven only to gaze upon him—to note the changes of that majestic countenance—to set down as food for memory every look and every movement. But when the look turns to me—when the voice utters my name, ah! Ellinor, then it is not a wonder that I love him thus much: but that any others should think they have known love, and yet not loved him! And, indeed, I feel assured that what the world calls love is not my love. Are there more Eugenes in the world than one? Who but Eugene could be loved as I love?"

"What! are there none as worthy?" said Ellinor, half smiling.

"Can you ask it?" answered Madeline, with a simple wonder in her voice; "Whom would you compare—compare! nay, place within a hundred grades of the height which Eugene Aram holds in this little world?"

"This is folly—dotage;" said Ellinor, indignantly: "Surely there are others, as brave, as gentle, as kind, and if not so wise, yet more fitted for the world."

"You mock me," replied Madeline, incredulously; "whom could you select?"

Ellinor blushed deeply—blushed from her snowy temples to her yet whiter bosom, as she answered,

"If I said Walter Lester, could you deny it?"

"Walter!" repeated Madeline, "the equal to Eugene Aram!"

"Ay, and more than equal," said Ellinor, with spirit, and a warm and angry tone. "And indeed, Madeline," she continued, after a pause, "I lose something of that respect, which, passing a sister's love, I have always borne towards you, when I see the unthinking and lavish idolatry you manifest to one, who, but for a silver tongue and florid words, would rather want attractions than be the wonder you esteem him. Fie, Madeline! I blush for you when you speak, it is unmaidenly so to love any one!"

Madeline rose from the window, but the angry word died on her lips when she saw that Ellinor, who had worked her mind beyond her self-control, had thrown herself back on the pillow, and now sobbed aloud.

The natural temper of the elder sister had always been much more calm and even than that of the younger, who united with her vivacity something of the passionate caprice and fitfulness of her sex. And Madeline's affection for her had been tinged by that character of forbearance and soothing, which a superior nature often manifests to one more imperfect, and which in this instance did not desert her. She gently closed the window, and, gliding to the bed, threw her arms round her sister's neck, and kissed away her tears with a caressing fondness, that, if Ellinor resisted for one moment, she returned with equal tenderness the next.

"Indeed, dearest," said Madeline, gently, "I cannot guess how I hurt you, and still less, how Eugene has offended you?"

"He has offended me in nothing," replied Ellinor, still weeping, "if he has not stolen away all your affection from me. But I was a foolish girl, forgive me, as you always do; and at this time I need your kindness, for I am very—very unhappy."

"Unhappy, dearest Nell, and why?"

Ellinor wept on without answering.

Madeline persisted in pressing for a reply; and at length her sister sobbed out:

"I know that—that—Walter only has eyes for you, and a heart for you, who neglect, who despise his love; and I—I—but no matter, he is going to leave us, and of me—poor me, he will think no more!"

Ellinor's attachment to their cousin, Madeline had long half suspected, and she had often rallied her sister upon it; indeed it might have been this suspicion which made her at the first steel her breast against Walter's evident preference to herself. But Ellinor had never till now seriously confessed how much her heart was affected; and Madeline, in the natural engrossment of her own ardent and devoted love, had not of late spared much observation to the tokens of her sister's. She was therefore dismayed, if not surprised, as she now perceived the cause of the peevishness Ellinor had just manifested, and by the nature of the love she felt herself, she judged, and perhaps somewhat overrated, the anguish that Ellinor endured.

She strove to comfort her by all the arguments which the fertile ingenuity of kindness could invent; she prophesied Walter's speedy return, with his boyish disappointment forgotten, and with eyes no longer blinded to the attractions of one sister, by a bootless fancy for another. And though Ellinor interrupted her from time to time with assertions, now of Walter's eternal constancy to his present idol; now, with yet more vehement declarations of the certainty of his finding new objects for his affections in new scenes; she yet admitted, by little and little, the persuasive power of Madeline to creep into her heart, and brighten away its griefs with hope, till at last, with the tears yet wet on her cheek, she fell asleep in her sister's arms.

And Madeline, though she would not stir from her post lest the movement should awaken her sister, was yet prevented from closing her eyes in a similar repose; ever and anon she breathlessly and gently raised herself to steal a glimpse of that solitary light afar; and ever, as she looked, the ray greeted her eyes with an unswerving and melancholy stillness, till the dawn crept greyly over the heavens, and that speck of light, holier to her than the stars, faded also with them beneath the broader lustre of the day.

The next week was passed in preparations for Walter's departure. At that time, and in that distant part of the country, it was greatly the fashion among the younger travellers to perform their excursions on horseback, and it was this method of conveyance that Walter preferred. The best steed in the squire's stables was therefore appropriated to his service, and a strong black horse with a Roman nose and a long tail, was consigned to the mastery of Corporal Bunting. The Squire was delighted that his nephew had secured such an attendant. For the soldier, though odd and selfish, was a man of some sense and experience, and Lester thought such qualities might not be without their use to a young master, new to the common frauds and daily usages of the world he was about to enter.

As for Bunting himself, he covered his secret exultation at the prospect of change, and board-wages, with the cool semblance of a man sacrificing his wishes to his affections. He made it his peculiar study to impress upon the Squire's mind the extent of the sacrifice he was about to make. The bit cot had been just white-washed, the pet cat just lain in; then too, who would dig, and gather seeds, in the garden, defend the plants, (plants! the Corporal could scarce count a dozen, and nine out of them were cabbages!) from the impending frosts? It was exactly, too, the time of year when the rheumatism paid flying visits to the bones and loins of the worthy Corporal; and to think of his "galavanting about the country," when he ought to be guarding against that sly foe the lumbago, in the fortress of his chimney corner!

To all these murmurs and insinuations the good Lester seriously inclined, not with the less sympathy, in that they invariably ended in the Corporal's slapping his manly thigh, and swearing that he loved Master Walter like gunpowder, and that were it twenty times as much, he would cheerfully do it for the sake of his handsome young honour. Ever at this peroration, the eyes of the Squire began to twinkle, and new thanks were given to the veteran for his disinterested affection, and new promises pledged him in inadequate return.

The pious Dealtry felt a little jealousy at the trust imparted to his friend. He halted, on his return from his farm, by the spruce stile which led to the demesne of the Corporal, and eyed the warrior somewhat sourly, as he now, in the cool of the evening, sate without his door, arranging his fishing-tackle and flies, in various little papers, which he carefully labelled by the help of a stunted pen which had seen at least as much service as himself.

"Well, neighbour Bunting," said the little landlord, leaning over the stile, but not passing its boundary, "and when do you go?—you will have wet weather of it (looking up to the skies)—you must take care of the rumatiz. At your age it's no trifle, eh—hem."

"My age! should like to know—what mean by that! my age indeed!—augh!—bother!" grunted Bunting, looking up from his occupation. Peter chuckled inly at the Corporal's displeasure, and continued, as in an apologetic tone,

"Oh, I ax your pardon, neighbour. I don't mean to say you are too old to travel. Why there was Hal Whittol, eighty-two come next Michaelmas, took a trip to Lunnun last year—

"For young and old, the stout—the poorly,—The eye of God be on them surely."

"Bother!" said the Corporal, turning round on his seat.

"And what do you intend doing with the brindled cat? put'un up in the saddle-bags? You won't surely have the heart to leave'un."

"As to that," quoth the Corporal, sighing, "the poor dumb animal makes me sad to think on't." And putting down his fish-hooks, he stroked the sides of an enormous cat, who now, with tail on end, and back bowed up, and uttering her lenes susurros—anglicae, purr;—rubbed herself to and fro, athwart the Corporal's legs.

"What staring there for? won't ye step in, man? Can climb the stile I suppose?—augh!"

"No thank'ye, neighbour. I do very well here, that is, if you can hear me; your deafness is not so troublesome as it was last win—"

"Bother!" interrupted the Corporal, in a voice that made the little landlord start bolt upright from the easy confidence of his position. Nothing on earth so offended the perpendicular Jacob Bunting, as any insinuation of increasing years or growing infirmities; but at this moment, as he meditated putting Dealtry to some use, he prudently conquered the gathering anger, and added, like the man of the world he justly plumed himself on being—in a voice gentle as a dying howl, "What 'fraid on? come in, there's good fellow, want to speak to ye. Come do—a-u-g-h!" the last sound being prolonged into one of unutterable coaxingness, and accompanied with a beck of the hand and a wheedling wink.

These allurements the good Peter could not resist—he clambered the stile, and seated himself on the bench beside the Corporal.

"There now, fine fellow, fit for the forty-second;" said Bunting, clapping him on the back. "Well, and—a—nd—a beautiful cat, isn't her?"

"Ah!" said Peter very shortly—for though a remarkably mild man, Peter did not love cats: moreover, we must now inform the reader, that the cat of Jacob Bunting was one more feared than respected throughout the village. The Corporal was a cunning teacher of all animals: he could learn goldfinches the use of the musket; dogs, the art of the broadsword; horses, to dance hornpipes and pick pockets; and he had relieved the ennui of his solitary moments by imparting sundry accomplishments to the ductile genius of his cat. Under his tuition, Puss had learned to fetch and carry; to turn over head and tail, like a tumbler; to run up your shoulder when you least expected it; to fly, as if she were mad, at any one upon whom the Corporal thought fit to set her; and, above all, to rob larders, shelves, and tables, and bring the produce to the Corporal, who never failed to consider such stray waifs lawful manorial acquisitions. These little feline cultivations of talent, however delightful to the Corporal, and creditable to his powers of teaching the young idea how to shoot, had nevertheless, since the truth must be told, rendered the Corporal's cat a proverb and byeword throughout the neighbourhood. Never was cat in such bad odour: and the dislike in which it was held was wonderfully increased by terror; for the creature was singularly large and robust, and withal of so courageous a temper, that if you attempted to resist its invasion of your property, it forthwith set up its back, put down its ears, opened its mouth, and bade you fully comprehend that what it feloniously seized it could gallantly defend. More than one gossip in the village had this notable cat hurried into premature parturition, as, on descending at day-break into her kitchen, the dame would descry the animal perched on the dresser, having entered, God knows how, and gleaming upon her with its great green eyes, and a malignant, brownie expression of countenance.

Various deputations had indeed, from time to time, arrived at the Corporal's cottage, requesting the death, expulsion, or perpetual imprisonment of the favourite. But the stout Corporal received them grimly, and dismissed them gruffly; and the cat still went on waxing in size and wickedness, and baffling, as if inspired by the devil, the various gins and traps set for its destruction. But never, perhaps, was there a greater disturbance and perturbation in the little hamlet, than when, some three weeks since, the Corporal's cat was known to be brought to bed, and safely delivered of a numerous offspring. The village saw itself overrun with a race and a perpetuity of Corporal's cats! Perhaps, too, their teacher growing more expert by practice, the descendants might attain to even greater accomplishment than their nefarious progenitor. No longer did the faint hope of being delivered from their tormentor by an untimely or even natural death, occur to the harassed Grassdalians. Death was an incident natural to one cat, however vivacious, but here was a dynasty of cats! Principes mortales, respublica eterna!

Now the Corporal loved this creature better, yes better than any thing in the world, except travelling and board-wages; and he was sorely perplexed in his mind how he should be able to dispose of her safely in his absence. He was aware of the general enmity she had inspired, and trembled to anticipate its probable result, when he was no longer by to afford her shelter and protection. The Squire had, indeed, offered her an asylum at the manor-house; but the Squire's cook was the cat's most embittered enemy; and who can answer for the peaceable behaviour of his cook? The Corporal, therefore, with a reluctant sigh, renounced the friendly offer, and after lying awake three nights, and turning over in his own mind the characters, consciences, and capabilities of all his neighbours, he came at last to the conviction that there was no one with whom he could so safely entrust his cat as Peter Dealtry. It is true, as we said before, that Peter was no lover of cats, and the task of persuading him to afford board and lodging to a cat, of all cats the most odious and malignant, was therefore no easy matter. But to a man of the world, what intrigue is impossible?

The finest diplomatist in Europe might have taken a lesson from the Corporal, as he now proceeded earnestly towards the accomplishment of his project.

He took the cat, which by the by we forgot to say that he had thought fit to christen after himself, and to honour with a name, somewhat lengthy for a cat, (but indeed this was no ordinary cat!) viz. Jacobina. He took Jacobina then, we say, upon his lap, and stroking her brindled sides with great tenderness, he bade Dealtry remark how singularly quiet the animal was in its manners. Nay, he was not contented until Peter himself had patted her with a timorous hand, and had reluctantly submitted the said hand to the honour of being licked by the cat in return. Jacobina, who, to do her justice, was always meek enough in the presence, and at the will, of her master, was, fortunately this day, on her very best behaviour.

"Them dumb animals be mighty grateful," quoth the Corporal.

"Ah!" rejoined Peter, wiping his hand with his pocket handkerchief.

"But, Lord! what scandal there be in the world!"

"'Though slander's breath may raise a storm, It quickly does decay!'" muttered Peter.

"Very well, very true; sensible verses those," said the Corporal, approvingly; "and yet mischief's often done before the amends come. Body o' me, it makes a man sick of his kind, ashamed to belong to the race of men, to see the envy that abounds in this here sublunary wale of tears!" said the Corporal, lifting up his eyes.

Peter stared at him with open mouth; the hypocritical rascal continued, after a pause,—

"Now there's Jacobina, 'cause she's a good cat, a faithful servant, the whole village is against her: such lies as they tell on her, such wappers, you'd think she was the devil in garnet! I grant, I grant," added the Corporal, in a tone of apologetic candour, "that she's wild, saucy, knows her friends from her foes, steals Goody Solomon's butter; but what then? Goody Solomon's d—d b—h! Goody Solomon sold beer in opposition to you, set up a public;—you do not like Goody Solomons, Peter Dealtry?"

"If that were all Jacobina had done!" said the landlord, grinning.

"All! what else did she do? Why she eat up John Tomkins's canary-bird; and did not John Tomkins, saucy rascal, say you could not sing better nor a raven?"

"I have nothing to say against the poor creature for that," said Peter, stroking the cat of his own accord. "Cats will eat birds, 'tis the 'spensation of Providence. But what! Corporal!" and Peter hastily withdrawing his hand, hurried it into his breeches pocket—"but what! did not she scratch Joe Webster's little boy's hand into ribbons, because the boy tried to prevent her running off with a ball of string?"

"And well," grunted the Corporal, "that was not Jacobina's doing, that was my doing. I wanted the string—offered to pay a penny for it—think of that!"

"It was priced three pence ha'penny," said Peter.

"Augh—baugh! you would not pay Joe Webster all he asks! What's the use of being a man of the world, unless one makes one's tradesmen bate a bit? Bargaining is not cheating, I hope?"

"God forbid!" said Peter.

"But as to the bit string, Jacobina took it solely for your sake. Ah, she did not think you were to turn against her!"

So saying, the Corporal, got up, walked into his house, and presently came back with a little net in his hand.

"There, Peter, net for you, to hold lemons. Thank Jacobina for that; she got the string. Says I to her one day, as I was sitting, as I might be now, without the door, 'Jacobina, Peter Dealtry's a good fellow, and he keeps his lemons in a bag: bad habit,—get mouldy,—we'll make him a net: and Jacobina purred, (stroke the poor creature, Peter!)—so Jacobina and I took a walk, and when we came to Joe Webster's I pointed out the ball o'twine to her. So, for your sake, Peter, she got into this here scrape—augh."

"Ah!" quoth Peter laughing, "poor Puss! poor Pussy! poor little Pussy!"

"And now, Peter," said the Corporal, taking his friend's hand, "I am going to prove friendship to you—going to do you great favour."

"Aha!" said Peter, "my good friend, I'm very much obliged to you. I know your kind heart, but I really don't want any"—

"Bother!" cried the Corporal, "I'm not the man as makes much of doing a friend a kindness. Hold jaw! tell you what,—tell you what: am going away on Wednesday at day-break, and in my absence you shall—"

"What? my good Corporal."

"Take charge of Jacobina!"

"Take charge of the devil!" cried Peter.

"Augh!—baugh!—what words are those? Listen to me."

"I won't!"

"You shall!"

"I'll be d—d if I do!" quoth Peter sturdily. It was the first time he had been known to swear since he was parish clerk.

"Very well, very well!" said the Corporal chucking up his chin, "Jacobina can take care of herself! Jacobina knows her friends and her foes as well as her master! Jacobina never injures her friends, never forgives foes. Look to yourself! look to yourself! insult my cat, insult me! Swear at Jacobina, indeed!"

"If she steals my cream!" cried Peter—

"Did she ever steal your cream?"

"No! but, if—"

"Did she ever steal your cream?"

"I can't say she ever did."

"Or any thing else of yours?"

"Not that I know of; but—"

"Never too late to mend."

"If—"

"Will you listen to me, or not?"

"Well."

"You'll listen?"

"Yes."

"Know then, that I wanted to do you kindness."

"Humph!"

"Hold jaw! I taught Jacobina all she knows."

"More's the pity!"

"Hold jaw! I taught her to respect her friends,—never to commit herself in doors—never to steal at home—never to fly at home—never to scratch at home—to kill mice and rats—to bring all she catches to her master—to do what he tells her—and to defend his house as well as a mastiff: and this invaluable creature I was going to lend you:—won't now, d—d if I do!"

"Humph."

"Hold jaw! When I'm gone, Jacobina will have no one to feed her. She'll feed herself—will go to every larder, every house in the place—your's best larder, best house;—will come to you oftenest. If your wife attempts to drive her away, scratch her eyes out; if you disturb her, serve you worse than Joe Webster's little boy:—wanted to prevent this—won't now, d—d if I do!"

"But, Corporal, how would it mend the matter to take the devil in-doors?"

"Devil! Don't call names. Did not I tell you, only one Jacobina does not hurt is her master?—make you her master: now d'ye see?"

"It is very hard," said Peter grumblingly, "that the only way I can defend myself from this villainous creature is to take her into my house."

"Villainous! You ought to be proud of her affection. She returns good for evil—she always loved you; see how she rubs herself against you—and that's the reason why I selected you from the whole village, to take care of her; but you at once injure yourself and refuse to do your friend a service. Howsomever, you know I shall be with young Squire, and he'll be master here one of these days, and I shall have an influence over him—you'll see—you'll see. Look that there's not another 'Spotted Dog' set up—augh!—bother!"

"But what would my wife say, if I took the cat? she can't abide its name."

"Let me alone to talk to your wife. What would she say if I bring her from Lunnun Town a fine silk gown, or a neat shawl, with a blue border—blue becomes her; or a tay-chest—that will do for you both, and would set off the little back parlour. Mahogany tay-chest—inlaid at top—initials in silver—J. B. to D. and P. D.—two boxes for tay, and a bowl for sugar in the middle.—Ah! ah! Love me, love my cat! When was Jacob Bunting ungrateful?—augh!"

"Well, well! will you talk to Dorothy about it?"

"I shall have your consent, then? Thanks, my dear, dear Peter; 'pon my soul you're a fine fellow! you see, you're great man of the parish. If you protect her, none dare injure; if you scout her, all set upon her. For as you said, or rather sung, t'other Sunday—capital voice you were in too—

"The mighty tyrants without cause Conspire her blood to shed!"

"I did not think you had so good a memory, Corporal," said Peter smiling;—the cat was now curling itself up in his lap: "after all, Jacobina—what a deuce of a name—seems gentle enough."

"Gentle as a lamb—soft as butter—kind as cream—and such a mouser!"

"But I don't think Dorothy—"

"I'll settle Dorothy."

"Well, when will you look up?"

"Come and take a dish of tay with you in half an hour;—you want a new tay-chest; something new and genteel."

"I think we do," said Peter, rising and gently depositing the cat on the ground.

"Aha! we'll see to it!—we'll see! Good b'ye for the present—in half an hour be with you!"

The Corporal left alone with Jacobina, eyed her intently, and burst into the following pathetic address.

"Well, Jacobina! you little know the pains I takes to serve you—the lies I tells for you—endangered my precious soul for your sake, you jade! Ah! may well rub your sides against me. Jacobina! Jacobina! you be the only thing in the world that cares a button for me. I have neither kith nor kin. You are daughter—friend—wife to me: if any thing happened to you, I should not have the heart to love any thing else. Any body o' me, but you be as kind as any mistress, and much more tractable than any wife; but the world gives you a bad name, Jacobina. Why? Is it that you do worse than the world do? You has no morality in you, Jacobina; well, but has the world?—no! But it has humbug—you have no humbug, Jacobina. On the faith of a man, Jacobina, you be better than the world!—baugh! You takes care of your own interest, but you takes care of your master's too!—You loves me as well as yourself. Few cats can say the same, Jacobina! and no gossip that flings a stone at your pretty brindled skin, can say half as much. We must not forget your kittens, Jacobina;—you have four left—they must be provided for. Why not a cat's children as well as a courtier's? I have got you a comfortable home, Jacobina—take care of yourself, and don't fall in love with every Tomcat in the place. Be sober, and lead a single life till my return. Come, Jacobina, we will lock up the house, and go and see the quarters I have provided for you.—Heigho!"

As he finished his harangue, the Corporal locked the door of his cottage, and Jacobina trotting by his side, he stalked with his usual stateliness to the Spotted Dog.

Dame Dorothy Dealtry received him with a clouded brow, but the man of the world knew whom he had to deal with. On Wednesday morning Jacobina was inducted into the comforts of the hearth of mine host;—and her four little kittens mewed hard by, from the sinecure of a basket lined with flannel.

Reader. Here is wisdom in this chapter: it is not every man who knows how to dispose of his cat!

CHAPTER XII.

```
A STRANGE HABIT.—WALTER'S INTERVIEW WITH MADELINE.—HER
GENEROUS AND CONFIDING DISPOSITION.—WALTER'S ANGER.—THE
PARTING MEAL.—CONVERSATION BETWEEN THE UNCLE AND NEPHEW.—
   WALTER ALONE.—SLEEP THE BLESSING OF THE YOUNG.


   Fall. Out, out, unworthy to speak where he breatheth....

   Punt. Well now, my whole venture is forth, I will resolve
      to depart.
         —Ben Jonson.—Every Man out of his Humour.
```

It was now the eve before Walter's departure, and on returning home from a farewell walk among his favourite haunts, he found Aram, whose visit had been made during Walter's absence, now standing on the threshold of the door, and taking leave of Madeline and her father. Aram and Walter had only met twice before since the interview we recorded, and each time Walter had taken care that the meeting should be but of short duration. In these brief encounters, Aram's manner had been even more gentle than heretofore; that of Walter's, more cold and distant. And now, as they thus unexpectedly met at the door, Aram, looking at him earnestly, said:

"Farewell, Sir! You are to leave us for some time, I hear. Heaven speed you!" Then he added in a lower tone, "Will you take my hand, now, in parting?"

As he said, he put forth his hand,—it was the left.

"Let it be the right hand," observed the elder Lester, smiling: "it is a luckier omen."

"I think not," said Aram, drily. And Walter noted that he had never remembered him to give his right hand to any one, even to Madeline; the peculiarity of this habit might, however, arise from an awkward early habit, it was certainly scarce worth observing, and Walter had already coldly touched the hand extended to him: when Lester carelessly renewed the subject.

"Is there any superstition," said he gaily, "that makes you think, as some of the ancients did, the left hand luckier than the right?"

"Yes," replied Aram; "a superstition. Adieu."

The Student departed; Madeline slowly walked up one of the garden alleys, and thither Walter, after whispering to his uncle, followed her.

There is something in those bitter feelings, which are the offspring of disappointed love; something in the intolerable anguish of well-founded jealousy, that when the first shock is over, often hardens, and perhaps elevates the character. The sterner powers that we arouse within us to combat a passion that can no longer be worthily indulged, are never afterwards wholly allayed. Like the allies which a nation summons to its bosom to defend it from its foes, they expel the enemy only to find a settlement for themselves. The mind of every man who conquers an unfortunate attachment, becomes stronger than before; it may be for evil, it may be for good, but the capacities for either are more vigorous and collected.

The last few weeks had done more for Walter's character than years of ordinary, even of happy emotion, might have effected. He had passed from youth to manhood, and with the sadness, had acquired also something of the dignity, of experience. Not that we would say that he had subdued his love, but he had made the first step towards it; he had resolved that at all hazards it should be subdued.

As he now joined Madeline, and she perceived him by her side, her embarrassment was more evident than his. She feared some avowal, and from his temper, perhaps some violence on his part. However, she was the first to speak: women, in such cases, always are.

"It is a beautiful evening," said she, "and the sun set in promise of a fine day for your journey to-morrow."

Walter walked on silently; his heart was full. "Madeline," he said at length, "dear Madeline, give me your hand. Nay, do not fear me; I know what you think, and you are right; I loved—I still love you! but I know well that I can have no hope in making this confession; and when I ask you for your hand, Madeline, it is only to convince you that I have no suit to press; had I, I would not dare to touch that hand."

Madeline, wondering and embarrassed, gave him her hand; he held it for a moment with a trembling clasp, pressed it to his lips, and then resigned it.

"Yes, Madeline, my cousin, my sweet cousin; I have loved you deeply, but silently, long before my heart could unravel the mystery of the feelings with which it glowed. But this—all this—it were now idle to repeat. I know that I have no hope of return; that the heart whose possession would have made my whole life a dream, a transport, is given to another. I have not sought you now, Madeline, to repine at this, or to vex you by the tale of any suffering I may endure: I am come only to give you the parting wishes, the parting blessing, of one, who, wherever he goes, or whatever befall him, will always think of you as the brightest and loveliest of human beings. May you be happy, yes even with another!"

"Oh, Walter!" said Madeline, affected to tears, "if I ever encouraged—if I ever led you to hope for more than the warm, the sisterly affection I bear you, how bitterly I should reproach myself!"

"You never did, dear Madeline; I asked for no inducement to love you,—I never dreamed of seeking a motive, or inquiring if I had cause to hope. But as I am now about to quit you, and as you confess you feel for me a sister's affection, will you give me leave to speak to you as a brother might?"

Madeline held her hand to him in frank cordiality: "Yes!" said she, "speak!"

"Then," said Walter, turning away his head in a spirit of delicacy that did him honour, "is it yet all too late for me to say one word of caution as relates to—Eugene Aram?"

"Of caution! you alarm me, Walter; speak, has aught happened to him? I saw him as lately as yourself. Does aught threaten him? Speak, I implore you,—quick?"

"I know of no danger to him!" replied Walter, stung to perceive the breathless anxiety with which Madeline spoke; "but pause, my cousin, may there be no danger to you from this man?"

"Walter!"

"I grant him wise, learned, gentle,—nay, more than all, bearing about him a spell, a fascination, by which he softens, or awes at will, and which even I cannot resist. But yet his abstracted mood, his gloomy life, certain words that have broken from him unawares,—certain tell-tale emotions, which words of mine, heedlessly said, have fiercely aroused, all united, inspire me,—shall I say it,—with fear and distrust. I cannot think him altogether the calm and pure being he appears. Madeline, I have asked myself again and again, is this suspicion the effect of jealousy? do I scan his bearing with the jaundiced eye of disappointed rivalship? And I have satisfied my conscience that my judgment is not thus biassed. Stay! listen yet a little while! You have a high—a thoughtful mind. Exert it now. Consider your whole happiness rests on one step! Pause, examine, compare! Remember, you have not of Aram, as of those whom you have hitherto mixed with, the eye-witness of a life! You can know but little of his real temper, his secret qualities; still less of the tenor of his former life. I only ask of you, for your own sake, for my sake, your sister's sake, and your good father's, not to judge too rashly! Love him, if you will; but observe him!"

"Have you done?" said Madeline, who had hitherto with difficulty contained herself; "then hear me. Was it I? was it Madeline Lester whom you asked to play the watch, to enact the spy upon the man whom she exults in loving? Was it not enough that you should descend to mark down each incautious look—to chronicle every heedless word—to draw dark deductions from the unsuspecting confidence of my father's friend—to lie in wait—to hang with a foe's malignity upon the unbendings of familiar intercourse—to extort anger from gentleness itself, that you might wrest the anger into crime! Shame, shame upon you, for the meanness! And must you also suppose that I, to whose trust he has given his noble heart, will receive it only to play the eavesdropper to its secrets? Away!"

The generous blood crimsoned the cheek and brow of this high-spirited girl as she uttered her galling reproof; her eyes sparkled, her lip quivered, her whole frame seemed to have grown larger with the majesty of indignant love.

"Cruel, unjust, ungrateful!" ejaculated Walter, pale with rage, and trembling under the conflict of his roused and wounded feelings. "Is it thus you answer the warning of too disinterested and self-forgetful a love?"

"Love!" exclaimed Madeline. "Grant me patience!—Love! It was but now I thought myself honoured by the affection you said you bore me. At this instant, I blush to have called forth a single sentiment in one who knows so little what love is! Love!—methought that word denoted all that was high and noble in human nature—confidence, hope, devotion, sacrifice of all thought of self! but you would make it the type and concentration of all that lowers and debases!—suspicion—cavil—fear—selfishness in all its shapes! Out on you—love!"

"Enough, enough! Say no more, Madeline, say no more. We part not as I had hoped; but be it so. You are changed indeed, if your conscience smite you not hereafter for this injustice. Farewell, and may you never regret, not only the heart you have rejected, but the friendship you have belied." With these words, and choked by his emotions, Walter hastily strode away.

He hurried into the house, and into a little room adjoining the chamber in which he slept, and which had been also appropriated solely to his use. It was now spread with boxes and trunks, some half packed, some corded, and inscribed with the address to which they were to be sent in London. All these mute tokens of his approaching departure struck upon his excited feelings with a suddenness that overpowered him.

"And it is thus—thus," said he aloud, "that I am to leave, for the first time, my childhood's home."

He threw himself on his chair, and covering his face with his hands, burst, fairly subdued and unmanned, into a paroxysm of tears.

When this emotion was over, he felt as if his love for Madeline had also disappeared; a sore and insulted feeling was all that her image now recalled to him. This idea gave him some consolation. "Thank God!" he muttered, "thank God, I am cured at last!"

The thanksgiving was scarcely over, before the door opened softly, and Ellinor, not perceiving him where he sat, entered the room, and laid on the table a purse which she had long promised to knit him, and which seemed now designed as a parting gift.

She sighed heavily as she laid it down, and he observed that her eyes seemed red as with weeping.

He did not move, and Ellinor left the room without discovering him; but he remained there till dark, musing on her apparition, and before he went down-stairs, he took up the little purse, kissed it, and put it carefully into his bosom.

He sate next to Ellinor at supper that evening, and though he did not say much, his last words were more to her than words had ever been before. When he took leave of her for the night, he whispered, as he kissed her cheek; "God bless you, dearest Ellinor, and till I return, take care of yourself, for the sake of one, who loves you now, better than any thing on earth."

Lester had just left the room to write some letters for Walter; and Madeline, who had hitherto sat absorbed and silent by the window, now approached Walter, and offered him her hand.

"Forgive me, my dear cousin," she said, in her softest voice. "I feel that I was hasty, and to blame. Believe me, I am now at least grateful, warmly grateful, for the kindness of your motives."

"Not so," said Walter, bitterly, "the advice of a friend is only meanness."

"Come, come, forgive me; pray, do not let us part unkindly. When did we ever quarrel before? I was wrong, grievously wrong—I will perform any penance you may enjoin."

"Agreed then, follow my admonitions."

"Ah! any thing else," said Madeline, gravely, and colouring deeply.

Walter said no more; he pressed her hand lightly and turned away.

"Is all forgiven?" said she, in so bewitching a tone, and with so bright a smile, that Walter, against his conscience, answered, "Yes."

The sisters left the room. I know not which of the two received his last glance.

Lester now returned with the letters. "There is one charge, my dear boy," said he, in concluding the moral injunctions and experienced suggestions with which the young generally leave the ancestral home (whether practically benefited or not by the legacy, may be matter of question)—"there is one charge which I need not entrust to your ingenuity and zeal. You know my strong conviction, that your father, my poor brother, still lives. Is it necessary for me to tell you to exert yourself by all ways and in all means to discover some clue to his fate? Who knows," added Lester, with a smile, "but that you may find him a rich nabob. I confess that I should feel but little surprise if it were so; but at all events you will make every possible inquiry. I have written down in this paper the few particulars concerning him which I have been enabled to glean since he left his home; the places where he was last seen, the false names he assumed, I shall watch with great anxiety for any fuller success to your researches."

"You needed not, my dear uncle," said Walter seriously, "to have spoken to me on this subject. No one, not even yourself, can have felt what I have; can have cherished the same anxiety, nursed the same hope, indulged the same conjecture. I have not, it is true, often of late years spoken to you on a matter so near to us both, but I have spent whole hours in guesses at my father's fate, and in dreams that for me was reserved the proud task to discover it. I will not say indeed that it makes at this moment the chief motive for my desire to travel, but in travel it will become my chief object. Perhaps I may find him not only rich,—that for my part is but a minor wish,—but sobered and reformed from the errors and wildness of his earlier manhood. Oh, what should be his gratitude to you for all the care with which you have supplied to the forsaken child the father's place; and not the least, that you have, in softening the colours of his conduct, taught me still to prize and seek for a father's love!"

"You have a kind heart, Walter," said the good old man, pressing his nephew's hand, "and that has more than repaid me for the little I have done for you; it is better to sow a good heart with kindness, than a field with corn, for the heart's harvest is perpetual."

Many, keen, and earnest were that night the meditations of Walter Lester. He was about to quit the home in which youth had been passed, in which first love had been formed and blighted: the world was before him; but there was something more grave than pleasure, more steady than enterprise, that beckoned him to its paths. The deep mystery that for so many years had hung over the fate of his parent, it might indeed be his lot to pierce; and with a common waywardness in our nature, the restless son felt his interest in that parent the livelier from the very circumstance of remembering nothing of his person. Affection had been nursed by curiosity and imagination, and the bad father was thus more fortunate in winning the heart of the son, than had he perhaps, by the tenderness of years, deserved that affection.

Oppressed and feverish, Walter opened the lattice of his room, and looked forth on the night. The broad harvest-moon was in the heavens, and filled the air as with a softer and holier day. At a distance its light just gave the dark outline of Aram's house, and beneath the window it lay bright and steady on the green, still church-yard that adjoined the house. The air and the light allayed the fitfulness at the young man's heart, but served to solemnize the project and desire with which it beat. Still leaning from the casement, with his eyes fixed upon the tranquil scene below, he poured forth a prayer, that to his hands might the discovery of his lost sire be granted. The prayer seemed to lift the oppression from his breast; he felt cheerful and relieved, and flinging himself on his bed, soon fell into the sound and healthful sleep of youth. And oh! let Youth cherish that happiest of earthly boons while yet it is at its command;—for there cometh the day to all, when "neither the voice of the lute or the birds"

[Quotation from Horace]

shall bring back the sweet slumbers that fell on their young eyes, as unbidden as the dews. It is a dark epoch in a man's life when Sleep forsakes him; when he tosses to and fro, and Thought will not be silenced; when the drug and draught are the courters of stupefaction, not sleep; when the down pillow is as a knotted log; when the eyelids close but with an effort, and there is a drag and a weight, and a dizziness in the eyes at morn. Desire and Grief, and Love, these are the young man's torments, but they are the creatures of Time; Time removes them as it brings, and the vigils we keep, "while the evil days come not," if weary, are brief and few. But Memory, and Care, and Ambition, and Avarice, these are the demon-gods that defy the Time that fathered them. The worldlier passions are the growth of mature years, and their grave is dug but in our own. As the dark Spirits in the Northern tale, that watch against the coming of one of a brighter and holier race, lest if he seize them unawares, he bind them prisoners in his chain, they keep ward at night over the entrance of that deep cave—the human heart—and scare away the angel Sleep!

BOOK II.

CHAPTER I.

THE MARRIAGE SETTLED.—LESTER'S HOPES AND SCHEMES.—GAIETY OF
TEMPER A GOOD SPECULATION.—THE TRUTH AND FERVOUR OF
ARAM'S LOVE.

Love is better than a pair of spectacles, to make every thing seem greater which is seen through it.
—Sir Philip Sydney's Arcadia.

Aram's affection to Madeline having now been formally announced to Lester, and Madeline's consent having been somewhat less formally obtained, it only remained to fix the time for their wedding. Though Lester forbore to question Aram as to his circumstances, the Student frankly confessed, that if not affording what the generality of persons would consider even a competence, they enabled one of his moderate wants and retired life to dispense, especially in the remote and cheap district in which they lived, with all fortune in a wife, who, like Madeline, was equally with himself enamoured of obscurity. The good Lester, however, proposed to bestow upon his daughter such a portion as might allow for the wants of an increased family, or the probable contingencies of Fate. For though Fortune may often slacken her wheel, there is no spot in which she suffers it to be wholly still.

It was now the middle of September, and by the end of the ensuing month it was agreed that the spousals of the lovers should be held. It is certain that Lester felt one pang for his nephew, as he subscribed to this proposal; but he consoled himself with recurring to a hope he had long cherished, viz. that Walter would return home not only cured of his vain attachment to Madeline, but of the disposition to admit the attractions of her sister. A marriage between these two cousins had for years been his favourite project. The lively and ready temper of Ellinor, her household turn, her merry laugh, a winning playfulness that characterised even her defects, were all more after Lester's secret heart than the graver and higher nature of his elder daughter. This might mainly be, that they were traits of disposition that more reminded him of his lost wife, and were therefore more accordant with his ideal standard of perfection; but I incline also to believe that the more persons advance in years, the more, even if of staid and sober temper themselves, they love gaiety and elasticity in youth. I have often pleased myself by observing in some happy family circle embracing all ages, that it is the liveliest and wildest child that charms the grandsire the most. And after all, it is perhaps with characters as with books, the grave and thoughtful may be more admired than the light and cheerful, but they are less liked; it is not only that the former, being of a more abstruse and recondite nature, find fewer persons capable of judging of their merits, but also that the great object of the majority of human beings is to be amused, and that they naturally incline to love those the best who amuse them most. And to so great a practical extent is this preference pushed, that I think were a nice observer to make a census of all those who have received legacies, or dropped unexpectedly into fortunes; he would find that where one grave disposition had so benefited, there would be at least twenty gay. Perhaps, however, it may be said that I am taking the cause for the effect!

But to return from our speculative disquisitions; Lester then, who, though he so slowly discovered his nephew's passion for Madeline, had long since guessed the secret of Ellinor's affection for him, looked forward with a hope rather sanguine than anxious to the ultimate realization of his cherished domestic scheme. And he pleased himself with thinking that when all soreness would, by this double wedding, be banished from Walter's mind, it would be impossible to conceive a family group more united or more happy.

And Ellinor herself, ever since the parting words of her cousin, had seemed, so far from being inconsolable for his absence, more bright of cheek and elastic of step than she had been for months before. What a world of all feelings, which forbid despondence, lies hoarded in the hearts of the young! As one fountain is filled by the channels that exhaust another; we cherish wisdom at the expense of hope. It thus happened from one cause or another, that Walter's absence created a less cheerless blank in the family circle than might have been expected, and the approaching bridals of Madeline and her lover, naturally diverted in a great measure the thoughts of each, and engrossed their conversation.

Whatever might be Madeline's infatuation as to the merits of Aram, one merit—the greatest of all in the eyes of a woman who loves, he at least possessed. Never was mistress more burningly and deeply loved than she, who, for the first time, awoke the long slumbering passions in the heart of Eugene Aram. Every day the ardour of his affections seemed to increase. With what anxiety he watched her footsteps!—with what idolatry he hung upon her words!—with what unspeakable and yearning emotion he gazed upon the changeful eloquence of her cheek. Now that Walter was gone, he almost took up his abode at the manor-house. He came thither in the early morning, and rarely returned home before the family retired for the night; and even then, when all was hushed, and they believed him in his solitary home, he lingered for hours around the house, to look up to Madeline's window, charmed to the spot which held the intoxication of her presence. Madeline discovered this habit, and chid it; but so tenderly, that it was not cured. And still at times, by the autumnal moon, she marked from her window his dark figure gliding among the shadows of the trees, or pausing by the lowly tombs in the still churchyard—the resting-place of hearts that once, perhaps, beat as wildly as his own.

It was impossible that a love of this order, and from one so richly gifted as Aram; a love, which in substance was truth, and yet in language poetry, could fail wholly to subdue and inthral a girl so young, so romantic, so enthusiastic, as Madeline Lester. How intense and delicious must have been her sense of happiness! In the pure heart of a girl loving for the first time—love is far more ecstatic than in man, inasmuch as it is unfevered by desire—love then and there makes the only state of human existence which is at once capable of calmness and transport!

CHAPTER II.

A FAVOURABLE SPECIMEN OF A NOBLEMAN AND A COURTIER.—A MAN OF SOME FAULTS AND MANY ACCOMPLISHMENTS.

> Titinius Capito is to rehearse. He is a man of an excellent
> disposition, and to be numbered among the chief ornaments of
> his age. He cultivates literature—he loves men of learning,
> etc.
> —Lord Orrery: Pliny.

About this time the Earl of _____, the great nobleman of the district, and whose residence was within four miles of Grassdale, came down to pay his wonted yearly visit to his country domains. He was a man well known in the history of the times; though, for various reasons, I conceal his name. He was a courtier;—deep—wily—accomplished; but capable of generous sentiments and enlarged views. Though, from regard to his interests, he seized and lived as it were upon the fleeting spirit of the day—the penetration of his intellect went far beyond its reach. He claims the merit of having been the one of all his co-temporaries (Lord Chesterfield alone excepted), who most clearly saw, and most distinctly prophesied, the dark and fearful storm that at the close of the century burst over the vices, in order to sweep away the miseries, of France—a terrible avenger—a salutary purifier.

From the small circle of sounding trifles, in which the dwellers of a court are condemned to live, and which he brightened by his abilities and graced by his accomplishments, the sagacious and far-sighted mind of Lord—comprehended the vast field without, usually invisible to those of his habits and profession. Men who the best know the little nucleus which is called the world, are often the most ignorant of mankind; but it was the peculiar attribute of this nobleman, that he could not only analyse the external customs of his species, but also penetrate their deeper and more hidden interests.

The works, and correspondence he has left behind him, though far from voluminous, testify a consummate knowledge of the varieties of human nature The refinement of his taste appears less remarkable than the vigour of his understanding. It might be that he knew the vices of men better than their virtues; yet he was no shallow disbeliever in the latter: he read the heart too accurately not to know that it is guided as often by its affections as its interests. In his early life he had incurred, not without truth, the charge of licentiousness; but even in pursuit of pleasure, he had been neither weak on the one hand, nor gross on the other;—neither the headlong dupe, nor the callous sensualist: but his graces, his rank, his wealth, had made his conquests a matter of too easy purchase; and hence, like all voluptuaries, the part of his worldly knowledge, which was the most fallible, was that which related to the sex. He judged of women by a standard too distinct from that by which he judged of men, and considered those foibles peculiar to the sex, which in reality are incident to human nature.

His natural disposition was grave and reflective; and though he was not without wit, it was rarely used. He lived, necessarily, with the frivolous and the ostentatious, yet ostentation and frivolity were charges never brought against himself. As a diplomatist and a statesman, he was of the old and erroneous school of intriguers; but his favourite policy was the science of conciliation. He was one who would so far have suited the present age, that no man could better have steered a nation from the chances of war; James the First could not have been inspired with a greater affection for peace; but the Peer's dexterity would have made that peace as honourable as the King's weakness could have made it degraded. Ambitious to a certain extent, but neither grasping nor mean, he never obtained for his genius the full and extensive field it probably deserved. He loved a happy life above all things; and he knew that while activity is the spirit, fatigue is the bane, of happiness.

In his day he enjoyed a large share of that public attention which generally bequeaths fame; yet from several causes (of which his own moderation is not the least) his present reputation is infinitely less great than the opinions of his most distinguished cotemporaries foreboded.

It is a more difficult matter for men of high rank to become illustrious to posterity, than for persons in a sterner and more wholesome walk of life. Even the greatest among the distinguished men of the patrician order, suffer in the eyes of the after-age for the very qualities, mostly dazzling defects, or brilliant eccentricities, which made them most popularly remarkable in their day. Men forgive Burns his amours and his revellings with greater ease than they will forgive Bolingbroke and Byron for the same offences.

Our Earl was fond of the society of literary men; he himself was well, perhaps even deeply, read. Certainly his intellectual acquisitions were more profound than they have been generally esteemed, though with the common subtlety of a ready genius, he could make the quick adaptation of a timely fact, acquired for the occasion, appear the rich overflowing of a copious erudition. He was a man who instantly perceived, and liberally acknowledged, the merits of others. No connoisseur had a more felicitous knowledge of the arts, or was more just in the general objects of his patronage. In short, what with all his advantages, he was one whom an aristocracy may boast of, though a people may forget; and if not a great man, was at least a most remarkable lord.

The Earl of—, in his last visit to his estates, had not forgotten to seek out the eminent scholar who shed an honour upon his neighbourhood; he had been greatly struck with the bearing and conversation of Aram, and with the usual felicity with which the accomplished Earl adapted his nature to those with whom he was thrown, he had succeeded in ingratiating himself with Aram in return. He could not indeed persuade the haughty and solitary Student to visit him at the castle; but the Earl did not disdain to seek any one from whom he could obtain instruction, and he had twice or thrice voluntarily encountered Aram, and effectually drawn him from his reserve. The Earl now heard with some pleasure, and more surprise, that the austere Recluse was about to be married to the beauty of the county, and he resolved to seize the first occasion to call at the manor-house to offer his compliments and congratulations to its inmates.

Sensible men of rank, who, having enjoyed their dignity from their birth, may reasonably be expected to grow occasionally tired of it; often like mixing with those the most who are the least dazzled by the condescension; I do not mean to say, with the vulgar parvenus who mistake rudeness for independence;—no man forgets respect to another who knows the value of respect to himself; but the respect should be paid easily; it is not every Grand Seigneur, who like Louis XIVth., is only pleased when he puts those he addresses out of countenance.

There was, therefore, much in the simplicity of Lester's manners, and those of his nieces, which rendered the family at the manor-house, especial favourites with Lord—; and the wealthier but less honoured squirearchs of the county, stiff in awkward pride, and bustling with yet more awkward veneration, heard with astonishment and anger of the numerous visits which his Lordship, in his brief sojourn at the castle, always contrived to pay to the Lesters, and the constant invitations, which they received to his most familiar festivities.

Lord—was no sportsman, and one morning, when all his guests were engaged among the stubbles of September, he mounted his quiet palfrey, and gladly took his way to the Manor-house.

It was towards the latter end of the month, and one of the earliest of the autumnal fogs hung thinly over the landscape. As the Earl wound along the sides of the hill on which his castle was built, the scene on which he gazed below received from the grey mists capriciously hovering over it, a dim and melancholy wildness. A broader and whiter vapour, that streaked the lower part of the valley, betrayed the course of the rivulet; and beyond, to the left, rose wan and spectral, the spire of the little church adjoining Lester's abode. As the horseman's eye wandered to this spot, the sun suddenly broke forth, and lit up as by enchantment, the quiet and lovely hamlet embedded, as it were, beneath,—the cottages, with their gay gardens and jasmined porches, the streamlet half in mist, half in light, while here and there columns of vapour rose above its surface like the chariots of the water genii, and broke into a thousand hues beneath the smiles of the unexpected sun: But far to the right, the mists around it yet unbroken, and the outline of its form only visible, rose the lone house of the Student, as if there the sadder spirits of the air yet rallied their broken armament of mist and shadow.

The Earl was not a man peculiarly alive to scenery, but he now involuntarily checked his horse, and gazed for a few moments on the beautiful and singular aspect which the landscape had so suddenly assumed. As he so gazed, he observed in a field at some little distance, three or four persons gathered around a bank, and among them he thought he recognised the comely form of Rowland Lester. A second inspection convinced him that he was right in his conjecture, and, turning from the road through a gap in the hedge, he made towards the group in question. He had not proceeded far, before he saw, that the remainder of the party was composed of Lester's daughters, the lover of the elder, and a fourth, whom he recognised as a celebrated French botanist who had lately arrived in England, and who was now making an amateur excursion throughout the more attractive districts of the island.

The Earl guessed rightly, that Monsieur de N—had not neglected to apply to Aram for assistance in a pursuit which the latter was known to have cultivated with such success, and that he had been conducted hither, as a place affording some specimen or another not unworthy of research. He now, giving his horse to his groom, joined the group.

CHAPTER III.

WHEREIN THE EARL AND THE STUDENT CONVERSE ON GRAVE BUT
DELIGHTFUL MATTERS.—THE STUDENT'S NOTION OF THE ONLY EARTHLY
HAPPINESS.

```
ARAM. If the witch Hope forbids us to be wise,
      Yet when I turn to these—Woe's only friends,
      And with their weird and eloquent voices calm
      The stir and Babel of the world within,
      I can but dream that my vex'd years at last
      Shall find the quiet of a hermit's cell:—
      And, neighbouring not this hacked and jaded world,
      Beneath the lambent eyes of the loved stars,
      And, with the hollow rocks and sparry caves,
      The tides, and all the many-music'd winds

      My oracles and co-mates;—watch my life
      Glide down the Stream of Knowledge, and behold
      Its waters with a musing stillness glass
      The thousand hues of Nature and of Heaven.
         —From Eugene Aram, a MS. Tragedy.
```

The Earl continued with the party he had joined; and when their occupation was concluded and they turned homeward, he accepted the Squire's frank invitation to partake of some refreshment at the Manor-house. It so chanced, or perhaps the Earl so contrived it, that Aram and himself, in their way to the village lingered a little behind the rest, and that their conversation was thus, for a few minutes, not altogether general.

"Is it I, Mr. Aram?" said the Earl smiling, "or is it Fate that has made you a convert? The last time we sagely and quietly conferred together, you contended that the more the circle of existence was contracted, the more we clung to a state of pure and all self-dependent intellect, the greater our chance of happiness. Thus you denied that we were rendered happier by our luxuries, by our ambition, or by our affections. Love and its ties were banished from your solitary Utopia. And you asserted that the true wisdom of life lay solely in the cultivation—not of our feelings, but our faculties. You know, I held a different doctrine: and it is with the natural triumph of a hostile partizan, that I hear you are about to relinquish the practice of one of your dogmas;—in consequence, may I hope, of having forsworn the theory?"

"Not so, my Lord," answered Aram, colouring slightly; "my weakness only proves that my theory is difficult,—not that it is wrong. I still venture to think it true. More pain than pleasure is occasioned us by others—banish others, and you are necessarily the gainer. Mental activity and moral quietude are the two states which, were they perfected and united, would constitute perfect happiness. It is such a union which constitutes all we imagine of Heaven, or conceive of the majestic felicity of a God."

"Yet, while you are on earth you will be (believe me) happier in the state you are about to choose," said the Earl. "Who could look at that enchanting face (the speaker directed his eyes towards Madeline) and not feel that it gave a pledge of happiness that could not be broken?"

It was not in the nature of Aram to like any allusion to himself, and still less to his affections: he turned aside his head, and remained silent: the wary Earl discovered his indiscretion immediately.

"But let us put aside individual cases," said he,—"the meum and the tuum forbid all argument:—and confess, that there is for the majority of human beings a greater happiness in love than in the sublime state of passionless intellect to which you would so chillingly exalt us. Has not Cicero said wisely, that we ought no more to subject too slavishly our affections, than to elevate them too imperiously into our masters? Neque se nimium erigere, nec subjacere serviliter."

"Cicero loved philosophizing better than philosophy," said Aram, coldly; "but surely, my Lord, the affections give us pain as well as pleasure. The doubt, the dread, the restlessness of love,—surely these prevent the passion from constituting a happy state of mind; to me one knowledge alone seems sufficient to embitter all its enjoyments,—the knowledge that the object beloved must die. What a perpetuity of fear that knowledge creates! The avalanche that may crush us depends upon a single breath!"

"Is not that too refined a sentiment? Custom surely blunts us to every chance, every danger, that may happen to us hourly. Were the avalanche over you for a day,—I grant your state of torture,—but had an avalanche rested over you for years, and not yet fallen, you would forget that it could ever fall; you would eat, sleep, and make love, as if it were not!"

"Ha! my Lord, you say well—you say well," said Aram, with a marked change of countenance; and, quickening his pace, he joined Lester's side, and the thread of the previous conversation was broken off.

The Earl afterwards, in walking through the gardens (an excursion which he proposed himself, for he was somewhat of an horticulturist), took an opportunity to renew the subject.

"You will pardon me," said he, "but I cannot convince myself that man would be happier were he without emotions; and that to enjoy life he should be solely dependant on himself!"

"Yet it seems to me," said Aram, "a truth easy of proof; if we love, we place our happiness in others. The moment we place our happiness in others, comes uncertainty, but uncertainty is the bane of happiness. Children are the source of anxiety to their parents;—his mistress to the lover. Change, accident, death, all menace us in each person whom we regard. Every new tie opens new channels by which grief can invade us; but, you will say, by which joy also can flow in;—granted! But in human life is there not more grief than joy? What is it that renders the balance even? What makes the staple of our happiness,—endearing to us the life at which we should otherwise repine? It is the mere passive, yet stirring, consciousness of life itself!—of the sun and the air of the physical being; but this consciousness every emotion disturbs. Yet could you add to its tranquillity an excitement that never exhausts itself,—that becomes refreshed, not sated, with every new possession, then you would obtain happiness. There is only one excitement of this divine order,—that of intellectual culture. Behold now my theory! Examine it—it contains no flaw. But if," renewed Aram, after a pause, "a man is subject to fate solely in himself, not in others, he soon hardens his mind against all fear, and prepares it for all events. A little philosophy enables him to bear bodily pain, or the common infirmities of flesh: by a philosophy somewhat deeper, he can conquer the ordinary reverses of fortune, the dread of shame, and the last calamity of death. But what philosophy could ever thoroughly console him for the ingratitude of a friend, the worthlessness of a child, the death of a mistress? Hence, only when he stands alone, can a man's soul say to Fate, 'I defy thee.'"

"You think then," said the Earl, reluctantly diverting the conversation into a new channel "that in the pursuit of knowledge lies our only active road to real happiness. Yet here how eternal must be the disappointments even of the most successful! Does not Boyle tell us of a man who, after devoting his whole life to the study of one mineral, confessed himself, at last, ignorant of all its properties?"

"Had the object of his study been himself, and not the mineral, he would not have been so unsuccessful a student," said Aram, smiling. "Yet," added he, in a graver tone, "we do indeed cleave the vast heaven of Truth with a weak and crippled wing: and often we are appalled in our way by a dread sense of the immensity around us, and of the inadequacy of our own strength. But there is a rapture in the breath of the pure and difficult air, and in the progress by which we compass earth, the while we draw nearer to the stars,—that again exalts us beyond ourselves, and reconciles the true student unto all things,—even to the hardest of them all,—the conviction how feebly our performance can ever imitate the grandeur of our ambition! As you see the spark fly upward,—sometimes not falling to earth till it be dark and quenched,—thus soars, whither it recks not, so that the direction be above, the luminous spirit of him who aspires to Truth; nor will it back to the vile and heavy clay from which it sprang, until the light which bore it upward be no more!"

CHAPTER IV.

A DEEPER EXAMINATION INTO THE STUDENT'S HEART.—THE VISIT TO
    THE CASTLE.—PHILOSOPHY PUT TO THE TRIAL.

```
I weigh not fortune's frown or smile,
 I joy not much in earthly joys,
I seek not state, I seek not stile,
 I am not fond of fancy's toys;
I rest so pleased with what I have,
I wish no more, no more I crave.
    —Joshua Sylvester.
```

The reader must pardon me, if I somewhat clog his interest in my tale by the brief conversations I have given, and must for a short while cast myself on his indulgence and renew. It is not only the history of his life, but the character and tone of Aram's mind, that I wish to stamp upon my page. Fortunately, however, the path my story assumes is of such a nature, that in order to effect this object, I shall never have to desert, and scarcely again even to linger by, the way.

Every one knows the magnificent moral of Goethe's "Faust!" Every one knows that sublime discontent—that chafing at the bounds of human knowledge—that yearning for the intellectual Paradise beyond, which "the sworded angel" forbids us to approach—that daring, yet sorrowful state of mind—that sense of defeat, even in conquest, which Goethe has embodied,—a picture of the loftiest grief of which the soul is capable, and which may remind us of the profound and august melancholy which the Great Sculptor breathed into the repose of the noblest of mythological heroes, when he represented the God resting after his labours, as if more convinced of their vanity than elated with their extent!

In this portrait, the grandeur of which the wild scenes that follow in the drama we refer to, do not (strangely wonderful as they are) perhaps altogether sustain, Goethe has bequeathed to the gaze of a calmer and more practical posterity, the burning and restless spirit—the feverish desire for knowledge more vague than useful, which characterised the exact epoch in the intellectual history of Germany, in which the poem was inspired and produced.

At these bitter waters, the Marah of the streams of Wisdom, the soul of the man whom we have made the hero of these pages, had also, and not lightly, quaffed. The properties of a mind, more calm and stern than belonged to the visionaries of the Hartz and the Danube, might indeed have preserved him from that thirst after the impossibilities of knowledge, which gives so peculiar a romance, not only to the poetry, but the philosophy of the German people. But if he rejected the superstitions, he did not also reject the bewilderments of the mind. He loved to plunge into the dark and metaphysical subtleties which human genius has called daringly forth from the realities of things:—

```
        "To spin

A shroud of thought, to hide him from the sun

Of this familiar life, which seems to be,
```

```
But is not—or is but quaint mockery

Of all we would believe;—or sadly blame

The jarring and inexplicable frame

Of this wrong world: and then anatomize

The purposes and thoughts of man, whose eyes

Were closed in distant years; or widely guess

The issue of the earth's great business,

When we shall be, as we no longer are,

Like babbling gossips, safe, who hear the war

Of winds, and sigh!—but tremble not!"
```

Much in him was a type, or rather forerunner, of the intellectual spirit that broke forth when we were children, among our countrymen, and is now slowly dying away amidst the loud events and absorbing struggles of the awakening world. But in one respect he stood aloof from all his tribe—in his hard indifference to worldly ambition, and his contempt of fame. As some sages have seemed to think the universe a dream, and self the only reality, so in his austere and collected reliance upon his own mind—the gathering in, as it were, of his resources, he appeared to consider the pomps of the world as shadows, and the life of his own spirit the only substance. He had built a city and a tower within the Shinar of his own heart, whence he might look forth, unscathed and unmoved, upon the deluge that broke over the rest of earth.

Only in one instance, and that, as we have seen, after much struggle, he had given way to the emotions that agitate his kind, and had surrendered himself to the dominion of another. This was against his theories—but what theories ever resist love? In yielding, however, thus far, he seemed more on his guard than ever against a broader encroachment. He had admitted one 'fair spirit' for his 'minister,' but it was only with a deeper fervour to invoke 'the desert' as 'his dwelling-place.' Thus, when the Earl, who, like most practical judges of mankind, loved to apply to each individual the motives that actuate the mass, and who only unwillingly, and somewhat sceptically, assented to the exceptions, and was driven to search for peculiar clues to the eccentric instance,—finding, to his secret triumph, that Aram had admitted one intruding emotion into his boasted circle of indifference, imagined that he should easily induce him (the spell once broken) to receive another, he was surprised and puzzled to discover himself in the wrong.

Lord—at that time had been lately called into the administration, and he was especially anxious to secure the support of all the talent that he could enlist in its behalf. The times were those in which party ran high, and in which individual political writings were honoured with an importance which the periodical press in general has now almost wholly monopolized. On the side opposed to Government, writers of great name and high attainments had shone with peculiar effect, and the Earl was naturally desirous that they should be opposed by an equal array of intellect on the side espoused by himself. The name alone of Eugene Aram, at a day when scholarship was renown, would have been no ordinary acquisition to the cause of the Earl's party; but that judicious and penetrating nobleman perceived that Aram's abilities, his various research, his extended views, his facility of argument, and the heat and energy of his eloquence, might be rendered of an importance which could not have been anticipated from the name alone, however eminent, of a retired and sedentary scholar; he was not therefore without an interested motive in the attentions he now lavished upon the Student, and in his curiosity to put to the proof the disdain of all worldly enterprise and worldly temptation, which Aram affected. He could not but think, that to a man poor and lowly of circumstance, conscious of superior acquirements, about to increase his wants by admitting to them a partner, and arrived at that age when the calculations of interest and the whispers of ambition have usually most weight;—he could not but think that to such a man the dazzling prospects of social advancement, the hope of the high fortunes, and the powerful and glittering influence which political life, in England, offers to the aspirant, might be rendered altogether irresistible.

He took several opportunities in the course of the next week, of renewing his conversation with Aram, and of artfully turning it into the channels which he thought most likely to produce the impression he desired to create. He was somewhat baffled, but by no means dispirited, in his attempts; but he resolved to defer his ultimate proposition until it could be made to the fullest advantage. He had engaged the Lesters to promise to pass a day at the castle; and with great difficulty, and at the earnest intercession of Madeline, Aram was prevailed upon to accompany them. So extreme was his distaste to general society, and, from some motive or another more powerful than mere constitutional reserve, so invariably had he for years refused all temptations to enter it, that natural as this concession was rendered by his approaching marriage to one of the party, it filled him with a sort of terror and foreboding of evil. It was as if he were passing beyond the boundary of some law, on which the very tenure of his existence depended. After he had consented, a trembling came over him; he hastily left the room, and till the day arrived, was observed by his friends of the Manor-house to be more gloomy and abstracted than they ever had known him, even at the earliest period of acquaintance.

On the day itself, as they proceeded to the castle, Madeline perceived with a tearful repentance of her interference, that he sate by her side cold and rapt; and that once or twice when his eyes dwelt upon her, it was with an expression of reproach and distrust.

It was not till they entered the lofty hall of the castle, when a vulgar diffidence would have been most abashed, that Aram recovered himself. The Earl was standing—the centre of a group in the recess of a window in the saloon, opening upon an extensive and stately terrace. He came forward to receive them with the polished and warm kindness which he bestowed upon al his inferiors in rank. He complimented the sisters; he jested with Lester; but to Aram only, he manifested less the courtesy of kindness than of respect. He took his arm, and leaning on it with a light touch, led him to the group at the window. It was composed of the most distinguished public men in the country, and among them (the Earl himself was connected through an illegitimate branch with the reigning monarch,) was a prince of the blood royal.

To these, whom he had prepared for the introduction, he severally, and with an easy grace, presented Aram, and then falling back a few steps, he watched with a keen but seemingly careless eye, the effect which so sudden a contact with royalty itself would produce on the mind of the shy and secluded Student, whom it was his object to dazzle and overpower. It was at this moment that the native dignity of Aram, which his studies, unworldly as they were, had certainly tended to increase, displayed itself, in a trial which, poor as it was in abstract theory, was far from despicable in the eyes of the sensible and practised courtier. He received with his usual modesty, but not with his usual shrinking and embarrassment on such occasions, the compliments he received; a certain and far from ungraceful pride was mingled with his simplicity of demeanour; no fluttering of manner, betrayed that he was either dazzled or humbled by the presence in which he stood, and the Earl could not but confess that there was never a more favourable opportunity for comparing the aristocracy of genius with that of birth; it was one of those homely every-day triumphs of intellect, which please us more than they ought to do, for, after all, they are more common than the men of courts are willing to believe.

Lord—did not however long leave Aram to the support of his own unassisted presence of mind and calmness of nerve; he advanced, and led the conversation, with his usual tact, into a course which might at once please Aram, and afford him the opportunity to shine. The Earl had imported from Italy some of the most beautiful specimens of classic sculpture which this country now possesses. These were disposed in niches around the magnificent apartment in which the guest were assembled, and as the Earl pointed them out, and illustrated each from the beautiful anecdotes and golden allusions of antiquity, he felt that he was affording to Aram a gratification he could never have experienced before; and in the expression of which, the grace and copiousness of his learning would find vent. Nor was he disappointed. The cheek, which till then had retained its steady paleness, now caught the glow of enthusiasm; and in a few moments there was not a person in the group, who did not feel, and cheerfully feel, the superiority of the one who, in birth and fortune, was immeasurably the lowest of all.

The English aristocracy, whatever be the faults of their education, (and certainly the name of the faults is legion!) have at least the merit of being alive to the possession, and easily warmed to the possessor, of classical attainment: perhaps even from this very merit spring many of the faults we allude to; they are too apt to judge all talent by a classical standard, and all theory by classical experience. Without,—save in very rare instances,—the right to boast of any deep learning, they are far more susceptible than the nobility of any other nation to the spiritum Camoenae. They are easily and willingly charmed back to the studies which, if not eagerly pursued in youth, are still entwined with all their youth's brightest recollections; the schoolboy's prize, and the master's praise,—the first ambition, and its first reward. A felicitous quotation, a delicate allusion, is never lost upon their ear; and the veneration which at Eton they bore to the best verse-maker in the school, tinctures their judgment of others throughout life, mixing I know not what, both of liking and esteem, with their admiration of one who uses his classical weapons with a scholar's dexterity, not a pedant's inaptitude: for such a one there is a sort of agreeable confusion in their respect; they are inclined, unconsciously, to believe that he must necessarily be a high gentleman—ay, and something of a good fellow into the bargain.

It happened then that Aram could not have dwelt upon a theme more likely to arrest the spontaneous interest of those with whom he now conversed—men themselves of more cultivated minds than usual, and more capable than most (from that acute perception of real talent, which is produced by habitual political warfare,) of appreciating not only his endowments, but his facility in applying them.

"You are right, my Lord," said Sir—, the whipper-in of the—party, taking the Earl aside; "he would be an inestimable pamphleteer."

"Could you get him to write us a sketch of the state of parties; luminous, eloquent?'" whispered a lord of the bed-chamber.

The Earl answered by a bon mot, and turned to a bust of Caracalla.

The hours at that time were (in the country at least) not late, and the Earl was one of the first introducers of the polished fashion of France, by which we testify a preference of the society of the women to that of our own sex; so that, in leaving the dining-room, it was not so late but that the greater part of the guests walked out upon the terrace, and admired the expanse of country which it overlooked, and along which the thin veil of the twilight began now to hover.

Having safely deposited his royal guest at a whist table, and thus left himself a free agent, the Earl, inviting Aram to join him, sauntered among the loiterers on the terrace for a few moments, and then descended a broad flight of steps, which brought them into a more shaded and retired walk; on either side of which rows of orange-trees gave forth their fragrance, while, to the right, sudden and numerous vistas were cut among the more irregular and dense foliage, affording glimpses—now of some rustic statue—now of some lone temple—now of some quaint fountain, on the play of whose waters the first stars had begun to tremble.

It was one of those magnificent gardens, modelled from the stately glories of Versailles, which it is now the mode to decry, but which breathe so unequivocally of the Palace. I grant that they deck Nature with somewhat too prolix a grace; but is beauty always best seen in deshabille? And with what associations of the brightest traditions connected with Nature they link her more luxuriant loveliness! Must we breathe only the malaria of Rome to be capable of feeling the interest attached to the fountain or the statue?

"I am glad," said the Earl, "that you admired my bust of Cicero—it is from an original very lately discovered. What grandeur in the brow!—what energy in the mouth, and downward bend of the head! It is pleasant even to imagine we gaze upon the likeness of so bright a spirit;—and confess, at least of Cicero, that in reading the aspirations and outpourings of his mind, you have felt your apathy to Fame melting away; you have shared the desire to live to the future age,—'the longing after immortality?"

"Was it not that longing," replied Aram, "which gave to the character of Cicero its poorest and most frivolous infirmity? Has it not made him, glorious as he is despite of it, a byword in the mouths of every schoolboy? Wherever you mention his genius, do you not hear an appendix on his vanity?"

"Yet without that vanity, that desire for a name with posterity, would he have been equally great—would he equally have cultivated his genius?"

"Probably, my Lord, he would not have equally cultivated his genius, but in reality he might have been equally great. A man often injures his mind by the means that increase his genius. You think this, my Lord, a paradox, but examine it. How many men of genius have been but ordinary men, take them from the particular objects in which they shine. Why is this, but that in cultivating one branch of intellect they neglect the rest? Nay, the very torpor of the reasoning faculty has often kindled the imaginative. Lucretius composed his sublime poem under the influence of a delirium. The susceptibilities that we create or refine by the pursuit of one object, weaken our general reason; and I may compare with some justice the powers of the mind to the faculties of the body, in which squinting is occasioned by an inequality of strength in the eyes, and discordance of voice by the same inequality in the ears."

"I believe you are right," said the Earl; "yet I own I willingly forgive Cicero for his vanity, if it contributed to the production of his orations and his essays; and he is a greater man, even with his vanity unconquered, than if he had conquered his foible, and in doing so taken away the incitements to his genius."

"A greater man in the world's eye, my Lord, but scarcely in reality. Had Homer written his Iliad and then burnt it, would his genius have been less? The world would have known nothing of him, but would he have been a less extraordinary man on that account? We are too apt, my Lord, to confound greatness and fame.

"There is one circumstance," added Aram, after a pause, "that should diminish our respect for renown. Errors of life, as well as foibles of characters, are often the real enhancers of celebrity. Without his errors, I doubt whether Henri Quatre would have become the idol of a people. How many Whartons has the world known, who, deprived of their frailties, had been inglorious! The light that you so admire, reaches you only through the distance of time, on account of the angles and unevenness of the body whence it emanates. Were the surface of the moon smooth, it would be invisible."

"I admire your illustrations," said the Earl; "but I reluctantly submit to your reasonings. You would then neglect your powers, lest they should lead you into errors?"

"Pardon me, my Lord; it is because I think all the powers should be cultivated, that I quarrel with the exclusive cultivation of one. And it is only because I would strengthen the whole mind that I dissent from the reasonings of those who tell you to consult your genius."

"But your genius may serve mankind more than this general cultivation of intellect?"

"My Lord," replied Aram, with a mournful cloud upon his countenance; "that argument may have weight with those who think mankind can be effectually served, though they may be often dazzled, by the labours of an individual. But, indeed, this perpetual talk of 'mankind' signifies nothing: each of us consults his proper happiness, and we consider him a madman who ruins his own peace of mind by an everlasting fretfulness of philanthropy."

This was a doctrine that half pleased, half displeased the Earl—it shadowed forth the most dangerous notions which Aram entertained.

"Well, well," said the noble host, as, after a short contest on the ground of his guest's last remark, they left off where they began, "Let us drop these general discussions: I have a particular proposition to unfold. We have, I trust, Mr. Aram, seen enough of each other, to feel that we can lay a sure foundation for mutual esteem. For my part, I own frankly, that I have never met with one who has inspired me with a sincerer admiration. I am desirous that your talents and great learning should be known in the widest sphere. You may despise fame, but you must permit your friends the weakness to wish you justice, and themselves triumph. You know my post in the present administration—the place of my secretary is one of great trust—some influence, and large emolument. I offer it to you—accept it, and you will confer upon me an honour and an obligation. You will have your own separate house, or apartments in mine, solely appropriated to your use. Your privacy will never be disturbed. Every arrangement shall be made for yourself and your bride, that either of you can suggest. Leisure for your own pursuits you will have, too, in abundance—there are others who will perform all that is toilsome in your office. In London, you will see around you the most eminent living men of all nations, and in all pursuits. If you contract, (which believe me is possible—it is a tempting game,) any inclination towards public life, you will have the most brilliant opportunities afforded you, and I foretell you the most signal success. Stay yet one moment:—for this you will owe me no thanks. Were I not sensible that I consult my own interests in this proposal, I should be courtier enough to suppress it."

"My Lord," said Aram, in a voice which, in spite of its calmness, betrayed that he was affected, "it seldom happens to a man of my secluded habits, and lowly pursuits, to have the philosophy he affects put to so severe a trial. I am grateful to you—deeply grateful for an offer so munificent—so undeserved. I am yet more grateful that it allows me to sound the strength of my own heart, and to find that I did not too highly rate it. Look, my Lord, from the spot where we now stand" (the moon had risen, and they had now returned to the terrace): "in the vale below, and far among those trees, lies my home. More than two years ago, I came thither, to fix the resting-place of a sad and troubled spirit. There have I centered all my wishes and my hopes; and there may I breathe my last! My Lord, you will not think me ungrateful, that my choice is made; and you will not blame my motive, though you may despise my wisdom."

"But," said the Earl astonished, "you cannot foresee all the advantages you would renounce. At your age—with your intellect—to choose the living sepulchre of a hermitage—it was wise to reconcile yourself to it, but not to prefer it! Nay, nay; consider—pause. I am in no haste for your decision; and what advantages have you in your retreat, that you will not possess in a greater degree with me? Quiet?—I pledge it to you under my roof. Solitude?—you shall have it at your will. Books?—what are those which you, which any individual possesses, to the public institutions, the magnificent collections, of the metropolis? What else is it you enjoy yonder, and cannot enjoy with me?"

"Liberty!" said Aram energetically.—"Liberty! the wild sense of independence. Could I exchange the lonely stars and the free air, for the poor lights and feverish atmosphere of worldly life? Could I surrender my mood, with its thousand eccentricities and humours—its cloud and shadow—to the eyes of strangers, or veil it from their gaze by the irksomeness of an eternal hypocrisy? No, my Lord! I am too old to turn disciple to the world! You promise me solitude and quiet. What charm would they have for me, if I felt they were held from the generosity of another? The attraction of solitude is only in its independence. You offer me the circle, but not the magic which made it holy. Books! They, years since, would have tempted me; but those whose wisdom I have already drained, have taught me now almost enough: and the two Books, whose interest can never be exhausted—Nature and my own Heart—will suffice for the rest of life. My Lord, I require no time for consideration."

"And you positively refuse me?"

"Gratefully refuse you."

The Earl walked peevishly away for one moment; but it was not in his nature to lose himself for more.

"Mr. Aram," said he frankly, and holding out his hand; "you have chosen nobly, if not wisely; and though I cannot forgive you for depriving me of such a companion, I thank you for teaching me such a lesson. Henceforth, I will believe, that philosophy may exist in practice; and that a contempt for wealth and for honours, is not the mere profession of discontent. This is the first time, in a various and experienced life, that I have found a man sincerely deaf to the temptations of the world,—and that man of such endowments! If ever you see cause to alter a theory that I still think erroneous, though lofty—remember me; and at all times, and on all occasions," he added, with a smile, "when a friend becomes a necessary evil, call to mind our starlit walk on the castle terrace."

Aram did not mention to Lester, or even Madeline, the above conversation. The whole of the next day he shut himself up at home; and when he again appeared at the Manor-house, he heard with evident satisfaction that the Earl had been suddenly summoned on state affairs to London.

There was an unaccountable soreness in Aram's mind, which made him feel a resentment—a suspicion against all who sought to lure him from his retreat. "Thank Heaven!" thought he, when he heard of the Earl's departure; "we shall not meet for another year!" He was mistaken.—Another year!

CHAPTER V.

IN WHICH THE STORY RETURNS TO WALTER AND THE CORPORAL.—THE RENCONTRE WITH A STRANGER, AND HOW THE STRANGER PROVES TO BE NOT ALTOGETHER A STRANGER.

> Being got out of town in the road to Penaflor, master of my own action, and forty good ducats; the first thing I did was to give my mule her head, and to go at what pace she pleased.
> . . . .
> I left them in the inn, and continued my journey; I was hardly got half-a-mile farther, when I met a cavalier very genteel,
> —Gil Blas.

It was broad and sunny noon on the second day of their journey, as Walter Lester, and the valorous attendant with whom it had pleased Fate to endow him, rode slowly into a small town in which the Corporal in his own heart, had resolved to bait his roman-nosed horse and refresh himself. Two comely inns had the younger traveller of the twain already passed with an indifferent air, as if neither bait nor refreshment made any part of the necessary concerns of this habitable world. And in passing each of the said hostelries, the roman-nosed horse had uttered a snort of indignant surprise, and the worthy Corporal had responded to the quadrupedal remonstrance by a loud hem. It seemed, however, that Walter heard neither of the above significant admonitions; and now the town was nearly passed, and a steep hill that seemed winding away into eternity, already presented itself to the rueful gaze of the Corporal.

"The boy's clean mad," grunted Bunting to himself—"must do my duty to him—give him a hint."

Pursuant to this notable and conscientious determination, Bunting jogged his horse into a trot, and coming alongside of Walter, put his hand to his hat and said:

"Weather warm, your honour—horses knocked up—next town far as hell!—halt a bit here—augh!"

"Ha! that is very true, Bunting; I had quite forgotten the length of our journey. But see, there is a sign-post yonder, we will take advantage of it."

"Augh! and your honour's right—fit for the forty-second;" said the Corporal, falling back; and in a few moments he and his charger found themselves, to their mutual delight, entering the yard of a small, but comfortable-looking inn.

The Host, a man of a capacious stomach and a rosy cheek—in short, a host whom your heart warms to see, stepped forth immediately, held the stirrup for the young Squire, (for the Corporal's movements were too stately to be rapid,) and ushered him with a bow, a smile, and a flourish of his napkin, into one of those little quaint rooms, with cupboards bright with high glasses and old china, that it pleases us still to find extant in the old-fashioned inns, in our remoter roads and less Londonized districts.

Mine host was an honest fellow, and not above his profession; he stirred the fire, dusted the table, brought the bill of fare, and a newspaper seven days old, and then bustled away to order the dinner and chat with the Corporal. That accomplished hero had already thrown the stables into commotion, and frightening the two ostlers from their attendance on the steeds of more peaceable men, had set them both at leading his own horse and his master's to and fro' the yard, to be cooled into comfort and appetite.

He was now busy in the kitchen, where he had seized the reins of government, sent the scullion to see if the hens had laid any fresh eggs, and drawn upon himself the objurgations of a very thin cook with a squint.

"Tell you, ma'am, you are wrong—quite wrong—have seen the world—old soldier—and know how to fry eggs better than any she in the three kingdoms—hold jaw—mind your own business—where's the frying-pan?—baugh!"

So completely did the Corporal feel himself in his element, while he was putting everybody else out of the way; and so comfortable did he find his new quarters, that he resolved that the "bait" should be at all events prolonged until his good cheer had been deliberately digested, and his customary pipe duly enjoyed.

Accordingly, but not till Walter had dined, for our man of the world knew that it is the tendency of that meal to abate our activity, while it increases our good humour, the Corporal presented himself to his master, with a grave countenance.

"Greatly vexed, your honour—who'd have thought it?—but those large animals are bad on long march."

"Why what's the matter now, Bunting?"

"Only, Sir, that the brown horse is so done up, that I think it would be as much as life's worth to go any farther for several hours."

"Very well, and if I propose staying here till the evening?—we have ridden far, and are in no great hurry."

"To be sure not—sure and certain not," cried the Corporal. "Ah, Master, you know how to command, I see. Nothing like discretion—discretion, Sir, is a jewel. Sir, it is more than jewel—it's a pair of stirrups!"

"A what? Bunting."

"Pair of stirrups, your honour. Stirrups help us to get on, so does discretion; to get off, ditto discretion. Men without stirrups look fine, ride bold, tire soon: men without discretion cut dash, but knock up all of a crack. Stirrups—but what sinnifies? Could say much more, your honour, but don't love chatter."

"Your simile is ingenious enough, if not poetical," said Walter; "but it does not hold good to the last. When a man falls, his discretion should preserve him; but he is often dragged in the mud by his stirrups."

"Beg pardon—you're wrong," quoth the Corporal, nothing taken by surprise; "spoke of the new-fangled stirrups that open, crank, when we fall, and let us out of the scrape." [Note: Of course the Corporal does not speak of the patent stirrup: that would be an anachronism.]

Satisfied with this repartee, the Corporal now (like an experienced jester) withdrew to leave its full effect on the admiration of his master. A little before sunset the two travellers renewed their journey.

"I have loaded the pistols, Sir," said the Corporal, pointing to the holsters on Walter's saddle. "It is eighteen miles off to the next town—will be dark long before we get there."

"You did very right, Bunting, though I suppose there is not much danger to be apprehended from the gentlemen of the highway."

"Why the Landlord do say the revarse, your honour,—been many robberies lately in these here parts."

"Well, we are fairly mounted, and you are a formidable-looking fellow, Bunting."

"Oh! your honour," quoth the Corporal, turning his head stiffly away, with a modest simper, "You makes me blush; though, indeed, bating that I have the military air, and am more in the prime of life, your honour is well nigh as awkward a gentleman as myself to come across."

"Much obliged for the compliment!" said Walter, pushing his horse a little forward—the Corporal took the hint and fell back.

It was now that beautiful hour of twilight when lovers grow especially tender. The young traveller every instant threw his dark eyes upward, and thought—not of Madeline, but her sister. The Corporal himself grew pensive, and in a few moments his whole soul was absorbed in contemplating the forlorn state of the abandoned Jacobina.

In this melancholy and silent mood, they proceeded onward till the shades began to deepen; and by the light of the first stars Walter beheld a small, spare gentleman riding before him on an ambling nag, with cropped ears and mane. The rider, as he now came up to him, seemed to have passed the grand climacteric, but looked hale and vigorous; and there was a certain air of staid and sober aristocracy about him, which involuntarily begat your respect.

He looked hard at Walter as the latter approached, and still more hard at the Corporal. He seemed satisfied with the survey.

"Sir," said he, slightly touching his hat to Walter, and with an agreeable though rather sharp intonation of voice, "I am very glad to see a gentleman of your appearance travelling my road. Might I request the honour of being allowed to join you so far as you go? To say the truth, I am a little afraid of encountering those industrious gentlemen who have been lately somewhat notorious in these parts; and it may be better for all of us to ride in as strong a party as possible."

"Sir," replied Walter, eyeing in his turn the speaker, and in his turn also feeling satisfied with the scrutiny, "I am going to—, where I shall pass the night on my way to town; and shall be very happy in your company."

The Corporal uttered a loud hem; that penetrating man of the world was not too well pleased with the advances of a stranger.

"What fools them boys be!" thought he, very discontentedly; "howsomever, the man does seem like a decent country gentleman, and we are two to one: besides, he's old, little, and—augh, baugh—I dare say, we are safe enough, for all he can do."

The Stranger possessed a polished and well-bred demeanour; he talked freely and copiously, and his conversation was that of a shrewd and cultivated man. He informed Walter that, not only the roads had been infested by those more daring riders common at that day, and to whose merits we ourselves have endeavoured to do justice in a former work of blessed memory, but that several houses had been lately attempted, and two absolutely plundered.

"For myself," he added, "I have no money, to signify, about my person: my watch is only valuable to me for the time it has been in my possession; and if the rogues robbed one civilly, I should not so much mind encountering them; but they are a desperate set, and use violence when there is nothing to be got by it. Have you travelled far to-day, Sir?"

"Some six or seven-and-twenty miles," replied Walter. "I am proceeding to London, and not willing to distress my horses by too rapid a journey."

"Very right, very good; and horses, Sir, are not now what they used to be when I was a young man. Ah, what wagers I used to win then! Horses galloped, Sir, when I was twenty; they trotted when I was thirty-five; but they only amble now. Sir, if it does not tax your patience too severely, let us give our nags some hay and water at the half-way house yonder."

Walter assented; they stopped at a little solitary inn by the side of the road, and the host came out with great obsequiousness when he heard the voice of Walter's companion.

"Ah, Sir Peter!" said he, "and how be'st your honour—fine night, Sir Peter—hope you'll get home safe, Sir Peter."

"Safe—ay! indeed, Jock, I hope so too. Has all been quiet here this last night or two?"

"Whish, Sir!" whispered my host, jerking his thumb back towards the house; "there be two ugly customers within I does not know: they have got famous good horses, and are drinking hard. I can't say as I knows any thing agen 'em, but I think your honours had better be jogging."

"Aha! thank ye, Jock, thank ye. Never mind the hay now," said Sir Peter, pulling away the reluctant mouth of his nag; and turning to Walter, "Come, Sir, let us move on. Why, zounds! where is that servant of yours?"

Walter now perceived, with great vexation, that the Corporal had disappeared within the alehouse; and looking through the casement, on which the ruddy light of the fire played cheerily, he saw the man of the world lifting a little measure of "the pure creature" to his lips; and close by the hearth, at a small, round table, covered with glasses, pipes, he beheld two men eyeing the tall Corporal very wistfully, and of no prepossessing appearance themselves. One, indeed, as the fire played full on his countenance, was a person of singularly rugged and sinister features; and this man, he now remarked, was addressing himself with a grim smile to the Corporal, who, setting down his little "noggin," regarded him with a stare, which appeared to Walter to denote recognition. This survey was the operation of a moment; for Sir Peter took it upon himself to despatch the landlord into the house, to order forth the unseasonable carouser; and presently the Corporal stalked out, and having solemnly remounted, the whole trio set onward in a brisk trot. As soon as they were without sight of the ale-house, the Corporal brought the aquiline profile of his gaunt steed on a level with his master's horse.

"Augh, Sir!" said he, with more than his usual energy of utterance, "I see'd him!"

"Him! whom?"

"Man with ugly face what drank at Peter Dealtry's, and knew Master Aram,—knew him in a crack,—sure he's a Tartar!"

"What! does your servant recognize one of those suspicious fellows whom Jock warned us against?" cried Sir Peter, pricking up his ears.

"So it seems, Sir," said Walter: "he saw him once before, many miles hence; but I fancy he knows nothing really to his prejudice."

"Augh!" cried the Corporal; "he's d—d ugly any how!"

"That's a tall fellow of yours," said Sir Peter, jerking up his chin with that peculiar motion common to the brief in stature, when they are covetous of elongation. "He looks military:—has he been in the army? Ay, I thought so; one of the King of Prussia's grenadiers, I suppose? Faith, I hear hoofs behind!"

"Hem!" cried the Corporal, again coming alongside of his master. "Beg pardon, Sir—served in the 42nd—nothing like regular line—stragglers always cut off—had rather not straggle just now—enemy behind!"

Walter looked back, and saw two men approaching them at a hand-gallop. "We are a match at least for them, Sir," said he, to his new acquaintance.

"I am devilish glad I met you," was Sir Peter's rather selfish reply.

"'Tis he! 'tis the devil!" grunted the Corporal, as the two men now gained their side and pulled up; and Walter recognised the faces he had marked in the ale-house.

"Your servant, gentlemen," quoth the uglier of the two; "you ride fast—"

"And ready;—bother—baugh!" chimed in the Corporal, plucking a gigantic pistol from his holster, without any farther ceremony.

"Glad to hear it, Sir!" said the hard-featured Stranger, nothing dashed. "But I can tell you a secret!"

"What's that—augh?" said the Corporal, cocking his pistol.

"Whoever hurts you, friend, cheats the gallows!" replied the stranger, laughing, and spurring on his horse, to be out of reach of any practical answer with which the Corporal might favour him. But Bunting was a prudent man, and not apt to be choleric.

"Bother!" said he, and dropped his pistol, as the other stranger followed his ill-favoured comrade.

"You see we are too strong for them!" cried Sir Peter, gaily; "evidently highwaymen! How very fortunate that I should have fallen in with you!"

A shower of rain now began to fall. Sir Peter looked serious—he halted abruptly—unbuckled his cloak, which had been strapped before his saddle—wrapped himself up in it—buried his face in the collar—muffled his chin with a red handkerchief, which he took out of his pocket, and then turning to Walter, he said to him, "What! no cloak, Sir? no wrapper even? Upon my soul I am very sorry I have not another handkerchief to lend you!"

"Man of the world—baugh!" grunted the Corporal, and his heart quite warmed to the stranger he had at first taken for a robber.

"And now, Sir," said Sir Peter, patting his nag, and pulling up his cloak-collar still higher, "let us go gently; there is no occasion for hurry. Why distress our horses?—"

"Really, Sir," said Walter, smiling, "though I have a great regard for my horse, I have some for myself; and I should rather like to be out of this rain as soon as possible."

"Oh, ah! you have no cloak. I forgot that; to be sure—to be sure, let us trot on, gently—though—gently. Well, Sir, as I was saying, horses are not so swift as they were. The breed is bought up by the French! I remember once, Johnny Courtland and I, after dining at my house, till the champagne had played the dancing-master to our brains, mounted our horses, and rode twenty miles for a cool thousand the winner. I lost it, Sir, by a hair's breadth; but I lost it on purpose; it would have half ruined Johnny Courtland to have paid me, and he had that delicacy, Sir,—he had that delicacy, that he would not have suffered me to refuse taking his money,—so what could I do, but lose on purpose? You see I had no alternative!"

"Pray, Sir," said Walter, charmed and astonished at so rare an instance of the generosity of human friendships—"Pray, Sir, did I not hear you called Sir Peter, by the landlord of the little inn? can it be, since you speak so familiarly of Mr. Courtland, that I have the honour to address Sir Peter Hales?"

"Indeed that is my name," replied the gentleman, with some surprise in his voice. "But I have never had the honour of seeing you before."

"Perhaps my name is not unfamiliar to you," said Walter. "And among my papers I have a letter addressed to you from my uncle Rowland Lester.

"God bless me!" cried Sir Peter, "What Rowy!—well, indeed I am overjoyed to hear of him. So you are his nephew? Pray tell me all about him, a wild, gay, rollicking fellow still, eh?" Always fencing, sa—sa! or playing at billiards, or hot in a steeple chace; there was not a jollier, better-humoured fellow in the world than Rowy Lester.

"You forget, Sir Peter," said Walter, laughing at a description so unlike his sober and steady uncle, "that some years have passed since the time you speak of."

"Ah, and so there have," replied Sir Peter; "and what does your uncle say of me?"

"That, when he knew you, you were generosity, frankness, hospitality itself."

"Humph, humph!" said Sir Peter, looking extremely disconcerted, a confusion which Walter imputed solely to modesty. "I was hairbrained foolish fellow then, quite a boy, quite a boy; but bless me, it rains sharply, and you have no cloak. But we are close on the town now. An excellent inn is the 'Duke of Cumberland's Head,' you will have charming accommodation there."

"What, Sir Peter, you know this part of the country well!"

"Pretty well, pretty well; indeed I live near, that is to say not very far from, the town. This turn, if you please. We separate here. I have brought you a little out of your way—not above a mile or two—for fear the robbers should attack me if I was left alone. I had quite forgot you had no cloak. That's your road—this mine. Aha! so Rowy Lester is still alive and hearty, the same excellent, wild fellow, no doubt. Give my kindest remembrance to him when you write. Adieu, Sir."

This latter speech having been delivered during a halt, the Corporal had heard it: he grinned delightedly as he touched his hat to Sir Peter, who now trotted off, and muttered to his young master:—

"Most sensible man, that, Sir!"

CHAPTER VI.

```
SIR PETER DISPLAYED.—ONE MAN OF THE WORLD SUFFERS FROM
ANOTHER.—THE INCIDENT OF THE BRIDLE BEGETS THE INCIDENT OF
THE SADDLE; THE INCIDENT OF THE SADDLE BEGETS THE INCIDENT OF
THE WHIP; THE INCIDENT OF THE WHIP BEGETS WHAT THE READER MUST
              READ TO SEE.

      Nihil est aliud magnum quam multa minuta.
         —Vetus Auctor.

      [Nor is their anything that hath so great
       a power as the aggregate of small things.]
```

"And so," said Walter, the next morning to the head waiter, who was busied about their preparations for breakfast; "and so, Sir Peter Hales, you say, lives within a mile of the town?"

"Scarcely a mile, Sir,—black or green? you passed the turn to his house last night;—Sir, the eggs are quite fresh this morning. This inn belongs to Sir Peter."

"Oh!—Does Sir Peter see much company?"

The waiter smiled.

"Sir Peter gives very handsome dinners, Sir; twice a year! A most clever gentleman, Sir Peter! They say he is the best manager of property in the whole county. Do you like Yorkshire cake?—toast? yes, Sir!"

"So so," said Walter to himself, "a pretty true description my uncle gave me of this gentleman. 'Ask me too often to dinner, indeed!'—'offer me money if I want it!'—'spend a month at his house!'—'most hospitable fellow in the world!'—My uncle must have been dreaming."

Walter had yet to learn, that the men most prodigal when they have nothing but expectations, are often most thrifty when they know the charms of absolute possession. Besides, Sir Peter had married a Scotch lady, and was blessed with eleven children! But was Sir Peter Hales much altered? Sir Peter Hales was exactly the same man in reality that he always had been. Once he was selfish in extravagance; he was now selfish in thrift. He had always pleased himself, and damned other people; that was exactly what he valued himself on doing now. But the most absurd thing about Sir Peter was, that while he was for ever extracting use from every one else, he was mightily afraid of being himself put to use. He was in parliament, and noted for never giving a frank out of his own family. Yet withal, Sir Peter Hales was still an agreeable fellow; nay, he was more liked and much more esteemed than ever. There is something conciliatory in a saving disposition; but people put themselves in a great passion when a man is too liberal with his own. It is an insult on their own prudence. "What right has he to be so extravagant? What an example to our servants!" But your close neighbour does not humble you. You love your close neighbour; you respect your close neighbour; you have your harmless jest against him—but he is a most respectable man.

"A letter, Sir, and a parcel, from Sir Peter Hales," said the waiter, entering.

The parcel was a bulky, angular, awkward packet of brown paper, sealed once and tied with the smallest possible quantity of string; it was addressed to Mr. James Holwell, Saddler,—Street,—The letter was to—Lester Esq., and ran thus, written in a very neat, stiff, Italian character.

"Dr Sr,

"I trust you had no difficulty in findg ye Duke of Cumberland's Head, it is an excellent In.

"I greatly regt yt you are unavoidy oblig'd to go on to Londn; for, otherwise I shd have had the sincerest please in seeing you here at dinr, introducing you to Ly Hales. Anothr time I trust we may be more fortunate.

"As you pass thro' ye litte town of..., exactly 21 miles from hence, on the road to Londn, will you do me the favr to allow your servt to put the little parcel I send into his pockt, drop it as directd. It is a bridle I am forc'd to return. Country workn are such bungrs.

"I shd most certainy have had ye honr to wait on you persony, but the rain has given me a mo seve cold;—hope you have escap'd, tho' by ye by, you had no cloke, nor wrappr!

"My kindest regards to your mo excellent unce. I am quite sure he's the same fine merry fellw he always was,—tell him so!

"Dr Sr, Yours faithy,

"Peter Grindlescrew Hales.

"P.S. You know perhs yt poor Jno Courtd, your uncle's mo intime friend, lives in..., the town in which your servt will drop ye bride. He is much alter'd,—poor Jno!"

"Altered! alteration then seems the fashion with my uncle's friends!" thought Walter, as he rang for the Corporal, and consigned to his charge the unsightly parcel.

"It is to be carried twenty-one miles at the request of the gentleman we met last night,—a most sensible man, Bunting."

"Augh—whaugh,—your honour!" grunted the Corporal, thrusting the bridle very discontentedly into his pocket, where it annoyed him the whole journey, by incessantly getting between his seat of leather and his seat of honour. It is a comfort to the inexperienced, when one man of the world smarts from the sagacity of another; we resign ourselves more willingly to our fate. Our travellers resumed their journey, and in a few minutes, from the cause we have before assigned, the Corporal became thoroughly out of humour.

"Pray, Bunting," said Walter, calling his attendant to his side, "do you feel sure that the man we met yesterday at the alehouse, is the same you saw at Grassdale some months ago?"

"Damn it!" cried the Corporal quickly, and clapping his hand behind.

"How, Sir!"

"Beg pardon, your honour—slip tongue, but this confounded parcel!—augh—bother!"

"Why don't you carry it in your hand?"

"'Tis so ungainsome, and be d—d to it; and how can I hold parcel and pull in this beast, which requires two hands; his mouth's as hard as a brickbat,—augh!"

"You have not answered my question yet?"

"Beg pardon, your honour. Yes, certain sure the man's the same; phiz not to be mistaken."

"It is strange," said Walter, musing, "that Aram should know a man, who, if not a highwayman as we suspected, is at least of rugged manner and disreputable appearance; it is strange too, that Aram always avoided recurring to the acquaintance, though he confessed it." With this he broke into a trot, and the Corporal into an oath.

They arrived by noon, at the little town specified by Sir Peter, and in their way to the inn (for Walter resolved to rest there), passed by the saddler's house. It so chanced that Master Holwell was an adept in his craft, and that a newly-invented hunting-saddle at the window caught Walter's notice. The artful saddler persuaded the young traveller to dismount and look at "the most convenientest and handsomest saddle what ever was seed;" and the Corporal having lost no time in getting rid of his encumbrance, Walter dismissed him to the inn with the horses, and after purchasing the saddle, in exchange for his own, he sauntered into the shop to look at a new snaffle. A gentleman's servant was in the shop at the time, bargaining for a riding whip; and the shopboy, among others, shewed him a large old-fashioned one, with a tarnished silver handle. Grooms have no taste for antiquity, and in spite of the silverhandle, the servant pushed it aside with some contempt. Some jest he uttered at the time, chanced to attract Walter's notice to the whip; he took it up carelessly, and perceived with great surprise that it bore his own crest, a bittern, on the handle. He examined it now with attention, and underneath the crest were the letters G. L., his father's initials.

"How long have you had this whip?" said he to the saddler, concealing the emotion, which this token of his lost parent naturally excited.

"Oh, a nation long time, Sir," replied Mr. Holwell; "it is a queer old thing, but really is not amiss, if the silver was scrubbed up a bit, and a new lash put on; you may have it a bargain, Sir, if so be you have taken a fancy to it."

"Can you at all recollect how you came by it," said Walter, earnestly; "the fact is that I see by the crest and initials, that it belonged to a person whom I have some interest in discovering."

"Why let me see," said the saddler, scratching the tip of his right ear, "'tis so long ago sin I had it, I quite forgets how I came by it."

"Oh, is it that whip, John?" said the wife, who had been attracted from the back parlour by the sight of the handsome young stranger. "Don't you remember, it's a many year ago, a gentleman who passed a day with Squire Courtland, when he first come to settle here, called and left the whip to have a new thong put to it. But I fancies he forgot it, Sir, (turning to Walter,) for he never called for it again; and the Squire's people said as how he was a gone into Yorkshire; so there the whip's been ever sin. I remembers it, Sir, 'cause I kept it in the little parlour nearly a year, to be in the way like."

"Ah! I thinks I do remember it now," said Master Holwell. "I should think it's a matter of twelve yearn ago. I suppose I may sell it without fear of the gentleman's claiming it again."

"Not more than twelve years!" said Walter, anxiously, for it was some seventeen years since his father had been last heard of by his family.

"Why it may be thirteen, Sir, or so, more or less, I can't say exactly."

"More likely fourteen!" said the Dame, "it can't be much more, Sir, we have only been a married fifteen year come next Christmas! But my old man here, is ten years older nor I."

"And the gentleman, you say, was at Mr. Courtland's."

"Yes, Sir, that I'm sure of," replied the intelligent Mrs. Holwell; "they said he had come lately from Ingee."

Walter now despairing of hearing more, purchased the whip; and blessing the worldly wisdom of Sir Peter Hales, that had thus thrown him on a clue, which, however faint and distant, he resolved to follow up, he inquired the way to Squire Courtland's, and proceeded thither at once.

CHAPTER VII.

WALTER VISITS ANOTHER OF HIS UNCLE'S FRIENDS.—MR. COURTLAND'S STRANGE COMPLAINT.—WALTER LEARNS NEWS OF HIS FATHER, WHICH SURPRISES HIM.—THE CHANGE IN HIS DESTINATION.

God's my life, did you ever hear the like, what a strange man is this!

What you have possessed me withall, I'll discharge it amply.
—Ben Jonson's Every Man in his Humour.

Mr. Courtland's house was surrounded by a high wall, and stood at the outskirts of the town. A little wooden door buried deep within the wall, seemed the only entrance. At this Walter paused, and after twice applying to the bell, a footman of a peculiarly grave and sanctimonious appearance, opened the door.

In reply to Walter's inquiries, he informed him that Mr. Courtland was very unwell, and never saw "Company."—Walter, however, producing from his pocket-book the introductory letter given him by his father, slipped it into the servant's hand, accompanied by half a crown, and begged to be announced as a gentleman on very particular business.

"Well, Sir, you can step in," said the servant, giving way; "but my master is very poorly, very poorly indeed."

"Indeed, I am sorry to hear it: has he been long so?"

"Going on for ten—years, sir!" replied the servant, with great gravity; and opening the door of the house which stood within a few paces of the wall, on a singularly flat and bare grass-plot, he showed him into a room, and left him alone.

The first thing that struck Walter in this apartment, was its remarkable lightness. Though not large, it had no less than seven windows. Two sides of the wall, seemed indeed all window! Nor were these admittants of the celestial beam-shaded by any blind or curtain,—

"The gaudy, babbling, and remorseless day"

made itself thoroughly at home in this airy chamber. Nevertheless, though so light, it seemed to Walter any thing but cheerful. The sun had blistered and discoloured the painting of the wainscot, originally of a pale sea-green; there was little furniture in the apartment; one table in the centre, some half a dozen chairs, and a very small Turkey-carpet, which did not cover one tenth part of the clean, cold, smooth, oak boards, constituted all the goods and chattels visible in the room. But what particularly added effect to the bareness of all within, was the singular and laborious bareness of all without. From each of these seven windows, nothing but a forlorn green flat of some extent was to be seen; there was not a tree, or a shrub, or a flower in the whole expanse, although by several stumps of trees near the house, Walter perceived that the place had not always been so destitute of vegetable life.

While he was yet looking upon this singular baldness of scene, the servant re-entered with his master's compliments, and a message that he should be happy to see any relation of Mr. Lester.

Walter accordingly followed the footman into an apartment possessing exactly the same peculiarities as the former one; viz. a most disproportionate plurality of windows, a commodious scantiness of furniture, and a prospect without, that seemed as if the house had been built on the middle of Salisbury plain.

Mr. Courtland, himself a stout man, and still preserving the rosy hues and comely features, though certainly not the same hilarious expression, which Lester had attributed to him, sat in a large chair, close by the centre window, which was open. He rose and shook Walter by the hand with great cordiality.

"Sir, I am delighted to see you! How is your worthy uncle? I only wish he were with you—you dine with me of course. Thomas, tell the cook to add a tongue and chicken to the roast beef—no,—young gentleman, I will have no excuse; sit down, sit down; pray come near the window; do you not find it dreadfully close? not a breath of air? This house is so choked up; don't you find it so, eh? Ah, I see, you can scarcely gasp."

"My dear Sir, you are mistaken; I am rather cold, on the contrary: nor did I ever in my life see a more airy house than yours."

"I try to make it so, Sir, but I can't succeed; if you had seen what it was, when I first bought it! a garden here, Sir; a copse there; a wilderness, God wot! at the back: and a row of chesnut trees in the front! You may conceive the consequence, Sir; I had not been long here, not two years, before my health was gone, Sir, gone—the d—d vegetable life sucked it out of me. The trees kept away all the air—I was nearly suffocated, without, at first, guessing the cause. But at length, though not till I had been withering away for five years, I discovered the origin of my malady. I went to work, Sir; I plucked up the cursed garden, I cut down the infernal chesnuts, I made a bowling green of the diabolical wilderness, but I fear it is too late. I am dying by inches,—have been dying ever since. The malaria has effectually tainted my constitution."

Here Mr. Courtland heaved a deep sigh, and shook his head with a most gloomy expression of countenance.

"Indeed, Sir," said Walter, "I should not, to look at you, imagine that you suffered under any complaint. You seem still the same picture of health, that my uncle describes you to have been when you knew him so many years ago."

"Yes, Sir, yes; the confounded malaria fixed the colour to my cheeks; the blood is stagnant, Sir. Would to God I could see myself a shade paler!—the blood does not flow; I am like a pool in a citizen's garden, with a willow at each corner;—but a truce to my complaints. You see, Sir, I am no hypochondriac, as my fool of a doctor wants to persuade me: a hypochondriac shudders at every breath of air, trembles when a door is open, and looks upon a window as the entrance of death. But I, Sir, never can have enough air; thorough draught or east wind, it is all the same to me, so that I do but breathe. Is that like hypochondria?—pshaw! But tell me, young gentleman, about your uncle; is he quite well,—stout,—hearty,—does he breathe easily,—no oppression?"

"Sir, he enjoys exceedingly good health: he did please himself with the hope that I should give him good tidings of yourself, and another of his old friends whom I accidentally saw yesterday,—Sir Peter Hales."

"Hales, Peter Hales!—ah! a clever little fellow that: how delighted Lester's good heart will be to hear that little Peter is so improved;—no longer a dissolute, harum-scarum fellow, throwing away his money, and always in debt. No, no; a respectable steady character, an excellent manager, an active member of Parliament, domestic in private life,—Oh! a very worthy man, Sir, a very worthy man!"

"He seems altered indeed, Sir," said Walter, who was young enough in the world to be surprised at this eulogy; "but is still agreeable and fond of anecdote. He told me of his race with you for a thousand guineas."

"Ah, don't talk of those days," said Mr. Courtland, shaking his head pensively, "it makes me melancholy. Yes, Peter ought to recollect that, for he has never paid me to this day; affected to treat it as a jest, and swore he could have beat me if he would. But indeed it was my fault, Sir; Peter had not then a thousand farthings in the world, and when he grew rich, he became a steady character, and I did not like to remind him of our former follies. Aha! can I offer you a pinch of snuff?—You look feverish, Sir; surely this room must affect you, though you are too polite to say so. Pray open that door, and then this window, and put your chair right between the two. You have no notion how refreshing the draught is."

Walter politely declined the proffered ague, and thinking he had now made sufficient progress in the acquaintance of this singular non-hypochondriac to introduce the subject he had most at heart, hastened to speak of his father.

"I have chanced, Sir," said he, "very unexpectedly upon something that once belonged to my poor father;" here he showed the whip. "I find from the saddler of whom I bought it, that the owner was at your house some twelve or fourteen years ago. I do not know whether you are aware that our family have heard nothing respecting my father's fate for a considerably longer time than that which has elapsed since you appear to have seen him, if at least I may hope that he was your guest, and the owner of this whip; and any news you can give me of him, any clue by which he can possibly be traced, would be to us all—to me in particular—an inestimable obligation."

"Your father!" said Mr. Courtland. "Oh,—ay, your uncle's brother. What was his Christian name?—Henry?"

"Geoffrey."

"Ay, exactly; Geoffrey! What, not been heard of?—his family not know where he is? A sad thing, Sir; but he was always a wild fellow; now here, now there, like a flash of lightning. But it is true, it is true, he did stay a day here, several years ago, when I first bought the place. I can tell you all about it;—but you seem agitated,—do come nearer the window:—there, that's right. Well, Sir, it is, as I said, a great many years ago,—perhaps fourteen,—and I was speaking to the landlord of the Greyhound about some hay he wished to sell, when a gentleman rode into the yard full tear, as your father always did ride, and in getting out of his way I recognised Geoffrey Lester. I did not know him well—far from it; but I had seen him once or twice with your uncle, and though he was a strange pickle, he sang a good song, and was deuced amusing. Well, Sir, I accosted him, and, for the sake of your uncle, I asked him to dine with me, and take a bed at my new house. Ah! I little thought what a dear bargain it was to be. He accepted my invitation, for I fancy—no offence, Sir,—there were few invitations that Mr. Geoffrey Lester ever refused to accept. We dined tete-a-tete,—I am an old bachelor, Sir,—and very entertaining he was, though his sentiments seemed to me broader than ever. He was capital, however, about the tricks he had played his creditors,—such manoeuvres,—such escapes! After dinner he asked me if I ever corresponded with his brother. I told him no; that we were very good friends, but never heard from each other; and he then said, 'Well, I shall surprise him with a visit shortly; but in case you should unexpectedly have any communication with him, don't mention having seen me; for, to tell you the truth, I am just returned from India, where I should have scraped up a little money, but that I spent it as fast as I got it. However, you know that I was always proverbially the luckiest fellow in the world—(and so, Sir, your father was!)—and while I was in India, I saved an old Colonel's life at a tiger-hunt; he went home shortly afterwards, and settled in Yorkshire; and the other day on my return to England, to which my ill-health drove me, I learned that my old Colonel was really dead, and had left me a handsome legacy, with his house in Yorkshire. I am now going down to Yorkshire to convert the chattels into gold—to receive my money, and I shall then seek out my good brother, my household gods, and, perhaps, though it's not likely, settle into a sober fellow for the rest of my life.' I don't tell you, young gentleman, that those were your father's exact words,—one can't remember verbatim so many years ago;—but it was to that effect. He left me the next day, and I never heard any thing more of him: to say the truth, he was looking wonderfully yellow, and fearfully reduced. And I fancied at the time, he could not live long; he was prematurely old, and decrepit in body, though gay in spirit; so that I had tacitly imagined in never hearing of him more—that he had departed life. But, good Heavens! did you never hear of this legacy?"

"Never: not a word!" said Walter, who had listened to these particulars in great surprise. "And to what part of Yorkshire did he say he was going?"

"That he did not mention."

"Nor the Colonel's name?"

"Not as I remember; he might, but I think not. But I am certain that the county was Yorkshire, and the gentleman, whatever was his name, was a Colonel. Stay! I recollect one more particular, which it is lucky I do remember. Your father in giving me, as I said before, in his own humorous strain, the history of his adventures, his hair-breadth escapes from his duns, the various disguises, and the numerous aliases he had assumed, mentioned that the name he had borne in India, and by which, he assured me, he had made quite a good character—was Clarke: he also said, by the way, that he still kept to that name, and was very merry on the advantages of having so common an one. 'By which,' he said wittily, 'he could father all his own sins on some other Mr. Clarke, at the same time that he could seize and appropriate all the merits of all his other namesakes.' Ah, no offence; but he was a sad dog, that father of yours! So you see that, in all probability, if he ever reached Yorkshire, it was under the name of Clarke that he claimed and received his legacy."

"You have told me more," said Walter joyfully, "than we have heard since his disappearance, and I shall turn my horses' heads northward to-morrow, by break of day. But you say, 'if he ever reached Yorkshire,'—What should prevent him?"

"His health!" said the non-hypochondriac, "I should not be greatly surprised if—if—In short you had better look at the grave-stones by the way, for the name of Clarke."

"Perhaps you can give me the dates, Sir," said Walter, somewhat cast down from his elation.

"Ay! I'll see, I'll see, after dinner; the commonness of the name has its disadvantages now. Poor Geoffrey!—I dare say there are fifty tombs, to the memory of fifty Clarkes, between this and York. But come, Sir, there's the dinner-bell."

Whatever might have been the maladies entailed upon the portly frame of Mr. Courtland by the vegetable life of the departed trees, a want of appetite was not among the number. Whenever a man is not abstinent from rule, or from early habit, as in the case of Aram, Solitude makes its votaries particularly fond of their dinner. They have no other event wherewith to mark their day—they think over it, they anticipate it, they nourish its soft idea with their imagination; if they do look forward to any thing else more than dinner, it is—supper!

Mr. Courtland deliberately pinned the napkin to his waistcoat, ordered all the windows to be thrown open, and set to work like the good Canon in Gil Blas. He still retained enough of his former self, to preserve an excellent cook; so far at least as the excellence of a she-artist goes; and though most of his viands were of the plainest, who does not know what skill it requires to produce an unexceptionable roast, or a blameless boil? Talk of good professed cooks, indeed! they are plentiful as blackberries: it is the good, plain cook, who is the rarity!

Half a tureen of strong soup; three pounds, at least, of stewed carp; all the under part of a sirloin of beef; three quarters of a tongue; the moiety of a chicken; six pancakes and a tartlet, having severally disappeared down the jaws of the invalid,

```
"Et cuncta terrarum subacta
Praeter atrocem animum Catonis,"

[And everything of earth subdued,
 except the resolute mind of Cato.]
```

he still called for two deviled biscuits and an anchovy!

When these were gone, he had the wine set on a little table by the window, and declared that the air seemed closer than ever. Walter was no longer surprised at the singular nature of the nonhypochondriac's complaint.

Walter declined the bed that Mr. Courtland offered him—though his host kindly assured him that it had no curtains, and that there was not a shutter to the house—upon the plea of starting the next morning at daybreak, and his consequent unwillingness to disturb the regular establishment of the invalid: and Courtland, who was still an excellent, hospitable, friendly man, suffered his friend's nephew to depart with regret. He supplied him, however, by a reference to an old note-book, with the date of the year, and even month, in which he had been favoured by a visit from Mr. Clarke, who, it seemed, had also changed his Christian name from Geoffrey, to one beginning with D—; but whether it was David or Daniel the host remembered not. In parting with Walter, Courtland shook his head, and observed:—"Entre nous, Sir, I fear this may be a wildgoose chase. Your father was too facetious to confine himself to fact—excuse me, Sir—and perhaps the

Colonel and the legacy were merely inventions—pour passer le temps—there was only one reason indeed, that made me fully believe the story."

"What was that, Sir?" asked Walter, blushing deeply, at the universality of that estimation his father had obtained.

"Excuse me, my young friend."

"Nay, Sir, let me press you."

"Why, then, Mr. Geoffrey Lester did not ask me to lend him any money."

The next morning, instead of repairing to the gaieties of the metropolis, Walter had, upon this slight and dubious clue, altered his journey northward, and with an unquiet yet sanguine spirit, the adventurous son commenced his search after the fate of a father evidently so unworthy of the anxiety he had excited.

CHAPTER VIII.

WALTER'S MEDITATIONS.—THE CORPORAL'S GRIEF AND ANGER.—THE CORPORAL PERSONALLY DESCRIBED.—AN EXPLANATION WITH HIS MASTER.—THE CORPORAL OPENS HIMSELF TO THE YOUNG TRAVELLER.— HIS OPINIONS ON LOVE;—ON THE WORLD;—ON THE PLEASURE AND RESPECTABILITY OF CHEATING;—ON LADIES—AND A PARTICULAR CLASS OF LADIES;—ON AUTHORS;—ON THE VALUE OF WORDS;—ON FIGHTING; —WITH SUNDRY OTHER MATTERS OF EQUAL DELECTATION AND IMPROVEMENT.—AN UNEXPECTED EVENT.

Quale per incertam Lunam sub luce maligna
Est iter.
—Virgil.

[Even as a journey by the upropitious light of the uncertain moon.]

The road prescribed to our travellers by the change in their destination led them back over a considerable portion of the ground they had already traversed, and since the Corporal took care that they should remain some hours in the place where they dined, night fell upon them as they found themselves in the midst of the same long and dreary stage in which they had encountered Sir Peter Hales and the two suspected highwaymen.

Walter's mind was full of the project on which he was bent. The reader can fully comprehend how vivid must have been his emotions at thus chancing on what might prove a clue to the mystery that hung over his father's fate; and sanguinely did he now indulge those intense meditations with which the imaginative minds of the young always brood over every more favourite idea, until they exalt the hope into a passion. Every thing connected with this strange and roving parent, had possessed for the breast of his son, not only an anxious, but so to speak, indulgent interest. The judgment of a young man is always inclined to sympathize with the wilder and more enterprising order of spirits; and Walter had been at no loss for secret excuses wherewith to defend the irregular life and reckless habits of his parent. Amidst all his father's evident and utter want of principle, Walter clung with a natural and self-deceptive partiality to the few traits of courage or generosity which relieved, if they did not redeem, his character; traits which, with a character of that stamp, are so often, though always so unprofitably blended, and which generally cease with the commencement of age. He now felt elated by the conviction, as he had always been inspired by the hope, that it was to be his lot to discover one whom he still believed living, and whom he trusted to find amended. The same intimate persuasion of the "good luck" of Geoffrey Lester, which all who had known him appeared to entertain, was felt even in a more credulous and earnest degree by his son. Walter gave way now, indeed, to a variety of conjectures as to the motives which could have induced his father to persist in the concealment of his fate after his return to England; but such of those conjectures as, if the more rational, were also the more despondent, he speedily and resolutely dismissed. Sometimes he thought that his father, on learning the death of the wife he had abandoned, might have been possessed with a remorse which rendered him unwilling to disclose himself to the rest of his family, and a feeling that the main tie of home was broken; sometimes he thought that the wanderer had been disappointed in his expected legacy, and dreading the attacks of his creditors, or unwilling to throw himself once more on the generosity of his brother, had again suddenly quitted England and entered on some enterprise or occupation abroad. It was also possible, to one so reckless and changeful, that even, after receiving the legacy, a proposition from some wild comrade might have hurried him away on any continental project on the mere impulse of the moment, for the impulse of the moment had always been the guide of his life; and once abroad he might have returned to India, and in new connections forgotten the old ties at home. Letters from abroad too, miscarry; and it was not improbable that the wanderer might have written repeatedly, and receiving no answer to his communications, imagined that the dissoluteness of his life had deprived him of the affections of his family, and, deserving so well to have the proffer of renewed intercourse rejected, believed that it actually was so. These, and a hundred similar conjectures, found favour in the eyes of the young traveller; but the chances of a fatal accident, or sudden death, he pertinaciously refused at present to include in the number of probabilities. Had his father been seized with a mortal illness on the road, was it not likely that he would, in the remorse occasioned in the hardiest by approaching death, have written to his brother, and recommending his child to his care, have apprised him of the addition to his fortune? Walter then did not meditate embarrassing his present journey by those researches among the dead, which the worthy Courtland had so considerately recommended to his prudence: should his expedition, contrary to his hopes, prove wholly unsuccessful, it might then be well to retrace his steps and adopt the suggestion. But what man, at the age of twenty-one, ever took much precaution on the darker side of a question on which his heart was interested?

With what pleasure, escaping from conjecture to a more ultimate conclusion—did he, in recalling those words, in which his father had more than hinted to Courtland of his future amendment, contemplate recovering a parent made wise by years and sober by misfortunes, and restoring him to a hearth of tranquil virtues and peaceful enjoyments! He imaged to himself a scene of that domestic happiness, which is so perfect in our dreams, because in our dreams monotony is always excluded from the picture. And, in this creation of Fancy, the form of Ellinor—his bright-eyed and gentle cousin, was not the least conspicuous. Since his altercation with Madeline, the love he had once thought so ineffaceable, had faded into a dim and sullen hue; and, in proportion as the image of Madeline grew indistinct, that of her sister became more brilliant. Often, now, as he rode slowly onward, in the quiet of the deepening night, and the mellow stars softening all on which they shone, he pressed the little token of Ellinor's affection to his heart, and wondered that it was only within the last few days he had discovered that her eyes were more beautiful than Madeline's, and her smile more touching. Meanwhile the redoubted Corporal, who was by no means pleased with the change in his master's plans, lingered behind, whistling the most melancholy tune in his collection. No young lady, anticipative of balls or coronets, had ever felt more complacent satisfaction in a journey to London than that which had cheered the athletic breast of the veteran on finding himself, at last, within one day's gentle march of the metropolis. And no young lady, suddenly summoned back in the first flush of her debut, by an unseasonable fit of gout or economy in papa, ever felt more irreparably aggrieved than now did the dejected Corporal. His master had not yet even acquainted him with the cause of the countermarch; and, in his own heart, he believed it nothing but the wanton levity and unpardonable fickleness "common to all them ere boys afore they have seen the world." He certainly considered himself a singularly ill-used and injured man, and drawing himself up to his full height, as if it were a matter with which Heaven should be acquainted at the earliest possible opportunity, he indulged, as we before said, in the melancholy consolation of a whistled death-dirge, occasionally interrupted by a long-drawn interlude half sigh, half snuffle of his favourite augh—baugh.

And here, we remember, that we have not as yet given to our reader a fitting portrait of the Corporal on horseback. Perhaps no better opportunity than the present may occur; and perhaps, also, Corporal Bunting, as well as Melrose Abbey, may seem a yet more interesting picture when viewed by the pale moonlight.

The Corporal then wore on his head a small cocked hat, which had formerly belonged to the Colonel of the Forty-second—the prints of my uncle Toby may serve to suggest its shape;—it had once boasted a feather—that was gone; but the gold lace, though tarnished, and the cockade, though battered, still remained. From under this shade the profile of the Corporal assumed a particular aspect of heroism: though a good-looking man on the main, it was his air, height, and complexion, which made him so; and a side view, unlike Lucian's one-eyed prince, was not the most favourable point in which his features could be regarded. His eyes, which were small and shrewd, were half hid by a pair of thick shaggy brows, which, while he whistled, he moved to and fro, as a horse moves his ears when he gives warning that he intends to shy; his nose was straight—so far so good—but then it did not go far enough; for though it seemed no despicable proboscis in front, somehow or another it appeared exceedingly short in profile; to make up for this, the upper lip was of a length the more striking from being exceedingly straight;—it had learned to hold itself upright, and make the most of its length as well as its master! his under lip, alone protruded in the act of whistling, served yet more markedly to throw the nose into the background; and, as for the chin—talk of the upper lip being long indeed!—the chin would have made two of it; such a chin! so long, so broad, so massive, had it been put on a dish might have passed, without discredit, for a round of beef! it looked yet larger than it was from the exceeding tightness of the stiff black-leather stock below, which forced forth all the flesh it encountered into another chin,—a remove to the round. The hat, being somewhat too small for the Corporal, and being cocked knowingly in front, left the hinder half of the head exposed. And the hair, carried into a club according to the fashion, lay thick, and of a grizzled black, on the brawny shoulders below. The veteran was dressed in a blue coat, originally a frock; but the skirts, having once, to the imminent peril of the place they guarded, caught fire, as the Corporal stood basking himself at Peter Dealtry's, had been so far amputated, as to leave only the stump of a tail, which just covered, and no more, that part which neither Art in bipeds nor Nature in quadrupeds loves to leave wholly exposed. And that part, ah, how ample! had Liston seen it, he would have hid for ever his diminished—opposite to head!—No wonder the Corporal had been so annoyed by the parcel of the previous day, a coat so short, and a—; but no matter, pass we to the rest! It was not only in its skirts that this wicked coat was deficient; the Corporal, who had within the last few years thriven lustily in the inactive serenity of Grassdale, had outgrown it prodigiously across the chest and girth; nevertheless he managed to button it up. And thus the muscular proportions of the wearer bursting forth in all quarters, gave him the ludicrous appearance of a gigantic schoolboy. His wrists, and large sinewy hands, both employed at the bridle of his hard-mouthed charger, were markedly visible; for it was the Corporal's custom whenever he came into an obscure part of the road, carefully to take off, and prudently to pocket, a pair of scrupulously clean white leather gloves which smartened up his appearance prodigiously in passing through the towns in their route. His breeches were of yellow buckskin, and ineffably tight; his stockings were of grey worsted, and a pair of laced boots, that reached the ascent of a very mountainous calf, but declined any farther progress, completed his attire.

Fancy then this figure, seated with laborious and unswerving perpendicularity on a demi-pique saddle, ornamented with a huge pair of well-stuffed saddle-bags, and holsters revealing the stocks of a brace of immense pistols, the horse with its obstinate mouth thrust out, and the bridle drawn as tight as a bowstring! its ears laid sullenly down, as if, like the Corporal, it complained of going to Yorkshire, and its long thick tail, not set up in a comely and well-educated arch, but hanging sheepishly down, as if resolved that its buttocks should at least be better covered than its master's!

And now, reader, it is not our fault if you cannot form some conception of the physical perfections of the Corporal and his steed.

The reverie of the contemplative Bunting was interrupted by the voice of his master calling upon him to approach.

"Well, well!" muttered he, "the younker can't expect one as close at his heels as if we were trotting into Lunnon, which we might be at this time, sure enough, if he had not been so damned flighty,—augh!"

"Bunting, I say, do you hear?"

"Yes, your honour, yes; this ere horse is so 'nation sluggish."

"Sluggish! why I thought he was too much the reverse, Bunting? I thought he was one rather requiring the bridle than the spur."

"Augh! your honour, he's slow when he should not, and fast when he should not; changes his mind from pure whim, or pure spite; new to the world, your honour, that's all; a different thing if properly broke. There be a many like him!"

"You mean to be personal, Mr. Bunting," said Walter, laughing at the evident ill-humour of his attendant.

"Augh! indeed and no!—I daren't—a poor man like me—go for to presume to be parsonal,—unless I get hold of a poorer!"

"Why, Bunting, you do not mean to say that you would be so ungenerous as to affront a man because he was poorer than you?—fie!"

"Whaugh, your honour! and is not that the very reason why I'd affront him? surely it is not my betters I should affront; that would be ill bred, your honour,—quite want of discipline."

"But we owe it to our great Commander," said Walter, "to love all men."

"Augh! Sir, that's very good maxim,—none better—but shows ignorance of the world, Sir—great!"

"Bunting, your way of thinking is quite disgraceful. Do you know, Sir, that it is the Bible you were speaking of?"

"Augh, Sir! but the Bible was addressed to them Jew creturs! How somever, it's an excellent book for the poor; keeps 'em in order, favours discipline,—none more so." "Hold your tongue. I called you, Bunting, because I think I heard you say you had once been at York. Do you know what towns we shall pass on our road thither?"

"Not I, your honour; it's a mighty long way.—What would the Squire think?—just at Lunnon, too. Could have learnt the whole road, Sir, inns all, if you had but gone on to Lunnon first. Howsomever, young gentlemen will be hasty,—no confidence in those older, and who are experienced in the world. I knows what I knows," and the Corporal recommenced his whistle.

"Why, Bunting, you seem quite discontented at my change of journey. Are you tired of riding, or were you very eager to get to town?"

"Augh! Sir; I was only thinking of what best for your honour,—I!—'tis not for me to like or dislike. Howsomever, the horses, poor creturs, must want rest for some days. Them dumb animals can't go on for ever, bumpety, bumpety, as your honour and I do.—Whaugh!"

"It is very true, Bunting, and I have had some thoughts of sending you home again with the horses, and travelling post."

"Eh!" grunted the Corporal, opening his eyes; "hopes your honour ben't serious."

"Why if you continue to look so serious, I must be serious too; you understand, Bunting?"

"Augh—and that's all, your honour," cried the Corporal, brightening up, "shall look merry enough to-morrow, when one's in, as it were, like, to the change of road. But you see, Sir, it took me by surprise. Said I to myself, says I, it is an odd thing for you, Jacob Bunting, on the faith of a man, it is! to go tramp here, tramp there, without knowing why or wherefore, as if you was still a private in the Forty-second, 'stead of a retired Corporal. You see, your honour, my pride was a hurt; but it's all over now;—only spites those beneath me,—I knows the world at my time o' life."

"Well, Bunting, when you learn the reason of my change of plan, you'll be perfectly satisfied that I do quite right. In a word, you know that my father has been long missing; I have found a clue by which I yet hope to trace him. This is the reason of my journey to Yorkshire."

"Augh!" said the Corporal, "and a very good reason: you're a most excellent son, Sir;—and Lunnon so nigh!"

"The thought of London seems to have bewitched you; did you expect to find the streets of gold since you were there last?"

"A—well Sir; I hears they be greatly improved."

"Pshaw! you talk of knowing the world, Bunting, and yet you pant to enter it with all the inexperience of a boy. Why even I could set you an example."

"'Tis 'cause I knows the world," said the Corporal, exceedingly nettled, "that I wants to get back to it. I have heard of some spoonies as never kist a girl, but never heard of any one who had kist a girl once, that did not long to be at it again."

"And I suppose, Mr. Profligate, it is that longing which makes you so hot for London?"

"There have been worse longings nor that," quoth the Corporal gravely.

"Perhaps you meditate marrying one of the London belles; an heiress—eh?"

"Can't but say," said the Corporal very solemnly, "but that might be 'ticed to marry a fortin, if so be she was young, pretty, good-tempered, and fell desperately in love with me,—best quality of all."

"You're a modest fellow."

"Why, the longer a man lives, the more knows his value; would not sell myself a bargain now, whatever might at twenty-one!"

"At that rate you would be beyond all price at seventy," said Walter: "but now tell me, Bunting, were you ever in love,—really and honestly in love?"

"Indeed, your honour," said the Corporal, "I have been over head and ears; but that was afore I learnt to swim. Love's very like bathing. At first we go souse to the bottom, but if we're not drowned, then we gather pluck, grow calm, strike out gently, and make a deal pleasanter thing of it afore we've done. I'll tell you, Sir, what I thinks of love: 'twixt you and me, Sir, 'tis not that great thing in life, boys and girls want to make it out to be; if 'twere one's dinner, that would be summut, for one can't do without that; but lauk, Sir, Love's all in the fancy. One does not eat it, nor drink it; and as for the rest,—why it's bother!"

"Bunting, you're a beast," said Walter in a rage, for though the Corporal had come off with a slight rebuke for his sneer at religion, we grieve to say that an attack on the sacredness of love seemed a crime beyond all toleration to the theologian of twenty-one.

The Corporal bowed, and thrust his tongue in his cheek.

There was a pause of some moments.

"And what," said Walter, for his spirits were raised, and he liked recurring to the quaint shrewdness of the Corporal, "and what, after all, is the great charm of the world, that you so much wish to return to it?"

"Augh!" replied the Corporal, "'tis a pleasant thing to look about un with all one's eyes open; rogue here, rogue there—keeps one alive;—life in Lunnon, life in a village—all the difference 'twixt healthy walk, and a doze in arm-chair; by the faith of a man, 'tis!"

"What! it is pleasant to have rascals about one?"

"Surely yes," returned the Corporal drily; "what so delightful like as to feel one's cliverness and 'bility all set an end—bristling up like a porkypine; nothing makes a man tread so light, feel so proud, breathe so briskly, as the knowledge that he's all his wits about him, that he's a match for any one, that the Divil himself could not take him in. Augh! that's what I calls the use of an immortal soul—bother!"

Walter laughed.

"And to feel one is likely to be cheated is the pleasantest way of passing one's time in town, Bunting, eh?"

"Augh! and in cheating too!" answered the Corporal; "'cause you sees, Sir, there be two ways o' living; one to cheat,—one to be cheated. 'Tis pleasant enough to be cheated for a little while, as the younkers are, and as you'll be, your honour; but that's a pleasure don't last long—t'other lasts all your life; dare say your honour's often heard rich gentlemen say to their sons, 'you ought, for your own happiness' sake, like, my lad, to have summut to do—ought to have some profession, be you niver so rich,'—very true, your honour, and what does that mean? why it means that 'stead of being idle and cheated, the boy ought to be busy and cheat—augh!"

"Must a man who follows a profession, necessarily cheat, then?"

"Baugh! can your honour ask that? Does not the Lawyer cheat? and the Doctor cheat? and the Parson cheat, more than any? and that's the reason they all takes so much int'rest in their profession—bother!"

"But the soldier? you say nothing of him."

"Why, the soldier," said the Corporal, with dignity, "the private soldier, poor fellow, is only cheated; but when he comes for to get for to be as high as a corp'ral, or a sargent, he comes for to get to bully others, and to cheat. Augh! then 'tis not for the privates to cheat,—that would be 'sumpton indeed, save us!"

"The General, then, cheats more than any, I suppose?"

"'Course, your honour; he talks to the world 'bout honour an' glory, and love of his Country, and sich like—augh! that's proper cheating!"

"You're a bitter fellow, Mr. Bunting: and pray, what do you think of the Ladies—'are they as bad as the men?'"

"Ladies—augh! when they're married—yes! but of all them ere creturs, I respects the kept Ladies, the most—on the faith of a man, I do! Gad! how well they knows the world—one quite invies the she rogues; they beats the wives hollow! Augh! and your honour should see how they fawns and flatters, and butters up a man, and makes him think they loves him like winkey, all the time they ruins him. They kisses money out of the miser, and sits in their satins, while the wife, 'drot her, sulks in a gingham. Oh, they be cliver creturs, and they'll do what they likes with old Nick, when they gets there, for 'tis the old gentlemen they cozens the best; and then," continued the Corporal, waxing more and more loquacious, for his appetite in talking grew with that it fed on,—"then there be another set o' queer folks you'll see in Lunnon, Sir, that is, if you falls in with 'em,—hang all together, quite in a clink. I seed lots on 'em when lived with the Colonel—Colonel Dysart, you knows—augh?"

"And what are they?"

"Rum ones, your honour; what they calls Authors."

"Authors! what the deuce had you or the Colonel to do with Authors?"

"Augh! then, the Colonel was a very fine gentleman, what the larned calls a my-seen-ass, wrote little songs himself, 'crossticks, you knows, your honour: once he made a play—'cause why, he lived with an actress!"

"A very good reason, indeed, for emulating Shakespear; and did the play succeed?"

"Fancy it did, your honour; for the Colonel was a dab with the scissors."

"Scissors! the pen, you mean?"

"No! that's what the dirty Authors make plays with; a Lord and a Colonel, my-seen-asses, always takes the scissors."

"How?"

"Why the Colonel's Lady—had lots of plays—and she marked a scene here—a jest there—a line in one place—a sentiment in t' other—and the Colonel sate by with a great paper book—cut 'em out, pasted them in book. Augh! but the Colonel pleased the town mightily."

"Well, so he saw a great many authors; and did not they please you?"

"Why they be so damned quarrelsome," said the Corporal, "wringle, wrangle, wrongle, snap, growl, scratch; that's not what a man of the world does; man of the world niver quarrels; then, too, these creturs always fancy you forgets that their father was a clargyman; they always thinks more of their family, like, than their writings; and if they does not get money when they wants it, they bristles up and cries, 'not treated like a gentleman, by God!' Yet, after all, they've a deal of kindness in 'em, if you knows how to manage 'em—augh! but, cat-kindness, paw today, claw to-morrow. And then they always marries young, the poor things, and have a power of children, and live on the fame and forten they are to get one of these days; for, my eye! they be the most sanguinest folks alive!"

"Why, Bunting, what an observer you have been! who could ever have imagined that you had made yourself master of so many varieties in men!"

"Augh! your honour, I had nothing to do when I was the Colonel's valley, but to take notes to ladies and make use of my eyes. Always a 'flective man."

"It is odd that, with all your abilities, you did not provide better for yourself."

"'Twas not my fault," said the Corporal, quickly; "but somehow, do what will—'tis not always the cliverest as foresees the best. But I be young yet, your honour!"

Walter stared at the Corporal and laughed outright: the Corporal was exceedingly piqued.

"Augh! mayhap you thinks, Sir, that 'cause not so young as you, not young at all; but, what's forty, or fifty, or fifty-five, in public life? never hear much of men afore then. 'Tis the autumn that reaps, spring sows, augh!—bother!"

"Very true and very poetical. I see you did not live among authors for nothing."

"I knows summut of language, your honour," quoth the Corporal pedantically.

"It is evident."

"For, to be a man of the world, Sir, must know all the ins and outs of speechifying; 'tis words, Sir, that makes another man's mare go your road. Augh! that must have been a cliver man as invented language; wonders who 'twas—mayhap Moses, your honour?"

"Never mind who it was," said Walter gravely; "use the gift discreetly."

"Umph!" said the Corporal—"yes, your honour," renewed he after a pause. "It be a marvel to think on how much a man does in the way of cheating, as has the gift of the gab. Wants a Missis, talks her over—wants your purse, talks you out on it—wants a place, talks himself into it.—What makes the Parson? words!—the lawyer? words—the Parliament-man? words!—words can ruin a country, in the Big House—words save souls, in the Pulpits—words make even them ere authors, poor creturs, in every man's mouth.—Augh! Sir, take note of the words, and the things will take care of themselves—bother!"

"Your reflections amaze me, Bunting," said Walter smiling; "but the night begins to close in; I trust we shall not meet with any misadventure."

"'Tis an ugsome bit of road!" said the Corporal, looking round him.

"The pistols?"

"Primed and loaded, your honour."

"After all, Bunting, a little skirmish would be no bad sport—eh?—especially to an old soldier like you."

"Augh, baugh! 'tis no pleasant work, fighting, without pay, at least; 'tis not like love and eating, your honour, the better for being, what they calls, 'gratis!'"

"Yet I have heard you talk of the pleasure of fighting; not for pay, Bunting, but for your King and Country!"

"Augh! and that's when I wanted to cheat the poor creturs at Grassdale, your honour; don't take the liberty to talk stuff to my master!"

They continued thus to beguile the way, till Walter again sank into a reverie, while the Corporal, who began more and more to dislike the aspect of the ground they had entered on, still rode by his side.

The road was heavy, and wound down the long hill which had stricken so much dismay into the Corporal's stout heart on the previous day, when he had beheld its commencement at the extremity of the town, where but for him they had not dined. They were now little more than a mile from the said town, the whole of the way was taken up by this hill, and the road, very different from the smoothened declivities of the present day, seemed to have been cut down the very steepest part of its centre; loose stones, and deep ruts encreased the difficulty of the descent, and it was with a slow pace and a guarded rein that both our travellers now continued their journey. On the left side of the road was a thick and lofty hedge; to the right, a wild, bare, savage heath, sloped downward, and just afforded a glimpse of the spires and chimneys of the town, at which the Corporal was already supping in idea! That incomparable personage was, however, abruptly recalled to the present instant, by a most violent stumble on the part of his hard-mouthed, Romannosed horse. The horse was all but down, and the Corporal all but over.

"Damn it," said the Corporal, slowly recovering his perpendicularity, "and the way to Lunnon was as smooth as a bowling-green!"

Ere this rueful exclamation was well out of the Corporal's mouth, a bullet whizzed past him from the hedge; it went so close to his ear, that but for that lucky stumble, Jacob Bunting had been as the grass of the field, which flourisheth one moment and is cut down the next!

Startled by the sound, the Corporal's horse made off full tear down the hill, and carried him several paces beyond his master, ere he had power to stop its career. But Walter reining up his better managed steed, looked round for the enemy, nor looked in vain.

Three men started from the hedge with a simultaneous shout. Walter fired, but without effect; ere he could lay hand on the second pistol, his bridle was seized, and a violent blow from a long double-handed bludgeon, brought him to the ground.

BOOK III.

CHAPTER I.

FRAUD AND VIOLENCE ENTER EVEN GRASSDALE.—PETER'S NEWS.
—THE LOVERS' WALK.—THE REAPPEARANCE.

> AUF.—"Whence comest thou—what wouldst thou?"
> —Coriolanus.

One evening Aram and Madeline were passing through the village in their accustomed walk, when Peter Dealtry sallied forth from The Spotted Dog, and hurried up to the lovers with a countenance full of importance, and a little ruffled by fear.

"Oh, Sir, Sir,—(Miss, your servant!)—have you heard the news? Two houses at Checkington, (a small town some miles distant from Grassdale,) were forcibly entered last night,—robbed, your honour, robbed. Squire Tibson was tied to his bed, his bureau rifled, himself shockingly confused on the head; and the maidservant Sally—her sister lived with me, a very good girl she was,—was locked up in the—the—the—I beg pardon, Miss—was locked up in the cupboard. As to the other house, they carried off all the plate. There were no less than four men, all masked, your honour, and armed with pistols. What if they should come here! such a thing was never heard of before in these parts. But, Sir,—but, Miss,—do not be afraid, do not ye now, for I may say with the Psalmist,

> 'But wicked men shall drink the dregs
> Which they in wrath shall wring,
> For I will lift my voice, and make
> Them flee while I do sing!'"

"You could not find a more effectual method of putting them to flight, Peter," said Madeline smiling; "but go and talk to my uncle. I know we have a whole magazine of blunderbusses and guns at home: they may be useful now. But you are well provided in case of attack. Have you not the Corporal's famous cat Jacobina,—surely a match for fifty robbers?"

"Ay, Miss, on the principle of set a thief to catch a thief, perhaps she may; but really it is no jesting matter. Them ere robbers flourish like a green bay tree, for a space at least, and it is 'nation bad sport for us poor lambs till they be cut down and withered like grass. But your house, Mr. Aram, is very lonesome like; it is out of reach of all your neighbours. Hadn't you better, Sir, take up your lodgings at the Squire's for the present?"

Madeline pressed Aram's arm, and looked up fearfully in his face. "Why, my good friend," said he to Dealtry, "robbers will have little to gain in my house, unless they are given to learned pursuits. It would be something new, Peter, to see a gang of housebreakers making off with a telescope, or a pair of globes, or a great folio covered with dust."

"Ay, your honour, but they may be the more savage for being disappointed."

"Well, well, Peter, we will see," replied Aram impatiently; "meanwhile we may meet you again at the hall. Good evening for the present."

"Do, dearest Eugene, do, for Heaven's sake," said Madeline, with tears in her eyes, as they, now turning from Dealtry, directed their steps towards the quiet valley, at the end of which the Student's house was situated, and which was now more than ever Madeline's favourite walk, "do, dearest Eugene, come up to the Manor-house till these wretches are apprehended. Consider how open your house is to attack; and surely there can be no necessity to remain in it now."

Aram's calm brow darkened for a moment. "What! dearest," said he, "can you be affected by the foolish fears of yon dotard? How do we know as yet, whether this improbable story have any foundation in truth. At all events, it is evidently exaggerated. Perhaps an invasion of the poultry-yard, in which some hungry fox was the real offender, may be the true origin of this terrible tale. Nay, love, nay, do not look thus reproachfully; it will be time enough for us when we have sifted the grounds of alarm to take our precautions; meanwhile, do not blame me if in your presence I cannot admit fear. Oh Madeline, dear, dear Madeline, could you know, could you dream, how different life has become to me since I knew you! Formerly, I will frankly own to you, that dark and boding apprehensions were wont to lie heavy at my heart; the cloud was more familiar to me than the sunshine. But now I have grown a child, and can see around me nothing but hope; my life was winter—your love has breathed it into spring."

"And yet, Eugene—yet—" "Yet what, my Madeline?"

"There are still moments when I have no power over your thoughts; moments when you break away from me; when you mutter to yourself feelings in which I have no share, and which seem to steal the consciousness from your eye and the colour from your lip."

"Ah, indeed!" said Aram quickly; "what! you watch me so closely?"

"Can you wonder that I do?" said Madeline, with an earnest tenderness in her voice.

"You must not then, you must not," returned her lover, almost fiercely; "I cannot bear too nice and sudden a scrutiny; consider how long I have clung to a stern and solitary independence of thought, which allows no watch, and forbids account of itself to any one. Leave it to time and your love to win their inevitable way. Ask not too much from me now. And mark, mark, I pray you, whenever, in spite of myself, these moods you refer to darken over me, heed not, listen not—Leave me! solitude is their only cure! promise me this, love—promise."

"It is a harsh request, Eugene, and I do not think I will grant you so complete a monopoly of thought;" answered Madeline, playfully, yet half in earnest.

"Madeline," said Aram, with a deep solemnity of manner, "I ask a request on which my very love for you depends. From the depths of my soul, I implore you to grant it; yea, to the very letter."

"Why, why, this is—" began Madeline, when encountering the full, the dark, the inscrutable gaze of her strange lover, she broke off in a sudden fear, which she could not analyse; and only added in a low and subdued voice, "I promise to obey you."

As if a weight were lifted from his heart, Aram now brightened at once into himself in his happiest mood. He poured forth a torrent of grateful confidence, of buoyant love, that soon swept from the remembrance of the blushing and enchanted Madeline, the momentary fear, the sudden chillness, which his look had involuntarily stricken into her mind. And as they now wound along the most lonely part of that wild valley, his arm twined round her waist, and his low but silver voice pouring magic into the very air she breathed—she felt perhaps a more entire and unruffled sentiment of present, and a more credulous persuasion of future, happiness, than she had ever experienced before. And Aram himself dwelt with a more lively and detailed fulness, than he was wont, on the prospects they were to share, and the security and peace which retirement would instill into their mode of life.

"Is it not," said he, with a lofty triumph that we shall look from our retreat upon the shifting passions, and the hollow loves of the distant world? We can have no petty object, no vain allurement to distract the unity of our affection: we must be all in all to each other; for what else can there be to engross our thoughts, and occupy our feelings here?

"If, my beautiful love, you have selected one whom the world might deem a strange choice for youth and loveliness like yours; you have, at least, selected one who can have no idol but yourself. The poets tell you, and rightly, that solitude is the fit sphere for love; but how few are the lovers whom solitude does not fatigue! they rush into retirement, with souls unprepared for its stern joys and its unvarying tranquillity: they weary of each other, because the solitude itself to which they fled, palls upon and oppresses them. But to me, the freedom which low minds call obscurity, is the aliment of life; I do not enter the temples of Nature as the stranger, but the priest: nothing can ever tire me of the lone and august altars, on which I sacrificed my youth: and now, what Nature, what Wisdom once were to me—no, no, more, immeasurably more than these, you are! Oh, Madeline! methinks there is nothing under Heaven like the feeling which puts us apart from all that agitates, and fevers, and degrades the herd of men; which grants us to control the tenour of our future life, because it annihilates our dependence upon others, and, while the rest of earth are hurried on, blind and unconscious, by the hand of Fate, leaves us the sole lords of our destiny; and able, from the Past, which we have governed, to become the Prophets of our Future!"

At this moment Madeline uttered a faint shriek, and clung trembling to Aram's arm. Amazed, and roused from his enthusiasm, he looked up, and on seeing the cause of her alarm, seemed himself transfixed, as by a sudden terror, to the earth.

But a few paces distant, standing amidst the long and rank fern that grew on either side of their path, quite motionless, and looking on the pair with a sarcastic smile, stood the ominous stranger, whom the second chapter of our first volume introduced to the reader.

For one instant Aram seemed utterly appalled and overcome; his cheek grew the colour of death; and Madeline felt his heart beat with a loud, a fearful force beneath the breast to which she clung. But his was not the nature any earthly dread could long abash. He whispered to Madeline to come on; and slowly, and with his usual firm but gliding step, continued his way.

"Good evening, Eugene Aram," said the stranger; and as he spoke, he touched his hat slightly to Madeline.

"I thank you," replied the Student, in a calm voice; "do you want aught with me?"

"Humph!—yes, if it so please you?"

"Pardon me, dear Madeline," said Aram softly, and disengaging himself from her, "but for one moment."

He advanced to the stranger, and Madeline could not but note that, as Aram accosted him, his brow fell, and his manner seemed violent and agitated; but she could not hear the words of either; nor did the conference last above a minute. The stranger bowed, and turning away, soon vanished among the shrubs. Aram regained the side of his mistress.

"Who," cried she eagerly, "is that fearful man? What is his business? What his name?"

"He is a man whom I knew well some fourteen years ago," replied Aram coldly, and with ease; "I did not then lead quite so lonely a life, and we were thrown much together. Since that time, he has been in unfortunate circumstances—rejoined the army—he was in early life a soldier, and had been disbanded—entered into business, and failed; in short, he has partaken of those vicissitudes inseparable from the life of one driven to seek the world. When he travelled this road some months ago, he accidentally heard of my residence in the neighbourhood, and naturally sought me. Poor as I am, I was of some assistance to him. His route brings him hither again, and he again seeks me: I suppose too that I must again aid him."

"And is that indeed all," said Madeline, breathing more freely; "well, poor man, if he be your friend, he must be inoffensive—I have done him wrong. And does he want money? I have some to give him—here Eugene!" And the simple-hearted girl put her purse into Aram's hand.

"No, dearest," said he, shrinking back; "no, we shall not require your contribution; I can easily spare him enough for the present. But let us turn back, it grows chill."

"And why did he leave us, Eugene?"

"Because I desired him to visit me at home an hour hence."

"An hour! then you will not sup with us to-night?"

"No, not this night, dearest."

The conversation now ceased; Madeline in vain endeavoured to renew it. Aram, though without relapsing into any of his absorbed reveries, answered her only in monosyllables. They arrived at the Manor-house, and Aram at the garden gate took leave of her for the night, and hastened backward towards his home. Madeline, after watching his form through the deepening shadows until it disappeared, entered the house with a listless step; a nameless and thrilling presentiment crept to her heart; and she could have sate down and wept, though without a cause.

CHAPTER II.

THE INTERVIEW BETWEEN ARAM AND THE STRANGER.

> The spirits I have raised abandon me,
> The spells which I have studied baffle me.
> —Manfred.

Meanwhile Aram strode rapidly through the village, and not till he had regained the solitary valley did he relax his step.

The evening had already deepened into night. Along the sere and melancholy wood, the autumnal winds crept, with a lowly, but gathering moan. Where the water held its course, a damp and ghostly mist clogged the air, but the skies were calm, and chequered only by a few clouds, that swept in long, white, spectral streaks, over the solemn stars. Now and then, the bat wheeled swiftly round, almost touching the figure of the Student, as he walked musingly onward. And the owl [Note: That species called the short-eared owl.] that before the month waned many days, would be seen no more in that region, came heavily from the trees, like a guilty thought that deserts its shade. It was one of those nights, half dim, half glorious, which mark the early decline of the year. Nature seemed restless and instinct with change; there were those signs in the atmosphere which leave the most experienced in doubt, whether the morning may rise in storm or sunshine. And in this particular period, the skiey influences seem to tincture the animal life with their own mysterious and wayward spirit of change. The birds desert their summer haunts; an unaccountable inquietude pervades the brute creation; even men in this unsettled season have considered themselves, more (than at others) stirred by the motion and whisperings of their genius. And every creature that flows upon the tide of the Universal Life of Things, feels upon the ruffled surface, the mighty and solemn change, which is at work within its depths.

And now Aram had nearly threaded the valley, and his own abode became visible on the opening plain, when the stranger emerged from the trees to the right, and suddenly stood before the Student. "I tarried for you here, Aram," said he, "instead of seeking you at home, at the time you fixed; for there are certain private reasons which make it prudent I should keep as much as possible among the owls, and it was therefore safer, if not more pleasant, to lie here amidst the fern, than to make myself merry in the village yonder."

"And what," said Aram, "again brings you hither? Did you not say, when you visited me some months since, that you were about to settle in a different part of the country, with a relation?"

"And so I intended; but Fate, as you would say, or the Devil, as I should, ordered it otherwise. I had not long left you, when I fell in with some old friends, bold spirits and true; the brave outlaws of the road and the field. Shall I have any shame in confessing that I preferred their society, a society not unfamiliar to me, to the dull and solitary life that I might have led in tending my old bed-ridden relation in Wales, who after all, may live these twenty years, and at the end can scarce leave me enough for a week's ill luck at the hazard-table? In a word, I joined my gallant friends, and entrusted myself to their guidance. Since then, we have cruised around the country, regaled ourselves cheerily, frightened the timid, silenced the fractious, and by the help of your fate, or my devil, have found ourselves by accident, brought to exhibit our valour in this very district, honoured by the dwelling-place of my learned friend, Eugene Aram."

"Trifle not with me, Houseman," said Aram sternly; "I scarcely yet understand you. Do you mean to imply, that yourself, and the lawless associates you say you have joined, are lying out now for plunder in these parts?"

"You say it: perhaps you heard of our exploits last night, some four miles hence?"

"Ha! was that villainy yours?"

"Villainy!" repeated Houseman, in a tone of sullen offence. "Come, Master Aram, these words must not pass between you and me, friends of such date, and on such a footing."

"Talk not of the past," replied Aram with a livid lip, "and call not those whom Destiny once, in despite of Nature, drove down her dark tide in a momentary companionship, by the name of friends. Friends we are not; but while we live, there is a tie between us stronger than that of friendship."

"You speak truth and wisdom," said Houseman, sneeringly; "for my part, I care not what you call us, friends or foes."

"Foes, foes!" exclaimed Aram abruptly, "not that. Has life no medium in its ties?—pooh—pooh! not foes; we may not be foes to each other."

"It were foolish, at least at present," said Houseman carelessly.

"Look you, Houseman," continued Aram drawing his comrade from the path into a wilder part of the scene, and, as he spoke, his words were couched in a more low and inward voice than heretofore. "Look you, I cannot live and have my life darkened thus by your presence. Is not the world wide enough for us both? Why haunt each other? what have you to gain from me? Can the thoughts that my sight recalls to you be brighter, or more peaceful, than those which start upon me, when I gaze on you? Does not a ghastly air, a charnel breath, hover about us both? Why perversely incur a torture it is so easy to avoid? Leave me—leave these scenes. All earth spreads before you—choose your pursuits, and your resting place elsewhere, but grudge me not this little spot."

"I have no wish to disturb you, Eugene Aram, but I must live; and in order to live I must obey my companions; if I deserted them, it would be to starve. They will not linger long in this district; a week, it may be; a fortnight, at most; then, like the Indian animal, they will strip the leaves, and desert the tree. In a word, after we have swept the country, we are gone."

"Houseman, Houseman!" said Aram passionately, and frowning till his brows almost hid his eyes, but that part of the orb which they did not hide, seemed as living fire; "I now implore, but I can threaten—beware!—silence, I say;" (and he stamped his foot violently on the ground, as he saw Houseman about to interrupt him;) "listen to me throughout—Speak not to me of tarrying here—speak not of days, of weeks—every hour of which would sound upon my ear like a death-knell. Dream not of a sojourn in these tranquil shades, upon an errand of dread and violence—the minions of the law aroused against you, girt with the chances of apprehension and a shameful death—" "And a full confession of my past sins," interrupted Houseman, laughing wildly.

"Fiend! devil!" cried Aram, grasping his comrade by the throat, and shaking him with a vehemence that Houseman, though a man of great strength and sinew, impotently attempted to resist.

"Breathe but another word of such import; dare to menace me with the vengeance of such a thing as thou, and, by the God above us, I will lay thee dead at my feet!"

"Release my throat, or you will commit murder," gasped Houseman with difficulty, and growing already black in the face.

Aram suddenly relinquished his gripe, and walked away with a hurried step, muttering to himself. He then returned to the side of Houseman, whose flesh still quivered either with rage or fear, and, his own self-possession completely restored, stood gazing upon him with folded arms, and his usual deep and passionless composure of countenance; and Houseman, if he could not boldly confront, did not altogether shrink from, his eye. So there and thus they stood, at a little distance from each other, both silent, and yet with something unutterably fearful in their silence.

"Houseman," said Aram at length, in a calm, yet a hollow voice, "it may be that I was wrong; but there lives no man on earth, save you, who could thus stir my blood,—nor you with ease. And know, when you menace me, that it is not your menace that subdues or shakes my spirit; but that which robs my veins of their even tenor is that you should deem your menace could have such power, or that you,—that any man,—should arrogate to himself the thought that he could, by the prospect of whatsoever danger, humble the soul and curb the will of Eugene Aram. And now I am calm; say what you will, I cannot be vexed again."

"I have done," replied Houseman coldly; "I have nothing to say; farewell!" and he moved away among the trees.

"Stay," cried Aram in some agitation; "stay; we must not part thus. Look you, Houseman, you say you would starve should you leave your present associates. That may not be; quit them this night,—this moment: leave the neighbourhood, and the little in my power is at your will."

"As to that," said Houseman drily, "what is in your power is, I fear me, so little as not to counterbalance the advantages I should lose in quitting my companions. I expect to net some three hundreds before I leave these parts."

"Some three hundreds!" repeated Aram recoiling; "that were indeed beyond me. I told you when we last met that it is only by an annual payment I draw the little wealth I have."

"I remember it. I do not ask you for money, Eugene Aram; these hands can maintain me," replied Houseman, smiling grimly. "I told you at once the sum I expected to receive somewhere, in order to prove that you need not vex your benevolent heart to afford me relief. I knew well the sum I named was out of your power, unless indeed it be part of the marriage portion you are about to receive with your bride. Fie, Aram! what, secrets from your old friend! You see I pick up the news of the place without your confidence."

Again Aram's face worked, and his lip quivered; but he conquered his passion with a surprising self-command, and answered mildly, "I do not know, Houseman, whether I shall receive any marriage portion whatsoever: If I do, I am willing to make some arrangement by which I could engage you to molest me no more. But it yet wants several days to my marriage; quit the neighbourhood now, and a month hence let us meet again. Whatever at that time may be my resources, you shall frankly know them."

"It cannot be," said Houseman; "I quit not these districts without a certain sum, not in hope, but possession. But why interfere with me? I seek not my hoards in your coffer. Why so anxious that I should not breathe the same air as yourself?"

"It matters not," replied Aram, with a deep and ghastly voice; "but when you are near me, I feel as if I were with the dead; it is a spectre that I would exorcise in ridding me of your presence. Yet this is not what I now speak of. You are engaged, according to your own lips, in lawless and midnight schemes, in which you may, (and the tide of chances runs towards that bourne,) be seized by the hand of Justice."

"Ho," said Houseman, sullenly, "and was it not for saying that you feared this, and its probable consequences, that you well-nigh stifled me, but now?—so truth may be said one moment with impunity, and the next at peril of life! These are the subtleties of you wise schoolmen, I suppose. Your Aristotles, and your Zenos, your Platos, and your Epicurus's, teach you notable distinctions, truly!"

"Peace!" said Aram; "are we at all times ourselves? Are the passions never our masters? You maddened me into anger; behold, I am now calm: the subjects discussed between myself and you, are of life and death; let us approach them with our senses collected and prepared. What, Houseman, are you bent upon your own destruction, as well as mine, that you persevere in courses which must end in a death of shame?"

"What else can I do? I will not work, and I cannot live like you in a lone wilderness on a crust of bread. Nor is my name like yours, mouthed by the praise of honest men: my character is marked; those who once knew me, shun now. I have no resource for society, (for I cannot face myself alone,) but in the fellowship of men like myself, whom the world has thrust from its pale. I have no resource for bread, save in the pursuits that are branded by justice, and accompanied with snares and danger. What would you have me do?"

"Is it not better," said Aram, "to enjoy peace and safety upon a small but certain pittance, than to live thus from hand to mouth? vibrating from wealth to famine, and the rope around your neck, sleeping and awake? Seek your relation; in that quarter, you yourself said your character was not branded: live with him, and know the quiet of easy days, and I promise you, that if aught be in my power to make your lot more suitable to your wants, so long as you lead the life of honest men, it shall be freely yours. Is not this better, Houseman, than a short and sleepless career of dread?"

"Aram," answered Houseman, "are you, in truth, calm enough to hear me speak? I warn you, that if again you forget yourself, and lay hands on me—" "Threaten not, threaten not," interrupted Aram, "but proceed; all within me is now still and cold as ice. Proceed without fear of scruple."

"Be it so; we do not love one another: you have affected contempt for me—and I—I—no matter—I am not a stone or stick, that I should not feel. You have scorned me—you have outraged me—you have not assumed towards me even the decent hypocrisies of prudence—yet now you would ask of me, the conduct, the sympathy, the forbearance, the concession of friendship. You wish that I should quit these scenes, where, to my judgment, a certain advantage waits me, solely that I may lighten your breast of its selfish fears. You dread the dangers that await me on your own account. And in my apprehension, you forebode your own doom. You ask me, nay, not ask, you would command, you would awe me to sacrifice my will and wishes, in order to soothe your anxieties, and strengthen your own safety. Mark me! Eugene Aram, I have been treated as a tool, and I will not be governed as a friend. I will not stir from the vicinity of your home, till my designs be fulfilled,—I enjoy, I hug myself in your torments. I exult in the terror with which you will hear of each new enterprise, each new daring, each new triumph of myself and my gallant comrades. And now I am avenged for the affront you put upon me."

Though Aram trembled, with suppressed passions, from limb to limb, his voice was still calm, and his lip even wore a smile as he answered,—"I was prepared for this, Houseman, you utter nothing that surprises or appalls me. You hate me; it is natural; men united as we are, rarely look on each other with a friendly or a pitying eye. But Houseman; I know you!—you are a man of vehement passions, but interest with you is yet stronger than passion. If not, our conference is over. Go—and do your worst."

"You are right, most learned scholar; I can fetter the tiger within, in his deadliest rage, by a golden chain."

"Well, then, Houseman, it is not your interest to betray me—my destruction is your own."

"I grant it; but if I am apprehended, and to be hung for robbery?"

"It will be no longer an object to you, to care for my safety. Assuredly, I comprehend this. But my interest induces me to wish that you be removed from the peril of apprehension, and your interest replies, that if you can obtain equal advantages in security, you would forego advantages accompanied by peril. Say what we will, wander as we will, it is to this point that we must return at last."

"Nothing can be clearer; and were you a rich man, Eugene Aram, or could you obtain your bride's dowry (no doubt a respectable sum) in advance, the arrangement might at once be settled."

Aram gasped for breath, and as usual with him in emotion, made several strides forward, muttering rapidly, and indistinctly to himself, and then returned.

"Even were this possible, it would be but a short reprieve; I could not trust you; the sum would be spent, and I again in the state to which you have compelled me now; but without the means again to relieve myself. No, no! if the blow must fall, be it so one day as another."

"As you will," said Houseman; 'but—' Just at that moment, a long shrill whistle sounded below, as from the water. Houseman paused abruptly—"That signal is from my comrades; I must away. Hark, again! Farewell, Aram."

"Farewell, if it must be so," said Aram, in a tone of dogged sullenness; "but to-morrow, should you know of any means by which I could feel secure, beyond the security of your own word, from your future molestation, I might—yet how?"

"To-morrow," said Houseman, "I cannot answer for myself; it is not always that I can leave my comrades; a natural jealousy makes them suspicious of the absence of their friends. Yet hold; the night after to-morrow, the Sabbath night, most virtuous Aram, I can meet you—but not here—some miles hence. You know the foot of the Devil's Crag, by the waterfall; it is a spot quiet and shaded enough in all conscience for our interview; and I will tell you a secret I would trust to no other man—(hark, again!)—it is close by our present lurking-place. Meet me there!—it would, indeed, be pleasanter to hold our conference under shelter—but just at present, I would rather not trust myself beneath any honest man's roof in this neighbourhood. Adieu! on Sunday night, one hour before mid-night."

The robber, for such then he was, waved his hand, and hurried away in the direction from which the signal seemed to come.

Aram gazed after him, but with vacant eyes; and remained for several minutes rooted to the spot, as if the very life had left him.

"The Sabbath night!" said he, at length, moving slowly on; "and I must spin forth my existence in trouble and fear till then—till then! what remedy can I then invent? It is clear that I can have no dependance on his word, if won; and I have not even aught wherewith to buy it. But courage, courage, my heart; and work thou, my busy brain! Ye have never failed me yet!"

CHAPTER III.

```
FRESH ALARM IN THE VILLAGE.—LESTER'S VISIT TO ARAM.—A TRAIT
OF DELICATE KINDNESS IN THE STUDENT.—MADELINE.—HER PRONENESS
   TO CONFIDE.—THE CONVERSATION BETWEEN LESTER AND ARAM.
     —THE PERSONS BY WHOM IT IS INTERRUPTED.


     Not my own fears, nor the prophetic soul
     Of the wide world, dreaming on things to come,
     Can yet the lease of my true love controul.
        —Shakspeare: Sonnets.


     Commend me to their love, and I am proud, say,
     That my occasions have found time to use them
     Toward a supply of money; let the request
     Be fifty talents.
        —Timon Of Athens.
```

The next morning the whole village was alive and bustling with terror and consternation. Another, and a yet more daring robbery, had been committed in the neighbourhood, and the police of the county town had been summoned, and were now busy in search of the offenders. Aram had been early disturbed by the officious anxiety of some of his neighbours; and it wanted yet some hours of noon, when Lester himself came to seek and consult with the Student.

Aram was alone in his large and gloomy chamber, surrounded, as usual, by his books, but not as usual engaged in their contents. With his face leaning on his hand, and his eyes gazing on a dull fire, that crept heavily upward through the damp fuel, he sate by his hearth, listless, but wrapt in thought.

"Well, my friend," said Lester, displacing the books from one of the chairs, and drawing the seat near the Student's—"you have ere this heard the news, and indeed in a county so quiet as ours, these outrages appear the more fearful, from their being so unlooked for. We must set a guard in the village, Aram, and you must leave this defenceless hermitage and come down to us; not for your own sake,—but consider you will be an additional safeguard to Madeline. You will lock up the house, dismiss your poor old governante to her friends in the village, and walk back with me at once to the hall."

Aram turned uneasily in his chair.

"I feel your kindness," said he after a pause, "but I cannot accept it—Madeline," he stopped short at that name, and added in an altered voice; "no, I will be one of the watch, Lester; I will look to her—to your—safety; but I cannot sleep under another roof. I am superstitious, Lester—superstitious. I have made a vow, a foolish one perhaps, but I dare not break it. And my vow binds me, save on indispensable and urgent necessity, not to pass a night any where but in my own home."

"But there is necessity."

"My conscience says not," said Aram smiling: "peace, my good friend, we cannot conquer men's foibles, or wrestle with men's scruples."

Lester in vain attempted to shake Aram's resolution on this head; he found him immoveable, and gave up the effort in despair.

"Well," said he, "at all events we have set up a watch, and can spare you a couple of defenders. They shall reconnoitre in the neighbourhood of your house, if you persevere in your determination, and this will serve in some slight measure to satisfy poor Madeline."

"Be it so," replied Aram; "and dear Madeline herself, is she so alarmed?"

And now in spite of all the more wearing and haggard thoughts that preyed upon his breast, and the dangers by which he conceived himself beset, the Student's face, as he listened with eager attention to every word that Lester uttered concerning his niece, testified how alive he yet was to the least incident that related to Madeline, and how easily her innocent and peaceful remembrance could allure him from himself.

"This room," said Lester, looking round, "will be, I conclude, after Madeline's own heart; but will you always suffer her here? students do not sometimes like even the gentlest interruption."

"I have not forgotten that Madeline's comfort requires some more cheerful retreat than this," said Aram, with a melancholy expression of countenance. "Follow me, Lester; I meant this for a little surprise to her. But Heaven only knows if I shall ever show it to herself?"

"Why? what doubt of that can even your boding temper discover?"

"We are as the wanderers in the desert," answered Aram, "who are taught wisely to distrust their own senses: that which they gaze upon as the waters of existence, is often but a faithless vapour that would lure them to destruction."

In thus speaking he had traversed the room, and, opening a door, showed a small chamber with which it communicated, and which Aram had fitted up with evident, and not ungraceful care. Every article of furniture that Madeline might most fancy, he had sent for from the neighbouring town. And some of the lighter and more attractive books that he possessed, were ranged around on shelves, above which were vases, intended for flowers; the window opened upon a little plot that had been lately broken up into a small garden, and was already intersected with walks, and rich with shrubs.

There was something in this chamber that so entirely contrasted the one it adjoined, something so light, and cheerful, and even gay in its decoration and its tout ensemble, that Lester uttered an exclamation of delight and surprise. And indeed it did appear to him touching, that this austere scholar, so wrapt in thought, and so inattentive to the common forms of life, should have manifested this tender and delicate consideration. In another it would have been nothing, but in Aram, it was a trait, that brought involuntary tears to the eyes of the good Lester. Aram observed them: he walked hastily away to the window, and sighed heavily; this did not escape his friend's notice, and after commenting on the attractions of the little room—Lester said: "You seem oppressed in spirits, Eugene: can any thing have chanced to disturb you, beyond, at least, these alarms which are enough to agitate the nerves of the hardiest of us?"

"No," said Aram; "I had no sleep last night, and my health is easily affected, and with my health my mind; but let us go to Madeline; the sight of her will revive me."

They then strolled down to the Manor-house, and met by the way a band of the younger heroes of the village, who had volunteered to act as a patrole, and who were now marshalled by Peter Dealtry, in a fit of heroic enthusiasm.

Although it was broad daylight, and, consequently, there was little cause of immediate alarm, the worthy publican carried on his shoulder a musket on full cock; and each moment he kept peeping about, as if not only every bush, but every blade of grass contained an ambuscade, ready to spring up the instant he was off his guard. By his side the redoubted Jacobina, who had transferred to her new master, the attachment she had originally possessed for the Corporal, trotted peeringly along, her tail perpendicularly cocked, and her ears moving to and fro, with a most incomparable air of vigilant sagacity. The cautious Peter every now and then checked her ardour, as she was about to quicken her step, and enliven the march by the gambols better adapted to serener times.

"Soho, Jacobina, soho! gently, girl, gently; thou little knowest the dangers that may beset thee. Come up, my good fellows, come to the Spotted Dog; I will tap a barrel on purpose for you; and we will settle the plan of defence for the night. Jacobina, come in, I say, come in,—

```
"'Lest, like a lion, they thee tear,
 And rend in pieces small;
```

```
While there is none to succour thee,
And rid thee out of thrall.'
```
What ho, there! Oh! I beg your honour's pardon! Your servant, Mr. Aram."

"What, patroling already?" said the squire; "your men will be tired before they are wanted; reserve their ardour for the night."

"Oh, your Honour, I have only been beating up for recruits; and we are going to consult a bit at home. Ah! what a pity the Corporal isn't here: he would have been a tower of strength unto the righteous. But howsomever, I do my best to supply his place—Jacobina, child, be still: I can't say as I knows the musket-sarvice, your honour; but I fancy's as how, like Joe Roarjug, the Methodist, we can do it extemporaneous-like at a pinch."

"A bold heart, Peter, is the best preparation," said the squire.

"And," quoth Peter quickly, "what saith the worshipful Mister Sternhold, in the 45th psalm, 5th verse,—
```
'Go forth with godly speed, in meekness, truth, and might,
And thy right hand shall thee instruct in works of dreadful might.'"
```

Peter quoted these verses, especially the last, with a truculent frown, and a brandishing of the musket, that surprisingly encouraged the hearts of his little armament; and with a general murmur of enthusiasm, the warlike band marched off to The Spotted Dog.

Lester and his companion found Madeline and Ellinor standing at the window of the hall; and Madeline's light step was the first that sprang forward to welcome their return: even the face of the Student brightened, when he saw the kindling eye, the parted lip, the buoyant form, from which the pure and innocent gladness she felt on seeing him broke forth.

There was a remarkable trustingness, if I may so speak, in Madeline's disposition. Thoughtful and grave as she was, by nature, she was yet ever inclined to the more sanguine colourings of life; she never turned to the future with fear—a placid sentiment of Hope slept at her heart—she was one who surrendered herself with a fond and implicit faith to the guidance of all she loved; and to the chances of life. It was a sweet indolence of the mind, which made one of her most beautiful traits of character; there is something so unselfish in tempers reluctant to despond. You see that such persons are not occupied with their own existence; they are not fretting the calm of the present life, with the egotisms of care, and conjecture, and calculation: if they learn anxiety, it is for another; but in the heart of that other, how entire is their trust!

It was this disposition in Madeline which perpetually charmed, and yet perpetually wrung, the soul of her wild lover; and as she now delightedly hung upon his arm, uttering her joy at seeing him safe, and presently forgetting that there ever had been cause for alarm, his heart was filled with the most gloomy sense of horror and desolation. "What," thought he, "if this poor, unconscious girl could dream that at this moment I am girded with peril, from which I see no ultimate escape? Delay it as I will, it seems as if the blow must come at last. What, if she could think how fearful is my interest in these outrages, that in all probability, if their authors are detected, there is one who will drag me into their ruin; that I am given over, bound and blinded, into the hands of another; and that other, a man steeled to mercy, and withheld from my destruction by a thread—a thread that a blow on himself would snap. Great God! wherever I turn, I see despair! And she—she clings to me; and beholding me, thinks the whole earth is filled with hope!"

While these thoughts darkened his mind, Madeline drew him onward into the more sequestered walks of the garden, to show him some flowers she had transplanted. And when an hour afterwards he returned to the hall, so soothing had been the influence of her looks and words upon Aram, that if he had not forgotten the situation in which he stood, he had at least calmed himself to regard with a steady eye the chances of escape.

The meal of the day passed as cheerfully as usual, and when Aram and his host were left over their abstemious potations, the former proposed a walk before the evening deepened. Lester readily consented, and they sauntered into the fields. The Squire soon perceived that something was on Aram's mind, of which he felt evident embarrassment in ridding himself: at length the Student said rather abruptly: "My dear friend, I am but a bad beggar, and therefore let me get over my request as expeditiously as possible. You said to me once that you intended bestowing some dowry upon Madeline; a dowry I would and could willingly dispense with; but should you of that sum be now able to spare me some portion as a loan,—should you have some three hundred pounds with which you could accommodate me.—" "Say no more, Eugene, say no more," interrupted the Squire,—"you can have double that amount. Your preparations for your approaching marriage, I ought to have foreseen, must have occasioned you some inconvenience; you can have six hundred pounds from me to-morrow."

Aram's eyes brightened. "It is too much, too much, my generous friend," said he; "the half suffices—but, but, a debt of old standing presses me urgently, and to-morrow, or rather Monday morning, is the time fixed for payment."

"Consider it arranged," said Lester, putting his hand on Aram's arm, and then leaning on it gently, he added, "And now that we are on this subject, let me tell you what I intended as a gift to you, and my dear Madeline; it is but small, but my estates are rigidly entailed on Walter, and of poor value in themselves, and it is half the savings of many years."

The Squire then named a sum, which, however small it may seem to our reader, was not considered a despicable portion for the daughter of a small country squire at that day, and was in reality, a generous sacrifice for one whose whole income was scarcely, at the most, seven hundred a year. The sum mentioned doubled that now to be lent, and which was of course a part of it; an equal portion was reserved for Ellinor.

"And to tell you the truth," said the Squire, "you must give me some little time for the remainder—for not thinking some months ago it would be so soon wanted, I laid out eighteen hundred pounds, in the purchase of Winclose Farm, six of which, (the remainder of your share,) I can pay off at the end of the year; the other twelve, Ellinor's portion, will remain a mortgage on the farm itself. And between us," added the Squire, "I do hope that I need be in no hurry respecting her, dear girl. When Walter returns, I trust matters may be arranged, in a manner, and through a channel, that would gratify the most cherished wish of my heart. I am convinced that Ellinor is exactly suited to him; and, unless he should lose his senses for some one else in the course of his travels, I trust that he will not be long returned before he will make the same discovery. I think of writing to him very shortly after your marriage, and making him promise, at all events, to revisit us at Christmas. Ah! Eugene, we shall be a happy party, then, I trust. And be assured, that we shall beat up your quarters, and put your hospitality, and Madeline's housewifery to the test."

Therewith the good Squire ran on for some minutes in the warmth of his heart, dilating on the fireside prospects before them, and rallying the Student on those secluded habits, which he promised him he should no longer indulge with impunity.

"But it is growing dark," said he, awakening from the theme which had carried him away, "and by this time Peter and our patrole will be at the hall. I told them to look up in the evening, in order to appoint their several duties and stations—let us turn back. Indeed, Aram, I can assure you, that I, for my own part, have some strong reasons to take precautions against any attack; for besides the old family plate, (though that's not much,) I have,—you know the bureau in the parlour to the left of the hall—well, I have in that bureau three hundred guineas, which I have not as yet been able to take to safe hands at—, and which, by the way, will be your's to-morrow. So, you see, it would be no light misfortune to me to be robbed."

"Hist!" said Aram, stopping short, "I think I heard steps on the other side of the hedge."

The Squire listened, but heard nothing; the senses of his companion were, however, remarkably acute, more especially that of hearing.

"There is certainly some one; nay, I catch the steps of two persons," whispered he to Lester. "Let us come round the hedge by the gap below."

They both quickened their pace, and gaining the other side of the hedge, did indeed perceive two men in carters' frocks, strolling on towards the village.

"They are strangers too," said the Squire suspiciously, "not Grassdale men. Humph! could they have overheard us, think you?"

"If men whose business it is to overhear their neighbours—yes; but not if they be honest men," answered Aram, in one of those shrewd remarks which he often uttered, and which seemed almost incompatible with the tenor of the quiet and abstruse pursuits that he had adopted, and that generally deaden the mind to worldly wisdom.

They had now approached the strangers, who, however, appeared mere rustic clowns, and who pulled off their hats with the wonted obeisance of their tribe.

"Hollo, my men," said the Squire, assuming his magisterial air, for the mildest Squire in Christendom can play the Bashaw, when he remembers he is a Justice of the Peace. "Hollo! what are you doing here this time of day? you are not after any good, I fear."

"We ax pardon, your honour," said the elder clown, in the peculiar accent of the country, "but we be come from Gladsmuir; and be going to work at Squire Nixon's at Mow-hall, on Monday; so as I has a brother living on the green afore the Squire's, we be a-going to sleep there to-night and spend the Sunday, your honour."

"Humph! humph! What's your name?"

"Joe Wood, your honour, and this here chap is, Will Hutchings."

"Well, well, go along with you," said the Squire: "And mind what you are about. I should not be surprised if you snare one of Squire Nixon's hares by the way."

"Oh, well and indeed, your honour."—"Go along, go along," said the Squire, and away went the men.

"They seem honest bumpkins enough," observed Lester.

"It would have pleased me better," said Aram, "had the speaker of the two particularized less; and you observed that he seemed eager not to let his companion speak; that is a little suspicious."

"Shall I call them back?" asked the Squire.

"Why it is scarcely worth while," said Aram; "perhaps I over refine. And now I look again at them, they seem really what they affect to be. No, it is useless to molest the poor wretches any more. There is something, Lester, humbling to human pride in a rustic's life. It grates against the heart to think of the tone in which we unconsciously permit ourselves to address him. We see in him humanity in its simple state; it is a sad thought to feel that we despise it; that all we respect in our species is what has been created by art; the gaudy dress, the glittering equipage, or even the cultivated intellect; the mere and naked material of Nature, we eye with indifference or trample on with disdain. Poor child of toil, from the grey dawn to the setting sun, one long task!—no idea elicited—no thought awakened beyond those that suffice to make him the machine of others—the serf of the hard soil! And then too, mark how we scowl upon his scanty holidays, how we hedge in his mirth with laws, and turn his hilarity into crime! We make the whole of the gay world, wherein we walk and take our pleasure, to him a place of snares and perils. If he leave his labour for an instant, in that instant how many temptations spring up to him! And yet we have no mercy for his errors; the gaol—the transport-ship—the gallows; those are our sole lecture-books, and our only methods of expostulation—ah, fie on the disparities of the world! They cripple the heart, they blind the sense, they concentrate the thousand links between man and man, into the two basest of earthly ties—servility, and pride. Methinks the devils laugh out when they hear us tell the boor that his soul is as glorious and eternal as our own; and yet when in the grinding drudgery of his life, not a spark of that soul can be called forth; when it sleeps, walled around in its lumpish clay, from the cradle to the grave, without a dream to stir the deadness of its torpor."

"And yet, Aram," said Lester, "the Lords of science have their ills. Exalt the soul as you will, you cannot raise it above pain. Better, perhaps, to let it sleep, when in waking it looks only upon a world of trial."

"You say well, you say well," said Aram smiting his heart, "and I suffered a foolish sentiment to carry me beyond the sober boundaries of our daily sense."

CHAPTER IV.

MILITARY PREPARATIONS.—THE COMMANDER AND HIS MAN.—ARAM IS
PERSUADED TO PASS THE NIGHT AT THE MANOR-HOUSE.

> Falstaff.—"Bid my Lieutenant Peto meet me at the town's end.
> .. I pressed me none but such toasts and butter, with hearts
> in their bellies no bigger than pins' heads."
> —Henry IV.

They had scarcely reached the Manor-house, before the rain, which the clouds had portended throughout the whole day, began to descend in torrents, and to use the strong expression of the Roman poet—the night rushed down, black and sudden, over the face of the earth.

The new watch were not by any means the hardy and experienced soldiery, by whom rain and darkness are unheeded. They looked with great dismay upon the character of the night in which their campaign was to commence. The valorous Peter, who had sustained his own courage by repeated applications to a little bottle, which he never failed to carry about him in all the more bustling and enterprising occasions of life, endeavoured, but with partial success, to maintain the ardour of his band. Seated in the servants' hall of the Manor-house, in a large arm-chair, Jacobina on his knee, and his trusty musket, which, to the great terror of the womankind, had never been uncocked throughout the day, still grasped in his right hand, while the stock was grounded on the floor; he indulged in martial harangues, plentifully interlarded with plagiarisms from the worshipful translations of Messrs. Sternhold and Hopkins, and psalmodic versions of a more doubtful authorship. And when at the hour of ten, which was the appointed time, he led his warlike force, which consisted of six rustics, armed with sticks of incredible thickness, three guns, one pistol, a broadsword, and a pitchfork, (a weapon likely to be more effectively used than all the rest put together;) when at the hour of ten he led them up to the room above, where they were to be passed in review before the critical eye of the Squire, with Jacobina leading the on-guard, you could not fancy a prettier picture for a hero in a little way, than mine host of the Spotted Dog.

His hat was fastened tight on his brows by a blue pocket-handkerchief; he wore a spencer of a light brown drugget, a world too loose, above a leather jerkin; his breeches of corduroy, were met all of a sudden half way up the thigh, by a detachment of Hessians, formerly in the service of the Corporal, and bought some time since by Peter Dealtry to wear when employed in shooting snipes for the Squire, to whom he occasionally performed the office of game-keeper; suspended round his wrist by a bit of black ribbon, was his constable's baton; he shouldered his musket gallantly, and he carried his person as erect as if the least deflexion from its perpendicularity were to cost him his life. One may judge of the revolution that had taken place in the village, when so peaceable a man as Peter Dealtry was thus metamorphosed into a commander-in-chief. The rest of the regiment hung sheepishly back; each trying to get as near to the door, and as far from the ladies, as possible. But Peter having made up his mind, that a hero should only look straight forward, did not condescend to turn round, to perceive the irregularity of his line. Secure in his own existence, he stood truculently forth, facing the Squire, and prepared to receive his plaudits.

Madeline and Aram sat apart at one corner of the hearth, and Ellinor leaned over the chair of the former; the mirth that she struggled to suppress from being audible, mantling over her arch face and laughing eyes; while the Squire, taking the pipe from his mouth, turned round on his easy chair, and nodded complacently to the little corps, and the great commander.

"We are all ready now, your honour," said Peter, in a voice that did not seem to belong to his body, so big did it sound, "all hot, all eager."

"Why you yourself are a host, Peter," said Ellinor with affected gravity; "your sight alone would frighten an army of robbers: who could have thought you could assume so military an air? The Corporal himself was never so upright!"

"I have practised my present attitude all the day, Miss," said Peter, proudly, "and I believe I may now say as Mr. Sternhold says or sings, in the twenty-sixth Psalm, verse twelfth.

> 'My foot is stayed for all assays,
>   It standeth well and right,
> Wherefore to God—will I give praise
>   In all the people's sight!'

Jacobina, behave yourself, child. I don't think, your honour, that we miss the Corporal so much as I fancied at first, for we all does very well without him."

"Indeed you are a most worthy substitute, Peter; and now, Nell, just reach me my hat and cloak; I will set you at your posts: you will have an ugly night of it."

"Very indeed, your honour," cried all the army, speaking for the first time.

"Silence—order—discipline," said Peter gruffly. "March!"

But instead of marching across the hall, the recruits huddled up one after the other, like a flock of geese, whom Jacobina might be supposed to have set in motion, and each scraping to the ladies, as they shuffled, sneaked, bundled, and bustled out at the door.

"We are well guarded now, Madeline," said Ellinor; "I fancy we may go to sleep as safely as if there were not a housebreaker in the world."

"Why," said Madeline, "let us trust they will be more efficient than they seem, though I cannot persuade myself that we shall really need them. One might almost as well conceive a tiger in our arbour, as a robber in Grassdale. But dear, dear Eugene, do not—do not leave us this night; Walter's room is ready for you, and if it were only to walk across that valley in such weather, it would be cruel to leave us. Let me beseech you; come, you cannot, you dare not refuse me such a favour."

Aram pleaded his vow, but it was overruled; Madeline proved herself a most exquisite casuist in setting it aside. One by one his objections were broken down; and how, as he gazed into those eyes, could he keep any resolution, that Madeline wished him to break! The power she possessed over him seemed exactly in proportion to his impregnability to every one else. The surface on which the diamond cuts its easy way, will yield to no more ignoble instrument; it is easy to shatter it, but by only one substance can it be impressed. And in this instance Aram had but one secret and strong cause to prevent his yielding to Madeline's wishes;—if he remained at the house this night, how could he well avoid a similar compliance the next? And on the next was his interview with Houseman. This reason was not, however, strong enough to enable him to resist Madeline's soft entreaties; he trusted to the time to furnish him with excuses, and when Lester returned, Madeline with a triumphant air informed him that Aram had consented to be their guest for the night."

"Your influence is indeed greater than mine," said Lester, wringing his hat as the delicate fingers of Ellinor loosened his cloak; "yet one can scarcely think our friend sacrifices much in concession, after proving the weather without. I should pity our poor patrole most exceedingly, if I were not thoroughly assured that within two hours every one of them will have quietly slunk home; and even Peter himself, when he has exhausted his bottle, will be the first to set the example. However, I have stationed two of the men near our house, and the rest at equal distances along the village."

"Do you really think they will go home, Sir?" said Ellinor, in a little alarm; "why they would be worse than I thought them, if they were driven to bed by the rain. I knew they could not stand a pistol, but a shower, however hard, I did imagine would scarcely quench their valour."

"Never mind, girl," said Lester, gaily chucking her under the chin, "we are quite strong enough now to resist them. You see Madeline has grown as brave as a lioness—Come, girls, come, let's have supper, and stir up the fire. And, Nell, where are my slippers?"

And thus on the little family scene, the cheerful wood fire flickering against the polished wainscot; the supper table arranged, the Squire drawing his oak chair towards it, Ellinor mixing his negus; and Aram and Madeline, though three times summoned to the table, and having three times answered to the summons, still lingering apart by the hearth—let us drop the curtain.

We have only, ere we close our chapter, to observe, that when Lester conducted Aram to his chamber he placed in his hands an order payable at the county town, for three hundred pounds. "The rest," he said in a whisper, "is below, where I mentioned; and there in my secret drawer it had better rest till the morning."

The good Squire then, putting his finger to his lip, hurried away, to avoid the thanks, which, indeed, however he might feel them, Aram was no dexterous adept in expressing.

CHAPTER V.

```
         THE SISTERS ALONE.—THE GOSSIP OF LOVE.—AN ALARM
             —AND AN EVENT.


         Juliet.—My true love is grown to such excess,
         I cannot sum up half my sum of wealth.
              —Romeo and Juliet.


         Eros.—Oh, a man in arms;
         His weapon drawn, too!
              —The False One.
```

It was a custom with the two sisters, when they repaired to their chamber for the night, to sit conversing, sometimes even for hours, before they finally retired to bed. This indeed was the usual time for their little confidences, and their mutual dilations over those hopes and plans for the future, which always occupy the larger share of the thoughts and conversation of the young. I do not know any thing in the world more lovely than such conferences between two beings who have no secrets to relate but what arise, all fresh, from the springs of a guiltless heart,—those pure and beautiful mysteries of an unsullied nature which warm us to hear; and we think with a sort of wonder when we feel how arid experience has made ourselves, that so much of the dew and sparkle of existence still linger in the nooks and valleys, which are as yet virgin of the sun and of mankind.

The sisters this night were more than commonly indifferent to sleep. Madeline sate by the small but bright hearth of the chamber, in her night dress, and Ellinor, who was much prouder of her sister's beauty than her own, was employed in knotting up the long and lustrous hair which fell in rich luxuriance over Madeline's throat and shoulders.

"There certainly never was such beautiful hair!" said Ellinor admiringly; "and, let me see,—yes,—on Thursday fortnight I may be dressing it, perhaps, for the last time—heigho!"

"Don't flatter yourself that you are so near the end of your troublesome duties," said Madeline, with her pretty smile, which had been much brighter and more frequent of late than it was formerly wont to be, so that Lester had remarked "That Madeline really appeared to have become the lighter and gayer of the two."

"You will often come to stay with us for weeks together, at least till—till you have a double right to be mistress here. Ah! my poor hair,—you need not pull it so hard."

"Be quiet, then," said Ellinor, half laughing, and wholly blushing.

"Trust me, I have not been in love myself without learning its signs; and I venture to prophesy that within six months you will come to consult me whether or not,—for there is a great deal to be said on both sides of the question,—you can make up your mind to sacrifice your own wishes, and marry Walter Lester. Ah!—gently, gently. Nell—" "Promise to be quiet."

"I will—I will; but you began it."

As Ellinor now finished her task, and kissed her sister's forehead, she sighed deeply.

"Happy Walter!" said Madeline.

"I was not sighing for Walter, but for you."

"For me?—impossible! I cannot imagine any part of my future life that can cost you a sigh. Ah! that I were more worthy of my happiness."

"Well, then," said Ellinor, "I sighed for myself;—I sighed to think we should so soon be parted, and that the continuance of your society would then depend not on our mutual love, but the will of another."

"What, Ellinor, and can you suppose that Eugene,—my Eugene,—would not welcome you as warmly as myself? Ah! you misjudge him; I know you have not yet perceived how tender a heart lies beneath all that melancholy and reserve."

"I feel, indeed," said Ellinor warmly, "as if it were impossible that one whom you love should not be all that is good and noble; yet if this reserve of his should increase, as is at least possible, with increasing years; if our society should become again, as it once was, distasteful to him, should I not lose you, Madeline?"

"But his reserve cannot increase: do you not perceive how much it is softened already? Ah! be assured that I will charm it away."

"But what is the cause of the melancholy that even now, at times, evidently preys upon him?—has he never revealed it to you?"

"It is merely the early and long habit of solitude and study, Ellinor," replied Madeline; "and shall I own to you I would scarcely wish that away; his tenderness itself seems linked with his melancholy. It is like a sad but gentle music, that brings tears into our eyes, but which we would not change for gayer airs for the world."

"Well, I must own," said Ellinor, reluctantly, "that I no longer wonder at your infatuation; I can no longer chide you as I once did; there is, assuredly, something in his voice, his look, which irresistibly sinks into the heart. And there are moments when, what with his eyes and forehead, his countenance seems more beautiful, more impressive, than any I ever beheld. Perhaps, too, for you, it is better, that your lover should be no longer in the first flush of youth. Your nature seems to require something to venerate, as well as to love. And I have ever observed at prayers, that you seem more especially rapt and carried beyond yourself, in those passages which call peculiarly for worship and adoration."

"Yes, dearest," said Madeline fervently, "I own that Eugene is of all beings, not only of all whom I ever knew, but of whom I ever dreamed, or imagined, the one that I am most fitted to love and to appreciate. His wisdom, but more than that, the lofty tenor of his mind, calls forth all that is highest and best in my own nature. I feel exalted when I listen to him;—and yet, how gentle, with all that nobleness! And to think that he should descend to love me, and so to love me. It is as if a star were to leave its sphere!"

"Hark! one o'clock," said Ellinor, as the deep voice of the clock told the first hour of morning. "Heavens! how much louder the winds rave. And how the heavy sleet drives against the window! Our poor watch without! but you may be sure my uncle was right, and they are safe at home by this time; nor is it likely, I should think, that even robbers would be abroad in such weather!"

"I have heard," said Madeline, "that robbers generally choose these dark, stormy nights for their designs, but I confess I don't feel much alarm, and he is in the house. Draw nearer to the fire, Ellinor; is it not pleasant to see how serenely it burns, while the storm howls without! it is like my Eugene's soul, luminous, and lone, amidst the roar and darkness of this unquiet world!"

"There spoke himself," said Ellinor smiling to perceive how invariably women, who love, imitate the tone of the beloved one. And Madeline felt it, and smiled too.

"Hist!" said Ellinor abruptly, "did you not hear a low, grating noise below? Ah! the winds now prevent your catching the sound; but hush, hush!—now the wind pauses,—there it is again!"

"Yes, I hear it," said Madeline, turning pale, "it seems in the little parlour; a continued, harsh, but very low, noise. Good heavens! it seems at the window below."

"It is like a file," whispered Ellinor: "perhaps—" "You are right," said Madeline, suddenly rising, "it is a file, and at the bars my father had fixed against the window yesterday. Let us go down, and alarm the house."

"No, no; for God's sake, don't be so rash," cried Ellinor, losing all presence of mind: "hark! the sound ceases, there is a louder noise below,—and steps. Let us lock the door."

But Madeline was of that fine and high order of spirit which rises in proportion to danger, and calming her sister as well as she could, till she found her attempts wholly ineffectual, she seized the light with a steady hand, opened the door, and Ellinor still clinging to her, passed the landing-place, and hastened to her father's room; he slept at the opposite corner of the staircase. Aram's chamber was at the extreme end of the house. Before she reached the door of Lester's apartment, the noise below grew loud and distinct—a scuffle—voices—curses—and now—the sound of a pistol!—in a moment more the whole house was stirring. Lester in his night robe, his broadsword in his hand, and his long grey hair floating behind, was the first to appear; the servants, old and young, male and female, now came thronging simultaneously round; and in a general body, Lester several paces at their head, his daughters following next to him, they rushed to the apartment whence the noise, now suddenly stilled, had proceeded.

The window was opened, evidently by force; an instrument like a wedge was fixed in the bureau containing Lester's money, and seemed to have been left there, as if the person using it had been disturbed before the design for which it was introduced had been accomplished, and, (the only evidence of life,) Aram stood, dressed, in the centre of the room, a pistol in his left hand, a sword in his right; a bludgeon severed in two lay at his feet, and on the floor within two yards of him, towards the window, drops of blood yet warm, showed that the pistol had not been discharged in vain.

"And is it you, my brave friend, that I have to thank for our safety?" cried Lester in great emotion.

"You, Eugene!" repeated Madeline, sinking on his breast.

"But thanks hereafter," continued Lester; "let us now to the pursuit,—perhaps the villain may have perished beneath your bullet?"

"Ha!" muttered Aram, who had hitherto seemed unconscious of all around him; so fixed had been his eye, so colourless his cheek, so motionless his posture. "Ha! say you so?—think you I have slain him?—no, it cannot be—the ball did not slay, I saw him stagger; but he rallied—not so one who receives a mortal wound!—ha! ha!—there is blood, you say, that is true; but what then!—it is not the first wound that kills, you must strike again—pooh, pooh, what is a little blood!"

While he was thus muttering, Lester and the more active of the servants had already sallied through the window, but the night was so intensely dark that they could not penetrate a step beyond them. Lester returned, therefore, in a few moments; and met Aram's dark eye fixed upon him with an unutterable expression of anxiety.

"You have found no one," said he, "no dying man?—Ha!—well—well—well! they must both have escaped; the night must favour them."

"Do you fancy the villain was severely wounded?"

"Not so—I trust not so; he seemed able to—But stop—oh God!—stop!—your foot is dabbling in blood—blood shed by me,—off! off!"

Lester moved aside with a quick abhorrence, as he saw that his feet were indeed smearing the blood over the polished and slippery surface of the oak boards, and in moving he stumbled against a dark lantern in which the light still burnt, and which the robbers in their flight had left.

"Yes," said Aram observing it. "It was by that—their own light that I saw them—saw their faces—and—and—(bursting into a loud, wild laugh) they were both strangers!"

"Ah, I thought so, I knew so," said Lester plucking the instrument from the bureau. "I knew they could be no Grassdale men. What, did you fancy, they could be? But—bless me, Madeline—what ho! help!—Aram, she has fainted at your feet."

And it was indeed true and remarkable, that so utter had been the absorption of Aram's mind, that he had been insensible not only to the entrance of Madeline, but even that she had thrown herself on his breast. And she, overcome by her feelings, had slid to the ground from that momentary resting-place, in a swoon which Lester, in the general tumult and confusion, was now the first to perceive.

At this exclamation, at the sound of Madeline's name, the blood rushed back from Aram's heart, where it had gathered, icy and curdling; and, awakened thoroughly and at once to himself, he knelt down, and weaving his arms around her, supported her head on his breast, and called upon her with the most passionate and moving exclamations.

But when the faint bloom retinged her cheek, and her lips stirred, he printed a long kiss on that cheek—on those lips, and surrendered his post to Ellinor; who, blushingly gathering the robe over the beautiful breast from which it had been slightly drawn; now entreated all, save the women of the house, to withdraw till her sister was restored.

Lester, eager to hear what his guest could relate, therefore took Aram to his own apartment, where the particulars were briefly told.

Suspecting, which indeed was the chief reason that excused him to himself in yielding to Madeline's request, that the men Lester and himself had encountered in their evening walk, might be other than they seemed, and that they might have well overheard Lester's communication, as to the sum in his house, and the place where it was stored; he had not undressed himself, but kept the door of his room open to listen if any thing stirred. The keen sense of hearing, which we have before remarked him to possess, enabled him to catch the sound of the file at the bars, even before Ellinor, notwithstanding the distance of his own chamber from the place, and seizing the sword which had been left in his room, (the pistol was his own) he had descended to the room below.

"What!" said Lester, "and without a light?"

"The darkness is familiar to me," said Aram. "I could walk by the edge of a precipice in the darkest night without one false step, if I had but once passed it before. I did not gain the room, however, till the window had been forced; and by the light of a dark lantern which one of them held, I perceived two men standing by the bureau—the rest you can imagine; my victory was easy, for the bludgeon, with which one of them aimed at me, gave way at once to the edge of your good sword, and my pistol delivered me of the other.—There ends the history."

Lester overwhelmed him with thanks and praises, but Aram, glad to escape them, hurried away to see after Madeline, whom he now met on the landing-place, leaning on Ellinor's arm and still pale.

She gave him her hand, which he for one moment pressed passionately to his lips, but dropped, the next, with an altered and chilled air. And hastily observing he would not now detain her from a rest which she must so much require, he turned away and descended the stairs. Some of the servants were grouped around the place of encounter; he entered the room, and again started at the sight of the blood.

"Bring water," said he fiercely: "will you let the stagnant gore ooze and rot into the boards, to startle the eye, and still the heart with its filthy, and unutterable stain—water, I say! water!"

They hurried to obey him, and Lester coming into the room to see the window reclosed by the help of boards found the Student bending over the servants as they performed their reluctant task, and rating them with a raised and harsh voice for the hastiness with which he accused them of seeking to slur it over.

CHAPTER VI.

ARAM ALONE AMONG THE MOUNTAINS.—HIS SOLILOQUY AND PROJECT.—
SCENE BETWEEN HIMSELF AND MADELINE.

>   Luce non grata fruor;
> Trepidante semper corde, non mortis metu
> Sed—
>   —Seneca: Octavia, act i.

The two men servants of the house remained up the rest of the night; but it was not till the morning had progressed far beyond the usual time of rising in the fresh shades of Grassdale, that Madeline and Ellinor became visible; even Lester left his bed an hour later than his wont; and knocking at Aram's door, found the Student was already abroad, while it was evident that his bed had not been pressed during the whole of the night. Lester descended into the garden, and was there met by Peter Dealtry, and a detachment of the band; who, as common sense and Lester had predicted, were indeed, at a very early period of the watch, driven to their respective homes. They were now seriously concerned for their unmanliness, which they passed off as well as they could upon their conviction "that nobody at Grassdale could ever really be robbed;" and promised with sincere contrition, that they would be most excellent guards for the future. Peter was, in sooth, singularly chop-fallen; and could only defend himself by an incoherent mutter, from which the Squire turned somewhat impatiently, when he heard, louder than the rest, the words "seventy-seventh psalm, seventeenth verse,

"The clouds that were both thick and black,

> Did rain full plenteously."

Leaving the Squire to the edification of the pious host, let us follow the steps of Aram, who at the early dawn had quitted his sleepless chamber, and, though the clouds at that time still poured down in a dull and heavy sleet, wandered away, whither he neither knew, nor heeded. He was now hurrying, with unabated speed, though with no purposed bourne or object, over the chain of mountains that backed the green and lovely valleys, among which his home was cast.

"Yes!" said he, at last halting abruptly, with a desperate resolution stamped on his countenance, "yes! I will so determine. If, after this interview, I feel that I cannot command and bind Houseman's perpetual secrecy, I will surrender Madeline at once. She has loved me generously and trustingly. I will not link her life with one that may be called hence in any hour, and to so dread an account. Neither shall the grey hairs of Lester be brought with the sorrow of my shame, to a dishonoured and untimely grave. And after the outrage of last night, the daring outrage, how can I calculate on the safety of a day? though Houseman was not present, though I can scarce believe that he knew or at least abetted the attack; yet they were assuredly of his gang: had one been seized, the clue might have traced to his detection—and he detected, what should I have to dread! No, Madeline! no; not while this sword hangs over me, will I subject thee to share the horror of my fate!"

This resolution, which was certainly generous, and yet no more than honest, Aram had no sooner arrived at, than he dismissed, at once, by one of those efforts which powerful minds can command, all the weak and vacillating thoughts that might interfere with the sternness of his determination. He seemed to breathe more freely, and the haggard wanness of his brow, relaxed at least from the workings that, but the moment before, distorted its wonted serenity, with a maniac wildness.

He pursued his desultory way now with a calmer step.

"What a night!" said he, again breaking into the low murmur in which he was accustomed to hold commune with himself. "Had Houseman been one of the ruffians! a shot might have freed me, and without a crime, for ever! And till the light flashed on their brows, I thought the smaller man bore his aspect. Ha, out, tempting thought! out on thee!" he cried aloud, and stamping with his foot, then recalled by his own vehemence, he cast a jealous and hurried glance round him, though at that moment his step was on the very height of the mountains, where not even the solitary shepherd, save in search of some more daring straggler of the flock, ever brushed the dew from the cragged, yet fragrant soil. "Yet," he said, in a lower voice, and again sinking into the sombre depths of his reverie, "it is a tempting, a wondrously tempting thought. And it struck athwart me, like a flash of lightning when this hand was at his throat—a tighter strain, another moment, and Eugene Aram had not had an enemy, a witness against him left in the world. Ha! are the dead no foes then? Are the dead no witnesses?" Here he relapsed into utter silence, but his gestures continued wild, and his eyes wandered round, with a bloodshot and unquiet glare. "Enough," at length he said calmly; and with the manner of one 'who has rolled a stone from his heart;' [Note: Eastern saying.] "enough! I will not so sully myself; unless all other hope of self-preservation be extinct. And why despond? the plan I have thought of seems well-laid, wise, consummate at all points. Let me consider—forfeited the moment he enters England—not given till he has left it—paid periodically, and of such extent as to supply his wants, preserve him from crime, and forbid the possibility of extorting more: all this sounds well; and if not feasible at last, why farewell Madeline, and I myself leave this land for ever. Come what will to me—death in its vilest shape—let not the stroke fall on that breast. And if it be," he continued, his face lighting up, "if it be, as it may yet, that I can chain this hell-hound, why, even then, the instant that Madeline is mine, I will fly these scenes; I will seek a yet obscurer and remoter corner of earth: I will choose another name—Fool! why did I not so before? But matters it? What is writ is writ. Who can struggle with the invisible and giant hand, that launched the world itself into motion; and at whose predecree we hold the dark boon of life and death?"

It was not till evening that Aram, utterly worn out and exhausted, found himself in the neighbourhood of Lester's house. The sun had only broken forth at its setting; and it now glittered from its western pyre over the dripping hedges, and spread a brief, but magic glow along the rich landscape around; the changing woods clad in the thousand dies of Autumn; the scattered and peaceful cottages, with their long wreaths of smoke curling upward, and the grey and venerable walls of the Manor-house, with the Church hard by, and the delicate spire, which, mixing itself with heaven, is at once the most touching and solemn emblem of the Faith to which it is devoted. It was a sabbath eve; and from the spot on which Aram stood, he might discern many a rustic train trooping slowly up the green village lane towards the Church; and the deep bell which summoned to the last service of the day now swung its voice far over the sunlit and tranquil scene.

But it was not the setting sun, nor the autumnal landscape, nor the voice of the holy bell that now arrested the step of Aram. At a little distance before him, leaning over a gate, and seemingly waiting till the ceasing of the bell should announce the time to enter the sacred mansion, he beheld the figure of Madeline Lester. Her head, at the moment, was averted from him, as if she were looking after Ellinor and her uncle, who were in the churchyard among a little group of their homely neighbours; and he was half in doubt whether to shun her presence, when she suddenly turned round, and seeing him, uttered an exclamation of joy. It was now too late for avoidance; and calling to his aid that mastery over his features, which, in ordinary times, few more eminently possessed, he approached his beautiful mistress with a smile as serene, if not as glowing, as her own. But she had already opened the gate, and bounding forward, met him half way.

"Ah, truant, truant," said she, the whole day absent, without inquiry or farewell! After this, when shall I believe that thou really lovest me?

"But," continued Madeline, gazing on his countenance, which bore witness, in its present languor, to the fierce emotions which had lately raged within, "but, heavens! dearest, how pale you look; you are fatigued; give me your hand, Eugene,—it is parched and dry. Come into the house;—you must need rest and refreshment."

"I am better here, my Madeline,—the air and the sun revive me: let us rest by the stile yonder. But you were going to Church? and the bell has ceased."

"I could attend, I fear, little to the prayers now," said Madeline, "unless you feel well enough and will come to Church with me."

"To Church!" said Aram, with a half shudder, "no; my thoughts are in no mood for prayer."

"Then you shall give your thoughts to me and I, in return, will pray for you before I rest."

And so saying, Madeline, with her usual innocent frankness of manner, wound her arm in his, and they walked onward towards the stile Aram had pointed out. It was a little rustic stile, with chesnut-trees hanging over it on either side. It stands to this day, and I have pleased myself with finding Walter Lester's initials, and Madeline's also, with the date of the year, carved in half-worn letters on the wood, probably by the hand of the former.

They now rested at this spot. All around them was still and solitary; the groups of peasants had entered the Church, and nothing of life, save the cattle grazing in the distant fields, or the thrush starting from the wet bushes, was visible. The winds were lulled to rest, and, though somewhat of the chill of autumn floated on the air, it only bore a balm to the harassed brow and fevered veins of the Student; and Madeline!—she felt nothing but his presence. It was exactly what we picture to ourselves of a sabbath eve, unutterably serene and soft, and borrowing from the very melancholy of the declining year an impressive, yet a mild solemnity.

There are seasons, often in the most dark or turbulent periods of our life, when, why we know not, we are suddenly called from ourselves, by the remembrances of early childhood: something touches the electric chain, and, lo! a host of shadowy and sweet recollections steal upon us. The wheel rests, the oar is suspended, we are snatched from the labour and travail of present life; we are born again, and live anew. As the secret page in which the characters once written seem for ever effaced, but which, if breathed upon, gives them again into view; so the memory can revive the images invisible for years: but while we gaze, the breath recedes from the surface, and all one moment so vivid, with the next moment has become once more a blank!

"It is singular," said Aram, "but often as I have paused at this spot, and gazed upon this landscape, a likeness to the scenes of my childish life, which it now seems to me to present, never occurred to me before. Yes, yonder, in that cottage, with the sycamores in front, and the orchard extending behind, till its boundary, as we now stand, seems lost among the woodland, I could fancy that I looked upon my father's home. The clump of trees that lies yonder to the right could cheat me readily to the belief that I saw the little grove in which, enamoured with the first passion of study, I was wont to pore over the thrice-read book through the long summer days;—a boy,—a thoughtful boy; yet, oh! how happy! What worlds appeared then to me, to open in every page! how exhaustless I thought the treasures and the hopes of life! and beautiful on the mountain tops seemed to me the steps of Knowledge! I did not dream of all that the musing and lonely passion that I nursed was to entail upon me. There, in the clefts of the valley, or the ridges of the hill, or the fragrant course of the stream, I began already to win its history from the herb or flower; I saw nothing, that I did not long to unravel its secrets; all that the earth nourished ministered to one desire:—and what of low or sordid did there mingle with that desire? The petty avarice, the mean ambition, the debasing love, even the heat, the anger, the fickleness, the caprice of other men, did they allure or bow down my nature from its steep and solitary eyrie? I lived but to feed my mind; wisdom was my thirst, my dream, my aliment, my sole fount and sustenance of life. And have I not sown the whirlwind and reaped the wind? The glory of my youth is gone, my veins are chilled, my frame is bowed, my heart is gnawed with cares, my nerves are unstrung as a loosened bow: and what, after all, is my gain? Oh, God! what is my gain?"

"Eugene, dear, dear Eugene!" murmured Madeline soothingly, and wrestling with her tears, "is not your gain great? is it no triumph that you stand, while yet young, almost alone in the world, for success in all that you have attempted?"

"And what," exclaimed Aram, breaking in upon her, "what is this world which we ransack, but a stupendous charnel-house? Every thing that we deem most lovely, ask its origin?—Decay! When we rifle nature, and collect wisdom, are we not like the hags of old, culling simples from the rank grave, and extracting sorceries from the rotting bones of the dead? Every thing around us is fathered by corruption, battened by corruption, and into corruption returns at last. Corruption is at once the womb and grave of Nature, and the very beauty on which we gaze and hang,—the cloud, and the tree, and the swarming waters,—all are one vast panorama of death! But it did not always seem to me thus; and even now I speak with a heated pulse and a dizzy brain. Come, Madeline, let us change the theme."

And dismissing at once from his language, and perhaps, as he proceeded, also from his mind, all of its former gloom, except such as might shade, but not embitter, the natural tenderness of remembrance, Aram now related, with that vividness of diction, which, though we feel we can very inadequately convey its effect, characterised his conversation, and gave something of poetic interest to all he uttered; those reminiscences which belong to childhood, and which all of us take delight to hear from the lips of any one we love.

It was while on this theme that the lights which the deepening twilight had now made necessary, became visible in the Church, streaming afar through its large oriel window, and brightening the dark firs that overshadowed the graves around: and just at that moment the organ, (a gift from a rich rector, and the boast of the neighbouring country,) stole upon the silence with its swelling and solemn note. There was something in the strain of this sudden music that was so kindred with the holy repose of the scene, and which chimed so exactly to the chord that now vibrated in Aram's mind, that it struck upon him at once with an irresistible power. He paused abruptly "as if an angel spoke!" that sound so peculiarly adapted to express sacred and unearthly emotion none who have ever mourned or sinned can hear, at an unlooked for moment, without a certain sentiment, that either subdues, or elevates, or awes. But he,—he was a boy once more!—he was again in the village church of his native place: his father, with his silver hair, stood again beside him! there was his mother, pointing to him the holy verse; there the half arch, half reverent face of his little sister, (she died young!)—there the upward eye and hushed countenance of the preacher who had first raised his mind to knowledge, and supplied its food,—all, all lived, moved, breathed, again before him,—all, as when he was young and guiltless, and at peace; hope and the future one word!

He bowed his head lower and lower; the hardness and hypocrisies of pride, the sense of danger and of horror, that, in agitating, still supported, the mind of this resolute and scheming man, at once forsook him. Madeline felt his tears drop fast and burning on her hand, and the next moment, overcome by the relief it afforded to a heart preyed upon by fiery and dread secrets, which it could not reveal, and a frame exhausted by the long and extreme tension of all its powers, he laid his head upon that faithful bosom, and wept aloud.

CHAPTER VII.

ARAM'S SECRET EXPEDITION.—A SCENE WORTHY THE ACTORS.—ARAM'S ADDRESS AND POWERS OF PERSUASION OR HYPOCRISY.—THEIR RESULT. —A FEARFUL NIGHT.—ARAM'S SOLITARY RIDE HOMEWARD. —WHOM HE MEETS BY THE WAY, AND WHAT HE SEES.

>   Macbeth. Now o'er the one half world
>   Nature seems dead.
>
>   Donalbain. Our separated fortune
>   Shall keep us both the safer.
>
>   Old Man. Hours dreadful and things strange.
>   —Macbeth.

"And you must really go to ——— to pay your importunate creditor this very evening. Sunday is a bad day for such matters; but as you pay him by an order, it does not much signify; and I can well understand your impatience to feel discharged of the debt. But it is already late; and if it must be so, you had better start."

"True," said Aram to the above remark of Lester's, as the two stood together without the door; "but do you feel quite secure and guarded against any renewed attack?"

"Why, unless they bring a regiment, yes! I have put a body of our patrole on a service where they can scarce be inefficient, viz. I have stationed them in the house, instead of without; and I shall myself bear them company through the greater part of the night: to-morrow I shall remove all that I possess of value to—(the county town) including those unlucky guineas, which you will not ease me of."

"The order you have kindly given me will amply satisfy my purpose," answered Aram: "And so, there has been no clue to these robberies discovered throughout the day?"

"None: to-morrow, the magistrates are to meet at—, and concert measures: it is absolutely impossible, but that we should detect the villains in a few days, viz. if they remain in these parts. I hope to heaven you will not meet them this evening."

"I shall go well armed," answered Aram, "and the horse you lend me is fleet and strong. And now farewell for the present; I shall probably not return to Grassdale this night, or if I do, it will be at so late an hour, that I shall seek my own domicile without disturbing you."

"No, no; you had better remain in the town, and not return till morning," said the Squire; "and now let us come to the stables."

To obviate all chance of suspicion as to the real place of his destination, Aram deliberately rode to the town he had mentioned, as the one in which his pretended creditor expected him. He put up at an inn, walked forth as if to visit some one in the town, returned, remounted, and by a circuitous route, came into the neighbourhood of the place in which he was to meet Houseman: then turning into a long and dense chain of wood, he fastened his horse to a tree, and looking to the priming of his pistols, which he carried under his riding-cloak, proceeded to the spot on foot.

The night was still, and not wholly dark; for the clouds lay scattered though dense, and suffered many stars to gleam through the heavy air; the moon herself was abroad, but on her decline, and looked forth with a man and saddened aspect, as she travelled from cloud to cloud. It has been the necessary course of our narrative, to pourtray Aram, more often than to give an exact notion of his character we could have altogether wished, in his weaker moments; but whenever he stood in the actual presence of danger, his whole soul was in arms to cope with it worthily: courage, sagacity, even cunning, all awakened to the encounter; and the mind which his life had so austerely cultivated repaid him in the urgent season, with its acute address, and unswerving hardihood. The Devil's Crag, as it was popularly called, was a spot consecrated by many a wild tradition, which would not, perhaps, be wholly out of character with the dark thread of this tale, were we in accordance with certain of our brethren, who seem to think a novel like a bundle of wood, the more faggots it contains the greater its value, allowed by the rapidity of our narrative to relate them.

The same stream which lent so soft an attraction to the valleys of Grassdale, here assumed a different character; broad, black, and rushing, it whirled along a course, overhung by shagged and abrupt banks. On the opposite side to that by which Aram now pursued his path, an almost perpendicular mountain was covered with gigantic pine and fir, that might have reminded a German wanderer of the darkest recesses of the Hartz; and seemed, indeed, no unworthy haunt for the weird huntsman, or the forest fiend. Over this wood the moon now shimmered, with the pale and feeble light we have already described; and only threw into a more sombre shade the motionless and gloomy foliage. Of all the offspring of the forest, the Fir bears, perhaps, the most saddening and desolate aspect. Its long branches, without absolute leaf or blossom; its dead, dark, eternal hue, which the winter seems to wither not, nor the spring to revive, have, I know not what of a mystic and unnatural life. Around all woodland, there is that horror umbrarum which becomes more remarkably solemn and awing amidst the silence and depth of night: but this is yet more especially the characteristic of that sullen evergreen. Perhaps, too, this effect is increased by the sterile and dreary soil, on which, when in groves, it is generally found; and its very hardiness, the very pertinacity with which it draws its strange unfluctuating life, from the sternest wastes and most reluctant strata, enhance, unconsciously, the unwelcome effect it is calculated to create upon the mind. At this place, too, the waters that dashed beneath gave yet additional wildness to the rank verdure of the wood, and contributed, by their rushing darkness partially broken by the stars, and the hoarse roar of their chafed course, a yet more grim and savage sublimity to the scene.

Winding a narrow path, (for the whole country was as familiar as a garden to his footstep) that led through the tall wet herbage, almost along the perilous brink of the stream, Aram was now aware, by the increased and deafening sound of the waters, that the appointed spot was nearly gained; and presently the glimmering and imperfect light of the skies, revealed the dim shape of a gigantic rock, that rose abruptly from the middle of the stream; and which, rude, barren, vast, as it really was, seemed now, by the uncertainty of night, like some monstrous and deformed creature of the waters, suddenly emerging from their vexed and dreary depths. This was the far-famed Crag, which had borrowed from tradition its evil and ominous name. And now, the stream, bending round with a broad and sudden swoop, showed at a little distance, ghostly and indistinct through the darkness, the mighty Waterfall, whose roar had been his guide. Only in one streak a-down the giant cataract, the stars were reflected; and this long train of broken light glittered preternaturally forth through the rugged crags and the sombre verdure, that wrapped either side of the waterfall in utter and rayless gloom.

Nothing could exceed the forlorn and terrific grandeur of the spot; the roar of the waters supplied to the ear what the night forbade to the eye. Incessant and eternal they thundered down into the gulf; and then shooting over that fearful basin, and forming another, but a mimic fall, dashed on, till they were opposed by the sullen and abrupt crag below; and besieging its base with a renewed roar, sent their foamy and angry spray half way up the hoar ascent.

At this stern and dreary spot, well suited for such conferences as Aram and Houseman alone could hold; and which, whatever was the original secret that linked the two men thus strangely, seemed of necessity to partake of a desperate and lawless character, with danger for its main topic, and death itself for its colouring, Aram now paused, and with an eye accustomed to the darkness, looked around for his companion.

He did not wait long: from the profound shadow that girded the space immediately around the fall, Houseman now emerged and joined the Student. The stunning noise of the cataract in the place where they met, forbade any attempt to converse; and they walked on by the course of the stream, to gain a spot less in reach of the deafening shout of the mountain giant as he rushed with his banded waters, upon the valley like a foe.

It was noticeable that as they proceeded, Aram walked on with an unsuspicious and careless demeanour; but Houseman pointing out the way with his hand, not leading it, kept a little behind Aram, and watched his motions with a vigilant and wary eye. The Student, who had diverged from the path at Houseman's direction, now paused at a place where the matted bushes seemed to forbid any farther progress; and said, for the first time breaking the silence, "We cannot proceed; shall this be the place of our conference?"

"No," said Houseman, "we had better pierce the bushes. I know the way, but will not lead it."

"And wherefore?"

"The mark of your gripe is still on my throat," replied Houseman, significantly; "you know as well as I, that it is not always safe to have a friend lagging behind."

"Let us rest here, then," said Aram, calmly, the darkness veiling any alteration of his countenance, which his comrade's suspicion might have created.

"Yet it were much better," said Houseman, doubtingly, "could we gain the cave below."

"The cave!" said Aram, starting, as if the word had a sound of fear.

"Ay, ay: but not St. Robert's," said Houseman; and the grin of his teeth was visible through the dullness of the shade. "But come, give me your hand, and I will venture to conduct you through the thicket:—that is your left hand," observed Houseman with a sharp and angry suspicion in his tone; "give me the right."

"As you will," said Aram in a subdued, yet meaning voice, that seemed to come from his heart; and thrilled, for an instant, to the bones of him who heard it; "as you will; but for fourteen years I have not given this right hand, in pledge of fellowship, to living man; you alone deserve the courtesy—there!"

Houseman hesitated, before he took the hand now extended to him.

"Pshaw!" said he, as if indignant at himself, "what! scruples at a shadow! Come," (grasping the hand) "that's well—so, so; now we are in the thicket—tread firm—this way—hold," continued Houseman, under his breath, as suspicion anew seemed to cross him; "hold! we can see each other's face not even dimly now: but in this hand, my right is free, I have a knife that has done good service ere this; and if I feel cause to suspect that you meditate to play me false, I bury it in your heart; do you heed me?"

"Fool!" said Aram, scornfully, "I should dread you dead yet more than living."

Houseman made no answer; but continued to grope on through the path in the thicket, which he evidently knew well; though even in daylight, so thick were the trees, and so artfully had their boughs been left to cover the track, no path could have been discovered by one unacquainted with the clue.

They had now walked on for some minutes, and of late their steps had been threading a rugged, and somewhat precipitous descent: all this while, the pulse of the hand Houseman held, beat with as steadfast and calm a throb, as in the most quiet mood of learned meditation; although Aram could not but be conscious that a mere accident, a slip of the foot, an entanglement in the briars, might awaken the irritable fears of his ruffian comrade, and bring the knife to his breast. But this was not that form of death that could shake the nerves of Aram; nor, though arming his whole soul to ward off one danger, was he well sensible of another, that might have seemed equally near and probable, to a less collected and energetic nature. Houseman now halted, again put aside the boughs, proceeded a few steps, and by a certain dampness and oppression in the air, Aram rightly conjectured himself in the cavern Houseman had spoken of.

"We are landed now," said Houseman, "but wait, I will strike a light; I do not love darkness, even with another sort of companion than the one I have now the honour to entertain!"

In a few moments a light was produced, and placed aloft on a crag in the cavern; but the ray it gave was feeble and dull, and left all beyond the immediate spot in which they stood, in a darkness little less Cimmerian than before.

"'Fore Gad, it is cold," said Houseman shivering, "but I have taken care, you see, to provide for a friend's comfort;" so saying, he approached a bundle of dry sticks and leaves, piled at one corner of the cave, applied the light to the fuel, and presently, the fire rose crackling, breaking into a thousand sparks, and freeing itself gradually from the clouds of smoke in which it was enveloped. It now mounted into a ruddy and cheering flame, and the warm glow played picturesquely upon the grey sides of the cavern, which was of a rugged shape, and small dimensions, and cast its reddening light over the forms of the two men.

Houseman stood close to the flame, spreading his hands over it, and a sort of grim complacency stealing along features singularly ill-favoured, and sinister in their expression, as he felt the animal luxury of the warmth.

Across his middle was a broad leathern belt, containing a brace of large horse pistols, and the knife, or rather dagger, with which he had menaced Aram, an instrument sharpened on both sides, and nearly a foot in length. Altogether, what with his muscular breadth of figure, his hard and rugged features, his weapons, and a certain reckless, bravo air which indescribably marked his attitude and bearing, it was not well possible to imagine a fitter habitant for that grim cave, or one from whom men of peace, like Eugene Aram, might have seemed to derive more reasonable cause of alarm.

The Scholar stood at a little distance, waiting till his companion was entirely prepared for the conference, and his pale and lofty features, hushed in their usual deep, but at such a moment, almost preternatural repose. He stood leaning with folded arms against the rude wall; the light reflected upon his dark garments, with the graceful riding-cloak of the day half falling from his shoulder, and revealing also the pistols in his belt, and the sword, which, though commonly worn at that time, by all pretending to superiority above the lower and trading orders, Aram usually waived as a distinction, but now carried as a defence. And nothing could be more striking, than the contrast between the ruffian form of his companion, and the delicate and chiselled beauty of the Student's features, with their air of mournful intelligence and serene command, and the slender, though nervous symmetry of his frame.

"Houseman," said Aram, now advancing, as his comrade turned his face from the flame, towards him; "before we enter on the main subject of our proposed commune—tell me, were you engaged on the attempt last night upon Lester's house?"

"By the Fiend, no!" answered Houseman, nor did I learn it till this morning; it was unpremeditated till within a few hours of the time, by the two fools who alone planned it. The fact is, that myself and the greater part of our little band, were engaged some miles off, in the western part of the county. Two—our general—spies, had been, of their own accord, into your neighbourhood, to reconnoitre. They marked Lester's house during the day, and gathered, (as I can say by experience it was easy to do) from unsuspected inquiry in the village, for they wore a clown's dress, several particulars which induced them to think it contained what might repay the trouble of breaking into it. And walking along the fields, they overheard the good master of the house tell one of his neighbours of a large sum at home; nay, even describe the place where it was kept: that determined them;—they feared, (as the old man indeed observed,) that the sum might be removed the next day; they had noted the house sufficiently to profit by the description given: they resolved, then, of themselves, for it was too late to reckon on our assistance, to break into the room in which the money was kept—though from the aroused vigilance of the frightened hamlet and the force within the house, they resolved to attempt no farther booty. They reckoned on the violence of the storm, and the darkness of the night to prevent their being heard or seen; they were mistaken—the house was alarmed, they were no sooner in the luckless room, than—"Well, I know the rest; was the one wounded dangerously hurt?"

"Oh, he will recover, he will recover; our men are no chickens. But I own I thought it natural that you might suspect me of sharing in the attack; and though, as I have said before, I do not love you, I have no wish to embroil matters so far as an outrage on the house of your father-in-law, might be reasonably expected to do:—at all events, while the gate to an amicable compromise between us is still open."

"I am satisfied on this head," said Aram, "and I can now treat with you in a spirit of less distrustful precaution than before. I tell you, Houseman, that the terms are no longer at your control; you must leave this part of the country, and that forthwith, or you inevitably perish.

The whole population is alarmed, and the most vigilant of the London Police have been already sent for. Life is sweet to you, as to us all, and I cannot imagine you so mad, as to incur not the risk, but the certainty, of losing it. You can no longer therefore, hold the threat of your presence over my head. Besides, were you able to do so, I at least have the power, which you seem to have forgotten, of freeing myself from it. Am I chained to yonder valleys? have I not the facility of quitting them at any moment I will? of seeking a hiding-place, which might baffle, not only your vigilance to discover me, but that of the Law? True, my approaching marriage puts some clog upon my wing, but you know that I, of all men, am not likely to be the slave of passion. And what ties are strong enough to arrest the steps of him who flies from a fearful death? Am I using sophistry here, Houseman? Have I not reason on my side?"

"What you say is true enough," said Houseman reluctantly; "I do not gainsay it. But I know you have not sought me, in this spot, and at this hour, for the purpose of denying my claims: the desire of compromise alone can have brought you hither."

"You speak well," said Aram, preserving the admirable coolness of his manner; and continuing the deep and sagacious hypocrisy by which he sought to baffle the dogged covetousness and keen sense of interest with which he had to contend. "It is not easy for either of us to deceive the other. We are men, whose perceptions a life of danger, has sharpened upon all points; I speak to you frankly, for disguise is unavailing. Though I can fly from your reach—though I can desert my present home and my intended bride, I would fain think I have free and secure choice to preserve that exact path and scene of life which I have chalked out for myself: I would fain be rid of all apprehension from you. There are two ways only by which this security can be won: the first is through your death;—nay, start not, nor put your hand on your pistol; you have not now cause to fear me. Had I chosen that method of escape, I could have effected it long since: When, months ago, you slept under my roof—ay, slept—what should have hindered me from stabbing you during the slumber? Two nights since, when my blood was up, and the fury upon me, what should have prevented me tightening the grasp that you so resent, and laying you breathless at my feet? Nay, now, though you keep your eye fixed on my motions, and your hand upon your weapon, you would be no match for a desperate and resolved man, who might as well perish in conflict with you, as by the protracted accomplishment of your threats. Your ball might fail—(even now I see your hand trembles)—mine, if I so will it, is certain death. No, Houseman, it would be as vain for your eye to scan the dark pool into whose breast you cataract casts its waters, as for your intellect to pierce the depths of my mind and motives. Your murder, though in self-defence, would lay a weight upon my soul, which would sink it for ever: I should see, in your death, new chances of detection spread themselves before me: the terrors of the dead are not to be bought or awed into silence; I should pass from one peril into another; and the law's dread vengeance might fall upon me, through the last peril, even yet more surely than through the first. Be composed, then, on this point! From my hand, unless you urge it madly upon yourself, you are wholly safe. Let us turn to my second method of attaining security. It lies, not in your momentary cessation from persecutions; not in your absence from this spot alone; you must quit the country—you must never return to it—your home must be cast, and your very grave dug in a foreign soil. Are you prepared for this? If not, I can say no more; and I again cast myself passive into the arms of Fate."

"You ask," said Houseman, whose fears were allayed by Aram's address, though, at the same time, his dissolute and desperate nature was subdued and tamed in spite of himself, by the very composure of the loftier mind with which it was brought in contact: "You ask," said he, "no trifling favour of a man—to desert his country for ever; but I am no dreamer, to love one spot better than another. I should, perhaps, prefer a foreign clime, as the safer and the freer from old recollections, if I could live in it as a man who loves the relish of life should do. Show me the advantages I am to gain by exile, and farewell to the pale cliffs of England for ever!"

"Your demand is just," answered Aram; "listen, then. I am willing to coin all my poor wealth, save alone the barest pittance wherewith to sustain life; nay, more, I am prepared also to melt down the whole of my possible expectations from others, into the form of an annuity to yourself. But mark, it will be taken out of my hands, so that you can have no power over me to alter the conditions with which it will be saddled. It will be so vested that it shall commence the moment you touch a foreign clime; and wholly and for ever cease the moment you set foot on any part of English ground; or, mark also, at the moment of my death. I shall then know that no farther hope from me can induce you to risk this income; for, as I should have spent my all in attaining it, you cannot even meditate the design of extorting more. I shall know that you will not menace my life; for my death would be the destruction of your fortunes. We shall live thus separate and secure from each other; you will have only cause to hope for my safety; and I shall have no reason to shudder at yours. Through one channel alone could I then fear; namely, that in dying, you should enjoy the fruitless vengeance of criminating me. But this chance I must patiently endure: you, if older, are more robust and hardy than myself—your life will probably be longer than mine; and, even were it otherwise, why should we destroy one another? At my death-bed I will solemnly swear to respect your secret; why not on your part, I say not swear, but resolve, to respect mine? We cannot love one another; but why hate with a gratuitous and demon vengeance? No, Houseman, however circumstances may have darkened or steeled your heart, it is touched with humanity yet—you will have owed to me the bread of a secure and easy existence—you will feel that I have stripped myself, even to penury, to purchase the comforts I cheerfully resign to you—you will remember that, instead of the sacrifices enjoined by this alternative, I might have sought only to counteract your threats, by attempting a life that you strove to make a snare and torture to my own. You will remember this; and you will not grudge me the austere and gloomy solitude in which I seek to forget, or the one solace with which I, perhaps vainly, endeavour to cheer my passage to a quiet grave. No, Houseman, no; dislike, hate, menace me as you will, I still feel I shall have no cause to dread the mere wantonness of your revenge."

These words, aided by a tone of voice, and an expression of countenance that gave them perhaps their chief effect, took even the hardened nature of Houseman by surprise; he was affected by an emotion which he could not have believed it possible the man who till then had galled him by the humbling sense of inferiority, could have created. He extended his hand to Aram.

"By—," he exclaimed, with an oath which we spare the reader, "you are right! you have made me as helpless in your hands, as an infant. I accept your offer—if I were to refuse it, I should be driven to the same courses I now pursue. But look you; I know not what may be the amount of the annuity you can raise. I shall not, however, require more than will satisfy wants, which, if not so scanty as your own, are not at least very extravagant or very refined. As for the rest, if there be any surplus, in God's name keep it for yourself, and rest assured that, so far as I am concerned, you shall be molested no more."

"No, Houseman," said Aram, with a half smile, "you shall have all I first mentioned; that is, all beyond what nature craves, honourably and fully. Man's best resolutions are weak: if you knew I possessed aught to spare, a fancied want, a momentary extravagance might tempt you to demand it. Let us put ourselves beyond the possible reach of temptation. But do not flatter yourself by the hope that the income will be magnificent. My own annuity is but trifling, and the half of the dowry I expect from my future father-in-law, is all that I can at present obtain. The whole of that dowry is insignificant as a sum. But if this does not suffice for you, I must beg or borrow elsewhere."

"This, after all, is a pleasanter way of settling business," said Houseman, "than by threats and anger. And now I will tell you exactly the sum on which, if I could receive it yearly, I could live without looking beyond the pale of the Law for more—on which I could cheerfully renounce England, and commence 'the honest man.' But then, hark you, I must have half settled on my little daughter."

"What! have you a child?" said Aram eagerly, and well pleased to find an additional security for his own safety.

"Ay, a little girl, my only one, in her eighth year; she lives with her grandmother, for she is motherless, and that girl must not be left quite penniless should I be summoned hence before my time. Some twelve years hence—as poor Jane promises to be pretty—she may be married off my hands, but her childhood must not be left to the chances of beggary or shame."

"Doubtless not, doubtless not. Who shall say now that we ever outlive feeling?" said Aram, "Half the annuity shall be settled upon her, should she survive you; but on the same conditions, ceasing when I die, or the instant of your return to England. And now, name the sum that you deem sufficing."

"Why," said Houseman, counting on his fingers, and muttering "twenty—fifty—wine and the creature cheap abroad—humph! a hundred for living, and half as much for pleasure. Come, Aram, one hundred and fifty guineas per annum, English money, will do for a foreign life—you see I am easily satisfied."

"Be it so," said Aram, "I will engage by one means or another to procure it. For this purpose I shall set out for London to-morrow; I will not lose a moment in seeing the necessary settlement made as we have specified. But meanwhile, you must engage to leave this neighbourhood, and if possible, cause your comrades to do the same, although you will not hesitate, for the sake of your own safety, immediately to separate from them."

"Now that we are on good terms," replied Houseman, "I will not scruple to oblige you in these particulars. My comrades intend to quit the country before to-morrow; nay, half are already gone; by daybreak I myself will be some miles hence, and separated from each of them. Let us meet in London after the business is completed, and there conclude our last interview on earth."

"What will be your address?"

"In Lambeth there is a narrow alley that leads to the water-side, called Peveril Lane. The last house to the right, towards the river, is my usual lodging; a safe resting-place at all times, and for all men."

"There then will I seek you. And now, Houseman, fare-you-well! As you remember your word to me, may life flow smooth for your child."

"Eugene Aram," said Houseman, "there is about you something against which the fiercer devil within me would rise in vain. I have read that the tiger can be awed by the human eye, and you compel me into submission by a spell equally unaccountable. You are a singular man, and it seems to me a riddle, how we could ever have been thus connected; or how—but we will not rip up the past, it is an ugly sight, and the fire is just out. Those stories do not do for the dark. But to return;—were it only for the sake of my child, you might depend upon me now; better too an arrangement of this sort, than if I had a larger sum in hand which I might be tempted to fling away, and in looking for more, run my neck into a halter, and leave poor Jane upon charity. But come, it is almost dark again, and no doubt you wish to be stirring: stay, I will lead you back, and put you on the right track, lest you stumble on my friends."

"Is this cavern one of their haunts?" said Aram.

"Sometimes: but they sleep the other side of the Devil's Crag to-night. Nothing like a change of quarters for longevity—eh?"

"And they easily spare you."

"Yes, if it be only on rare occasions, and on the plea of family business. Now then, your hand, as before. Jesu! how it rains—lightning too—I could look with less fear on a naked sword, than those red, forked, blinding flashes—Hark! thunder."

The night had now, indeed, suddenly changed its aspect; the rain descended in torrents, even more impetuously than on the former night, while the thunder burst over their very heads, as they wound upward through the brake. With every instant, the lightning broke from the riven chasm of the blackness that seemed suspended as in a solid substance above, brightened the whole heaven into one livid and terrific flame, and showed to the two men the faces of each other, rendered deathlike and ghastly by the glare. Houseman was evidently affected by the fear that sometimes seizes even the sturdiest criminals, when exposed to those more fearful phenomena of the Heavens, which seem to humble into nothing the power and the wrath of man. His teeth chattered, and he muttered broken words about the peril of wandering near trees when the lightning was of that forked character, accelerating his pace at every sentence, and sometimes interrupting himself with an ejaculation, half oath, half prayer, or a congratulation that the rain at least diminished the danger. They soon cleared the thicket, and a few minutes brought them once more to the banks of the stream, and the increased roar of the cataract. No earthly scene perhaps could surpass the appalling sublimity of that which they beheld;—every instant the lightning, which became more and more frequent, converting the black waters into billows of living fire, or wreathing itself in lurid spires around the huge crag that now rose in sight; and again, as the thunder rolled onward, darting its vain fury upon the rushing cataract, and the tortured breast of the gulf that raved below low. And the sounds that filled the air were even more fraught with terror and menace than the scene;—the waving, the groans, the crash of the pines on the hill, the impetuous force of the rain upon the whirling river, and the everlasting roar of the cataract, answered anon by the yet more awful voice that burst above it from the clouds.

They halted while yet sufficiently distant from the cataract to be heard by each other. "My path," said Aram, as the lightning now paused upon the scene, and seemed literally to wrap in a lurid shroud the dark figure of the Student, as he stood, with his hand calmly raised, and his cheek pale, but dauntless and composed; "My path now lies yonder: in a week we shall meet again."

"By the fiend," said Houseman, shuddering, "I would not, for a full hundred, ride alone through the moor you will pass. There stands a gibbet by the road, on which a parricide was hanged in chains. Pray Heaven this night be no omen of the success of our present compact!"

"A steady heart, Houseman," answered Aram, striking into the separate path, "is its own omen."

The Student soon gained the spot in which he had left his horse; the animal had not attempted to break the bridle, but stood trembling from limb to limb, and testified by a quick short neigh the satisfaction with which it hailed the approach of its master, and found itself no longer alone.

Aram remounted, and hastened once more into the main road. He scarcely felt the rain, though the fierce wind drove it right against his path; he scarcely marked the lightning, though at times it seemed to dart its arrows on his very form; his heart was absorbed in the success of his schemes.

"Let the storm without howl on," thought he, "that within hath a respite at last. Amidst the winds and rains I can breathe more freely than I have done on the smoothest summer day. By the charm of a deeper mind and a subtler tongue, I have then conquered this desperate foe; I have silenced this inveterate spy: and, Heaven be praised, he too has human ties; and by those ties I hold him! Now, then, I hasten to London—I arrange this annuity—see that the law tightens every cord of the compact; and when all is done, and this dangerous man fairly departed on his exile, I return to Madeline, and devote to her a life no longer the vassal of accident and the hour: but I have been taught caution. Secure as my own prudence may have made me from farther apprehension of Houseman, I will yet place myself wholly beyond his power: I will still consummate my former purpose, adopt a new name, and seek a new retreat; Madeline may not know the real cause; but this brain is not barren of excuse. Ah!" as drawing his cloak closer round him, he felt the purse hid within his breast which contained the order he had obtained from Lester; "Ah! this will now add its quota to purchase, not a momentary relief, but the stipend of perpetual silence. I have passed through the ordeal easier than I had hoped for. Had the devil at his heart been more difficult to lay, so necessary is his absence, that I must have purchased it at any cost. Courage, Eugene Aram! thy mind, for which thou hast lived, and for which thou hast hazarded thy soul—if soul and mind be distinct from each other—thy mind can support thee yet through every peril: not till thou art stricken into idiotcy, shalt thou behold thyself defenceless. How cheerfully," muttered he, after a momentary pause, "how cheerfully, for safety, and to breathe with a quiet heart, the air of Madeline's presence, shall I rid myself of all save enough to defy want. And want can never now come to me, as of old. He who knows the sources of every science from which wealth is wrought holds even wealth at his will."

Breaking at every interval into these soliloquies, Aram continued to breast the storm until he had won half his journey, and had come upon a long and bleak moor, which was the entrance to that beautiful line of country in which the valleys around Grassdale are embosomed: faster and faster came the rain; and though the thunder-clouds were now behind, they yet followed loweringly, in their black array, the path of the lonely horseman.

But now he heard the sound of hoofs making towards him; he drew his horse on one side of the road, and at that instant a broad flash of lightning illumining the space around, he beheld four horsemen speeding along at a rapid gallop; they were armed, and conversing loudly—their oaths were heard jarringly and distinctly amidst all the more solemn and terrific sounds of the night. They came on, sweeping by the Student, whose hand was on his pistol, for he recognised in one of the riders the man who had escaped unwounded from Lester's house. He and his comrades were evidently, then, Houseman's desperate associates; and they too, though they were borne too rapidly by Aram to be able to rein in their horses on the spot, had seen the solitary traveller, and already wheeled round, and called upon him to halt!

The lightning was again gone, and the darkness snatched the robbers and their intended victim from the sight of each other. But Aram had not lost a moment; fast fled his horse across the moor, and when, with the next flash, he looked back, he saw the ruffians, unwilling even for booty to encounter the horrors of the night, had followed him but a few paces, and again turned round; still he dashed on, and had now nearly passed the moor; the thunder rolled fainter and fainter from behind, and the lightning only broke forth at prolonged intervals, when suddenly, after a pause of unusual duration, it brought the whole scene into a light, if less intolerable, even more livid than before. The horse, that had hitherto sped on without start or stumble, now recoiled in abrupt affright; and the horseman, looking up at the cause, beheld the Gibbet of which Houseman had spoken immediately fronting his path, with its ghastly tenant waving to and fro, as the winds rattled through the parched and arid bones; and the inexpressible grin of the skull fixed, as in mockery, upon his countenance.

BOOK IV.

CHAPTER I.

```
IN WHICH WE RETURN TO WALTER.—HIS DEBT OF GRATITUDE TO
   MR. PERTINAX FILLGRAVE.—THE CORPORAL'S ADVICE,
      AND THE CORPORAL'S VICTORY.


   Let a Physician be ever so excellent,
   there will be those that censure him.
      —Gil Blas.
```

We left Walter in a situation of that critical nature, that it would be inhuman to delay our return to him any longer. The blow by which he had been felled, stunned him for an instant; but his frame was of no common strength and hardihood, and the imminent peril in which he was placed, served to recall him from the momentary insensibility. On recovering himself, he felt that the ruffians were dragging him towards the hedge, and the thought flashed upon him that their object was murder. Nerved by this idea, he collected his strength, and suddenly wresting himself from the grasp of one of the ruffians who had seized him by the collar, he had already gained his knee, and now his feet, when a second blow once more deprived him of sense.

When a dim and struggling consciousness recurred to him; he found that the villains had dragged him to the opposite side of the hedge and were deliberately robbing him. He was on the point of renewing an useless and dangerous struggle, when one of the ruffians said, "I think he stirs, I had better draw my knife across his throat."

"Pooh, no!" replied another voice, "never kill if it can be helped: trust me 'tis an ugly thing to think of afterwards. Besides, what use is it? A robbery, in these parts, is done and forgotten; but a murder rouses the whole country."

"Damnation, man! why, the deed's done already, he's as dead as a door-nail."

"Dead!" said the other in a startled voice; "no, no!" and leaning down, the ruffian placed his hand on Walter's heart. The unfortunate traveller felt his flesh creep as the hand touched him, but prudently abstained from motion or exclamation. He thought, however, as with dizzy and half-shut eyes he caught the shadowy and dusk outline of the face that bent over him, so closely that he felt the breath of its lips, that it was one that he had seen before; and as the man now rose, and the wan light of the skies gave a somewhat clearer view of his features, the supposition was heightened, though not absolutely confirmed. But Walter had no farther power to observe his plunderers: again his brain reeled; the dark trees, the grim shadows of human forms, swam before his glazing eye; and he sunk once more into a profound insensibility.

Meanwhile, the doughty Corporal had at the first sight of his master's fall, halted abruptly at the spot to which his steed had carried him; and coming rapidly to the conclusion that three men were best encountered at a distance, he fired his two pistols, and without staying to see if they took effect, which, indeed, they did not, galloped down the precipitous hill with as much despatch, as if it had been the last stage to "Lunnun."

"My poor young master!" muttered he: "But if the worst comes to the worst, the chief part of the money's in the saddle-bags any how; and so, messieurs thieves, you're bit—baugh!"

The Corporal was not long in reaching the town, and alarming the loungers at the inn-door. A posse comitatus was soon formed; and, armed as if they were to have encountered all the robbers between Hounslow and the Apennine, a band of heroes, with the Corporal, who had first deliberately reloaded his pistols, at their head, set off to succour "the poor gentleman what was already murdered."

They had not got far before they found Walter's horse, which had luckily broke from the robbers, and was now quietly regaling himself on a patch of grass by the roadside. "He can get his supper, the beast," grunted the Corporal, thinking of his own; and bid one of the party try to catch the animal, which, however, would have declined all such proffers, had not a long neigh of recognition from the roman nose of the Corporal's steed, striking familiarly on the straggler's ear, called it forthwith, to the Corporal's side; and (while the two chargers exchanged greeting) the Corporal seized its rein.

When they came to the spot from which the robbers had made their sally, all was still and tranquil; no Walter was to be seen: the Corporal cautiously dismounted, and searched about with as much minuteness as if he were looking for a pin; but the host of the inn at which the travellers had dined the day before, stumbled at once on the right track. Gouts of blood on the white chalky soil directed him to the hedge, and creeping through a small and recent gap, he discovered the yet breathing body of the young traveller.

Walter was now conducted with much care to the inn; a Surgeon was already in attendance; for having heard that a gentleman had been murdered without his knowledge, Mr. Pertinax Fillgrave had rushed from his house, and placed himself on the road, that the poor creature might not, at least, be buried without his assistance. So eager was he to begin, that he scarce suffered the unfortunate Walter to be taken within, before he whipped out his instruments, and set to work with the smack of an amateur.

Although the Surgeon declared his patient to be in the greatest possible danger, the sagacious Corporal, who thought himself more privileged to know about wounds than any man of peace, by profession, however destructive by practice, could possibly be, had himself examined those his master had received, before he went down to taste his long-delayed supper; and he now confidently assured the landlord, and the rest of the good company in the kitchen, that the blows on the head had been mere fly-bites, and that his master would be as well as ever in a week at the farthest.

And, indeed, when Walter the very next morning woke from the stupor, rather than sleep, he had undergone, he felt himself surprisingly better than the Surgeon, producing his probe, hastened to assure him he possibly could be.

By the help of Mr. Pertinax Fillgrave, Walter was detained several days in the town; nor is it wholly improbable, but that for the dexterity of the Corporal, he might be in the town to this day; not, indeed in the comfortable shelter of the old-fashioned inn, but in the colder quarters of a certain green spot, in which, despite of its rural attractions, few persons are willing to fix a permanent habitation.

Luckily, however, one evening, the Corporal, who had been, to say truth, very regular in his attendance on his master; for, bating the selfishness, consequent, perhaps, on his knowledge of the world, Jacob Bunting was a good-natured man on the whole, and liked his master as well as he did any thing, always excepting Jacobina, and board-wages; one evening, we say, the Corporal coming into Walter's apartment, found him sitting up in his bed, with a very melancholy and dejected expression of countenance.

"And well, Sir, what does the Doctor say?" asked the Corporal, drawing aside the curtains.

"Ah, Bunting, I fancy it's all over with me!"

"The Lord forbid, Sir! you're a-jesting, surely?"

"Jesting! my good fellow, ah! just get me that phial."

"The filthy stuff!" said the Corporal, with a wry face; "Well, Sir, if I had had the dressing of you—been half way to Yorkshire by this. Man's a worm; and when a doctor gets un on his hook, he is sure to angle for the devil with the bait—augh!"

"What! you really think that damned fellow, Fillgrave, is keeping me on in this way?"

"Is he a fool, to give up three phials a day, 4s. 6d. item, ditto, ditto?" cried the Corporal, as if astonished at the question; "but don't you feel yourself getting a deal better every day? Don't you feel all this ere stuff revive you?"

No, indeed, I was amazingly better the first day than I am now; I progress from worse to worse. Ah! Bunting, if Peter Dealtry were here, he might help me to an appropriate epitaph: as it is, I suppose I shall be very simply labelled. Fillgrave will do the whole business, and put it down in his bill—item, nine draughts—item, one epitaph.

"Lord-a-mercy, your honour," said the Corporal, drawing out a little red-spotted pocket-handkerchief; "how can—jest so?—it's quite moving."

"I wish we were moving!" sighed the patient.

"And so we might be," cried the Corporal; "so we might, if you'd pluck up a bit. Just let me look at your honour's head; I knows what a confusion is better nor any of 'em."

The Corporal having obtained permission, now removed the bandages wherewith the Doctor had bound his intended sacrifice to Pluto, and after peering into the wounds for about a minute, he thrust out his under lip, with a contemptuous, "Pshaugh! augh! And how long," said he, "does Master Fillgrave say you be to be under his hands,—augh!"

"He gives me hopes that I may be taken out an airing very gently, (yes, hearses always go very gently!) in about three weeks!"

The Corporal started, and broke into a long whistle. He then grinned from ear to ear, snapped his fingers, and said, "Man of the world, Sir,—man of the world every inch of him!"

"He seems resolved that I shall be a man of another world," said Walter.

"Tell ye what, Sir—take my advice—your honour knows I be no fool—throw off them ere wrappers; let me put on scrap of plaister—pitch phials to devil—order out horses to-morrow, and when you've been in the air half an hour, won't know yourself again!"

"Bunting! the horses out to-morrow?—faith, I don't think I could walk across the room."

"Just try, your honour."

"Ah! I'm very weak, very weak—my dressing-gown and slippers—your arm, Bunting—well, upon my honour, I walk very stoutly, eh? I should not have thought this! leave go: why I really get on without your assistance!"

"Walk as well as ever you did."

"Now I'm out of bed, I don't think I shall go back again to it."

"Would not, if I was your honour."

"And after so much exercise, I really fancy I've a sort of an appetite."

"Like a beefsteak?"

"Nothing better."

"Pint of wine?"

"Why that would be too much—eh?"

"Not it."

"Go, then, my good Bunting; go and make haste—stop, I say that d—d fellow—" "Good sign to swear," interrupted the Corporal; "swore twice within last five minutes—famous symptom!"

"Do you choose to hear me? That d—d fellow, Fillgrave, is coming back in an hour to bleed me: do you mount guard—refuse to let him in—pay him his bill—you have the money. And harkye, don't be rude to the rascal."

"Rude, your honour! not I—been in the Forty-second—knows discipline—only rude to the privates!"

The Corporal, having seen his master conduct himself respectably toward the viands with which he supplied him—having set his room to rights, brought him the candles, borrowed him a book, and left him for the present in extremely good spirits, and prepared for the flight of the morrow; the Corporal, I say, now lighting his pipe, stationed himself at the door of the inn, and waited for Mr. Pertinax Fillgrave. Presently the Doctor, who was a little thin man, came bustling across the street, and was about, with a familiar "Good evening," to pass by the Corporal, when that worthy, dropping his pipe, said respectfully, "Beg pardon, Sir—want to speak to you—a little favour. Will your honour walk in the back-parlour?"

"Oh! another patient," thought the Doctor; "these soldiers are careless fellows—often get into scrapes. Yes, friend, I'm at your service."

The Corporal showed the man of phials into the back-parlour, and, hemming thrice, looked sheepish, as if in doubt how to begin. It was the Doctor's business to encourage the bashful.

"Well, my good man," said he, brushing off, with the arm of his coat, some dust that had settled on his inexpressibles, "so you want to consult me?"

"Indeed, your honour, I do; but—feel a little awkward in doing so—a stranger and all."

"Pooh!—medical men are never strangers. I am the friend of every man who requires my assistance."

"Augh!—and I do require your honour's assistance very sadly."

"Well—well—speak out. Any thing of long standing?"

"Why, only since we have been here, Sir."

"Oh, that's all! Well."

"Your honour's so good—that—won't scruple in telling you all. You sees as how we were robbed—master at least was—had some little in my pockets—but we poor servants are never too rich. You seems such a kind gentleman—so attentive to master—though you must have felt how disinterested it was to 'tend a man what had been robbed—that I have no hesitation in making bold to ask you to lend us a few guineas, just to help us out with the bill here,—bother!"

"Fellow!" said the Doctor, rising, "I don't know what you mean; but I'd have you to learn that I am not to be cheated out of my time and property. I shall insist upon being paid my bill instantly, before I dress your master's wound once more."

"Augh!" said the Corporal, who was delighted to find the Doctor come so immediately into the snare;—"won't be so cruel surely,—why, you'll leave us without a shiner to pay my host here."

"Nonsense!—Your master, if he's a gentleman, can write home for money."

"Ah, Sir, all very well to say so;—but, between you and me and the bed-post—young master's quarrelled with old master—old master won't give him a rap,—so I'm sure, since your honour's a friend to every man who requires your assistance—noble saying, Sir!—you won't refuse us a few guineas;—and as for your bill—why—" "Sir, you're an impudent vagabond!" cried the Doctor, as red as a rose-draught, and flinging out of the room; "and I warn you, that I shall bring in my bill, and expect to be paid within ten minutes."

The Doctor waited for no answer—he hurried home, scratched off his account, and flew back with it in as much haste as if his patient had been a month longer under his care, and was consequently on the brink of that happier world, where, since the inhabitants are immortal, it is very evident that doctors, as being useless, are never admitted.

The Corporal met him as before.

"There, Sir," cried the Doctor, breathlessly, and then putting his arms akimbo, "take that to your master, and desire him to pay me instantly."

"Augh! and shall do no such thing."

"You won't?"

"No, for shall pay you myself. Where's your wee stamp—eh?"

And with great composure the Corporal drew out a well-filled purse, and discharged the bill. The Doctor was so thunderstricken, that he pocketed the money without uttering a word. He consoled himself, however, with the belief that Walter, whom he had tamed into a becoming hypochondria, would be sure to send for him the next morning. Alas, for mortal expectations!—the next morning Walter was once more on the road.

CHAPTER II.

NEW TRACES OF THE FATE OF GEOFFREY LESTER.—WALTER AND THE CORPORAL PROCEED ON A FRESH EXPEDITION.—THE CORPORAL IS ESPECIALLY SAGACIOUS ON THE OLD TOPIC OF THE WORLD.—HIS OPINIONS ON THE MEN WHO CLAIM 'KNOWLEDGE THEREOF.—ON THE ADVANTAGES ENJOYED BY A VALET.—ON THE SCIENCE OF SUCCESSFUL LOVE.—ON VIRTUE AND THE CONSTITUTION.—ON QUALITIES TO BE DESIRED IN A MISTRESS,—A LANDSCAPE.

> This way of talking of his very much enlivens the conversation among us of a more sedate turn.
> —Spectator, No. 3.

Walter found, while he made search himself, that it was no easy matter, in so large a county as Yorkshire, to obtain even the preliminary particulars, viz. the place of residence, and the name of the Colonel from India whose dying gift his father had left the house of the worthy Courtland, to claim and receive. But the moment he committed the inquiry to the care of an active and intelligent lawyer, the case seemed to brighten up prodigiously; and Walter was shortly informed that a Colonel Elmore, who had been in India, had died in the year 17—; that by a reference to his will it appeared that he had left to Daniel Clarke the sum of a thousand pounds, and the house in which he resided before his death, the latter being merely leasehold at a high rent, was specified in the will to be of small value: it was situated in the outskirts of Knaresborough. It was also discovered that a Mr. Jonas Elmore, the only surviving executor of the will, and a distant relation of the deceased Colonel's, lived about fifty miles from York, and could, in all probability, better than any one, afford Walter those farther particulars of which he was so desirous to be informed. Walter immediately proposed to his lawyer to accompany him to this gentleman's house; but it so happened that the lawyer could not, for three or four days, leave his business at York, and Walter, exceedingly impatient to proceed on the intelligence thus granted him, and disliking the meagre information obtained from letters, when a personal interview could be obtained, resolved himself to repair to Mr. Jonas Elmore's without farther delay; and behold, therefore, our worthy Corporal and his master again mounted, and commencing a new journey.

The Corporal, always fond of adventure, was in high spirits.

"See, Sir," said he to his master, patting with great affection the neck of his steed, "See, Sir, how brisk the creturs are; what a deal of good their long rest at York city's done'em. Ah, your honour, what a fine town that ere be!—yet," added the Corporal, with an air of great superiority, "it gives you no notion of Lunnun, like—on the faith of a man, no!"

"Well, Bunting, perhaps we may be in London within a month hence."

"And afore we gets there, your honour,—no offence,—but should like to give you some advice; 'tis ticklish place, that Lunnun, and though you be by no manner of means deficient in genus, yet, Sir, you be young, and I be—" "Old,—true, Bunting," added Walter very gravely.

"Augh—bother! old, Sir, old, Sir!—A man in the prime of life,—hair coal black, (bating a few grey ones that have had, since twenty—care, and military service, Sir,)—carriage straight,—teeth strong,—not an ail in the world, bating the rheumatics—is not old, Sir,—not by no manner of means,—baugh!"

"You are very right, Bunting; when I said old, I meant experienced. I assure you I shall be very grateful for your advice; and suppose, while we walk our horses up this hill, you begin lecture the first. London's a fruitful subject. All you can say on it won't be soon exhausted."

"Ah, may well say that," replied the Corporal, exceedingly flattered with the permission he had obtained, "and any thing my poor wit can suggest, quite at your honour's sarvice—ehem!—hem! You must know by Lunnun, I means the world, and by the world means Lunnun,—know one—know t'other. But 'tis not them as affects to be most knowing as be so at bottom. Begging your honour's pardon, I thinks gentlefolks what lives only with gentlefolks, and call themselves men of the world, be often no wiser nor Pagan creturs, and live in a gentile darkness."

"The true knowledge of the world," said Walter, "is only then for the Corporals of the Forty-second,—eh, Bunting?"

"As to that, Sir," quoth the Corporal, "'tis not being of this calling or of that calling that helps one on; 'tis an inborn sort of genus the talent of observing, and growing wise by observing. One picks up crumb here, crumb there: but if one has not good digestion, Lord, what sinnifies a feast?—Healthy man thrives on a 'tatoe, sickly looks pale on a haunch. You sees, your honour, as I said afore, I was own sarvant to Colonel Dysart; he was a Lord's nephy, a very gay gentleman, and great hand with the ladies,—not a man more in the world;—so I had the opportunity of larning what's what among the best set; at his honour's expense, too,—augh! To my mind, Sir, there is not a place from which a man has a better view of things than the bit carpet behind a gentleman's chair. The gentleman eats, and talks, and swears, and jests, and plays cards and makes love, and tries to cheat, and is cheated, and his man stands behind with his eyes and ears open,—augh!"

"One should go to service to learn diplomacy, I see," said Walter, greatly amused.

"Does not know what 'plomacy be, Sir, but knows it would be better for many a young master nor all the Colleges;—would not be so many bubbles if my Lord could take a turn now and then with John. A-well, Sir!—how I used to laugh in my sleeve like, when I saw my master, who was thought the knowingest gentleman about Court, taken in every day smack afore my face. There was one lady whom he had tried hard, as he thought, to get away from her husband; and he used to be so mighty pleased at every glance from her brown eyes—and be d—d to them!—and so careful the husband should not see—so pluming himself on his discretion here, and his conquest there,—when, Lord bless you, it was all settled 'twixt man and wife aforehand! And while the Colonel laughed at the cuckold, the cuckold laughed at the dupe. For you sees, Sir, as how the Colonel was a rich man, and the jewels as he bought for the lady went half into the husband's pocket—he! he!—That's the way of the world, Sir,—that's the way of the world!"

"Upon my word, you draw a very bad picture of the world: you colour highly; and, by the way, I observe that whenever you find any man committing a roguish action, instead of calling him a scoundrel, you show those great teeth of yours, and chuckle out 'A man of the world! a man of the world!'"

"To be sure, your honour; the proper name, too. 'Tis your green-horns who fly into a passion, and use hard words. You see, Sir, there's one thing we larn afore all other things in the world—to butter bread. Knowledge of others, means only the knowledge which side bread's buttered. In short, Sir, the wiser grow, the more take care of oursels. Some persons make a mistake, and, in trying to take care of themsels, run neck into halter—baugh! they are not rascals—they are would-be men of the world. Others be more prudent, (for, as I said afore, Sir, discretion is a pair of stirrups;) they be the true men of the world."

"I should have thought," said Walter, "that the knowledge of the world might be that knowledge which preserves us from being cheated, but not that which enables us to cheat."

"Augh!" quoth the Corporal, with that sort of smile with which you see an old philosopher put down a sounding error from the lips of a young disciple who flatters himself he has uttered something prodigiously fine,—"Augh! and did not I tell you, t'other day, to look at the professions, your honour? What would a laryer be if he did not know how to cheat a witness and humbug a jury?—knows he is lying,—why is he lying? for love of his fees, or his fame like, which gets fees;—Augh! is not that cheating others?—The doctor, too, Master Fillgrave, for instance?—" "Say no more of doctors; I abandon them to your satire, without a word."

"The lying knaves! Don't they say one's well when one's ill—ill when one's well?—profess to know what don't know?—thrust solemn phizzes into every abomination, as if larning lay hid in a—? and all for their neighbours' money, or their own reputation, which makes money—augh! In short, Sir—look where will, impossible to see so much cheating allowed, praised, encouraged, and feel very angry with a cheat who has only made a mistake. But when I sees a man butter his bread carefully—knife steady—butter thick, and hungry fellows looking on and licking chops—mothers stopping their brats—'See, child—respectable man—how thick his bread's buttered!—pull off your hat to him:'—When I sees that, my heart warms: there's the true man of the world—augh!"

"Well, Bunting," said Walter, laughing, "though you are thus lenient to those unfortunate gentlemen whom others call rogues, and thus laudatory of gentlemen who are at best discreetly selfish, I suppose you admit the possibility of virtue, and your heart warms as much when you see a man of worth as when you see a man of the world?"

"Why, you knows, your honour," answered the Corporal, "so far as vartue's concerned, there's a deal in constitution; but as for knowledge of the world, one gets it oneself!"

"I don't wonder, Bunting—as your opinion of women is much the same as your opinion of men—that you are still unmarried."

"Augh! but your honour mistakes!—I am no mice-and-trope. Men are neither one thing nor t'other—neither good nor bad. A prudent parson has nothing to fear from 'em—nor a foolish one any thing to gain—baugh! As to the women creturs, your honour, as I said, vartue's a deal in the constitution. Would not ask what a lassie's mind be—nor what her eddycation;—but see what her habits be, that's all—habits and constitution all one—play into one another's hands."

"And what sort of signs, Bunting, would you mostly esteem in a lady?"

"First place, Sir—woman I'd marry, must not mope when alone!—must be able to 'muse herself; must be easily 'mused. That's a great sign, Sir, of an innocent mind, to be tickled with straws. Besides, employments keeps 'em out of harm's way. Second place, should observe, if she was very fond of places, your honour—sorry to move—that's a sure sign she won't tire easily; but that if she like you now from fancy, she'll like you by and by from custom. Thirdly, your honour, she should not be avarse to dress—a leaning that way shows she has a desire to please: people who don't care about pleasing, always sullen. Fourthly, she must bear to be crossed—I'd be quite sure that she might be contradicted, without mumping or storming;—'cause then, you knows, your honour, if she wanted any thing expensive—need not give it—augh! Fifthly, must not be over religious, your honour; they pyehouse she-creturs always thinks themsels so much better nor we men;—don't understand our language and ways, your honour: they wants us not only to belave, but to tremble—bother!"

"I like your description well enough, on the whole," said Walter, "and when I look out for a wife, I shall come to you for advice."

"Your honour may have it already—Miss Ellinor's jist the thing."

Walter turned away his head, and told Bunting, with great show of indignation, not to be a fool.

The Corporal, who was not quite certain of his ground here, but who knew that Madeline, at all events, was going to be married to Aram, and deemed it, therefore, quite useless to waste any praise upon her, thought that a few random shots of eulogium were worth throwing away on a chance, and consequently continued.

"Augh, your honour—'tis not 'cause I have eyes, that I be's a fool. Miss Ellinor and your honour be only cousins, to be sure; but more like brother and sister, nor any thing else. Howsomever, she's a rare cretur, whoever gets her has a face that puts one in good-humour with the world, if one sees it first thing in the morning—'tis as good as the sun in July—augh! But, as I was saying, your honour—'bout the women-creturs in general—" "Enough of them, Bunting; let us suppose you have been so fortunate as to find one to suit you—how would you woo her? Of course, there are certain secrets of courtship, which you will not hesitate to impart to one, who, like me, wants such assistance from art—much more than you can do, who are so bountifully favoured by Nature."

"As to Nature," replied the Corporal, with considerable modesty, for he never disputed the truth of the compliment—"'tis not 'cause a man be six feet without's shoes, that he's any nearer to lady's heart. Sir, I will own to you, howsomever it makes 'gainst your honour and myself, for that matter—that don't think one is a bit more lucky with the ladies for being so handsome! 'Tis all very well with them ere willing ones, your honour—caught at a glance; but as for the better sort, one's beauty's all bother! Why, Sir, when we see some of the most fortunatest men among she-creturs—what poor little minnikens they be! One's a dwarf—another knock-kneed—a third squints—and a fourth might be shown for a hape! Neither, Sir, is it your soft, insiniivating, die-away youths, as seem at first so seductive; they do very well for lovers, your honour; but then it's always rejected ones! Neither, your honour, does the art of succeeding with the ladies 'quire all those finniken, nimini-pimini's, flourishes, and maxims, and saws, which the Colonel, my old master, and the great gentlefolks, as be knowing, call the art of love—baugh! The whole science, Sir, consists in these two rules—'Ask soon, and ask often.'"

"There seems no great difficulty in them, Bunting."

"Not to us who has gumption, Sir; but then there is summut in the manner of axing—one can't be too hot—can't flatter too much—and, above all, one must never take a refusal. There, Sir, now—if you takes my advice—may break the peace of all the husbands in Lunnun—bother—whaugh!"

"My uncle little knows what a praiseworthy tutor he has secured me in you, Bunting," said Walter, laughing: "And now, while the road is so good, let us make the most of it."

As they had set out late in the day, and the Corporal was fearful of another attack from a hedge, he resolved, that about evening, one of the horses should be seized with a sudden lameness, (which he effected by slily inserting a stone between the shoe and the hoof,) that required immediate attention and a night's rest; so that it was not till the early noon of the next day that our travellers entered the village in which Mr. Jonas Elmore resided.

It was a soft, tranquil day, though one of the very last in October; for the reader will remember that Time had not stood still during Walter's submission to the care of Mr. Pertinax Fillgrave, and his subsequent journey and researches.

The sun-light rested on a broad patch of green heath, covered with furze, and around it were scattered the cottages and farm-houses of the little village. On the other side, as Walter descended the gentle hill that led into this remote hamlet, wide and flat meadows, interspersed with several fresh and shaded ponds, stretched away towards a belt of rich woodland gorgeous with the melancholy pomp by which the "regal year" seeks to veil its decay. Among these meadows you might now see groups of cattle quietly grazing, or standing half hid in the still and sheltered pools. Still farther, crossing to the woods, a solitary sportsman walked careless on, surrounded by some half a dozen spaniels, and the shrill small tongue of one younger straggler of the canine crew, who had broke indecorously from the rest, and already entered the wood, might be just heard, softened down by the distance, into a wild, cheery sound, that animated, without disturbing, the serenity of the scene.

"After all," said Walter aloud, "the scholar was right—there is nothing like the country!"

```
"'Oh, happiness of sweet retired content,
  To be at once secure and innocent!'"
```

"Be them Verses in the Psalms, Sir?" said the Corporal, who was close behind.

"No, Bunting; but they were written by one who, if I recollect right, set the Psalms to verse:—[Denham.] I hope they meet with your approbation?"

"Indeed, Sir, and no—since they ben't in the Psalms, one has no right to think about 'em at all."

"And why, Mr. Critic?"

"'Cause what's the use of security, if one's innocent, and does not mean to take advantage of it—baugh! One does not lock the door for nothing, your honour!"

"You shall enlarge on that honest doctrine of yours another time; meanwhile, call that shepherd, and ask the way to Mr. Elmore's."

The Corporal obeyed, and found that a clump of trees, at the farther corner of the waste land, was the grove that surrounded Mr. Elmore's house; a short canter across the heath brought them to a white gate, and having passed this, a comfortable brick mansion of moderate size stood before them.

CHAPTER III.

A SCHOLAR, BUT OF A DIFFERENT MOULD FROM THE STUDENT OF GRASSDALE.—NEW PARTICULARS CONCERNING GEOFFREY LESTER.—THE JOURNEY RECOMMENCED.

Upon inquiring for Mr. Elmore, Walter was shown into a handsome library, that appeared well-stocked with books, of that good, old-fashioned size and solidity, which are now fast passing from the world, or at least shrinking into old shops and public collections. The time may come, when the mouldering remains of a folio will attract as much philosophical astonishment as the bones of the mammoth. For behold, the deluge of writers hath produced a new world of small octavo! and in the next generation, thanks to the popular libraries, we shall only vibrate between the duodecimo and the diamond edition. Nay, we foresee the time when a very handsome collection may be carried about in one's waistcoat-pocket, and a whole library of the British Classics be neatly arranged in a well-compacted snuff-box.

In a few minutes Mr. Elmore made his appearance; he was a short, well-built man, about the age of fifty. Contrary to the established mode, he wore no wig, and was very bald; except at the sides of the head, and a little circular island of hair in the centre. But this defect was rendered the less visible by a profusion of powder. He was dressed with evident care and precision; a snuff-coloured coat was adorned with a respectable profusion of gold lace; his breeches were of plum-coloured satin; his salmon-coloured stockings, scrupulously drawn up, displayed a very handsome calf; and a pair of steel buckles in his high-heeled and square-toed shoes, were polished into a lustre which almost rivalled the splendour of diamonds. Mr. Jonas Elmore was a beau, a wit, and a scholar of the old school. He abounded in jests, in quotations, in smart sayings, and pertinent anecdotes: but, withal, his classical learning, (out of the classics he knew little enough,) was at once elegant, but wearisome; pedantic, but profound.

To this gentleman Walter presented a letter of introduction which he had obtained from a distinguished clergyman in York. Mr. Elmore received it with a profound salutation—"Aha, from my friend, Dr. Hebraist," said he, glancing at the seal, "a most worthy man, and a ripe scholar. I presume at once, Sir, from his introduction, that you yourself have cultivated the literas humaniores. Pray sit down—ay—I see, you take up a book, an excellent symptom; it gives me an immediate insight into your character. But you have chanced, Sir, on light reading,—one of the Greek novels, I think,—you must not judge of my studies by such a specimen."

"Nevertheless, Sir, it does not seem to my unskilful eye very easy Greek."

"Pretty well, Sir; barbarous, but amusing,—pray continue it. The triumphal entry of Paulus Emilius is not ill told. I confess, that I think novels might be made much higher works than they have been yet. Doubtless, you remember what Aristotle says concerning Painters and Sculptors, 'that they teach and recommend virtue in a more efficacious and powerful manner, than Philosophers by their dry precepts, and are more capable of amending the vicious, than the best moral lessons without such aid.' But how much more, Sir, can a good novelist do this, than the best sculptor or painter in the world! Every one can be charmed by a fine novel, few by a fine painting. 'Indocti rationem artis intelligunt, indocti voluptatem.' A happy sentence that in Quinctilian, Sir, is it not? But, bless me, I am forgetting the letter of my good friend Dr. Hebraist. The charms of your conversation carry me away. And indeed I have seldom the happiness to meet a gentleman so well-informed as yourself. I confess, Sir, I confess that I still retain the tastes of my boyhood; the Muses cradled my childhood, they now smooth the pillow of my footstool—Quem tu, Melpomene, are not yet subject to gout, dira podagra: By the way, how is the worthy Doctor since his attack?—Ah, see now, if you have not still, by your delightful converse, kept me from his letter—yet, positively I need no introduction to you, Apollo has already presented you to me. And as for the Doctor's letter, I will read it after dinner; for as Seneca—" "I beg your pardon a thousand times, Sir," said Walter, who began to despair of ever coming to the matter which seemed lost sight of beneath this battery of erudition, "but you will find by Dr. Hebraist's letter, that it is only on business of the utmost importance that I have presumed to break in upon the learned leisure of Mr. Jonas Elmore."

"Business!" replied Mr. Elmore, producing his spectacles, and deliberately placing them athwart his nose,

"'His mane edictum, post prandia Callirhoen, etc.

"Business in the morning, and the ladies after dinner. Well, Sir, I will yield to you in the one, and you must yield to me in the other: I will open the letter, and you shall dine here, and be introduced to Mrs. Elmore;—What is your opinion of the modern method of folding letters? I—but I see you are impatient." Here Mr. Elmore at length broke the seal; and to Walter's great joy fairly read the contents within.

"Oh! I see, I see!" he said, refolding the epistle, and placing it in his pocket-book; "my friend, Dr. Hebraist, says you are anxious to be informed whether Mr. Clarke ever received the legacy of my poor cousin, Colonel Elmore; and if so, any tidings I can give you of Mr. Clarke himself; or any clue to discover him will be highly acceptable. I gather, Sir, from my friend's letter, that this is the substance of your business with me, caput negotii;—although, like Timanthes, the painter, he leaves more to be understood than is described, 'intelligitur plus quam pingitur,' as Pliny has it."

"Sir," said Walter, drawing his chair close to Mr. Elmore, and his anxiety forcing itself to his countenance, "that is indeed the substance of my business with you; and so important will be any information you can give me that I shall esteem it a—" "Not a very great favour, eh?—not very great?"

"Yes, indeed, a very great obligation."

"I hope not, Sir; for what says Tacitus—that profound reader of the human heart,—'beneficia eo usque loeta sunt,' favours easily repaid beget affection—favours beyond return engender hatred. But, Sir, a truce to trifling;" and here Mr. Elmore composed his countenance, and changed,—which he could do at will, so that the change was not expected to last long—the pedant for the man of business.

"Mr. Clarke did receive his legacy: the lease of the house at Knaresborough was also sold by his desire, and produced the sum of seven hundred and fifty pounds; which being added to the farther sum of a thousand pounds, which was bequeathed to him, amounted to seventeen hundred and fifty pounds. It so happened, that my cousin had possessed some very valuable jewels, which were bequeathed to myself. I, Sir, studious, and a cultivator of the Muse, had no love and no use for these baubles; I preferred barbaric gold to barbaric pearl; and knowing that Clarke had been in India, from whence these jewels had been brought, I showed them to him, and consulted his knowledge on these matters, as to the best method of obtaining a sale. He offered to purchase them of me, under the impression that he could turn them to a profitable speculation in London. Accordingly we came to terms: I sold the greater part of them to him for a sum a little exceeding a thousand pounds. He was pleased with his bargain; and came to borrow the rest of me, in order to look at them more considerately at home, and determine whether or not he should buy them also. Well, Sir, (but here comes the remarkable part of the story,) about three days after this last event, Mr. Clarke and my jewels both disappeared in rather a strange and abrupt manner. In the middle of the night he left his lodging at Knaresborough, and never returned; neither himself nor my jewels were ever heard of more!"

"Good God!" exclaimed Walter, greatly agitated; "what was supposed to be the cause of his disappearance?"

"That," replied Elmore, "was never positively traced. It excited great surprise and great conjecture at the time. Advertisements and handbills were circulated throughout the country, but in vain. Mr. Clarke was evidently a man of eccentric habits, of a hasty temper, and a wandering manner of life; yet it is scarcely probable that he took this sudden manner of leaving the country either from whim or some secret but honest motive never divulged. The fact is, that he owed a few debts in the town—that he had my jewels in his possession, and as (pardon me for saying this, since you take an interest in him,) his connections were entirely unknown in these parts, and his character not very highly estimated,—(whether from his manner, or his conversation, or some undefined and vague rumours, I cannot say)—it was considered by no means improbable that he had decamped with his property in this sudden manner in order to save himself that trouble of settling accounts which a more seemly and public method of departure might have rendered necessary. A man of the name of Houseman, with whom he was acquainted, (a resident in Knaresborough,) declared that Clarke had borrowed rather a considerable sum from him, and did not scruple openly to accuse him of the evident design to avoid repayment. A few more dark but utterly groundless conjectures were afloat; and since the closest search—the minutest inquiry was employed without any result, the supposition that he might have been robbed and murdered was strongly entertained for some time; but as his body was never found, nor suspicion directed against any particular person, these conjectures insensibly died away; and being so complete a stranger to these parts, the very circumstance of his disappearance was not likely to occupy, for very long, the attention of that old gossip the Public, who, even in the remotest parts, has a thousand topics to fill up her time and talk. And now, Sir, I think you know as much of the particulars of the case as any one in these parts can inform you."

We may imagine the various sensations which this unsatisfactory intelligence caused in the adventurous son of the lost wanderer. He continued to throw out additional guesses, and to make farther inquiries concerning a tale which seemed to him so mysterious, but without effect; and he had the mortification to perceive, that the shrewd Jonas was, in his own mind, fully convinced that the permanent disappearance of Clark was accounted for only by the most dishonest motives.

"And," added Elmore, I am confirmed in this belief by discovering afterwards from a tradesman in York who had seen my cousin's jewels—that those I had trusted to Mr. Clarke's hands were more valuable than I had imagined them, and therefore it was probably worth his while to make off with them as quietly as possible. He went on foot, leaving his horse, a sorry nag, to settle with me and the other claimants.

"I, pedes quo te rapiunt et aurae!"

"Heavens!" thought Walter, sinking back in his chair sickened and disheartened, "what a parent, if the opinions of all men who knew him be true, do I thus zealously seek to recover!"

The good-natured Elmore, perceiving the unwelcome and painful impression his account had produced on his young guest, now exerted himself to remove, or at least to lessen it; and turning the conversation into a classical channel, which with him was the Lethe to all cares, he soon forgot that Clarke had ever existed, in expatiating on the unappreciated excellences of Propertius, who, to his mind, was the most tender of all elegiac poets, solely because he was the most learned. Fortunately this vein of conversation, however tedious to Walter, preserved him from the necessity of rejoinder, and left him to the quiet enjoyment of his own gloomy and restless reflections.

At length the time touched upon dinner; Elmore, starting up, adjourned to the drawing-room, in order to present the handsome stranger to the placens uxor—the pleasing wife, whom, in passing through the hall, he eulogized with an amazing felicity of diction.

The object of these praises was a tall, meagre lady, in a yellow dress carried up to the chin, and who added a slight squint to the charms of red hair, ill concealed by powder, and the dignity of a prodigiously high nose. "There is nothing, Sir," said Elmore, "nothing, believe me, like matrimonial felicity. Julia, my dear, I trust the chickens will not be overdone."

"Indeed, Mr. Elmore, I cannot tell; I did not boil them."

"Sir," said Elmore, turning to his guest, I do not know whether you will agree with me, but I think a slight tendency to gourmandism is absolutely necessary to complete the character of a truly classical mind. So many beautiful touches are there in the ancient poets—so many delicate allusions in history and in anecdote relating to the gratification of the palate, that if a man have no correspondent sympathy with the illustrious epicures of old, he is rendered incapable of enjoying the most beautiful passages, that—Come, Sir, the dinner is served:

"'Nutrimus lautis mollissima corpora mensis.'"

As they crossed the hall to the dining-room, a young lady, whom Elmore hastily announced as his only daughter, appeared descending the stairs, having evidently retired for the purpose of re-arranging her attire for the conquest of the stranger. There was something in Miss Elmore that reminded Walter of Ellinor, and, as the likeness struck him, he felt, by the sudden and involuntary sigh it occasioned, how much the image of his cousin had lately gained ground upon his heart.

Nothing of any note occurred during dinner, until the appearance of the second course, when Elmore, throwing himself back with an air of content, that signified the first edge of his appetite was blunted, observed, Sir, the second course I always opine to be the more dignified and rational part of a repast—

"'Quod nunc ratio est, impetus ante fuit.'"
[That which is now reason, at first was but desire.]

"Ah! Mr. Elmore," said the lady, glancing towards a brace of very fine pigeons, "I cannot tell you how vexed I am at a mistake of the gardener's: you remember my poor pet pigeons, so attached to each other—would not mix with the rest—quite an inseparable friendship, Mr. Lester—well, they were killed by mistake, for a couple of vulgar pigeons. Ah! I could not touch a bit of them for the world."

"My love," said Elmore, pausing, and with great solemnity, "hear how beautiful a consolation is afforded to you in Valerius Maximus:—'Ubi idem et maximus et honestissimus amor est, aliquando praestat morte jungi quam vitae distrahi;' which being interpreted, means, that wherever, as in the case of your pigeons, a thoroughly high and sincere affection exists, it is sometimes better to be joined in death than divided in life.—Give me half the fatter one, if you please, Julia."

"Sir," said Elmore, when the ladies withdrew, "I cannot tell you how pleased I am to meet with a gentleman so deeply imbued with classic lore. I remember, several years ago, before my poor cousin died, it was my lot, when I visited him at Knaresborough, to hold some delightful conversations on learned matters with a very rising young scholar who then resided at Knaresborough,—Eugene Aram. Conversations as difficult to obtain as delightful to remember, for he was exceedingly reserved."

"Aram!" repeated Walter.

"What, you know him then?—and where does he live now?"

"In—, very near my uncle's residence. He is certainly a remarkable man."

"Yes, indeed he promised to become so. At the time I refer to, he was poor to penury, and haughty as poor; but it was wonderful to note the iron energy with which he pursued his progress to learning. Never did I see a youth,—at that time he was no more,—so devoted to knowledge for itself.

'Doctrin' pretium triste magister habet.'"

"Methinks," added Elmore, "I can see him now, stealing away from the haunts of men,

'With even step and musing gait,'—

across the quiet fields, or into the woods, whence he was certain not to re-appear till night-fall. Ah! he was a strange and solitary being, but full of genius, and promise of bright things hereafter. I have often heard since of his fame as a scholar, but could never learn where he lived or what was now his mode of life. Is he yet married?"

"Not yet, I believe; but he is not now so absolutely poor as you describe him to have been then, though certainly far from rich."

"Yes, yes, I remember that he received a legacy from a relation shortly before he left Knaresborough. He had very delicate health at that time: has he grown stronger with increasing years?"

"He does not complain of ill health. And pray, was he then of the same austere and blameless habits of life that he now professes?"

"Nothing could be so faultless as his character appeared; the passions of youth—(ah! I was a wild fellow at his age,) never seemed to venture near one.

'Quem casto erudit docta Minerva sinu.'

Well, I am surprised he has not married. We scholars, Sir, fall in love with abstractions, and fancy the first woman we see is—Sir, let us drink the ladies."

The next day Walter, having resolved to set out for Knaresborough, directed his course towards that town; he thought it yet possible that he might, by strict personal inquiry, continue the clue that Elmore's account had, to present appearance, broken. The pursuit in which he was engaged, combined, perhaps, with the early disappointment to his affections, had given a grave and solemn tone to a mind naturally ardent and elastic. His character acquired an earnestness and a dignity from late events; and all that once had been hope within him, deepened into thought. As now, on a gloomy and clouded day he pursued his course along a bleak and melancholy road, his mind was filled with that dark presentiment—that shadow from the coming event, which superstition believes the herald of the more tragic discoveries, or the more fearful incidents of life; he felt steeled, and prepared for some dread denouement,—to a journey to which the hand of Providence seemed to conduct his steps; and he looked on the shroud that Time casts over all beyond the present moment with the same intense and painful resolve with which, in the tragic representations of life, we await the drawing up of the curtain before the last act, which contains the catastrophe—that while we long, we half shudder to behold.

Meanwhile, in following the adventures of Walter Lester, we have greatly outstript the progress of events of Grassdale, and thither we now return.

CHAPTER IV.

ARAM'S DEPARTURE.—MADELINE.—EXAGGERATION OF SENTIMENT NATURAL IN LOVE.—MADELINE'S LETTER.—WALTER'S.—THE WALK.—TWO VERY DIFFERENT PERSONS, YET BOTH INMATES OF THE SAME COUNTRY VILLAGE.—THE HUMOURS OF LIFE, AND ITS DARK PASSIONS, ARE FOUND IN JUXTA-POSITION EVERYWHERE.

>   Her thoughts as pure as the chaste morning's breath,
>   When from the Night's cold arms it creeps away,
>   Were clothed in words.
>   —Sir J. Suckling—Detraction Execrated

"You positively leave us then to-day, Eugene?" said the Squire.

"Indeed," answered Aram, "I hear from my creditor, (now no longer so, thanks to you,) that my relation is so dangerously ill, that if I have any wish to see her alive, I have not an hour to lose. It is the last surviving relative I have in the world."

"I can say no more, then," rejoined the Squire shrugging his shoulders: "When do you expect to return?"

"At least, ere the day fixed for the wedding," answered Aram, with a grave and melancholy smile.

"Well, can you find time, think you, to call at the lodging in which my nephew proposed to take up his abode,—my old lodging;—I will give you the address,—and inquire if Walter has been heard of there: I confess that I feel considerable alarm on his account. Since that short and hurried letter which I read to you, I have heard nothing of him."

"You may rely on my seeing him if in London, and faithfully reporting to you all that I can learn towards removing your anxiety."

"I do not doubt it; no heart is so kind as yours, Eugene. You will not depart without receiving the additional sum you are entitled to claim from me, since you think it may be useful to you in London, should you find a favourable opportunity of increasing your annuity. And now I will no longer detain you from taking your leave of Madeline."

The plausible story which Aram had invented of the illness and approaching death of his last living relation, was readily believed by the simple family to whom it was told; and Madeline herself checked her tears that she might not, for his sake, sadden a departure that seemed inevitable. Aram accordingly repaired to London that day,—the one that followed the night which witnessed his fearful visit to the "Devil's Crag."

It is precisely at this part of my history that I love to pause for a moment; a sort of breathing interval between the cloud that has been long gathering, and the storm that is about to burst. And this interval is not without its fleeting gleam of quiet and holy sunshine.

It was Madeline's first absence from her lover since their vows had plighted them to each other; and that first absence, when softened by so many hopes as smiled upon her, is perhaps one of the most touching passages in the history of a woman's love. It is marvellous how many things, unheeded before, suddenly become dear. She then feels what a power of consecration there was in the mere presence of the one beloved; the spot he touched, the book he read, have become a part of him—are no longer inanimate—are inspired, and have a being and a voice. And the heart, too, soothed in discovering so many new treasures, and opening so delightful a world of memory, is not yet acquainted with that weariness—that sense of exhaustion and solitude which are the true pains of absence, and belong to the absence not of hope but regret.

"You are cheerful, dear Madeline," said Ellinor, "though you did not think it possible, and he not here!"

"I am occupied," replied Madeline, "in discovering how much I loved him."

We do wrong when we censure a certain exaggeration in the sentiments of those who love. True passion is necessarily heightened by its very ardour to an elevation that seems extravagant only to those who cannot feel it. The lofty language of a hero is a part of his character; without that largeness of idea he had not been a hero. With love, it is the same as with glory: what common minds would call natural in sentiment, merely because it is homely, is not natural, except to tamed affections. That is a very poor, nay, a very coarse, love, in which the imagination makes not the greater part. And the Frenchman, who censured the love of his mistress because it was so mixed with the imagination, quarrelled with the body, for the soul which inspired and preserved it.

Yet we do not say that Madeline was so possessed by the confidence of her love, that she did not admit the intrusion of a single doubt or fear; when she recalled the frequent gloom and moody fitfulness of her lover—his strange and mysterious communings with self—the sorrow which, at times, as on that Sabbath eve when he wept upon her bosom, appeared suddenly to come upon a nature so calm and stately, and without a visible cause; when she recalled all these symptoms of a heart not now at rest, it was not possible for her to reject altogether a certain vague and dreary apprehension. Nor did she herself, although to Ellinor she so affected, ascribe this cloudiness and caprice of mood merely to the result of a solitary and meditative life; she attributed them to the influence of an early grief, perhaps linked with the affections, and did not doubt but that one day or another she should learn its secret. As for remorse—the memory of any former sin—a life so austerely blameless, a disposition so prompt to the activity of good, and so enamoured of its beauty—a mind so cultivated, a temper so gentle, and a heart so easily moved—all would have forbidden, to natures far more suspicious than Madeline's, the conception of such a thought. And so, with a patient gladness, though not without some mixture of anxiety, she suffered herself to glide onward to a future, which, come cloud, come shine, was, she believed at least, to be shared with him.

On looking over the various papers from which I have woven this tale, I find a letter from Madeline to Aram, dated at this time. The characters, traced in the delicate and fair Italian hand coveted at that period, are fading, and, in one part, wholly obliterated by time; but there seems to me so much of what is genuine in the heart's beautiful romance in this effusion, that I will lay it before the reader without adding or altering a word.

"Thank you, thank you, dearest Eugene! I have received, then, the first letter you ever wrote me. I cannot tell you how strange it seemed to me, and how agitated I felt on seeing it, more so, I think, than if it had been yourself who had returned. However, when the first delight of reading it faded away, I found that it had not made me so happy as it ought to have done—as I thought at first it had done. You seem sad and melancholy; a certain nameless gloom appears to me to hang over your whole letter. It affects my spirits—why I know not—and my tears fall even while I read the assurances of your unaltered, unalterable love—and yet this assurance your Madeline—vain girl!—never for a moment disbelieves. I have often read and often heard of the distrust and jealousy that accompany love; but I think that such a love must be a vulgar and low sentiment. To me there seems a religion in love, and its very foundation is in faith. You say, dearest, that the noise and stir of the great city oppress and weary you even more than you had expected. You say those harsh faces, in which business, and care, and avarice, and ambition write their lineaments, are wholly unfamiliar to you;—you turn aside to avoid them,—you wrap yourself up in your solitary feelings of aversion to those you see, and you call upon those not present—upon your Madeline! and would that your Madeline were with you! It seems to me—perhaps you will smile when I say this—that I alone can understand you—I alone can read your heart and your emotions;—and oh! dearest Eugene, that I could read also enough of your past history to know all that has cast so habitual a shadow over that lofty heart and that calm and profound nature! You smile when I ask you—but sometimes you sigh,—and the sigh pleases and soothes me better than the smile.

"We have heard nothing more of Walter, and my father begins at times to be seriously alarmed about him. Your account, too, corroborates that alarm. It is strange that he has not yet visited London, and that you can obtain no clue of him. He is evidently still in search of his lost parent, and following some obscure and uncertain track. Poor Walter! God speed him! The singular fate of his father, and the many conjectures respecting him, have, I believe, preyed on Walter's mind more than he acknowledged. Ellinor found a paper in his closet, where we had occasion to search the other day for something belonging to my father, which was scribbled with all the various fragments of guess or information concerning my uncle, obtained from time to time, and interspersed with some remarks by Walter himself, that affected me strangely. It seems to have been from early childhood the one desire of my cousin to discover his father's fate. Perhaps the discovery may be already made;—perhaps my long-lost uncle may yet be present at our wedding.

"You ask me, Eugene, if I still pursue my botanical researches. Sometimes I do; but the flower now has no fragrance—and the herb no secret, that I care for; and astronomy, which you had just begun to teach me, pleases me more;—the flowers charm me when you are present; but the stars speak to me of you in absence. Perhaps it would not be so, had I loved a being less exalted than you. Every one, even my father, even Ellinor, smile when they observe how incessantly I think of you—how utterly you have become all in all to me. I could not tell this to you, though I write it: is it not strange that letters should be more faithful than the tongue? And even your letter, mournful as it is, seems to me kinder, and dearer, and more full of yourself, than with all the magic of your language, and the silver sweetness of your voice, your spoken words are. I walked by your house yesterday; the windows were closed—there was a strange air of lifelessness and dejection about it. Do you remember the evening in which I first entered that house? Do you—or rather is there one hour in which it is not present to you? For me, I live in the past,—it is the present—(which is without you,) in which I have no life. I passed into the little garden, that with your own hands you have planted for me, and filled with flowers. Ellinor was with me, and she saw my lips move. She asked me what I was saying to myself. I would not tell her—I was praying for you, my kind, my beloved Eugene. I was praying for the happiness of your future years—praying that I might requite your love. Whenever I feel the most, I am the most inclined to prayer. Sorrow, joy, tenderness, all emotion, lift up my heart to God. And what a delicious overflow of the heart is prayer! When I am with you—and I feel that you love me—my happiness would be painful, if there were no God whom I might bless for its excess. Do those, who believe not, love?—have they deep emotions?—can they feel truly—devotedly? Why, when I talk thus to you—do you always answer me with that chilling and mournful smile? You would make religion only the creation of reason—as well might you make love the same—what is either, unless you let it spring also from the feelings?

"When—when—when will you return? I think I love you now more than ever. I think I have more courage to tell you so. So many things I have to say—so many events to relate. For what is not an event to US? the least incident that has happened to either—the very fading of a flower, if you have worn it, is a whole history to me.

"Adieu, God bless you—God reward you—God keep your heart with Him, dearest, dearest Eugene. And may you every day know better and better how utterly you are loved by your

"Madeline."

The epistle to which Lester referred as received from Walter, was one written on the day of his escape from Mr. Pertinax Fillgrave, a short note, rather than letter, which ran as follows.

"My dear Uncle, I have met with an accident which confined me to my bed;—a rencontre, indeed, with the Knights of the Road—nothing serious, (so do not be alarmed!) though the Doctor would fain have made it so. I am just about to recommence my journey, but not towards London; on the contrary, northward.

"I have, partly through the information of your old friend Mr. Courtland, partly by accident, found what I hope may prove a clue to the fate of my father. I am now departing to put this hope to the issue. More I would fain say; but lest the expectation should prove fallacious, I will not dwell on circumstances which would in that case only create in you a disappointment similar to my own. Only this take with you, that my father's proverbial good luck seems to have visited him since your latest news of his fate; a legacy, though not a large one, awaited his return to England from India; but see if I am not growing prolix already—I must break off in order to reserve you the pleasure (may it be so!) of a full surprise!

"God bless you, my dear Uncle! I write in spirits and hope; kindest love to all at home.

"Walter Lester.

"P. S. Tell Ellinor that my bitterest misfortune in the adventure I have referred to, was to be robbed of her purse. Will she knit me another? By the way, I encountered Sir Peter Hales; such an open-hearted, generous fellow as you said! 'thereby hangs a tale.'"

This letter, which provoked all the curiosity of our little circle, made them anxiously look forward to every post for additional explanation, but that explanation came not. And they were forced to console themselves with the evident exhilaration under which Walter wrote, and the probable supposition that he delayed farther information until it could be ample and satisfactory.—"Knights of the Road," quoth Lester one day, "I wonder if they were any of the gang that have just visited us. Well, but poor boy! he does not say whether he has any money left; yet if he were short of the gold, he would be very unlike his father, (or his uncle for that matter,) had he forgotten to enlarge on that subject, however brief upon others."

"Probably," said Ellinor, "the Corporal carried the main sum about him in those well-stuffed saddle-bags, and it was only the purse that Walter had about his person that was stolen; and it is probable that the Corporal might have escaped, as he mentions nothing about that excellent personage."

"A shrewd guess, Nell: but pray, why should Walter carry the purse about him so carefully? Ah, you blush: well, will you knit him another?"

"Pshaw, Papa! Good b'ye, I am going to gather you a nosegay."

But Ellinor was seized with a sudden fit of industry, and somehow or other she grew fonder of knitting than ever.

The neighbourhood was now tranquil and at peace; the nightly depredators that had infested the green valleys of Grassdale were heard of no more; it seemed a sudden incursion of fraud and crime, which was too unnatural to the character of the spot invaded to do more than to terrify and to disappear. The truditur dies die; the serene steps of one calm day chasing another returned, and the past alarm was only remembered as a tempting subject of gossip to the villagers, and (at the Hall) a theme of eulogium on the courage of Eugene Aram.

"It is a lovely day," said Lester to his daughters, as they sate at the window; "come, girls, get your bonnets, and let us take a walk into the village."

"And meet the postman," said Ellinor, archly.

"Yes," rejoined Madeline in the same vein, but in a whisper that Lester might not hear, "for who knows but that we may have a letter from Walter?"

How prettily sounds such raillery on virgin lips. No, no; nothing on earth is so lovely as the confidence between two happy sisters, who have no secrets but those of a guileless love to reveal!

As they strolled into the village, they were met by Peter Dealtry, who was slowly riding home on a large ass which carried himself and his panniers to the neighbouring market in a more quiet and luxurious indolence of action than would the harsher motions of the equine species.

"A fine day, Peter: and what news at market?" said Lester.

"Corn high,—hay dear, your honour," replied the clerk.

"Ah, I suppose so; a good time to sell ours, Peter;—we must see about it on Saturday. But, pray, have you heard any thing from the Corporal since his departure?"

"Not I, your honour, not I; though I think as he might have given us a line, if it was only to thank me for my care of his cat, but—

  'Them as comes to go to roam,
  Thinks slight of they as stays at home.'"

"A notable distich, Peter; your own composition, I warrant."

"Mine! Lord love your honour, I has no genus, but I has memory; and when them ere beautiful lines of poetry-like comes into my head, they stays there, and stays till they pops out at my tongue like a bottle of ginger-beer. I do loves poetry, Sir, 'specially the sacred."

"We know it,—we know it."

"For there be summut in it," continued the clerk, "which smooths a man's heart like a clothes-brush, wipes away the dust and dirt, and sets all the nap right; and I thinks as how 'tis what a clerk of the parish ought to study, your honour."

"Nothing better; you speak like an oracle."

"Now, Sir, there be the Corporal, honest man, what thinks himself mighty clever,—but he has no soul for varse. Lord love ye, to see the faces he makes when I tells him a hymn or so; 'tis quite wicked, your honour,—for that's what the heathen did, as you well know, Sir.

  "'And when I does discourse of things
  Most holy, to their tribe;
  What does they do?—they mocks at me,
  And makes my harp a gibe.'

"'Tis not what I calls pretty, Miss Ellinor."

"Certainly not, Peter; I wonder, with your talents for verse, you never indulge in a little satire against such perverse taste."

"Satire! what's that? Oh, I knows; what they writes in elections. Why, Miss, mayhap—" here Peter paused, and winked significantly—"but the Corporal's a passionate man, you knows: but I could so sting him—Aha! we'll see, we'll see.—Do you know, your honour," here Peter altered his air to one of serious importance, as if about to impart a most sagacious conjecture, "I thinks there be one reason why the Corporal has not written to me."

"And what's that, Peter?"

"Cause, your honour, he's ashamed of his writing: I fancy as how his spelling is no better than it should be—but mum's the word. You sees, your honour, the Corporal's got a tarn for conversation-like—he be a mighty fine talker surely! but he be shy of the pen—'tis not every man what talks biggest what's the best schollard at bottom. Why, there's the newspaper I saw in the market, (for I always sees the newspaper once a week,) says as how some of them great speakers in the Parliament House, are no better than ninnies when they gets upon paper; and that's the Corporal's case, I sispect: I suppose as how they can't spell all them ere long words they make use on. For my part, I thinks there be mortal desate (deceit) like in that ere public speaking; for I knows how far a loud voice and a bold face goes, even in buying a cow, your honour; and I'm afraid the country's greatly bubbled in that ere partiklar; for if a man can't write down clearly what he means for to say, I does not thinks as how he knows what he means when he goes for to speak!"

This speech—quite a moral exposition from Peter, and, doubtless, inspired by his visit to market—for what wisdom cannot come from intercourse?—our good publican delivered with especial solemnity, giving a huge thump on the sides of his ass as he concluded.

"Upon my word, Peter," said Lester, laughing, "you have grown quite a Solomon; and, instead of a clerk, you ought to be a Justice of Peace, at the least: and, indeed, I must say that I think you shine more in the capacity of a lecturer than in that of a soldier."

"'Tis not for a clerk of the parish to have too great a knack at the weapons of the flesh," said Peter, sanctimoniously, and turning aside to conceal a slight confusion at the unlucky reminiscence of his warlike exploits; "But lauk, Sir, even as to that, why we has frightened all the robbers away. What would you have us do more?"

"Upon my word, Peter, you say right; and now, good day. Your wife's well, I hope? and Jacobina—is not that the cat's name?—in high health and favour."

"Hem, hem!—why, to be sure, the cat's a good cat; but she steals Goody Truman's cream as she sets for butter reg'larly every night."

"Oh! you must cure her of that," said Lester, smiling, "I hope that's the worst fault."

"Why, your gardiner do say," replied Peter, reluctantly, "as how she goes arter the pheasants in Copse-hole."

"The deuce!" cried the Squire; "that will never do: she must be shot, Peter, she must be shot. My pheasants! my best preserves! and poor Goody Truman's cream, too! a perfect devil. Look to it, Peter; if I hear any complaints again, Jacobina is done for—What are you laughing at, Nell?"

"Well, go thy ways, Peter, for a shrewd man and a clever man; it is not every one who could so suddenly have elicited my father's compassion for Goody Truman's cream."

"Pooh!" said the Squire, "a pheasant's a serious thing, child; but you women don't understand matters."

They had now crossed through the village into the fields, and were slowly sauntering by

> "Hedge-row elms on hillocks green,"

when, seated under a stunted pollard, they came suddenly on the ill-favoured person of Dame Darkmans: she sat bent (with her elbows on her knees, and her hands supporting her chin,) looking up to the clear autumnal sky; and as they approached, she did not stir, or testify by sign or glance that she even perceived them.

There is a certain kind-hearted sociality of temper that you see sometimes among country gentlemen, especially not of the highest rank, who knowing, and looked up to by, every one immediately around them, acquire the habit of accosting all they meet—a habit as painful for them to break, as it was painful for poor Rousseau to be asked 'how he did' by an applewoman. And the kind old Squire could not pass even Goody Darkmans, (coming thus abruptly upon her,) without a salutation.

"All alone, Dame, enjoying the fine weather—that's right—And how fares it with you?"

The old woman turned round her dark and bleared eyes, but without moving limb or posture. "'Tis well-nigh winter now: 'tis not easy for poor folks to fare well at this time o' year. Where be we to get the firewood, and the clothing, and the dry bread, carse it! and the drop o' stuff that's to keep out the cold. Ah, it's fine for you to ask how we does, and the days shortening, and the air sharpening."

"Well, Dame, shall I send to—for a warm cloak for you?" said Madeline.

"Ho! thankye, young leddy—thankye kindly, and I'll wear it at your widding, for they says you be going to git married to the larned man yander. Wish ye well, ma'am, wish ye well."

And the old hag grinned as she uttered this benediction, that sounded on her lips like the Lord's Prayer on a witch's; which converts the devotion to a crime, and the prayer to a curse.

"Ye're very winsome, young lady," she continued, eyeing Madeline's tall and rounded figure from head to foot. "Yes, very—but I was as bonny as you once, and if you lives—mind that—fair and happy as you stand now, you'll be as withered, and foul-faced, and wretched as me—ha! ha! I loves to look on young folk, and think o' that. But mayhap ye won't live to be old—more's the pity, for ye might be a widow and childless, and a lone 'oman, as I be; if you were to see sixty: an' wouldn't that be nice?—ha! ha!—much pleasure ye'd have in the fine weather then, and in people's fine speeches, eh?"

"Come, Dame," said Lester, with a cloud on his benign brow, "this talk is ungrateful to me, and disrespectful to Miss Lester; it is not the way to—" "Hout!" interrupted the old woman; "I begs pardon, Sir, if I offended—I begs pardon, young lady, 'tis my way, poor old soul that I be. And you meant me kindly, and I would not be uncivil, now you are a-going to give me a bonny cloak,—and what colour shall it be?"

"Why, what colour would you like best, Dame—red?"

"Red!—no!—like a gypsy-quean, indeed! Besides, they all has red cloaks in the village, yonder. No; a handsome dark grey—or a gay, cheersome black, an' then I'll dance in mourning at your wedding, young lady; and that's what ye'll like. But what ha'ye done with the merry bridegroom, Ma'am? Gone away, I hear. Ah, ye'll have a happy life on it, with a gentleman like him. I never seed him laugh once. Why does not ye hire me as your sarvant—would not I be a favourite thin! I'd stand on the thrishold, and give ye good morrow every day. Oh! it does me a deal of good to say a blessing to them as be younger and gayer than me. Madge Darkman's blessing!—Och! what a thing to wish for!"

"Well, good day, mother," said Lester, moving on.

"Stay a bit, stay a bit, Sir;—has ye any commands, Miss, yonder, at Master Aram's? His old 'oman's a gossip of mine—we were young togither—and the lads did not know which to like the best. So we often meets, and talks of the old times. I be going up there now.—Och! I hope I shall be asked to the widding. And what a nice month to wid in; Novimber—Novimber, that's the merry month for me! But 'tis cold—bitter cold, too. Well, good day—good day. Ay," continued the hag, as Lester and the sisters moved on, "ye all goes and throws niver a look behind. Ye despises the poor in your hearts. But the poor will have their day. Och! an' I wish ye were dead—dead—dead, an' I dancing in my bonny black cloak about your graves;—for an't all mine dead—cold—cold—rotting, and one kind and rich man might ha' saved them all."

Thus mumbling, the wretched creature looked after the father and his daughters, as they wound onward, till her dim eyes caught them no longer; and then, drawing her rags round her, she rose, and struck into the opposite path that led to Aram's house.

"I hope that hag will be no constant visitor at your future residence, Madeline," said the younger sister; "it would be like a blight on the air."

"And if we could remove her from the parish," said Lester, "it would be a happy day for the village. Yet, strange as it may seem, so great is her power over them all, that there is never a marriage, nor a christening in the village, from which she is absent—they dread her spite and foul tongue enough, to make them even ask humbly for her presence."

"And the hag seems to know that her bad qualities are a good policy, and obtain more respect than amiability would do," said Ellinor. "I think there is some design in all she utters."

"I don't know how it is, but the words and sight of that woman have struck a damp into my heart," said Madeline, musingly.

"It would be wonderful if they had not, child," said Lester, soothingly; and he changed the conversation to other topics.

As concluding their walk, they re-entered the village, they encountered that most welcome of all visitants to a country village, the postman—a tall, thin pedestrian, famous for swiftness of foot, with a cheerful face, a swinging gait, and Lester's bag slung over his shoulder. Our little party quickened their pace—one letter—for Madeline—Aram's handwriting. Happy blush—bright smile! Ah! no meeting ever gives the delight that a letter can inspire in the short absences of a first love "And none for me," said Lester, in a disappointed tone, and Ellinor's hand hung more heavily on his arm, and her step moved slower. "It is very strange in Walter; but I am more angry than alarmed."

"Be sure," said Ellinor, after a pause, "that it is not his fault. Something may have happened to him. Good Heavens! if he has been attacked again—those fearful highwaymen!"

"Nay," said Lester, "the most probable supposition after all is, that he will not write until his expectations are realized or destroyed. Natural enough, too; it is what I should have done, if I had been in his place."

"Natural," said Ellinor, who now attacked where she before defended—"Natural not to give us one line, to say he is well and safe—natural; I could not have been so remiss!"

"Ay, child, you women are so fond of writing,—'tis not so with us, especially when we are moving about: it is always—'Well, I must write to-morrow—well, I must write when this is settled—well, I must write when I arrive at such a place;'—and, meanwhile, time slips on, till perhaps we get ashamed of writing at all. I heard a great man say once, that 'Men must have something effeminate about them to be good correspondents;' and 'faith, I think it's true enough on the whole."

"I wonder if Madeline thinks so?" said Ellinor, enviously glancing at her sister's absorption, as, lingering a little behind, she devoured the contents of her letter.

"He is coming home immediately, dear father; perhaps he may be here to-morrow," cried Madeline abruptly; "think of that, Ellinor! Ah! and he writes in spirits!"—and the poor girl clapped her hands delightedly, as the colour danced joyously over her cheek and neck.

"I am glad to hear it," quoth Lester; "we shall have him at last beat even Ellinor in gaiety!"

"That may easily be," sighed Ellinor to herself, as she glided past them into the house, and sought her own chamber.

CHAPTER V.

```
A REFLECTION NEW AND STRANGE.—THE STREETS OF LONDON.—A GREAT
   MAN'S LIBRARY.—A CONVERSATION BETWEEN THE STUDENT AND AN
      ACQUAINTANCE OF THE READER'S.—ITS RESULT.
```

```
         Rollo. Ask for thyself.
         Lat. What more can concern me than this?
              —The Tragedy of Rollo.
```

It was an evening in the declining autumn of 1758; some public ceremony had occurred during the day, and the crowd, which it had assembled was only now gradually lessening, as the shadows darkened along the streets. Through this crowd, self-absorbed as usual—with them—not one of them—Eugene Aram slowly wound his uncompanioned way. What an incalculable field of dread and sombre contemplation is opened to every man who, with his heart disengaged from himself, and his eyes accustomed to the sharp observance of his tribe, walks through the streets of a great city! What a world of dark and troublous secrets in the breast of every one who hurries by you! Goethe has said somewhere, that each of us, the best as the worst, hides within him something—some feeling, some remembrance that, if known, would make you hate him. No doubt the saying is exaggerated; but still, what a gloomy and profound sublimity in the idea!—what a new insight it gives into the hearts of the common herd!—with what a strange interest it may inspire us for the humblest, the tritest passenger that shoulders us in the great thoroughfare of life! One of the greatest pleasures in the world is to walk alone, and at night, (while they are yet crowded,) through the long lamplit streets of this huge metropolis. There, even more than in the silence of woods and fields, seems to me the source of endless, various meditation.

There was that in Aram's person which irresistibly commanded attention. The earnest composure of his countenance, its thoughtful paleness, the long hair falling back, the peculiar and estranged air of his whole figure, accompanied as it was, by a mildness of expression, and that lofty abstraction which characterises one who is a brooder over his own heart—a ponderer and a soothsayer to his own dreams;—all these arrested from time to time the second gaze of the passenger, and forced on him the impression, simple as was the dress, and unpretending as was the gait of the stranger, that in indulging that second gaze, he was in all probability satisfying the curiosity which makes us love to fix our regard upon any remarkable man.

At length Aram turned from the more crowded streets, and in a short time paused before one of the most princely houses in London. It was surrounded by a spacious court-yard, and over the porch, the arms of the owner, with the coronet and supporters, were raised in stone.

"Is Lord—within?" asked Aram of the bluff porter who appeared at the gate.

"My Lord is at dinner," replied the porter, thinking the answer quite sufficient, and about to reclose the gate upon the unseasonable visitor.

"I am glad to find he is at home," rejoined Aram, gliding past the servant, with an air of quiet and unconscious command, and passing the court-yard to the main building.

At the door of the house, to which you ascended by a flight of stone steps, the valet of the nobleman—the only nobleman introduced in our tale, and consequently the same whom we have presented to our reader in the earlier part of this work, happened to be lounging and enjoying the smoke of the evening air. High-bred, prudent, and sagacious, Lord—knew well how often great men, especially in public life, obtain odium for the rudeness of their domestics, and all those, especially about himself, had been consequently tutored into the habits of universal courtesy and deference, to the lowest stranger, as well as to the highest guest. And trifling as this may seem, it was an act of morality as well as of prudence. Few can guess what pain may be saved to poor and proud men of merit by a similar precaution. The valet, therefore, replied to Aram's inquiry with great politeness; he recollected the name and repute of Aram, and as the Earl, taking delight in the company of men of letters, was generally easy of access to all such—the great man's great man instantly conducted the Student to the Earl's library, and informing him that his Lordship had not yet left the dining-room, where he was entertaining a large party, assured him that he should be informed of Aram's visit the moment he did so.

Lord—was still in office: sundry boxes were scattered on the floor; papers, that seemed countless, lay strewed over the immense library-table; but here and there were books of a more seductive character than those of business, in which the mark lately set, and the pencilled note still fresh, showed the fondness with which men of cultivated minds, though engaged in official pursuits, will turn, in the momentary intervals of more arid and toilsome life, to those lighter studies which perhaps they in reality the most enjoy.

One of these books, a volume of Shaftesbury, Aram carefully took up; it opened of its own accord in that most beautiful and profound passage which contains perhaps the justest sarcasm, to which that ingenious and graceful reasoner has given vent.

"The very spirit of Faction, for the greatest part, seems to be no other than the abuse or irregularity of that social love and common affection which is natural to mankind—for the opposite of sociableness, is selfishness, and of all characters, the thorough selfish one—is the least forward in taking party. The men of this sort are, in this respect, true men of moderation. They are secure of their temper, and possess themselves too well to be in danger of entering warmly into any cause, or engaging deeply with any side or faction."

On the margin of the page was the following note, in the handwriting of Lord—.

"Generosity hurries a man into party—philosophy keeps him aloof from it; the Emperor Julian says in his epistle to Themistius, 'If you should form only three or four philosophers, you would contribute more essentially to the happiness of mankind than many kings united.' Yet, if all men were philosophers, I doubt whether, though more men would be virtuous, there would be so many instances of an extraordinary virtue. The violent passions produce dazzling irregularities."

The Student was still engaged with this note when the Earl entered the room. As the door through which he passed was behind Aram, and he trod with a soft step, he was not perceived by the Scholar till he had reached him, and, looking over Aram's shoulder, the Earl said:—"You will dispute the truth of my remark, will you not? Profound calm is the element in which you would place all the virtues."

"Not all, my Lord," answered Aram, rising, as the Earl now shook him by the hand, and expressed his delight at seeing the Student again. Though the sagacious nobleman had no sooner heard the Student's name, than, in his own heart, he was convinced that Aram had sought him for the purpose of soliciting a renewal of the offers he had formerly refused; he resolved to leave his visitor to open the subject himself, and appeared courteously to consider the visit as a matter of course, made without any other object than the renewal of the mutual pleasure of intercourse.

"I am afraid, my Lord," said Aram, "that you are engaged. My visit can be paid to-morrow if—" "Indeed," said the Earl interrupting him, and drawing a chair to the table, "I have no engagements which should deprive me of the pleasure of your company. A few friends have indeed dined with me, but as they are now with Lady—, I do not think they will greatly miss me; besides, an occasional absence is readily forgiven in us happy men of office—we, who have the honour of exciting the envy of all England, for being made magnificently wretched."

"I am glad you allow so much, my Lord," said Aram smiling, "I could not have said more. Ambition only makes a favourite to make an ingrate;—she has lavished her honours on Lord—, and see how he speaks of her bounty?"

"Nay," said the Earl, "I spoke wantonly, and stand corrected. I have no reason to complain of the course I have chosen. Ambition, like any other passion, gives us unhappy moments; but it gives us also an animated life. In its pursuit, the minor evils of the world are not felt; little crosses, little vexations do not disturb us. Like men who walk in sleep, we are absorbed in one powerful dream, and do not even know the obstacles in our way, or the dangers that surround us: in a word, we have no private life. All that is merely domestic, the anxiety and the loss which fret other men, which blight the happiness of other men, are not felt by us: we are wholly public;—so that if we lose much comfort, we escape much care."

The Earl broke off for a moment; and then turning the subject, inquired after the Lesters, and making some general and vague observations about that family, came purposely to a pause.

Aram broke it:—"My Lord," said he, with a slight, but not ungraceful, embarrassment, "I fear that, in the course of your political life, you must have made one observation, that he who promises to-day, will be called upon to perform to-morrow. No man who has any thing to bestow, can ever promise with impunity. Some time since, you tendered me offers that would have dazzled more ardent natures than mine; and which I might have advanced some claim to philosophy in refusing. I do not now come to ask a renewal of those offers. Public life, and the haunts of men, are as hateful as ever to my pursuits: but I come, frankly and candidly, to throw myself on that generosity, which proffered to me then so large a bounty. Certain circumstances have taken from me the small pittance which supplied my wants;—I require only the power to pursue my quiet and obscure career of study—your Lordship can afford me that power: it is not against custom for the Government to grant some small annuity to men of letters—your Lordship's interest could obtain for me this favour. Let me add, however, that I can offer nothing in return! Party politics—Sectarian interests—are for ever dead to me: even my common studies are of small general utility to mankind—I am conscious of this—would it were otherwise!—Once I hoped it would be—but—" Aram here turned deadly pale, gasped for breath, mastered his emotion, and proceeded—"I have no great claim, then, to this bounty, beyond that which all poor cultivators of the abstruse sciences can advance. It is well for a country that those sciences should be cultivated; they are not of a nature which is ever lucrative to the possessor—not of a nature that can often be left, like lighter literature, to the fair favour of the public—they call, perhaps, more than any species of intellectual culture, for the protection of a government; and though in me would be a poor selection, the principle would still be served, and the example furnish precedent for nobler instances hereafter. I have said all, my Lord!"

Nothing, perhaps, more affects a man of some sympathy with those who cultivate letters, than the pecuniary claims of one who can advance them with justice, and who advances them also with dignity. If the meanest, the most pitiable, the most heart-sickening object in the world, is the man of letters, sunk into the habitual beggar, practising the tricks, incurring the rebuke, glorying in the shame, of the mingled mendicant and swindler;—what, on the other hand, so touches, so subdues us, as the first, and only petition, of one whose intellect dignifies our whole kind; and who prefers it with a certain haughtiness in his very modesty; because, in asking a favour to himself, he may be only asking the power to enlighten the world?

"Say no more, Sir," said the Earl, affected deeply, and giving gracefully way to the feeling; "the affair is settled. Consider it utterly so. Name only the amount of the annuity you desire."

With some hesitation Aram named a sum so moderate, so trivial, that the Minister, accustomed as he was to the claims of younger sons and widowed dowagers—accustomed to the hungry cravings of petitioners without merit, who considered birth the only just title to the right of exactions from the public—was literally startled by the contrast. "More than this," added Aram, "I do not require, and would decline to accept. We have some right to claim existence from the administrators of the common stock—none to claim affluence."

"Would to Heaven!" said the Earl, smiling, "that all claimants were like you: pension lists would not then call for indignation; and ministers would not blush to support the justice of the favours they conferred. But are you still firm in rejecting a more public career, with all its deserved emoluments and just honours? The offer I made you once, I renew with increased avidity now."

"'Despiciam dites,'" answered Aram, "and, thanks to you, I may add, 'despiciamque famem.'"

CHAPTER VI.

THE THAMES AT NIGHT.—A THOUGHT.—THE STUDENT RE-SEEKS THE
RUFFIAN.—A HUMAN FEELING EVEN IN THE WORST SOIL.

>   Clem. 'Tis our last interview!
>   Stat. Pray Heav'n it be.
>   —Clemanthes.

On leaving Lord ———'s, Aram proceeded, with a lighter and more rapid step, towards a less courtly quarter of the metropolis.

He had found, on arriving in London, that in order to secure the annual sum promised to Houseman, it had been necessary to strip himself even of the small stipend he had hoped to retain. And hence his visit, and hence his petition to Lord—. He now bent his way to the spot in which Houseman had appointed their meeting. To the fastidious reader these details of pecuniary matters, so trivial in themselves, may be a little wearisome, and may seem a little undignified; but we are writing a romance of real life, and the reader must take what is homely with what may be more epic—the pettiness and the wants of the daily world, with its loftier sorrows and its grander crimes. Besides, who knows how darkly just may be that moral which shows us a nature originally high, a soul once all a-thirst for truth, bowed (by what events?) to the manoeuvres and the lies of the worldly hypocrite?

The night had now closed in, and its darkness was only relieved by the wan lamps that vista'd the streets, and a few dim stars that struggled through the reeking haze that curtained the great city. Aram had now gained one of the bridges 'that arch the royal Thames,' and, in no time dead to scenic attraction, he there paused for a moment, and looked along the dark river that rushed below.

Oh, God! how many wild and stormy hearts have stilled themselves on that spot, for one dread instant of thought—of calculation—of resolve—one instant the last of life! Look at night along the course of that stately river, how gloriously it seems to mock the passions of them that dwell beside it;—Unchanged—unchanging—all around it quick death, and troubled life; itself smiling up to the grey stars, and singing from its deep heart as it bounds along. Beside it is the Senate, proud of its solemn triflers, and there the cloistered Tomb, in which as the loftiest honour, some handful of the fiercest of the strugglers may gain forgetfulness and a grave! There is no moral to a great city like the River that washes its walls.

There was something in the view before him, that suggested reflections similar to these, to the strange and mysterious breast of the lingering Student. A solemn dejection crept over him, a warning voice sounded on his ear, the fearful Genius within him was aroused, and even in the moment when his triumph seemed complete and his safety secured, he felt it only as

```
"The torrent's smoothness ere it dash below."
```

The mist obscured and saddened the few lights scattered on either side the water. And a deep and gloomy quiet brooded round;

```
"The very houses seemed asleep,
And all that mighty heart was lying still."
```

Arousing himself from his short and sombre reverie, Aram resumed his way, and threading some of the smaller streets on the opposite side of the water, arrived at last in the street in which he was to seek Houseman.

It was a narrow and dark lane, and seemed altogether of a suspicious and disreputable locality. One or two samples of the lowest description of alehouses broke the dark silence of the spot;—from them streamed the only lights which assisted the single lamp that burned at the entrance of the alley; and bursts of drunken laughter and obscene merriment broke out every now and then from these wretched theatres of Pleasure As Aram passed one of them, a crowd of the lowest order of ruffian and harlot issued noisily from the door, and suddenly obstructed his way; through this vile press reeking with the stamp and odour of the most repellent character of vice was the lofty and cold Student to force his path! The darkness, his quick step, his downcast head, favoured his escape through the unhallowed throng, and he now stood opposite the door of a small and narrow house. A ponderous knocker adorned the door, which seemed of uncommon strength, being thickly studded with large nails. He knocked twice before his summons was answered, and then a voice from within, cried, "Who's there? What want you?"

"I seek one called Houseman."

No answer was returned—some moments elapsed. Again the Student knocked, and presently he heard the voice of Houseman himself call out, "Who's there—Joe the Cracksman?"

"Richard Houseman, it is I," answered Aram, in a deep tone, and suppressing the natural feelings of loathing and abhorrence.

Houseman uttered a quick exclamation; the door was hastily unbarred All within was utterly dark; but Aram felt with a thrill of repugnance, the gripe of his strange acquaintance on his hand.

"Ha! it is you!—Come in, come in!—let me lead you. Have a care—cling to the wall—the right hand—now then—stay. So—so"—(opening the door of a room, in which a single candle, wellnigh in its socket, broke on the previous darkness;) "here we are! here we are! And, how goes it—eh!"

Houseman, now bustling about, did the honours of his apartment with a sort of complacent hospitality. He drew two rough wooden chairs, that in some late merriment seemed to have been upset, and lay, cumbering the unwashed and carpetless floor, in a position exactly contrary to that destined them by their maker;—he drew these chairs near a table strewed with drinking horns, half-emptied bottles, and a pack of cards. Dingy caricatures of the large coarse fashion of the day, decorated the walls; and carelessly thrown on another table, lay a pair of huge horse-pistols, an immense shovel hat, a false moustache, a rouge-pot, and a riding-whip. All this the Student comprehended with a rapid glance—his lip quivered for a moment—whether with shame or scorn of himself, and then throwing himself on the chair Houseman had set for him, he said, "I have come to discharge my part of our agreement."

"You are most welcome," replied Houseman, with that tone of coarse, yet flippant jocularity, which afforded to the mien and manner of Aram a still stronger contrast than his more unrelieved brutality.

"There," said Aram, giving him a paper; "there you will perceive that the sum mentioned is secured to you, the moment you quit this country. When shall that be? Let me entreat haste."

"Your prayer shall be granted. Before day-break to-morrow, I will be on the road."

Aram's face brightened.

"There is my hand upon it," said Houseman, earnestly. "You may now rest assured that you are free of me for life. Go home—marry—enjoy your existence—as I have done. Within four days, if the wind set fair, I am in France."

"My business is done; I will believe you," said Aram, frankly, and rising.

"You may," answered Houseman. "Stay—I will light you to the door. Devil and death—how the d—d candle flickers."

Across the gloomy passage, as the candle now flared—and now was dulled—by quick fits and starts,—Houseman, after this brief conference, reconducted the Student. And as Aram turned from the door, he flung his arms wildly aloft, and exclaimed in the voice of one, from whose heart a load is lifted—"Now, now, for Madeline. I breathe freely at last."

Meanwhile, Houseman turned musingly back, and regained his room, muttering, "Yes—yes—my business here is also done! Competence and safety abroad—after all, what a bugbear is this conscience!—fourteen years have rolled away—and lo! nothing discovered! nothing known! And easy circumstances—the very consequence of the deed—wait the remainder of my days:—my child, too—my Jane—shall not want—shall not be a beggar nor a harlot."

So musing, Houseman threw himself contentedly on the chair, and the last flicker of the expiring light, as it played upward on his rugged countenance—rested on one of those self-hugging smiles, with which a sanguine man contemplates a satisfactory future.

He had not been long alone, before the door opened; and a woman with a light in her hand appeared. She was evidently intoxicated, and approached Houseman with a reeling and unsteady step.

"How now, Bess? drunk as usual. Get to bed, you she shark, go!"

"Tush, man, tush! don't talk to your betters," said the woman, sinking into a chair; and her situation, disgusting as it was, could not conceal the rare, though somewhat coarse beauty of her face and person.

Even Houseman, (his heart being opened, as it were, by the cheering prospects of which his soliloquy had indulged the contemplation,) was sensible of the effect of the mere physical attraction, and drawing his chair closer to her, he said in a tone less harsh than usual.

"Come, Bess, come, you must correct that d—d habit of yours; perhaps I may make a lady of you after all. What if I were to let you take a trip with me to France, old girl, eh? and let you set off that handsome face, for you are devilish handsome, and that's the truth of it, with some of the French gewgaws you women love. What if. I were? would you be a good girl, eh?"

"I think I would, Dick,—I think I would," replied the woman, showing a set of teeth as white as ivory, with pleasure partly at the flattery, partly at the proposition: "you are a good fellow, Dick, that you are."

"Humph!" said Houseman, whose hard, shrewd mind was not easily cajoled, "but what's that paper in your bosom, Bess? a love-letter, I'll swear."

"'Tis to you then; came to you this morning, only somehow or other, I forgot to give it you till now!"

"Ha! a letter to me?" said Houseman, seizing the epistle in question. "Hem! the Knaresbro' postmark—my mother-in-law's crabbed hand, too! what can the old crone want?"

He opened the letter, and hastily scanning its contents, started up.

"Mercy, mercy!" cried he, "my child is ill, dying. I may never see her again,—my only child,—the only thing that loves me,—that does not loath me as a villain!"

"Heyday, Dicky!" said the woman, clinging to him, "don't take on so, who so fond of you as me?—what's a brat like that!"

"Curse on you, hag!" exclaimed Houseman, dashing her to the ground with a rude brutality, "you love me! Pah! My child,—my little Jane,—my pretty Jane,—my merry Jane,—my innocent Jane—I will seek her instantly—instantly; what's money? what's ease,—if—if—" And the father, wretch, ruffian as he was, stung to the core of that last redeeming feeling of his dissolute nature, struck his breast with his clenched hand, and rushed from the room—from the house.

CHAPTER VII.

```
       MADELINE, HER HOPES.—A MILD AUTUMN CHARACTERISED.
         —A LANDSCAPE.—A RETURN.

         'Tis late, and cold—stir up the fire,
          Sit close, and draw the table nigher;
          Be merry and drink wine that's old,
          A hearty medicine 'gainst a cold,
          Welcome—welcome shall fly round!
       —Beaumont and Fletcher: Song in the Lover's Progress.
```
As when the Great Poet,—
```
              Escaped the Stygian pool, though long detained
              In that obscure sojourn; while, in his flight
              Through utter and through middle darkness borne,
              He sang of chaos, and eternal night:—
```
As when, revisiting the "Holy Light, offspring of heaven first-born," the sense of freshness and glory breaks upon him, and kindles into the solemn joyfulness of adjuring song: so rises the mind from the contemplation of the gloom and guilt of life, "the utter and the middle darkness," to some pure and bright redemption of our nature—some creature of "the starry threshold," "the regions mild of calm and serene air." Never was a nature more beautiful and soft than that of Madeline Lester—never a nature more inclined to live "above the smoke and stir of this dim spot, which men call earth"—to commune with its own high and chaste creations of thought—to make a world out of the emotions which this world knows not—a paradise, which sin, and suspicion, and fear, had never yet invaded—where God might recognise no evil, and Angels forebode no change.

Aram's return was now daily, nay, even hourly expected. Nothing disturbed the soft, though thoughtful serenity, with which his betrothed relied upon the future. Aram's letters had been more deeply impressed with the evidence of love, than even his spoken vows: those letters had diffused not so much an agitated joy, as a full and mellow light of happiness over her heart. Every thing, even Nature, seemed inclined to smile with approbation on her hopes. The autumn had never, in the memory of man, worn so lovely a garment: the balmy and freshening warmth, which sometimes characterises that period of the year, was not broken, as yet, by the chilling winds, or the sullen mists, which speak to us so mournfully of the change that is creeping over the beautiful world. The summer visitants among the feathered tribe yet lingered in flocks, showing no intention of departure; and their song—but above all, the song of the sky-lark—which, to the old English poet, was what the nightingale is to the Eastern—seemed even to grow more cheerful as the sun shortened his daily task;—the very mulberry-tree, and the rich boughs of the horse chesnut, retained something of their verdure; and the thousand glories of the woodland around Grassdale were still chequered with the golden hues that herald, but beautify Decay. Still, no news had been received of Walter: and this was the only source of anxiety that troubled the domestic happiness of the Manor-house. But the Squire continued to remember, that in youth he himself had been but a negligent correspondent; and the anxiety he felt, assumed rather the character of anger at Walter's forgetfulness, than of fear for his safety. There were moments when Ellinor silently mourned and pined; but she loved her sister not less even than her cousin; and in the prospect of Madeline's happiness, did not too often question the future respecting her own.

One evening, the sisters were sitting at their work by the window of the little parlour, and talking over various matters of which the Great World, strange as it may seem, never made a part.

They conversed in a low tone, for Lester sat by the hearth in which a wood fire had been just kindled, and appeared to have fallen into an afternoon slumber. The sun was sinking to repose, and the whole landscape lay before them bathed in light, till a cloud passing overhead, darkened the heavens just immediately above them, and one of those beautiful sun showers, that rather characterize the spring than autumn, began to fall; the rain was rather sharp, and descended with a pleasant and freshening noise through the boughs, all shining in the sun light; it did not, however, last long, and presently there sprang up the glorious rainbow, and the voices of the birds, which a minute before were mute, burst into a general chorus, the last hymn of the declining day. The sparkling drops fell fast and gratefully from the trees, and over the whole scene there breathed an inexpressible sense of gladness—

"The odour and the harmony of eve."

"How beautiful!" said Ellinor, pausing from her work—"Ah, see the squirrel, is that our pet one? he is coming close to the window, poor fellow! Stay, I will get him some bread."

"Hush!" said Madeline, half rising, and turning quite pale, "Do you hear a step without?"

"Only the dripping of the boughs," answered Ellinor.

"No—no—it is he—it is he!" cried Madeline, the blood rushing back vividly to her cheeks, "I know his step!"

And—yes—winding round the house till he stood opposite the window, the sisters now beheld Eugene Aram; the diamond rain glittered on the locks of his long hair; his cheeks were flushed by exercise, or more probably the joy of return; a smile, in which there was no shade or sadness, played over his features, which caught also a fictitious semblance of gladness from the rays of the setting sun which fell full upon them.

"My Madeline, my love, my Madeline!" broke from his lips.

"You are returned—thank God—thank God—safe—well?"

"And happy!" added Aram, with a deep meaning in the tone of his voice.

"Hey day, hey day!" cried the Squire, starting up, "what's this? bless me, Eugene.—wet through too, seemingly! Nell, run and open the door—more wood on the fire—the pheasants for supper—and stay, girl, stay—there's the key of the cellar—the twenty-one port—you know it. Ah! ah! God willing, Eugene Aram shall not complain of his welcome back to Grassdale!"

CHAPTER VIII.

AFFECTION: ITS GODLIKE NATURE.—THE CONVERSATION BETWEEN ARAM
    AND MADELINE.—THE FATALIST FORGETS FATE.

    Hope is a lover's staff; walk hence with that,
    And manage it against despairing thoughts.
        —Two Gentlemen of Verona.

If there be any thing thoroughly lovely in the human heart, it is Affection! All that makes hope elevated, or fear generous, belongs to the capacity of loving. For my own part, I do not wonder, in looking over the thousand creeds and sects of men, that so many religionists have traced their theology,—that so many moralists have wrought their system from—Love. The errors thus originated have something in them that charms us even while we smile at the theology, or while we neglect the system. What a beautiful fabric would be human nature—what a divine guide would be human reason—if Love were indeed the stratum of the one, and the inspiration of the other! What a world of reasonings, not immediately obvious, did the sage of old open to our inquiry, when he said the pathetic was the truest part of the sublime. Aristides, the painter, created a picture in which an infant is represented sucking a mother wounded to the death, who, even in that agony, strives to prevent the child from injuring itself by imbibing the blood mingled with the milk. [Note: Intelligitur sentire mater et timere, ne mortuo lacte sanguinem lambat.] How many emotions, that might have made us permanently wiser and better, have we lost in losing that picture!

Certainly, Love assumes a more touching and earnest semblance, when we find it in some retired and sequestered hollow of the world; when it is not mixed up with the daily frivolities and petty emotions of which a life passed in cities is so necessarily composed: we cannot but believe it a deeper and a more absorbing passion: perhaps we are not always right in the belief.

Had one of that order of angels to whom a knowledge of the future, or the seraphic penetration into the hidden heart of man is forbidden, stayed his wings over the lovely valley in which the main scene of our history has been cast, no spectacle might have seemed to him more appropriate to that lovely spot, or more elevated in the character of its tenderness above the fierce and short-lived passions of the ordinary world, than the love that existed between Madeline and her betrothed. Their natures seemed so suited to each other! the solemn and undiurnal mood of the one was reflected back in hues so gentle, and yet so faithful, from the purer, but scarce less thoughtful character of the other! Their sympathies ran through the same channel, and mingled in a common fount; and whatever was dark and troubled in the breast of Aram, was now suffered not to appear. Since his return, his mood was brighter and more tranquil; and he seemed better fitted to appreciate and respond to the peculiar tenderness of Madeline's affection. There are some stars which, viewed by the naked eye, seem one, but in reality are two separate orbs revolving round each other, and drinking, each from each, a separate yet united existence: such stars seemed a type of them.

Had anything been wanting to complete Madeline's happiness, the change in Aram supplied the want. The sudden starts, the abrupt changes of mood and countenance, that had formerly characterized him, were now scarcely, if ever, visible. He seemed to have resigned himself with confidence to the prospects of the future, and to have forsworn the haggard recollections of the past; he moved, and looked, and smiled like other men; he was alive to the little circumstances around him, and no longer absorbed in the contemplation of a separate and strange existence within himself. Some scattered fragments of his poetry bear the date of this time: they are chiefly addressed to Madeline, and, amidst the vows of love, a spirit, sometimes of a wild and bursting—sometimes of a profound and collected happiness, are visible. There is great beauty in many of these fragments, and they bear a stronger impress of heart—they breathe more of nature and truth, than the poetry that belongs of right to that time.

And thus day rolled on day, till it was now the eve before their bridals. Aram had deemed it prudent to tell Lester, that he had sold his annuity, and that he had applied to the Earl for the pension which we have seen he had been promised. As to his supposed relation—the illness he had created he suffered now to cease; and indeed the approaching ceremony gave him a graceful excuse for turning the conversation away form any topics that did not relate to Madeline, or to that event.

It was the eve before their marriage; Aram and Madeline were walking along the valley that led to the house of the former.

"How fortunate it is!" said Madeline, "that our future residence will be so near my father's. I cannot tell you with what delight he looks forward to the pleasant circle we shall make. Indeed, I think he would scarce have consented to our wedding, if it had separated us from him."

Aram stopped, and plucked a flower.

"Ah! indeed, indeed, Madeline! Yet in the course of the various changes of life, how more than probable it is that we shall be divided from him—that we shall leave this spot."

"It is possible, certainly; but not probable, is it, Eugene?"

"Would it grieve thee irremediably, dearest, were it so?" rejoined Aram, evasively.

"Irremediably! What could grieve me irremediably, that did not happen to you?"

"Should, then, circumstances occur to induce us to leave this part of the country, for one yet more remote, you could submit cheerfully to the change?"

"I should weep for my father—I should weep for Ellinor; but—"

"But what?"

"I should comfort myself in thinking that you would then be yet more to me than ever!"

"Dearest!"

"But why do you speak thus; only to try me? Ah! that is needless."

"No, my Madeline; I have no doubt of your affection. When you loved such as me, I knew at once how blind, how devoted must be that love. You were not won through the usual avenues to a woman's heart; neither wit nor gaiety, nor youth nor beauty, did you behold in me. Whatever attracted you towards me, that which must have been sufficiently powerful to make you overlook these ordinary allurements, will be also sufficiently enduring to resist all ordinary changes. But listen, Madeline. Do not yet ask me wherefore; but I fear, that a certain fatality will constrain us to leave this spot, very shortly after our wedding."

"How disappointed my poor father will be!" said Madeline, sighing.

"Do not, on any account, mention this conversation to him, or to Ellinor; 'sufficient for the day is the evil thereof.'"

Madeline wondered, but said no more. There was a pause for some minutes.

"Do you remember," observed Madeline, "that it was about here we met that strange man whom you had formerly known?"

"Ha! was it?—Here, was it?"

"What has become of him?"

"He is abroad, I hope," said Aram, calmly. "Yes, let me think; by this time he must be in France. Dearest, let us rest here on this dry mossy bank for a little while;" and Aram drew his arm round her waist, and, his countenance brightening as if with some thought of increasing joy, he poured out anew those protestations of love, and those anticipations of the future, which befitted the eve of a morrow so full of auspicious promise.

The heaven of their fate seemed calm and glowing, and Aram did not dream that the one small cloud of fear which was set within it, and which he alone beheld afar, and unprophetic of the storm, was charged with the thunderbolt of a doom, he had protracted, not escaped.

CHAPTER IX.

WALTER AND THE CORPORAL ON THE ROAD.—THE EVENING SETS IN.—
THE GIPSEY TENTS.—ADVENTURE WITH THE HORSEMAN.—THE CORPORAL
DISCOMFITED, AND THE ARRIVAL AT KNARESBOROUGH.

> Long had he wandered, when from far he sees
> A ruddy flame that gleamed betwixt the trees.
> .... Sir Gawaine prays him tell
> Where lies the road to princely Corduel.
> —The Knight of the Sword.

"Well, Bunting, we are not far from our night's resting-place," said Walter, pointing to a milestone on the road.

"The poor beast will be glad when we gets there, your honour," answered the Corporal, wiping his brows.

"Which beast, Bunting?"

"Augh!—now your honour's severe! I am glad to see you so merry."

Walter sighed heavily; there sat no mirth at his heart at that moment.

"Pray Sir," said the Corporal after a pause, "if not too bold, has your honour heard how they be doing at Grassdale?"

"No, Bunting; I have not held any correspondence with my uncle since our departure. Once I wrote to him on setting off to Yorkshire, but I could give him no direction to write to me again. The fact is, that I have been so sanguine in this search, and from day to day I have been so led on in tracing a clue, which I fear is now broken, that I have constantly put off writing till I could communicate that certain intelligence which I flattered myself I should be able ere this to procure. However, if we are unsuccessful at Knaresbro' I shall write from that place a detailed account of our proceedings."

"And I hopes you will say as how I have given your honour satisfaction."

"Depend upon that."

"Thank you Sir, thank you humbly; I would not like the Squire to think I'm ungrateful!—augh,—and mayhap I may have more cause to be grateful by and by, whenever the Squire, God bless him, in consideration of your honour's good offices, should let me have the bit cottage rent free."

"A man of the world, Bunting; a man of the world!"

"Your honour's mighty obleeging," said the Corporal, putting his hand to his hat; "I wonders," renewed he, after a short pause, "I wonders how poor neighbour Dealtry is. He was a sufferer last year; I should like to know how Peter be getting on—'tis a good creature."

Somewhat surprised at this sudden sympathy on the part of the Corporal, for it was seldom that Bunting expressed kindness for any one, Walter replied,—

"When I write, Bunting, I will not fail to inquire how Peter Dealtry is;—does your kind heart suggest any other message to him?"

"Only to ask arter Jacobina, poor thing; she might get herself into trouble if little Peter fell sick and neglected her like—augh. And I hopes as how Peter airs the bit cottage now and then; but the Squire, God bless him, will see to that, and the tato garden, I'm sure."

"You may rely on that, Bunting," said Walter sinking into a reverie, from which he was shortly roused by the Corporal.

"I'spose Miss Madeline be married afore now, your honour: well, pray Heaven she be happy with that ere larned man!"

Walter's heart beat faster for a moment at this sudden remark, but he was pleased to find that the time when the thought of Madeline's marriage was accompanied with painful emotion was entirely gone by; the reflection however induced a new train of idea, and without replying to the Corporal, he sank into a deeper meditation than before.

The shrewd Bunting saw that it was not a favourable moment for renewing the conversation; he therefore suffered his horse to fall back, and taking a quid from his tobacco-box, was soon as well entertained as his master. In this manner they rode on for about a couple of miles, the evening growing darker as they proceeded, when a green opening in the road brought them within view of a gipsy's encampment; the scene was so sudden and so picturesque, that it aroused the young traveller from his reverie, and as his tired horse walked slowly on, the bridle about its neck, he looked with an earnest eye on the vagrant settlement beside his path. The moon had just risen above a dark copse in the rear, and cast a broad, deep shadow along the green, without lessening the vivid effect of the fires which glowed and sparkled in the darker recess of the waste land, as the gloomy forms of the Egyptians were seen dimly cowering round the blaze. A scene of this sort is perhaps one of the most striking that the green lanes of Old England afford,—to me it has always an irresistible attraction, partly from its own claims, partly from those of association. When I was a mere boy, and bent on a solitary excursion over parts of England and Scotland, I saw something of that wild people,—though not perhaps so much as the ingenious George Hanger, to whose memoirs the reader may be referred, for some rather amusing pages on gipsy life. As Walter was still eyeing the encampment, he in return had not escaped the glance of an old crone, who came running hastily up to him, and begged permission to tell his fortune and to have her hand crossed with silver.

Very few men under thirty ever sincerely refuse an offer of this sort. Nobody believes in these predictions, yet every one likes hearing them: and Walter, after faintly refusing the proposal twice, consented the third time; and drawing up his horse submitted his hand to the old lady. In the mean while, one of the younger urchins who had accompanied her had run to the encampments for a light, and now stood behind the old woman's shoulder, rearing on high a pine brand, which cast over the little group a red and weird-like glow.

The reader must not imagine we are now about to call his credulity in aid to eke out any interest he may feel in our story; the old crone was but a vulgar gipsy, and she predicted to Walter the same fortune she always predicted to those who paid a shilling for the prophecy—an heiress with blue eyes—seven children—troubles about the epoch of forty-three, happily soon over—and a healthy old age with an easy death. Though Walter was not impressed with any reverential awe for these vaticinations, he yet could not refrain from inquiring, whether the journey on which he was at present bent was likely to prove successful in its object.

"'Tis an ill night," said the old woman, lifting up her wild face and elfin locks with a mysterious air—"'Tis an ill night for them as seeks, and for them as asks.—He's about—"

"He—who?"

"No matter!—you may be successful, young Sir, yet wish you had not been so. The moon thus, and the wind there—promise that you will get your desires, and find them crosses."

The Corporal had listened very attentively to these predictions, and was now about to thrust forth his own hand to the soothsayer, when from a cross road to the right came the sound of hoofs, and presently a horseman at full trot pulled up beside them.

"Hark ye, old she Devil, or you, Sirs—is this the road to Knaresbro'?"

The Gipsy drew back, and gazed on the countenance of the rider, on which the red glare of the pine-brand shone full.

"To Knaresbro', Richard, the dare-devil? Ay, and what does the ramping bird want in the ould nest? Welcome back to Yorkshire, Richard, my ben cove!"

"Ha!" said the rider, shading his eyes with his hand, as he returned the gaze of the Gipsy—"is it you, Bess Airlie: your welcome is like the owl's, and reads the wrong way. But I must not stop. This takes to Knaresbro' then?"

"Straight as a dying man's curse to hell," replied the crone, in that metaphorical style in which all her tribe love to speak, and of which their proper language is indeed almost wholly composed.

The horseman answered not, but spurred on.

"Who is that?" asked Walter earnestly, as the old woman stretched her tawny neck after the rider.

"An ould friend, Sir," replied the Egyptian, drily. "I have not seen him these fourteen years; but it is not Bess Airlie who is apt to forget friend or foe. Well, Sir, shall I tell your honour's good luck?"—(Here she turned to the Corporal, who sat erect on his saddle with his hand on his holster)—"the colour of the lady's hair—and—"

"Hold your tongue, you limb of Satan!" interrupted the Corporal fiercely, as if his whole tide of thought, so lately favourable to the Soothsayer, had undergone a deadly reversion. "Please your honour, it's getting late, we had better be jogging!"

"You are right," said Walter spurring his jaded horse, and nodding his adieu to the Gipsy,—he was soon out of sight of the encampment.

"Sir," said the Corporal joining his master, "that is a man as I have seed afore; I knowed his ugly face again in a crack—'tis the man what came to Grassdale arter Mr. Aram, and we saw arterwards the night we chanced on Sir Peter Thingumybob."

"Bunting," said Walter, in a low voice, "I too have been trying to recal the face of that man, and I too am persuaded I have seen it before. A fearful suspicion, amounting almost to conviction, creeps over me, that the hour in which I last saw it was one when my life was in peril. In a word, I do believe that I beheld that face bending over me on the night when I lay under the hedge, and so nearly escaped murder! If I am right, it was, however, the mildest of the ruffians; the one who counselled his comrades against despatching me."

The Corporal shuddered.

"Pray, Sir!" said he, after a moment's pause, "do see if your pistols are primed—so—so. 'Tis not out o' nature that the man may have some 'complices hereabout, and may think to way-lay us. The old Gipsy, too, what a face she had! depend on it, they are two of a trade—augh!—bother!—whaugh!"

And the Corporal grunted his most significant grunt.

"It is not at all unlikely, Bunting; and as we are now not far from Knaresbro', it will be prudent to ride on as fast as our horses will allow us. Keep up alongside."

"Certainly—I'll purtect your honour," said the Corporal, getting on that side where the hedge being thinnest, an ambush was less likely to be laid. "I care more for your honour's safety than my own, or what a brute I should be—augh!"

The master and man had trotted on for some little distance, when they perceived a dark object moving along by the grass on the side of the road. The Corporal's hair bristled—he uttered an oath, which by him was always intended for a prayer. Walter felt his breath grow a little thick as he watched the motions of the object so imperfectly beheld; presently, however, it grew into a man on horseback, trotting very slowly along the grass; and as they now neared him, they recognised the rider they had just seen, whom they might have imagined, from the pace at which he left them before, to have been considerably a-head of them.

The horseman turned round as he saw them.

"Pray, gentlemen," said he, in a tone of great and evident anxiety, "how far is it to Knaresbro'?"

"Don't answer him, your honour!" whispered the Corporal.

"Probably," replied Walter, unheeding this advice, "you know this road better than we do. It cannot however be above three or four miles hence."

"Thank you, Sir,—it is long since I have been in these parts. I used to know the country, but they have made new roads and strange enclosures, and I now scarcely recognise any thing familiar. Curse on this brute! curse on it, I say!" repeated the horseman through his ground teeth in a tone of angry vehemence, "I never wanted to ride so quick before, and the beast has fallen as lame as a tree. This comes of trying to go faster than other folks.—Sir, are you a father?"

This abrupt question, which was uttered in a sharp, strained voice, a little startled Walter. He replied shortly in the negative, and was about to spur onward, when the horseman continued—and there was something in his voice and manner that compelled attention: "And I am in doubt whether I have a child or not.—By G—! it is a bitter gnawing state of mind.—I may reach Knaresbro' to find my only daughter dead, Sir!—dead!"

Despite of Walter's suspicions of the speaker, he could not but feel a thrill of sympathy at the visible distress with which these words were said.

"I hope not," said he involuntarily.

"Thank you, Sir," replied the Horseman, trying ineffectually to spur on his steed, which almost came down at the effort to proceed. "I have ridden thirty miles across the country at full speed, for they had no post-horses at the d—d place where I hired this brute. This was the only creature I could get for love or money; and now the devil only knows how important every moment may be.—While I speak, my child may breathe her last!—" and the man brought his clenched fist on the shoulder of his horse in mingled spite and rage.

"All sham, your honour," whispered the Corporal.

"Sir," cried the horseman, now raising his voice, "I need not have asked if you had been a father—if you had, you would have had compassion on me ere this,—you would have lent me your own horse."

"The impudent rogue!" muttered the Corporal.

"Sir," replied Walter, "it is not to the tale of every stranger that a man gives belief."

"Belief!—ah, well, well, 'tis no matter," said the horseman, sullenly. "There was a time, man, when I would have forced what I now solicit; but my heart's gone. Ride on, Sir—ride on,—and the curse of—"

"If," interrupted Walter, irresolutely—"if I could believe your statement:—but no. Mark me, Sir: I have reasons—fearful reasons, for imagining you mean this but as a snare!"

"Ha!" said the horseman, deliberately, "have we met before?"

"I believe so."

"And you have had cause to complain of me? It may be—it may be: but were the grave before me, and if one lie would smite me into it, I solemnly swear that I now utter but the naked truth."

"It would be folly to trust him, Bunting?" said Walter, turning round to his attendant.

"Folly!—sheer madness—bother!"

"If you are the man I take you for," said Walter, "you once lifted your voice against the murder, though you assisted in the robbery of a traveller:—that traveller was myself. I will remember the mercy—I will forget the outrage: and I will not believe that you have devised this tale as a snare. Take my horse, Sir; I will trust you."

Houseman, for it was he, flung himself instantly from his saddle. "I don't ask God to bless you: a blessing in my mouth would be worse than a curse. But you will not repent this: you will not repent it!"

Houseman said these few words with a palpable emotion; and it was more striking on account of the evident coarseness and hardened vulgarity of his nature. In a moment more he had mounted Walter's horse, and turning ere he sped on, inquired at what place at Knaresborough the horse should be sent. Walter directed him to the principal inn; and Houseman, waving his hand, and striking his spurs into the animal, wearied as it was, was out of sight in a moment.

"Well, if ever I seed the like!" quoth the Corporal. "Lira, lira, la, la, la! lira, lara, la, la, la!—augh!—whaugh!—bother!"

"So my good-nature does not please you, Bunting."

"Oh, Sir, it does not sinnify: we shall have our throats cut—that's all.

"What! you don't believe the story."

"I? Bless your honour, I am no fool."

"Bunting!"

"Sir."

"You forget yourself."

"Augh!"

"So you don't think I should have lent the horse?"

"Sartainly not."

"On occasions like these, every man ought to take care of himself? Prudence before generosity?"

"Of a sartainty, Sir."

"Dismount, then,—I want my horse. You may shift with the lame one."

"Augh, Sir,—baugh!"

"Rascal, dismount, I say!" said Walter angrily: for the Corporal was one of those men who aim at governing their masters; and his selfishness now irritated Walter as much as his impertinent tone of superior wisdom.

The Corporal hesitated. He thought an ambuscade by the road of certain occurrence; and he was weighing the danger of riding a lame horse against his master's displeasure. Walter, perceiving he demurred, was seized with so violent a resentment, that he dashed up to the Corporal, and, grasping him by the collar, swung him, heavy as he was,—being wholly unprepared for such force,—to the ground.

Without deigning to look at his condition, Walter mounted the sound horse, and throwing the bridle of the lame one over a bough, left the Corporal to follow at his leisure.

There is not perhaps a more sore state of mind than that which we experience when we have committed an act we meant to be generous, and fear to be foolish.

"Certainly," said Walter, soliloquizing, "certainly the man is a rascal: yet he was evidently sincere in his emotion. Certainly he was one of the men who robbed me; yet, if so, he was also the one who interceded for my life. If I should now have given strength to a villain;—if I should have assisted him to an outrage against myself! What more probable? Yet, on the other hand, if his story be true;—if his child be dying,—and if, through my means, he obtain a last interview with her! Well, well, let me hope so!"

Here he was joined by the Corporal, who, angry as he was, judged it prudent to smother his rage for another opportunity; and by favoring his master with his company, to procure himself an ally immediately at hand, should his suspicions prove true. But for once, his knowledge of the world deceived him: no sign of living creature broke the loneliness of the way. By and by the lights of the town gleamed upon them; and, on reaching the inn, Walter found his horse had been already sent there, and, covered with dust and foam, was submitting itself to the tutelary hands of the hostler.

CHAPTER X.

WALTER'S REFLECTIONS.—MINE HOST.—A GENTLE CHARACTER AND A GREEN OLD AGE.—THE GARDEN, AND THAT WHICH IT TEACHETH.—A DIALOGUE, WHEREIN NEW HINTS TOWARDS THE WISHED FOR DISCOVERY ARE SUGGESTED.—THE CURATE.—A VISIT TO A SPOT OF DEEP INTEREST TO THE ADVENTURER.

I made a posy while the day ran by,
Here will I smell my remnant out, and tie
My life within this band.
    —George Herbert.

    The time approaches,
That will with due precision make us know,
What—
    —Macbeth.

The next morning Walter rose early, and descending into the court-yard of the inn, he there met with the landlord, who—a hoe in his hand,—was just about to enter a little gate that led into the garden. He held the gate open for Walter.

"It is a fine morning, Sir; would you like to look into the garden," said mine host, with an inviting smile.

Walter accepted the offer, and found himself in a large and well-stocked garden, laid out with much neatness and some taste; the Landlord halted by a parterre which required his attention, and Walter walked on in solitary reflection.

The morning was serene and clear, but the frost mingled the freshness with an "eager and nipping air," and Walter unconsciously quickened his step as he paced to and fro the straight walk that bisected the garden, with his eyes on the ground, and his hat over his brows.

Now then he had reached the place where the last trace of his father seemed to have vanished; in how wayward and strange a manner! If no further clue could be here discovered by the inquiry he purposed; at this spot would terminate his researches and his hopes. But the young heart of the traveller was buoyed up with expectation. Looking back to the events of the last few weeks, he thought he recognised the finger of Destiny guiding him from step to step, and now resting on the scene to which it had brought his feet. How singularly complete had been the train of circumstance, which, linking things seemingly most trifling—most dissimilar, had lengthened into one continuous chain of evidence! the trivial incident that led him to the saddler's shop; the accident that brought the whip that had been his father's, to his eye; the account from Courtland, which had conducted him to this remote part of the country; and now the narrative of Elmore leading him to the spot, at which all inquiry seemed as yet to pause! Had he been led hither only to hear repeated that strange tale of sudden and wanton disappearance—to find an abrupt wall, a blank and impenetrable barrier to a course, hitherto so continuously guided on? had he been the sport of Fate, and not its instrument? No; he was filled with a serious and profound conviction, that a discovery that he of all men was best entitled by the unalienable claims of blood and birth to achieve was reserved for him, and that this grand dream and nursed object of his childhood was now about to be embodied and attained. He could not but be sensible, too, that as he had proceeded on his high enterprise, his character had acquired a weight and a thoughtful seriousness, which was more fitted to the nature of that enterprise than akin to his earlier temper. This consciousness swelled his bosom with a profound and steady hope. When Fate selects her human agents, her dark and mysterious spirit is at work within them; she moulds their hearts, she exalts their energies, she shapes them to the part she has allotted them, and renders the mortal instrument worthy of the solemn end.

Thus chewing the cud of his involved and deep reflection, the young adventurer paused at last opposite his host, who was still bending over his pleasant task, and every now and then, excited by the exercise and the fresh morning air, breaking into snatches of some old rustic song. The contrast in mood between himself and this!

"Unvexed loiterer by the world's green ways" struck forcibly upon him. Mine host, too, was one whose appearance was better suited to his occupation than his profession. He might have told some three-and-sixty years, but it was a comely and green old age; his cheek was firm and ruddy, not with nightly cups, but the fresh witness of the morning breezes it was wont to court; his frame was robust, not corpulent; and his long grey hair, which fell almost to his shoulder, his clear blue eyes, and a pleasant curve in a mouth characterized by habitual good humour, completed a portrait that even many a dull observer would have paused to gaze upon. And indeed the good man enjoyed a certain kind of reputation for his comely looks and cheerful manner. His picture had even been taken by a young artist in the neighbourhood; nay, the likeness had been multiplied into engravings, somewhat rude and somewhat unfaithful, which might be seen occupying no inconspicuous or dusty corner in the principal printshop of the town: nor was mine host's character a contradiction to his looks. He had seen enough of life to be intelligent, and had judged it rightly enough to be kind. He had passed that line so nicely given to man's codes in those admirable pages which first added delicacy of tact to the strong sense of English composition. "We have just religion enough," it is said somewhere in the Spectator, "to make us hate, but not enough to make us love one another." Our good landlord, peace be with his ashes! had never halted at this limit. The country innkeeper might have furnished Goldsmith with a counterpart to his country curate; his house was equally hospitable to the poor—his heart equally tender, in a nature wiser than experience, to error, and equally open, in its warm simplicity, to distress. Peace be with thee—Our grandsire was thy patron—yet a patron thou didst not want. Merit in thy capacity is seldom bare of reward. The public want no indicators to a house like thine. And who requires a third person to tell him how to appreciate the value of good nature and good cheer?

As Walter stood, and contemplated the old man bending over the sweet fresh earth, (and then, glancing round, saw the quiet garden stretching away on either side with its boundaries lost among the thick evergreen,) something of that grateful and moralizing stillness with which some country scene (the rura et silentium) generally inspires us, when we awake to its consciousness from the troubled dream of dark and unquiet thought, stole over his mind: and certain old lines which his uncle, who loved the soft and rustic morality that pervades the ancient race of English minstrels, had taught him, when a boy, came pleasantly into his recollection,

```
"With all, as in some rare-limn'd book, we see
Here painted lectures of God's sacred will.
The daisy teacheth lowliness of mind;
The camomile, we should be patient still;
The rue, our hate of Vice's poison ill;
The woodbine, that we should our friendship hold;
Our hope the savory in the bitterest cold."
    —[Henry Peacham.]
```

The old man stopped from his work, as the musing figure of his guest darkened the prospect before him, and said:

"A pleasant time, Sir, for the gardener!"

"Ay, is it so... you must miss the fruits and flowers of summer."

"Well, Sir,—but we are now paying back the garden, for the good things it has given us.—It is like taking care of a friend in old age, who has been kind to us when he was young."

Walter smiled at the quaint amiability of the idea.

"'Tis a winning thing, Sir, a garden!—It brings us an object every day; and that's what I think a man ought to have if he wishes to lead a happy life."

"It is true," said Walter; and mine host was encouraged to continue by the attention and affable countenance of the stranger, for he was a physiognomist in his way.

"And then, Sir, we have no disappointment in these objects:—the soil is not ungrateful, as, they say, men are—though I have not often found them so, by the by. What we sow we reap. I have an old book, Sir, lying in my little parlour, all about fishing, and full of so many pretty sayings about a country life, and meditation, and so forth, that it does one as much good as a sermon to look into it. But to my mind, all those sayings are more applicable to a gardener's life than a fisherman's."

"It is a less cruel life, certainly," said Walter.

"Yes, Sir; and then the scenes one makes oneself, the flowers one plants with one's own hand, one enjoys more than all the beauties which don't owe us any thing; at least, so it seems to me. I have always been thankful to the accident that made me take to gardening."

"And what was that?"

"Why, Sir, you must know there was a great scholar, though he was but a youth then, living in this town some years ago, and he was very curious in plants and flowers and such like. I have heard the parson say, he knew more of those innocent matters than any man in this county. At that time I was not in so flourishing a way of business as I am at present. I kept a little inn in the outskirts of the town; and having formerly been a gamekeeper of my Lord—'s, I was in the habit of eking out my little profits by accompanying gentlemen in fishing or snipe-shooting. So, one day, Sir, I went out fishing with a strange gentleman from London, and, in a very quiet retired spot some miles off, he stopped and plucked some herbs that seemed to me common enough, but which he declared were most curious and rare things, and he carried them carefully away. I heard afterwards he was a great herbalist, I think they call it, but he was a very poor fisher. Well, Sir, I thought the next morning of Mr. Aram, our great scholar and botanist, and thought it would please him to know of these bits of grass: so I went and called upon him, and begged leave to go and show the spot to him. So we walked there, and certainly, Sir, of all the men that ever I saw, I never met one that wound round your heart like this same Eugene Aram. He was then exceedingly poor, but he never complained;

and was much too proud for any one to dare to offer him relief. He lived quite alone, and usually avoided every one in his walks: but, Sir, there was something so engaging and patient in his manner, and his voice, and his pale, mild countenance, which, young as he was then, for he was not a year or two above twenty, was marked with sadness and melancholy, that it quite went to your heart when you met him or spoke to him.—Well, Sir, we walked to the place, and very much delighted he seemed with the green things I shewed him, and as I was always of a communicative temper, rather a gossip, Sir, my neighbours say, I made him smile now and then by my remarks. He seemed pleased with me, and talked to me going home about flowers, and gardening, and such like; and after that, when we came across one another, he would not shun me as he did others, but let me stop and talk to him; and then I asked his advice about a wee farm I thought of taking, and he told me many curious things which, sure enough, I found quite true, and brought me in afterwards a deal of money But we talked much about gardening, for I loved to hear him talk on those matters; and so, Sir, I was struck by all he said, and could not rest till I took to gardening myself, and ever since I have gone on, more pleased with it every day of my life. Indeed, Sir, I think these harmless pursuits make a man's heart better and kinder to his fellow-creatures; and I always take more pleasure in reading the Bible, specially the New Testament, after having spent the day in the garden. Ah! well, I should like to know, what has become of that poor gentleman."

"I can relieve your honest heart about him. Mr. Aram is living in—, well off in the world, and universally liked; though he still keeps to his old habits of reserve."

"Ay, indeed, Sir! I have not heard any thing that pleased me more this many a day."

"Pray," said Walter, after a moment's pause, "do you remember the circumstance of a Mr. Clarke appearing in this town, and leaving it in a very abrupt and mysterious manner?"

"Do I mind it, Sir? Yes, indeed. It made a great noise in Knaresbro'—there were many suspicions of foul play about it. For my part, I too had my thoughts, but that's neither here nor there;" and the old man recommenced weeding with great diligence.

"My friend," said Walter, mastering his emotion; "you would serve me more deeply than I can express, if you would give me any information, any conjecture, respecting this—this Mr. Clarke. I have come hither, solely to make inquiry after his fate: in a word, he is—or was—a near relative of mine!"

The old man looked wistfully in Walter's face. "Indeed," said he, slowly, "you are welcome, Sir, to all I know; but that is very little, or nothing rather. But will you turn up this walk, Sir? it's more retired. Did you ever hear of one Richard Houseman?"

"Houseman! yes. He knew my poor—, I mean he knew Clarke; he said Clarke was in his debt when he left the town so suddenly."

The old man shook his head mysteriously, and looked round. "I will tell you," said he, laying his hand on Walter's arm, and speaking in his ear—"I would not accuse any one wrongfully, but I have my doubts that Houseman murdered him."

"Great God!" murmured Walter, clinging to a post for support. "Go on—heed me not—heed me not—for mercy's sake go on."

"Nay, I know nothing certain—nothing certain, believe me," said the old man, shocked at the effect his words had produced: "it may be better than I think for, and my reasons are not very strong, but you shall hear them.

"Mr. Clarke, you know, came to this town to receive a legacy—you know the particulars."

Walter impatiently nodded assent.

"Well, though he seemed in poor health, he was a lively careless man, who liked any company who would sit and tell stories, and drink o'nights; not a silly man exactly, but a weak one. Now of all the idle persons of this town, Richard Houseman was the most inclined to this way of life. He had been a soldier—had wandered a good deal about the world—was a bold, talking, reckless fellow—of a character thoroughly profligate; and there were many stories afloat about him, though none were clearly made out. In short, he was suspected of having occasionally taken to the high road; and a stranger who stopped once at my little inn, assured me privately, that though he could not positively swear to his person, he felt convinced that he had been stopped a year before on the London road by Houseman. Notwithstanding all this, as Houseman had some respectable connections in the town—among his relations, by the by, was Mr. Aram—as he was a thoroughly boon companion—a good shot—a bold rider—excellent at a song, and very cheerful and merry, he was not without as much company as he pleased; and the first night, he and Mr. Clarke came together, they grew mighty intimate; indeed, it seemed as if they had met before. On the night Mr. Clarke disappeared, I had been on an excursion with some gentlemen, and in consequence of the snow which had been heavy during the latter part of the day, I did not return to Knaresbro' till past midnight. In walking through the town, I perceived two men engaged in earnest conversation: one of them, I am sure, was Clarke; the other was wrapped up in a great coat, with the cape over his face, but the watchman had met the same man alone at an earlier hour, and putting aside the cape, perceived that it was Houseman. No one else was seen with Clarke after that hour."

"But was not Houseman examined?"

"Slightly; and deposed that he had been spending the night with Eugene Aram; that on leaving Aram's house, he met Clarke, and wondering that he the latter, an invalid, should be out at so late an hour, he walked some way with him, in order to learn the cause; but that Clarke seemed confused, and was reserved, and on his guard, and at last wished him good-b'ye abruptly, and turned away. That he, Houseman, had no doubt he left the town that night, with the intention of defrauding his creditors, and making off with some jewels he had borrowed from Mr. Elmore."

"But, Aram? was this suspicious, nay, abandoned character—this Houseman, intimate with Aram?"

"Not at all; but being distantly related, and Houseman being a familiar, pushing sort of a fellow, Aram could not, perhaps, always shake him off; and Aram allowed that Houseman had spent the evening with him."

"And no suspicion rested on Aram?"

The host turned round in amazement.—"Heavens above, no! One might as well suspect the lamb of eating the wolf!"

But not thus thought Walter Lester; the wild words occasionally uttered by the Student—his lone habits—his frequent starts and colloquy with self, all of which had, even from the first, it has been seen, excited Walter's suspicion of former guilt, that had murdered the mind's wholesome sleep, now rushed with tenfold force upon his memory.

"But no other circumstance transpired? Is this your whole ground for suspicion; the mere circumstance of Houseman's being last seen with Clarke?"

"Consider also the dissolute and bold character of Houseman. Clarke evidently had his jewels and money with him—they were not left in the house. What a temptation to one who was more than suspected of having in the course of his life taken to plunder! Houseman shortly afterwards left the country. He has never returned to the town since, though his daughter lives here with his wife's mother, and has occasionally gone up to town to see him."

"And Aram—he also left Knaresbro' soon after this mysterious event?"

"Yes! an old Aunt at York, who had never assisted him during her life, died and bequeathed him a legacy, about a month afterwards. On receiving it, he naturally went to London—the best place for such clever scholars."

"Ha! But are you sure that the aunt died?—that the legacy was left? Might this be no tale to give an excuse to the spending of money otherwise acquired?"

Mine host looked almost with anger on Walter.

"It is clear," said he, "you know nothing of Eugene Aram, or you would not speak thus. But I can satisfy your doubts on this head. I knew the old lady well, and my wife was at York when she died. Besides, every one here knows something of the will, for it was rather an eccentric one."

Walter paused irresolutely. "Will you accompany me," he asked, "to the house in which Mr. Clarke lodged,—and indeed to any other place where it may be prudent to institute inquiry?"

"Certainly, Sir, with the biggest pleasure," said mine host: "but you must first try my dame's butter and eggs. It is time to breakfast."

We may suppose that Walter's simple meal was soon over; and growing impatient and restless to commence his inquiries, he descended from his solitary apartment to the little back-room behind the bar, in which he had, on the night before, seen mine host and his better-half at supper. It was a sung, small, wainscoted room; fishing-rods were neatly arranged against the wall, which was also decorated by a portrait of the landlord himself, two old Dutch pictures of fruit and game, a long, quaint-fashioned fowling-piece, and, opposite the fireplace, a noble stag's head and antlers. On the window-seat lay the Izaak Walton to which the old man had referred; the Family Bible, with its green baize cover, and the frequent marks peeping out from its venerable pages; and, close nestling to it, recalling that beautiful sentence, "suffer the little children to come unto me, and forbid them not," several of those little volumes with gay bindings, and marvellous contents of fay and giant, which delight the hearth-spelled urchin, and which were "the source of golden hours" to the old man's grandchildren, in their respite from "learning's little tenements,"

```
"Where sits the dame, disguised in look profound,
And eyes her fairy throng, and turns her wheel around."
    —[Shenstone's Schoolmistress.]
```

Mine host was still employed by a huge brown loaf and some baked pike; and mine hostess, a quiet and serene old lady, was alternately regaling herself and a large brindled cat from a plate of "toasten cheer."

While the old man was hastily concluding his repast, a little knock at the door was heard, and presently an elderly gentleman in black put his head into the room, and, perceiving the stranger, would have drawn back; but both landlady and landlord bustling up, entreated him to enter by the appellation of Mr. Summers. And then, as the gentleman smilingly yielded to the invitation, the landlady, turning to Walter, said: "Our clergyman, Sir: and though I say it afore his face, there is not a man who, if Christian vertues were considered, ought so soon to be a bishop."

"Hush! my good lady," said Mr. Summers, laughing as he bowed to Walter. "You see, Sir, that it is no trifling advantage to a Knaresbro' reputation to have our hostess's good word. But, indeed," turning to the landlady, and assuming a grave and impressive air, "I have little mind for jesting now. You know poor Jane Houseman,—a mild, quiet, blue-eyed creature, she died at daybreak this morning! Her father had come from London expressly to see her: she died in his arms, and, I hear, he is almost in a state of frenzy."

The host and hostess signified their commiseration. "Poor little girl!" said the latter, wiping her eyes; "her's was a hard fate, and she felt it, child as she was. Without the care of a mother,—and such a father! Yet he was fond of her."

"My reason for calling on you was this," renewed the Clergyman, addressing the host: "you knew Houseman formerly; me he always shunned, and, I fancy, ridiculed. He is in distress now, and all that is forgotten. Will you seek him, and inquire if any thing in my power can afford him consolation? He may be poor: I can pay for the poor child's burial. I loved her; she was the best girl at Mrs. Summers' school."

"Certainly, Sir, I will seek him," said the landlord, hesitating; and then, drawing the Clergyman aside, he informed him in a whisper of his engagement with Walter, and with the present pursuit and meditated inquiry of his guest; not forgetting to insinuate his suspicion of the guilt of the man whom he was now called upon to compassionate.

The Clergyman mused a little, and then, approaching Walter, offered his services in the stead of the Publican in so frank and cordial a manner, that Walter at once accepted them.

"Let us come now, then," said the good Curate—for he was but the Curate—seeing Walter's impatience; "and first we will go to the house in which Clarke lodged; I know it well."

The two gentlemen now commenced their expedition. Summers was no contemptible antiquary; and he sought to beguile the nervous impatience of his companion by dilating on the attractions of the antient and memorable town to which his purpose had brought him;—

"Remarkable," said the Curate, "alike in history and tradition: look yonder" (pointing above, as an opening in the road gave to view the frowning and beetled ruins of the shattered Castle); "you would be at some loss to recognize now the truth of old Leland's description of that once stout and gallant bulwark of the North, when he 'numbrid 11 or 12 towres in the walles of the Castel, and one very fayre beside in the second area.' In that castle, the four knightly murderers of the haughty Becket (the Wolsey of his age) remained for a whole year, defying the weak justice of the times. There, too, the unfortunate Richard the Second,—the Stuart of the Plantagenets—passed some portion of his bitter imprisonment. And there, after the battle of Marston Moor, waved the banners of the loyalists against the soldiers of Lilburne. It was made yet more touchingly memorable at that time, as you may have heard, by an instance of filial piety. The town was greatly straitened for want of provisions; a youth, whose father was in the garrison, was accustomed nightly to get into the deep dry moat, climb up the glacis, and put provisions through a hole, where the father stood ready to receive them. He was perceived at length; the soldiers fired on him. He was taken prisoner, and sentenced to be hanged in sight of the besieged, in order to strike terror into those who might be similarly disposed to render assistance to the garrison. Fortunately, however, this disgrace was spared the memory of Lilburne and the republican arms. With great difficulty, a certain lady obtained his respite; and after the conquest of the place, and the departure of the troops, the adventurous son was released."

"A fit subject for your local poets," said Walter, whom stories of this sort, from the nature of his own enterprise, especially affected.

"Yes: but we boast but few minstrels since the young Aram left us. The castle then, once the residence of Pierce Gaveston,—of Hubert III.—and of John of Gaunt, was dismantled and destroyed. Many of the houses we shall pass have been built from its massive ruins. It is singular, by the way, that it was twice captured by men of the name of Lilburn, or Lilleburn, once in the reign of Edward II., once as I have related. On looking over historical records, we are surprised to find how often certain names have been fatal to certain spots; and this reminds me, by the way, that we boast the origin of the English Sibyl, the venerable Mother Shipton. The wild rock, at whose foot she is said to have been born, is worthy of the tradition."

"You spoke just now," said Walter, who had not very patiently suffered the Curate thus to ride his hobby, "of Eugene Aram; you knew him well?"

"Nay: he suffered not any to do that! He was a remarkable youth. I have noted him from his childhood upward, long before he came to Knaresbro', till on leaving this place, fourteen years back, I lost sight of him.—Strange, musing, solitary from a boy! but what accomplishment of learning he had reached! Never did I see one whom Nature so emphatically marked to be GREAT. I often wonder that his name has not long ere this been more universally noised abroad: whatever he attempted was stamped with such signal success. I have by me some scattered pieces of poetry when a boy; they were given me by his poor father, long since dead; and are full of a dim, shadowy anticipation of future fame. Perhaps, yet, before he dies,—he is still young,—the presentiment will be realized. You too know him, then?"

"Yes! I have known him. Stay—dare I ask you a question, a fearful question? Did suspicion ever, in your mind, in the mind of any one, rest on Aram, as concerned in the mysterious disappearance of my—of Clarke? His acquaintance with Houseman who was suspected; Houseman's visit to Aram that night; his previous poverty—so extreme, if I hear rightly; his after riches—though they perhaps may be satisfactorily accounted for; his leaving this town so shortly after the disappearance I refer to;—these alone might not create suspicion in me, but I have seen the man in moments of reverie and abstraction, I have listened to strange and broken words, I have noted a sudden, keen, and angry susceptibility to any unmeant excitation of a less peaceful or less innocent remembrance. And there seems to me inexplicably to hang over his heart some gloomy recollection, which I cannot divest myself from imagining to be that of guilt."

Walter spoke quickly, and in great though half suppressed excitement; the more kindled from observing that as he spoke, Summers changed countenance, and listened as with painful and uneasy attention.

"I will tell you," said the Curate, after a short pause, (lowering his voice)—"I will tell you: Aram did undergo examination—I was present at it—but from his character and the respect universally felt for him, the examination was close and secret. He was not, mark me, suspected of the murder of the unfortunate Clarke, nor was any suspicion of murder generally entertained until all means of discovering Clarke were found wholly unavailing; but of sharing with Houseman, some part of the jewels with which Clarke was known to have left the town. This suspicion of robbery could not, however, be brought home, even to Houseman, and Aram was satisfactorily acquitted from the imputation. But in the minds of some present at that examination, a doubt lingered, and this doubt certainly deeply wounded a man so proud and susceptible. This, I believe, was the real reason of his quitting Knaresbro' almost immediately after that examination. And some of us, who felt for him and were convinced of his innocence, persuaded the others to hush up the circumstance of his examination, nor has it generally transpired, even to this day, when the whole business is well nigh forgot. But as to his subsequent improvement of circumstance, there is no doubt of his aunt's having left him a legacy sufficient to account for it."

Walter bowed his head, and felt his suspicions waver, when the Curate renewed.

"Yet it is but fair to tell you, who seem so deeply interested in the fate of Clarke, that since that period rumours have reached my ear that the woman at whose house Aram lodged has from time to time dropped words that require explanation—hints that she could tell a tale—that she knows more than men will readily believe—nay, once she was even reported to have said that the life of Eugene Aram was in her power."

"Father of mercy! and did Inquiry sleep on words so calling for its liveliest examination?"

"Not wholly—on their being brought to me, I went to the house, but found the woman, whose habits and character are low and worthless, was abrupt and insolent in her manner; and after in vain endeavouring to call forth some explanation of the words she was reported to have uttered, I left the house fully persuaded that she had only given vent to a meaningless boast, and that the idle words of a disorderly gossip could not be taken as evidence against a man of the blameless character and austere habits of Aram. Since, however, you have now re-awakened investigation, we will visit her before you leave the town; and it may be as well too, that Houseman should undergo a further investigation before we suffer him to depart."

"I thank you! I thank you—I will not let slip one thread of this dark clue."

"And now," said the Curate, pointing to a decent house, "we have reached the lodging Clarke occupied in the town!"

An old man of respectable appearance opened the door, and welcomed the Curate and his companion with an air of cordial respect which attested the well-deserved popularity of the former.

"We have come," said the Curate, "to ask you some questions respecting Daniel Clarke, whom you remember as your lodger. This gentleman is a relation of his, and interested deeply in his fate!"

"What, Sir!" quoth the old man, "and have you, his relation, never heard of Mr. Clarke since he left the town? Strange!—this room, this very room was the one Mr. Clarke occupied, and next to this,—here—(opening a door) was his bed-chamber!"

It was not without powerful emotion that Walter found himself thus within the apartment of his lost father. What a painful, what a gloomy, yet sacred interest every thing around instantly assumed! The old-fashioned and heavy chairs—the brown wainscot walls—the little cupboard recessed as it were to the right of the fire-place, and piled with morsels of Indian china and long taper wine glasses—the small window-panes set deep in the wall, giving a dim view of a bleak and melancholy-looking garden in the rear—yea, the very floor he trod—the very table on which he leant—the very hearth, dull and fireless as it was, opposite his gaze—all took a familiar meaning in his eye, and breathed a household voice into his ear. And when he entered the inner room, how, even to suffocation, were those strange, half sad, yet not all bitter emotions increased. There was the bed on which his father had rested on the night before—what? perhaps his murder! The bed, probably a relic from the castle, when its antique furniture was set up to public sale, was hung with faded tapestry, and above its dark and polished summit were hearselike and heavy trappings. Old commodes of rudely carved oak, a discoloured glass in a japan frame, a ponderous arm-chair of Elizabethan fashion, and covered with the same tapestry as the bed, altogether gave that uneasy and sepulchral impression to the mind so commonly produced by the relics of a mouldering and forgotten antiquity.

"It looks cheerless, Sir," said the owner, "but then we have not had any regular lodger for years; it is just the same as when Mr. Clarke lived here. But bless you, Sir, he made the dull rooms look gay enough. He was a blithesome gentleman. He and his friends, Mr. Houseman especially, used to make the walls ring again when they were over their cups!"

"It might have been better for Mr. Clarke," said the Curate, "had he chosen his comrades with more discretion. Houseman was not a creditable, perhaps not a safe companion."

"That was no business of mine then," quoth the lodging-letter; "but it might be now, since I have been a married man!"

The Curate smiled, "Perhaps you, Mr. Moor, bore a part in those revels?"

"Why, indeed, Mr. Clarke would occasionally make me take a glass or so, Sir."

"And you must then have heard the conversations that took place between Houseman and him? Did Mr. Clarke, ever, in those conversations, intimate an intention of leaving the town soon? and where, if so, did he talk of going?"

"Oh! first to London. I have often heard him talk of going to London, and then taking a trip to see some relations of his in a distant part of the country. I remember his caressing a little boy of my brother's; you know Jack, Sir, not a little boy now, almost as tall as this gentleman. 'Ah,' said he with a sort of sigh, 'ah! I have a boy at home about this age,—when shall I see him again?'"

"When indeed!" thought Walter, turning away his face at this anecdote, to him so naturally affecting.

"And the night that Clarke left you, were you aware of his absence?"

"No! he went to his room at his usual hour, which was late, and the next morning I found his bed had not been slept in, and that he was gone—gone with all his jewels, money, and valuables; heavy luggage he had none. He was a cunning gentleman; he never loved paying a bill. He was greatly in debt in different parts of the town, though he had not been here long. He ordered everything and paid for nothing."

Walter groaned. It was his father's character exactly; partly it might be from dishonest principles superadded to the earlier feelings of his nature; but partly also from that temperament at once careless and procrastinating, which, more often than vice, loses men the advantage of reputation.

"Then in your own mind, and from your knowledge of him," renewed the Curate, "you would suppose that Clarke's disappearance was intentional; that though nothing has since been heard of him, none of the blacker rumours afloat were well founded?"

"I confess, Sir, begging this gentleman's pardon who you say is a relation, I confess I see no reason to think otherwise."

"Was Mr. Aram, Eugene Aram, ever a guest of Clarke's? Did you ever see them together?"

"Never at this house. I fancy Houseman once presented Mr. Aram to Clarke; and that they may have met and conversed some two or three times, not more, I believe; they were scarcely congenial spirits, Sir."

Walter having now recovered his self-possession, entered into the conversation; and endeavoured by as minute an examination as his ingenuity could suggest, to obtain some additional light upon the mysterious subject so deeply at his heart. Nothing, however, of any effectual import was obtained from the good man of the house. He had evidently persuaded himself that Clarke's disappearance was easily accounted for, and would scarcely lend attention to any other suggestion than that of Clarke's dishonesty. Nor did his recollection of the meetings between Houseman and Clarke furnish him with any thing worthy of narration. With a spirit somewhat damped and disappointed, Walter, accompanied by the Curate, recommenced his expedition.

CHAPTER XI.

GRIEF IN A RUFFIAN.—THE CHAMBER OF EARLY DEATH.—A HOMELY YET MOMENTOUS CONFESSION.—THE EARTH'S SECRETS.—THE CAVERN.—THE ACCUSATION.

```
        ALL is not well;
    I doubt some foul play.
    . . . . . . . . . . . .
```

```
        Foul deeds will rise,
Though all the earth o'erwhelm them, to men's eyes.
                —Hamlet.
```

As they passed through the street, they perceived three or four persons standing round the open door of a house of ordinary description, the windows of which were partially closed.

"It is the house," said the curate, "in which Houseman's daughter died,—poor, poor child! Yet why mourn for the young? Better that the light cloud should fade away into heaven with the morning breath, than travel through the weary day to gather in darkness and end in storm."

"Ah, sir!" said an old man, leaning on his stick and lifting his hat, in obeisance to the curate, "the father is within, and takes on bitterly. He drives them all away from the room, and sits moaning by the bedside, as if he was a going out of his mind. Won't your reverence go in to him a bit?"

The curate looked at Walter inquiringly. "Perhaps," said the latter, "you had better go in: I will wait without." While the curate hesitated, they heard a voice in the passage; and presently Houseman was seen at the far end, driving some women before him with vehement gesticulations. "I tell you, ye hell-hags," shrieked his harsh and now straining voice, "that ye suffered her to die! Why did ye not send to London for physicians? Am I not rich enough to buy my child's life at any price? By the living ___, I would have turned your very bodies into gold to have saved her! But she's DEAD! and I ___ Out of my sight; out of my way!" And with his hands clenched, his brows knit, and his head uncovered, Houseman sallied forth from the door, and Walter recognized the traveller of the preceding night. He stopped abruptly as he saw the little knot without, and scowled round at each of them with a malignant and ferocious aspect. "Very well, it's very well, neighbors!" said he at length, with a fierce laugh; "this is kind! You have come to welcome Richard Houseman home, have ye? Good, good! Not to gloat at his distress? Lord, no! Ye have no idle curiosity, no prying, searching, gossiping devil within ye that makes ye love to flock and gape and chatter when poor men suffer! This is all pure compassion; and Houseman, the good, gentle, peaceful, honest Houseman, you feel for him,—I know you do! Hark ye, begone! Away, march, tramp, or—Ha, ha! there they go, there they go!" laughing wildly again as the frightened neighbors shrank from the spot, leaving only Walter and the clergyman with the childless man.

"Be comforted, Houseman!" said Summers, soothingly; "it is a dreadful affliction that you have sustained. I knew your daughter well: you may have heard her speak of me. Let us in, and try what heavenly comfort there is in prayer."

"Prayer! pooh! I am Richard Houseman!"

"Lives there one man for whom prayer is unavailing?"

"Out, canter, out! My pretty Jane! And she laid her head on my bosom, and looked up in my face, and so—died!"

"Come," said the curate, placing his hand on Houseman's arm, "come."

Before he could proceed, Houseman, who was muttering to himself, shook him off roughly, and hurried away up the street; but after he had gone a few paces, he turned back, and approaching the curate, said, in a more collected tone: "I pray you, sir, since you are a clergyman (I recollect your face, and I recollect Jane said you had been good to her),—I pray you go and say a few words over her. But stay,—don't bring in my name; you understand. I don't wish God to recollect that there lives such a man as he who now addresses you. Halloo! [shouting to the women] my hat, and stick too. Fal la! la! fal la!—why should these things make us play the madman? It is a fine day, sir; we shall have a late winter.

"Curse the b___, how long she is! Yet the hat was left below. But when a death is in the house, sir, it throws things into confusion: don't you find it so?"

Here one of the women, pale, trembling, and tearful, brought the ruffian his hat; and placing it deliberately on his head, and bowing with a dreadful and convulsive attempt to smile, he walked slowly away and disappeared.

"What strange mummers grief makes!" said the curate. "It is an appalling spectacle when it thus wrings out feeling from a man of that mould! But pardon me, my young friend; let me tarry here for a moment."

"I will enter the house with you," said Walter. And the two men walked in, and in a few moments they stood within the chamber of death.

The face of the deceased had not yet suffered the last withering change. Her young countenance was hushed and serene, and but for the fixedness of the smile, you might have thought the lips moved. So delicate, fair, and gentle were the features that it was scarcely possible to believe such a scion could spring from such a stock; and it seemed no longer wonderful that a thing so young, so innocent, so lovely, and so early blighted should have touched that reckless and dark nature which rejected all other invasion of the softer emotions. The curate wiped his eyes, and kneeling down prayed, if not for the dead (who, as our Church teaches, are beyond human intercession), perhaps for the father she had left on earth, more to be pitied of the two! Nor to Walter was the scene without something more impressive and thrilling than its mere pathos alone. He, now standing beside the corpse of Houseman's child, was son to the man of whose murder Houseman had been suspected. The childless and the fatherless,—might there be no retribution here?

When the curate's prayer was over, and he and Walter escaped from the incoherent blessings and complaints of the women of the house, they, with difficulty resisting the impression the scene had left upon their minds, once more resumed their errand.

"This is no time," said Walter, musingly, "for an examination of Houseman; yet it must not be forgotten."

The curate did not reply for some moments; and then, as an answer to the remark, observed that the conversation they anticipated with Aram's former hostess might throw some light on their researches. They now proceeded to another part of the town, and arrived at a lonely and desolate-looking house, which seemed to wear in its very appearance something strange, sad, and ominous. Some houses have an expression, as it were, in their outward aspect that sinks unaccountably into the heart,—a dim, oppressive eloquence which dispirits and affects. You say some story must be attached to those walls; some legendary interest, of a darker nature, ought to be associated with the mute stone and mortar; you feel a mingled awe and curiosity creep over you as you gaze. Such was the description of the house that the young adventurer now surveyed. It was of antique architecture, not uncommon in old towns; gable ends rose from the roof; dull, small, latticed panes were sunk deep in the gray, discolored wall; the pale, in part, was broken and jagged; and rank weeds sprang up in the neglected garden, through which they walked towards the porch. The door was open; they entered, and found an old woman of coarse appearance sitting by the fireside, and gazing on space with that vacant stare which so often characterizes the repose and relaxation of the uneducated poor. Walter felt an involuntary thrill of dislike come over him as he looked at the solitary inmate of the solitary house.

"Hey day, sir!" said she, in a grating voice, "and what now? Oh! Mr. Summers, is it you? You're welcome, sir! I wishes I could offer you a glass of summut, but the bottle's dry—he! he!" pointing, with a revolting grin, to an empty bottle that stood on a niche within the hearth. "I don't know how it is, sir, but I never wants to eat; but ah! 't is the liquor that does un good!"

"You have lived a long time in this house?" said the curate.

"A long time,—some thirty years an' more."

"You remember your lodger, Mr. Aram?"

"A—well—yes!"

"An excellent man—"

"Humph."

"A most admirable man!"

"A-humph! he!—humph! that's neither here nor there."

"Why, you don't seem to think as all the rest of the world does with regard to him?"

"I knows what I knows."

"Ah! by the by, you have some cock-and-a-bull story about him, I fancy, but you never could explain yourself,—it is merely for the love of seeming wise that you invented it, eh, Goody?"

The old woman shook her head, and crossing her hands on her knee, replied with peculiar emphasis, but in a very low and whispered voice, "I could hang him!"

"Pooh!"

"Tell you I could!"

"Well, let's have the story then!"

"No, no! I have not told it to ne'er a one yet, and I won't for nothing. What will you give me? Make it worth my while."

"Tell us all, honestly, fairly, and fully, and you shall have five golden guineas. There, Goody."

Roused by this promise, the dame looked up with more of energy than she had yet shown, and muttered to herself, rocking her chair to and fro: "Aha! why not? No fear now, both gone; can't now murder the poor old cretur, as the wretch once threatened. Five golden guineas,—five, did you say, sir, five?"

"Ah! and perhaps our bounty may not stop there," said the curate.

Still the old woman hesitated, and still she muttered to herself; but after some further prelude, and some further enticement from the curate, the which we spare our reader, she came at length to the following narration:—

"It was on the 7th of February, in the year '44,—yes, '44, about six o'clock in the evening, for I was a-washing in the kitchen,—when Mr. Aram called to me an' desired of me to make a fire upstairs, which I did; he then walked out. Some hours afterwards, it might be two in the morning, I was lying awake, for I was mighty bad with the toothache, when I heard a noise below, and two or three voices. On this I was greatly afeard, and got out o' bed, and opening the door, I saw Mr. Houseman and Mr. Clarke coming upstairs to Mr. Aram's room, and Mr. Aram followed them. They shut the door, and stayed there, it might be an hour. Well, I could not a think what could make so shy an' resarved a gentleman as Mr. Aram admit these 'ere wild madcaps like at that hour; an' I lay awake a thinking an' a thinking, till I heard the door open agin, an' I went to listen at the keyhole, an' Mr. Clarke said: 'It will soon be morning, and we must get off.' They then all three left the house. But I could not sleep, an' I got up afore five o'clock; and about that hour Mr. Aram an' Mr. Houseman returned, and they both glowered at me as if they did not like to find me a stirring; an' Mr. Aram went into his room, and Houseman turned and frowned at me as black as night. Lord have mercy on me, I see him now! An' I was sadly feared, an' I listened at the keyhole, an' I heard Houseman say: 'If the woman comes in, she'll tell.'

"'What can she tell?' said Mr. Aram; 'poor simple thing, she knows nothing.' With that, Houseman said, says he: 'If she tells that I am here, it will be enough; but however [with a shocking oath], we'll take an opportunity to shoot her.'

"On that I was so frighted that I went away back to my own room, and did not stir till they had gone out, and then—"

"What time was that?"

"About seven o'clock. Well—You put me out! where was I? Well, I went into Mr. Aram's, an' I seed they had been burning a fire, an' that all the ashes were taken out o' the grate; so I went an' looked at the rubbish behind the house, and there sure enough I seed the ashes, and among 'em several bits o' cloth and linen which seemed to belong to wearing apparel; and there, too, was a handkerchief which I had observed Houseman wear (for it was a very curious handkerchief, all spotted) many's the time, and there was blood on it, 'bout the size of a shilling. An' afterwards I seed Houseman, an' I showed him the handkerchief; and I said to him, 'What has come of Clarke?' An' he frowned, and, looking at me, said, 'Hark ye, I know not what you mean; but as sure as the devil keeps watch for souls, I will shoot you through the head if you ever let that d——d tongue of yours let slip a single word about Clarke or me or Mr. Aram,—so look to yourself!'

"An' I was all scared, and trimbled from limb to limb; an' for two whole yearn afterwards (long arter Aram and Houseman were both gone) I never could so much as open my lips on the matter; and afore he went, Mr. Aram would sometimes look at me, not sternly-like, as the villain Houseman, but as if he would read to the bottom of my heart. Oh! I was as if you had taken a mountain off o' me when he an' Houseman left the town; for sure as the sun shines I believes, from what I have now said, that they two murdered Clarke on that same February night. An' now, Mr. Summers, I feels more easy than I has felt for many a long day; an' if I have not told it afore, it is because I thought of Houseman's frown and his horrid words; but summut of it would ooze out of my tongue now an' then, for it's a hard thing, sir, to know a secret o' that sort and be quiet and still about it; and, indeed, I was not the same cretur when I knew it as I was afore, for it made me take to anything rather than thinking; and that's the reason, sir, I lost the good crackter I used to have."

Such, somewhat abridged from its "says he" and "says I," its involutions and its tautologies, was the story which Walter held his breath to hear. But events thicken, and the maze is nearly thridden.

"Not a moment now should be lost," said the curate, as they left the house. "Let us at once proceed to a very able magistrate, to whom I can introduce you, and who lives a little way out of the town."

"As you will," said Walter, in an altered and hollow voice. "I am as a man standing on an eminence, who views the whole scene he is to travel over, stretched before him, but is dizzy and bewildered by the height which he has reached. I know, I feel, that I am on the brink of fearful and dread discoveries; pray God that—But heed me not, sir, heed me not; let us on, on!"

It was now approaching towards the evening; and as they walked on, having left the town, the sun poured his last beams on a group of persons that appeared hastily collecting and gathering round a spot, well known in the neighborhood of Knaresborough, called Thistle Hill.

"Let us avoid the crowd," said the curate. "Yet what, I wonder, can be its cause?" While he spoke, two peasants hurried by towards the throng.

"What is the meaning of the crowd yonder?" asked the curate.

"I don't know exactly, your honor, but I hears as how Jem Ninnings, digging for stone for the limekiln, have dug out a big wooden chest."

A shout from the group broke in on the peasant's explanation,—a sudden simultaneous shout, but not of joy; something of dismay and horror seemed to breathe in the sound.

Walter looked at the curate. An impulse, a sudden instinct, seemed to attract them involuntarily to the spot whence that sound arose; they quickened their pace, they made their way through the throng. A deep chest, that had been violently forced, stood before them; its contents had been dragged to day, and now lay on the sward—a bleached and mouldering skeleton! Several of the bones were loose, and detached from the body. A general hubbub of voices from the spectators,—inquiry, guess, fear, wonder,—rang confusedly around.

"Yes!" said one old man, with gray hair, leaning on a pickaxe, "it is now about fourteen years since the Jew pedlar disappeared. These are probably his bones,—he was supposed to have been murdered!"

"Nay!" screeched a woman, drawing back a child who, all unalarmed, was about to touch the ghastly relics, "nay, the pedlar was heard of afterwards. I'll tell ye, ye may be sure these are the bones of Clarke,—Daniel Clarke,—whom the country was so stirred about when we were young!"

"Right, dame, right! It is Clarke's skeleton," was the simultaneous cry. And Walter, pressing forward, stood over the bones, and waved his hand as to guard them from further insult. His sudden appearance, his tall stature, his wild gesture, the horror, the paleness, the grief of his countenance, struck and appalled all present. He remained speechless, and a sudden silence succeeded the late clamor.

"And what do you here, fools?" said a voice, abruptly. The spectators turned: a new comer had been added to the throng,—it was Richard Houseman. His dress loose and disarranged, his flushed cheeks and rolling eyes, betrayed the source of consolation to which he had flown from his domestic affliction. "What do ye here?" said he, reeling forward. "Ha! human bones? And whose may they be, think ye?"

"They are Clarke's!" said the woman, who had first given rise to that supposition.

"Yes, we think they are Daniel Clarke's,—he who disappeared some years ago!" cried two or three voices in concert. "Clarke's?" repeated Houseman, stooping down and picking up a thigh-bone, which lay at a little distance from the rest; "Clarke's? Ha! ha! they are no more Clarke's than mine!"

"Behold!" shouted Walter, in a voice that rang from cliff to plain; and springing forward, he seized Houseman with a giant's grasp,— "behold the murderer!"

As if the avenging voice of Heaven had spoken, a thrilling, an electric conviction darted through the crowd. Each of the elder spectators remembered at once the person of Houseman, and the suspicion that had attached to his name.

"Seize him! seize him!" burst forth from twenty voices. "Houseman is the murderer!"

"Murderer!" faltered Houseman, trembling in the iron hands of Walter,—"murderer of whom? I tell ye these are not Clarke's bones!"

"Where then do they lie?" cried his arrester.

Pale, confused, conscience-stricken, the bewilderment of intoxication mingling with that of fear, Houseman turned a ghastly look around him, and, shrinking from the eyes of all, reading in the eyes of all his condemnation, he gasped out, "Search St. Robert's Cave, in the turn at the entrance!"

"Away!" rang the deep voice of Walter, on the instant; "away! To the cave, to the cave!"

On the banks of the River Nid, whose waters keep an everlasting murmur to the crags and trees that overhang them, is a wild and dreary cavern, hollowed from a rock which, according to tradition, was formerly the hermitage of one of those early enthusiasts who made their solitude in the sternest recesses of earth, and from the austerest thoughts and the bitterest penance wrought their joyless offerings to the great Spirit of the lovely world. To this desolate spot, called, from the name of its once celebrated eremite, St. Robert's Cave, the crowd now swept, increasing its numbers as it advanced.

The old man who had discovered the unknown remains, which were gathered up and made a part of the procession, led the way; Houseman, placed between two strong and active men, went next; and Walter followed behind, fixing his eyes mutely upon the ruffian. The curate had had the precaution to send on before for torches, for the wintry evening now darkened round them, and the light from the torch-bearers, who met them at the cavern, cast forth its red and lurid flare at the mouth of the chasm. One of these torches Walter himself seized, and his was the first step that entered the gloomy passage. At this place and time, Houseman, who till then, throughout their short journey, had seemed to have recovered a sort of dogged self-possession, recoiled, and the big drops of fear or agony fell fast from his brow.

He was dragged forward forcibly into the cavern; and now as the space filled, and the torches flickered against the grim walls, glaring on faces which caught, from the deep and thrilling contagion of a common sentiment, one common expression, it was not well possible for the wildest imagination to conceive a scene better fitted for the unhallowed burial-place of the murdered dead.

The eyes of all now turned upon Houseman; and he, after twice vainly endeavoring to speak, for the words died inarticulate and choked within him, advancing a few steps, pointed towards a spot on which, the next moment, fell the concentrated light of every torch. An indescribable and universal murmur, and then a breathless silence, ensued. On the spot which Houseman had indicated, with the head placed to the right, lay what once had been a human body!

"Can you swear," said the priest, solemnly, as he turned to Houseman, "that these are the bones of Clarke?"

"Before God, I can swear it!" replied Houseman, at length finding his voice.

"MY FATHER!" broke from Walter's lips as he sank upon his knees; and that exclamation completed the awe and horror which prevailed in the breasts of all present. Stung by a sense of the danger he had drawn upon himself, and despair and excitement restoring, in some measure, not only his natural hardihood, but his natural astuteness, Houseman, here mastering his emotions, and making that effort which he was afterwards enabled to follow up with an advantage to himself of which he could not then have dreamed,—Houseman, I say, cried aloud,

"But I did not do the deed; I am not the murderer."

"Speak out! Whom do you accuse?" said the curate. Drawing his breath hard, and setting his teeth as with some steeled determination, Houseman replied,—

"The murderer is Eugene Aram!"

"Aram!" shouted Walter, starting to his feet: "O God, thy hand hath directed me hither!" And suddenly and at once sense left him, and he fell, as if a shot had pierced through his heart, beside the remains of that father whom he had thus mysteriously discovered.

BOOK V.

> Surely the man that plotteth ill against his
> neighbor perpetrateth ill against himself,
> and the evil design is most evil to him that
> deviseth it.
>   —Hesiod

CHAPTER I.

GRASSDALE.—THE MORNING OF THE MARRIAGE.—THE CRONES GOSSIP.—THE BRIDE
    AT HER TOILET.—THE ARRIVAL.

> JAM veniet virgo, jam dicetur Hymenaeus,
>   Hymen, O Hymenae! Hymen ades, O Hymenae!
>   CATULLUS: Carmen Nuptiale.

It was now the morning in which Eugene Aram was to be married to Madeline Lester. The student's house had been set in order for the arrival of the bride; and though it was yet early morn, two old women, whom his domestic (now not the only one, for a buxom lass of eighteen had been transplanted from Lester's household to meet the additional cares that the change of circumstances brought to Aram's) had invited to assist her in arranging what was already arranged, were bustling about the lower apartments and making matters, as they call it, "tidy."

"Them flowers look but poor things, after all," muttered an old crone, whom our readers will recognize as Dame Darkmans, placing a bowl of exotics on the table. "They does not look nigh so cheerful as them as grows in the open air."

"Tush! Goody Darkmans," said the second gossip. "They be much prettier and finer, to my mind; and so said Miss Nelly when she plucked them last night and sent me down with them. They says there is not a blade o' grass that the master does not know. He must be a good man to love the things of the field so."

"Ho!" said Dame Darkmans, "ho! When Joe Wrench was hanged for shooting the lord's keeper, and he mounted the scaffold wid a nosegay in his hand, he said, in a peevish voice, says he: 'Why does not they give me a tarnation? I always loved them sort o' flowers,—I wore them when I went a courting Bess Lucas,—an' I would like to die with one in my hand!' So a man may like flowers, and be but a hempen dog after all!"

"Now don't you, Goody; be still, can't you? What a tale for a marriage day!"

"Tally vally!" returned the grim hag, "many a blessing carries a curse in its arms, as the new moon carries the old. This won't be one of your happy weddings, I tell ye."

"And why d' ye say that?"

"Did you ever see a man with a look like that make a happy husband? No, no! Can ye fancy the merry laugh o' childer in this house, or a babe on the father's knee, or the happy, still smile on the mother's winsome face, some few years hence? No, Madge! the devil has set his black claw on the man's brow."

"Hush, hush, Goody Darkmans; he may hear o' ye!" said the second gossip, who, having now done all that remained to do, had seated herself down by the window, while the more ominous crone, leaning over Aram's oak chair, uttered from thence her sibyl bodings.

"No," replied Mother Darkmans, "I seed him go out an hour agone, when the sun was just on the rise; and I said, when I seed him stroam into the wood yonder, and the ould leaves splashed in the damp under his feet, and his hat was aboon his brows, and his lips went so,—I said, says I, 't is not the man that will make a hearth bright that would walk thus on his marriage day. But I knows what I knows, and I minds what I seed last night."

"Why, what did you see last night?" asked the listener, with a trembling voice; for Plother Darkmans was a great teller of ghost and witch tales, and a certain ineffable awe of her dark gypsy features and malignant words had circulated pretty largely throughout the village.

"Why, I sat up here with the ould deaf woman, and we were a drinking the health of the man and his wife that is to be, and it was nigh twelve o' the clock ere I minded it was time to go home. Well, so I puts on my cloak, and the moon was up, an' I goes along by the wood, and up by Fairlegh Field, an' I was singing the ballad on Joe Wrench's hanging, for the spirats had made me gamesome, when I sees somemut dark creep, creep, but iver so fast, arter me over the field, and making right ahead to the village. And I stands still, an' I was not a bit afeared; but sure I thought it was no living cretur, at the first sight. And so it comes up faster and faster, and then I sees it was not one thing, but a many, many things, and they darkened the whole field afore me. And what d' ye think they was? A whole body o' gray rats, thousands and thousands on 'em; and they were making away from the outbuildings here. For sure they knew, the witch things, that an ill luck sat on the spot. And so I stood aside by the tree, an' I laughed to look on the ugsome creturs as they swept close by me, tramp, tramp! and they never heeded me a jot; but some on 'em looked aslant at me with their glittering eyes, and showed their white teeth, as if they grinned, and were saying to me, 'Ha, ha! Goody Darkmans, the house that we leave is a falling house, for the devil will have his own.'"

In some parts of the country, and especially in that where our scene is laid, no omen is more superstitiously believed evil than the departure of these loathsome animals from their accustomed habitation; the instinct which is supposed to make them desert an unsafe tenement is supposed also to make them predict, in desertion, ill fortune to the possessor. But while the ears of the listening gossip were still tingling with this narration, the dark figure of the student passed the window, and the old women, starting up, appeared in all the bustle of preparation, as Aram now entered the apartment.

"A happy day, your honor; a happy good morning," said both the crones in a breath; but the blessing of the worse-natured was vented in so harsh a croak that Arum turned round as if struck by the sound, and still more disliking the well-remembered aspect of the person from whom it came, waved his hand impatiently, and bade them begone.

"A-whish, a-whish!" muttered Dame Darkmans,—"to spake so to the poor; but the rats never lie, the bonny things!"

Aram threw himself into his chair, and remained for some moments absorbed in a revery, which did not bear the aspect of gloom. Then, walking once or twice to and fro the apartment, he stopped opposite the chimney-piece, over which were slung the firearms, which he never omitted to keep charged and primed.

"Humph!" he said, half aloud, "ye have been but idle servants; and now ye are but little likely ever to requite the care I have bestowed upon you."

With that a faint smile crossed his features; and turning away, he ascended the stairs that led to the lofty chamber in which he had been so often wont to outwatch the stars,—

"The souls of systems, and the lords of life,
    Through their wide empires."

Before we follow him to his high and lonely retreat we will bring the reader to the manor-house, where all was already gladness and quiet but deep joy.

It wanted about three hours to that fixed for the marriage; and Aram was not expected at the manor-house till an hour before the celebration of the event. Nevertheless, the bells were already ringing loudly and blithely; and the near vicinity of the church to the house brought that sound, so inexpressibly buoyant and cheering, to the ears of the bride with a noisy merriment that seemed like the hearty voice of an old-fashioned friend who seeks in his greeting rather cordiality than discretion. Before her glass stood the beautiful, the virgin, the glorious form of Madeline Lester; and Ellinor, with trembling hands (and a voice between a laugh and a cry), was braiding up her sister's rich hair, and uttering her hopes, her wishes, her congratulations. The small lattice was open, and the air came rather chillingly to the bride's bosom.

"It is a gloomy morning, dearest Nell," said she, shivering; "the winter seems about to begin at last."

"Stay, I will shut the window. The sun is struggling with the clouds at present, but I am sure it will clear up by and by. You don't, you don't leave us—the word must out—till evening."

"Don't cry!" said Madeline, half weeping herself, and sitting down, she drew Ellinor to her; and the two sisters, who had never been parted since birth, exchanged tears that were natural, though scarcely the unmixed tears of grief.

"And what pleasant evenings we shall have," said Madeline, holding her sister's hands, "in the Christmas time! You will be staying with us, you know; and that pretty old room in the north of the house Eugene has already ordered to be fitted up for you. Well, and my dear father, and dear Walter, who will be returned long ere then, will walk over to see us, and praise my housekeeping, and so forth. And then, after dinner, we will draw near the fire,—I next to Eugene, and my father, our guest, on the other side of me, with his long gray hair and his good fine face, with a tear of kind feeling in his eye,—you know that look he has whenever he is affected. And at a little distance on the other side of the hearth will be you—and Walter; I suppose we must make room for him. And Eugene, who will be then the liveliest of you all, shall read to us with his soft, clear voice, or tell us all about the birds and flowers and strange things in other countries. And then after supper we will walk half-way home across that beautiful valley—beautiful even in winter—with my father and Walter, and count the stars, and take new lessons in astronomy, and hear tales about the astrologers and the alchemists, with their fine old dreams. Ah! it will be such a happy Christmas! And then, when spring comes, some fine morning—finer than this—when the birds are about, and the leaves getting green, and the flowers springing up every day, I shall be called in to help your toilet, as you have helped mine, and to go with you to church, though not, alas! as your bridesmaid. Ah! whom shall we have for that duty?"

"Pshaw!" said Ellinor, smiling through her tears.

While the sisters were thus engaged, and Madeline was trying, with her innocent kindness of heart, to exhilarate the spirits, so naturally depressed, of her doting sister, the sound of carriage-wheels was heard in the distance,—nearer, nearer; now the sound stopped, as at the gate; now fast, faster,—fast as the postilions could ply whip and the horses tear along. While the groups in the church-yard ran forth to gaze, and the bells rang merrily all the while, two chaises whirled by Madeline's window and stopped at the porch of the house. The sisters had flown in surprise to the casement.

"It is, it is—good God! it is Walter," cried Ellinor; "but how pale he looks!"

"And who are those strange men with him?" faltered Madeline, alarmed, though she knew not why.

CHAPTER II.

THE STUDENT ALONE IN HIS CHAMBER.—THE INTERRUPTION.—FAITHFUL LOVE.

```
NEQUICQUAM thalamo graves
Hastas....
Vitabis strepitumque et celerem sequi
Ajacem.
    —HORACE: Od. xv. lib. 1.


["In vain within your nuptial chamber will you
shun the deadly spears,... the hostile shout,
and Ajax eager in pursuit."]
```

Alone in his favorite chamber, the instruments of science around him, and books, some of astronomical research, some of less lofty but yet abstruser lore, scattered on the tables, Eugene Aram indulged the last meditation he believed likely to absorb his thoughts before that great change of life which was to bless solitude with a companion.

"Yes," said he, pacing the apartment with folded arms, "yes, all is safe! He will not again return; the dead sleeps now without a witness. I may lay this working brain upon the bosom that loves me, and not start at night and think that the soft hand around my neck is the hangman's gripe. Back to thyself, henceforth and forever, my busy heart! Let not thy secret stir from its gloomy depth! The seal is on the tomb; henceforth be the spectre laid. Yes, I must smooth my brow, and teach my lip restraint, and smile and talk like other men. I have taken to my hearth a watch, tender, faithful, anxious,—but a watch. Farewell the unguarded hour! The soul's relief in speech, the dark and broken, yet how grateful, confidence with self, farewell! And come, thou veil! subtle, close, unvarying, the everlasting curse of entire hypocrisy, that under thee, as night, the vexed world within may sleep, and stir not! and all, in truth concealment, may seem repose!"

As he uttered these thoughts, the student paused and looked on the extended landscape that lay below. A heavy, chill, and comfortless mist sat saddening over the earth. Not a leaf stirred on the autumnal trees, but the moist damps fell slowly and with a mournful murmur upon the unwaving grass. The outline of the morning sun was visible, but it gave forth no lustre: a ring of watery and dark vapor girded the melancholy orb. Far at the entrance of the valley the wild fern showed red and faded, and the first march of the deadly winter was already heralded by that drear and silent desolation which cradles the winds and storms. But amidst this cheerless scene the distant note of the merry marriage-bell floated by, like the good spirit of the wilderness, and the student rather paused to hearken to the note than to survey the scene. "My marriage-bell!" said he. "Could I, two short years back, have dreamed of this? My marriage-bell! How fondly my poor mother, when first she learned pride for her young scholar, would predict this day, and blend its festivities with the honor and the wealth her son was to acquire! Alas! can we have no science to count the stars and forebode the black eclipse of the future? But peace! peace! peace! I am, I will, I shall be happy now! Memory, I defy thee!"

He uttered the last words in a deep and intense tone; and turning away as the joyful peal again broke distinctly on his ear,—

"My marriage-bell! Oh, Madeline, how wondrously beloved, how unspeakably dear thou art to me! What hast thou conquered! How many reasons for resolve, how vast an army in the Past, has thy bright and tender purity overthrown! But thou—No, never shalt thou repent!" And for several minutes the sole thought of the soliloquist was love. But scarce consciously to himself, a spirit, not, to all seeming, befitted to that bridal-day,—vague, restless, impressed with the dark and fluttering shadow of coming change,—had taken possession of his breast, and did not long yield the mastery to any brighter and more serene emotion.

"And why," he said, as this spirit regained its empire over him, and he paused before the "starred tubes" of his beloved science,—"and why this chill, this shiver, in the midst of hope? Can the mere breath of the seasons, the weight or lightness of the atmosphere, the outward gloom or smile of the brute mass called Nature, affect us thus? Out on this empty science, this vain knowledge, this little lore, if we are so fooled by the vile clay and the common air from our one great empire, self! Great God! hast thou made us in mercy, or in disdain? Placed in this narrow world, darkness and cloud around us; no fixed rule for men; creeds, morals, changing in every clime, and growing like herbs upon the mere soil,—we struggle to dispel the shadows; we grope around; from our own heart and our sharp and hard endurance we strike our only light. For what? To show us what dupes we are,—creatures of accident, tools of circumstance, blind instruments of the scorner Fate; the very mind, the very reason, a bound slave to the desires, the weakness of the clay; affected by a cloud, dulled by the damps of the foul marsh; stricken from power to weakness, from sense to madness, to gaping idiocy, or delirious raving, by a putrid exhalation! A rheum, a chill, and Caesar trembles! The world's gods, that slay or enlighten millions, poor puppets to the same rank imp which calls up the fungus or breeds the worm,—pah! How little worth is it in this life to be wise! Strange, strange, how my heart sinks. Well, the better sign, the better sign! In danger it never sank."

Absorbed in these reflections, Aram had not for some minutes noticed the sudden ceasing of the bell; but now, as he again paused from his irregular and abrupt pacings along the chamber, the silence struck him, and looking forth, and striving again to catch the note, he saw a little group of men, among whom he marked the erect and comely form of Rowland Lester, approaching towards the house.

"What!" he thought, "do they come for me? Is it so late? Have I played the laggard? Nay, it yet wants near an hour to the time they expected me. Well, some kindness, some attention from my good father-in-law; I must thank him for it. What! my hand trembles. How weak are these poor nerves; I must rest and recall my mind to itself!"

And indeed, whether or not from the novelty and importance of the event he was about to celebrate, or from some presentiment, occasioned, as he would fain believe, by the mournful and sudden change in the atmosphere, an embarrassment, a wavering, a fear, very unwonted to the calm and stately self-possession of Eugene Aram, made itself painfully felt throughout his frame. He sank down in his chair and strove to re-collect himself; it was an effort in which he had just succeeded, when a loud knocking was heard at the outer door; it swung open; several voices were heard. Aram sprang up, pale, breathless, his lips apart.

"Great God!" he exclaimed, clasping his hands. "'Murderer!'—was that the word I heard shouted forth? The voice, too, is Walter Lester's. Has he returned? Can he have learned—?"

To rush to the door, to throw across it a long, heavy iron bar, which would resist assaults of no common strength, was his first impulse. Thus enabled to gain time for reflection, his active and alarmed mind ran over the whole field of expedient and conjecture. Again, "Murderer!" "Stay me not," cried Walter, from below; "my hand shall seize the murderer!"

Guess was now over; danger and death were marching on him. Escape,—how? whither? The height forbade the thought of flight from the casement! The door?—he heard loud steps already hurrying up the stairs; his hands clutched convulsively at his breast, where his fire-arms were generally concealed,—they were left below. He glanced one lightning glance round the room; no weapon of any kind was at hand. His brain reeled for a moment, his breath gasped, a mortal sickness passed over his heart, and then the MIND triumphed over all. He drew up to his full height, folded his arms doggedly on his breast, and muttering, "The accuser comes,—I have it still to refute the charge!" he stood prepared to meet, nor despairing to evade, the worst.

As waters close over the object which divided them, all these thoughts, these fears, and this resolution had been but the work, the agitation, and the succeeding calm of the moment; that moment was past.

"Admit us!" cried the voice of Walter Lester, knocking fiercely at the door.

"Not so fervently, boy," said Lester, laying his hand on his nephew's shoulder; "your tale is yet to be proved,—I believe it not. Treat him as innocent, I pray,—I command,—till you have shown him guilty."

"Away, uncle!" said the fiery Walter; "he is my father's murderer. God hath given justice to my hands." These words, uttered in a lower key than before, were but indistinctly heard by Aram through the massy door.

"Open, or we force our entrance!" shouted Walter again; and Aram, speaking for the first time, replied in a clear and sonorous voice, so that an angel, had one spoken, could not have more deeply impressed the heart of Rowland Lester with a conviction of the student's innocence,

"Who knocks so rudely? What means this violence? I open my doors to my friends. Is it a friend who asks it?"

"I ask it," said Rowland Lester, in a trembling and agitated voice. "There seems some dreadful mistake: come forth, Eugene, and rectify it by a word."

"Is it you, Rowland Lester? It is enough. I was but with my books, and had secured myself from intrusion. Enter." The bar was withdrawn, the door was burst open, and even Walter Lester, even the officers of justice with him, drew back for a moment as they beheld the lofty brow, the majestic presence, the features so unutterably calm, of Eugene Aram. "What want you, sirs?" said he, unmoved and unfaltering, though in the officers of justice he recognized faces he had known before, and in that distant town in which all that he dreaded in the past lay treasured up. At the sound of his voice the spell that for an instant had arrested the step of the avenging son melted away.

"Seize him!" he cried to the officers; "you see your prisoner."

"Hold!" cried Aram, drawing back. "By what authority is this outrage,—for what am I arrested?"

"Behold," said Walter, speaking through his teeth, "behold our warrant! You are accused of murder! Know you the name of Richard Houseman,—pause, consider,—or that of Daniel Clarke?"

Slowly Aram lifted his eyes from the warrant, and it might be seen that his face was a shade more pale, though his look did not quail, or his nerves tremble. Slowly he turned his gaze upon Walter; and then, after one moment's survey, dropped it once more on the paper.

"The name of Houseman is not unfamiliar to me," said he calmly, but with effort.

"And knew you Daniel Clarke

"What mean these questions?" said Aram, losing temper, and stamping violently on the ground. "Is it thus that a man, free and guiltless, is to be questioned at the behest, or rather outrage, of every lawless boy? Lead me to some authority meet for me to answer; for you, boy, my answer is contempt."

"Big words shall not save thee, murderer!" cried Walter, breaking from his uncle, who in vain endeavored to hold him, and laying his powerful grasp upon Aram's shoulder. Livid was the glare that shot from the student's eye upon his assailer; and so fearfully did his features work and change with the passions within him that even Walter felt a strange shudder thrill through his frame.

"Gentlemen," said Aram at last, mastering his emotions, and resuming some portion of the remarkable dignity that characterized his usual bearing, as he turned towards the officers of justice, "I call upon you to discharge your duty. If this be a rightful warrant, I am your prisoner, but I am not this man's. I command your protection from him!"

Walter had already released his gripe, and said, in a muttered voice,

"My passion misled me; violence is unworthy my solemn cause. God and Justice—not these hands—are my avengers."

"Your avengers!" said Aram. "What dark words are these? This warrant accuses me of the murder of one Daniel Clarke. What is he to thee?"

"Mark me, man!" said Walter, fixing his eyes on Aram's countenance. "The name of Daniel Clarke was a feigned name; the real name was Geoffrey Lester: that murdered Lester was my father, and the brother of him whose daughter, had I not come to-day, you would have called your wife!"

Aram felt, while these words were uttered, that the eyes of all in the room were on him; and perhaps that knowledge enabled him not to reveal by outward sign what must have passed within during the awful trial of that moment.

"It is a dreadful tale," he said, "if true,—dreadful to me, so nearly allied to that family. But as yet I grapple with shadows."

"What! does not your conscience now convict you?" cried Walter, staggered by the calmness of the prisoner. But here Lester, who could no longer contain himself, interposed; he put by his nephew, and rushing to Aram, fell, weeping, upon his neck.

"I do not accuse thee, Eugene, my son, my son! I feel, I know thou art innocent of this monstrous crime; some horrid delusion darkens that poor boy's sight. You, you, who would walk aside to save a worm!" and the poor old man, overcome with his emotions, could literally say no more.

Aram looked down on Lester with a compassionate expression; and soothing him with kind words, and promises that all would be explained, gently moved from his hold, and, anxious to terminate the scene, silently motioned the officers to proceed. Struck with the calmness and dignity of his manner, and fully impressed by it with the notion of his innocence, the officers treated him with a marked respect; they did not even walk by his side, but suffered him to follow their steps. As they descended the stairs, Aram turned round to Walter, with a bitter and reproachful countenance,

"And so, young man, your malice against me has reached even to this! Will nothing but my life content you?"

"Is the desire of execution on my father's murderer but the wish of malice?" retorted Walter; though his heart yet well-nigh misgave him as to the grounds on which his suspicion rested.

Aram smiled, as half in scorn, half through incredulity; and, shaking his head gently, moved on without further words.

The three old women, who had remained in listening astonishment at the foot of the stairs, gave way as the men descended; but the one who so long had been Aram's solitary domestic, and who, from her deafness, was still benighted and uncomprehending as to the causes of his seizure, though from that very reason her alarm was the greater and more acute, she, impatiently thrusting away the officers, and mumbling some unintelligible anathema as she did so, flung herself at the feet of a master whose quiet habits and constant kindness had endeared him to her humble and faithful heart, and exclaimed,—

"What are they doing? Have they the heart to ill-use you? O master, God bless you! God shield you! I shall never see you, who was my only friend—who was every one's friend—any more!"

Aram drew himself from her, and said, with a quivering lip to Rowland Lester,—

"If her fears are true—if—if I never more return hither, see that her old age does not starve—does not want." Lester could not speak for sobbing, but the request was remembered. And now Aram, turning aside his proud head to conceal his emotion, beheld open the door of the room so trimly prepared for Madeline's reception: the flowers smiled upon him from their stands. "Lead on, gentlemen," he said quickly. And so Eugene Aram passed his threshold!

"Ho, ho!" muttered the old hag whose predictions in the morning had been so ominous,—"ho, ho! you'll believe Goody Darkmans another time! Providence respects the sayings of the ould. 'T was not for nothing the rats grinned at me last night. But let's in and have a warm glass. He, he! there will be all the strong liquors for us now; the Lord is merciful to the poor!"

As the little group proceeded through the valley, the officers first, Aram and Lester side by side, Walter, with his hand on his pistol and his eye on the prisoner, a little behind, Lester endeavored to cheer the prisoner's spirits and his own by insisting on the madness of the charge and the certainty of instant acquittal from the magistrate to whom they were bound, and who was esteemed the one both most acute and most just in the county. Aram interrupted him somewhat abruptly,

"My friend, enough of this presently. But Madeline, what knows she as yet?"

"Nothing; of course, we kept—"

"Exactly, exactly; you have done wisely. Why need she learn anything as yet? Say an arrest for debt, a mistake, an absence but of a day or so at most,—you understand?"

"Yes. Will you not see her, Eugene, before you go, and say this yourself?"

"I!—O God!—I! to whom this day was—No, no; save me, I implore you, from the agony of such a contrast,—an interview so mournful and unavailing. No, we must not meet! But whither go we now? Not, not, surely, through all the idle gossips of the village,—the crowd already excited to gape and stare and speculate on the—"

"No," interrupted Lester; "the carriages await us at the farther end of the valley. I thought of that,—for the rash boy behind seems to have changed his nature. I loved—Heaven knows how I loved my brother! But before I would let suspicion thus blind reason, I would suffer inquiry to sleep forever on his fate."

"Your nephew," said Aram, "has ever wronged me. But waste not words on him; let us think only of Madeline. Will you go back at once to her,—tell her a tale to lull her apprehensions, and then follow us with haste? I am alone among enemies till you come."

Lester was about to answer, when, at a turn in the road which brought the carriage within view, they perceived two figures in white hastening towards them; and ere Aram was prepared for the surprise, Madeline had sunk pale, trembling, and all breathless on his breast.

"I could not keep her back," said Ellinor, apologetically, to her father.

"Back! and why? Am I not in my proper place?" cried Madeline, lifting her face from Aram's breast; and then, as her eyes circled the group, and rested on Aram's countenance, now no longer calm, but full of woe, of passion, of disappointed love, of anticipated despair, she rose, and gradually recoiling with a fear which struck dumb her voice, thrice attempted to speak, and thrice failed.

"But what—what is—what means this?" exclaimed Ellinor. "Why do you weep, father? Why does Eugene turn away his face? You answer not. Speak, for God's sake! These strangers,—what are they? And you, Walter, you,—why are you so pale? Why do you thus knit your brows and fold your arms! You, you will tell me the meaning of this dreadful silence,—this scene. Speak, cousin, dear cousin, speak!"

"Speak!" cried Madeline, finding voice at length, but in the sharp and straining tone of wild terror, in which they recognized no note of the natural music. The single word sounded rather as a shriek than an adjuration; and so piercingly it ran through the hearts of all present that the very officers, hardened as their trade had made them, felt as if they would rather have faced death than answered that command.

A dead, long, dreary pause, and Aram broke it. "Madeline Lester," said he, "prove yourself worthy of the hour of trial. Exert yourself; arouse your heart; be prepared! You are the betrothed of one whose soul never quailed before man's angry word. Remember that, and fear not!"

"I will not, I will not, Eugene! Speak, only speak!"

"You have loved me in good report; trust me now in ill. They accuse me of a crime,—a heinous crime! At first I would not have told you the real charge. Pardon me, I wronged you,—now, know all! They accuse me, I say, of crime. Of what crime? you ask. Ay, I scarce know, so vague is the charge, so fierce the accuser; but prepare, Madeline,—it is of murder!"

Raised as her spirits had been by the haughty and earnest tone of Aram's exhortation, Madeline now, though she turned deadly pale, though the earth swam round and round, yet repressed the shriek upon her lips as those horrid words shot into her soul.

"You!—murder!—you! And who dares accuse you?"

"Behold him,—your cousin!"

Ellinor heard, turned, fixed her eyes on Walter's sullen brow and motionless attitude, and fell senseless to the earth. Not thus Madeline. As there is an exhaustion that forbids, not invites repose, so when the mind is thoroughly on the rack, the common relief to anguish is not allowed; the senses are too sharply strung, thus happily to collapse into forgetfulness; the dreadful inspiration that agony kindles, supports nature while it consumes it. Madeline passed, without a downward glance, by the lifeless body of her sister; and walking with a steady step to Walter, she laid her hand upon his arm, and fixing on his countenance that soft clear eye, which was now lit with a searching and preternatural glare, and seemed to pierce into his soul, she said,

"Walter, do I hear aright? Am I awake? Is it you who accuse Eugene Aram,—your Madeline's betrothed husband,—Madeline, whom you once loved? Of what? Of crimes which death alone can punish. Away! It is not you,—I know it is not. Say that I am mistaken,—that I am mad, if you will. Come, Walter, relieve me; let me not abhor the very air you breathe!"

"Will no one have mercy on me?" cried Walter, rent to the heart, and covering his face with his hands. In the fire and heat of vengeance he had not reeked of this. He had only thought of justice to a father, punishment to a villain, rescue for a credulous girl. The woe, the horror he was about to inflict on all he most loved: this had not struck upon him with a due force till now!

"Mercy—you talk of mercy! I knew it could not be true!" said Madeline, trying to pluck her cousin's hand from his face; "you could not have dreamed of wrong to Eugene and—and upon this day. Say we have erred, or that you have erred, and we will forgive and bless you even now!" Aram had not interfered in this scene; he kept his eyes fixed on the cousins, not uninterested to see what effect Madeline's touching words might produce on his accuser. Meanwhile she continued: "Speak to me, Walter, dear Walter, speak to me'. Are you, my cousin, my playfellow,—are you the one to blight our hopes, to dash our joys, to bring dread and terror into a home so lately all peace and sunshine, your own home, your childhood's home? What have you done? What have you dared to do? Accuse him! Of what? Murder! Speak, speak. Murder, ha! ha!—murder! nay, not so! You would not venture to come here, you would not let me take your hand, you would not look us, your uncle, your more than sisters, in the face if you could nurse in your heart this lie,—this black, horrid lie!"

Walter withdrew his hands, and as he turned his face said,—

"Let him prove his innocence. Pray God he do! I am not his accuser, Madeline. His accusers are the bones of my dead father! Save these, Heaven alone and the revealing earth are witness against him!"

"Your father!" said Madeline, staggering back,—"my lost uncle! Nay, now I know indeed what a shadow has appalled us all! Did you know my uncle, Eugene? Did you ever see Geoffrey Lester?"

"Never, as I believe, so help me God!" said Aram, laying his hand on his heart. "But this is idle now," as, recollecting himself, he felt that the case had gone forth from Walter's hands, and that appeal to him had become vain. "Leave us now, dearest Madeline, my beloved wife that shall be, that is! I go to disprove these charges. Perhaps I shall return to-night. Delay not my acquittal, even from doubt,—a boy's doubt. Come, sirs."

"O Eugene! Eugene!" cried Madeline, throwing herself on her knees before hint, "do not order me to leave you now, now in the hour of dread! I will not. Nay, look not so! I swear I will not! Father, dear father, come and plead for me,—say I shall go with you. I ask nothing more. Do not fear for my nerves,—cowardice is gone. I will not shame you, I will not play the woman. I know what is due to one who loves him. Try me, only try me. You weep, father, you shake your head. But you, Eugene,—you have not the heart to deny me? Think—think if I stayed here to count the moments till you return, my very senses would leave me. What do I ask? But to go with you, to be the first to hail your triumph! Had this happened two hours hence, you could not have said me nay,—I should have claimed the right to be with you; I now but implore the blessing. You relent, you relent; I see it!"

"O Heaven!" exclaimed Aram, rising, and clasping her to his breast, and wildly kissing her face, but with cold and trembling lips, "this is indeed a bitter hour; let me not sink beneath it. Yes, Madeline, ask your father if he consents; I hail your strengthening presence as that of an angel. I will not be the one to sever you from my side."

"You are right, Eugene," said Lester, who was supporting Ellinor, not yet recovered,—"let her go with us; it is but common kindness and common mercy."

Madeline uttered a cry of joy (joy even at such a moment!), and clung fast to Eugene's arm, as if for assurance that they were not indeed to be separated.

By this time some of Lester's servants, who had from a distance followed their young mistresses, reached the spot. To their care Lester gave the still scarce reviving Ellinor; and then, turning round with a severe countenance to Walter, said, "Come, sir, your rashness has done sufficient wrong for the present; come now, and see how soon your suspicions will end in shame."

"Justice, and blood for blood!" said Walter, sternly; but his heart felt as if it were broken. His venerable uncle's tears, Madeline's look of horror as she turned from him, Ellinor all lifeless, and he not daring to approach her,—this was HIS work! He pulled his hat over his eyes, and hastened into the carriage alone. Lester, Madeline, and Aram followed in the other vehicle; and the two officers contented themselves with mounting the box, certain the prisoner would attempt no escape.

CHAPTER III.

```
THE JUSTICE—THE DEPARTURE—THE EQUANIMITY OF THE CORPORAL IN
BEARING THE MISFORTUNES OF OTHER PEOPLE.—THE EXAMINATION; ITS
   RESULT.—ARAM'S CONDUCT IN PRISON.—THE ELASTICITY OF OUR
      HUMAN NATURE.—A VISIT FROM THE EARL.—WALTER'S
              DETERMINATION.—MADELINE.

       Bear me to prison, where I am committed.
          —Measure for Measure.
```

On arriving at Sir—'s, a disappointment, for which, had they previously conversed with the officers they might have been prepared, awaited them. The fact was, that the justice had only endorsed the warrant sent from Yorkshire; and after a very short colloquy, in which he expressed his regret at the circumstance, his conviction that the charge would be disproved, and a few other courteous common-places, he gave Aram to understand that the matter now did not rest with him, but that it was to Yorkshire that the officers were bound, and before Mr. Thornton, a magistrate of that country, that the examination was to take place. "All I can do," said the magistrate, "I have already done; but I wished for an opportunity of informing you of it. I have written to my brother justice at full length respecting your high character, and treating the habits and rectitude of your life alone as a sufficient refutation of so monstrous a charge."

For the first time a visible embarrassment came over the firm nerves of the prisoner: he seemed to look with great uneasiness at the prospect of this long and dreary journey, and for such an end. Perhaps, the very notion of returning as a suspected criminal to that part of the country where a portion of his youth had been passed, was sufficient to disquiet and deject him. All this while his poor Madeline seemed actuated by a spirit beyond herself; she would not be separated from his side—she held his hand in hers—she whispered comfort and courage at the very moment when her own heart most sank. The magistrate wiped his eyes when he saw a creature so young, so beautiful, in circumstances so fearful, and bearing up with an energy so little to be expected from her years and delicate appearance. Aram said but little; he covered his face with his right hand for a few moments, as if to hide a passing emotion, a sudden weakness. When he removed it, all vestige of colour had died away; his face was pale as that of one who has risen from the grave; but it was settled and composed.

"It is a hard pang, Sir," said he, with a faint smile; "so many miles—so many days—so long a deferment of knowing the best, or preparing to meet the worst. But, be it so! I thank you, Sir,—I thank you all,—Lester, Madeline, for your kindness; you two must now leave me; the brand is on my name—the suspected man is no fit object for love or friendship! Farewell!"

"We go with you!" said Madeline firmly, and in a very low voice.

Aram's eye sparkled, but he waved his hand impatiently.

"We go with you, my friend!" repeated Lester.

And so, indeed, not to dwell long on a painful scene, it was finally settled. Lester and his two daughters that evening followed Aram to the dark and fatal bourne to which he was bound.

It was in vain that Walter, seizing his uncle's hands, whispered,

"For Heaven's sake, do not be rash in your friendship! You have not yet learnt all. I tell you, that there can be no doubt of his guilt! Remember, it is a brother for whom you mourn! will you countenance his murderer?"

Lester, despite himself, was struck by the earnestness with which his nephew spoke, but the impression died away as the words ceased: so strong and deep had been the fascination which Eugene Aram had exercised over the hearts of all once drawn within the near circle of his attraction, that had the charge of murder been made against himself, Lester could not have repelled it with a more entire conviction of the innocence of the accused. Still, however, the deep sincerity of his nephew's manner in some measure served to soften his resentment towards him.

"No, no, boy!" said he, drawing away his hand, "Rowland Lester is not the one to desert a friend in the day of darkness and the hour of need. Be silent I say!—My brother, my poor brother, you tell me, has been murdered. I will see justice done to him: but, Aram! Fie! fie! it is a name that would whisper falsehood to the loudest accusation. Go, Walter! go! I do not blame you!—you may be right—a murdered father is a dread and awful memory to a son! What wonder that the thought warps your judgment? But go! Eugene was to me both a guide and a blessing; a father in wisdom, a son in love. I cannot look on his accuser's face without anguish. Go! we shall meet again.—How! Go!"

"Enough, Sir!" said Walter, partly in anger, partly in sorrow—"Time be the judge between us all!"

With those words he turned from the house, and proceeded on foot towards a cottage half way between Grassdale and the Magistrate's house, at which, previous to his return to the former place, he had prudently left the Corporal—not willing to trust to that person's discretion, as to the tales and scandal that he might propagate throughout the village on a matter so painful and so dark.

Let the world wag as it will, there are some tempers which its vicissitudes never reach. Nothing makes a picture of distress more sad than the portrait of some individual sitting indifferently looking on in the back-ground. This was a secret Hogarth knew well. Mark his deathbed scenes:—Poverty and Vice worked up into horror—and the Physicians in the corner wrangling for the fee!—or the child playing with the coffin—or the nurse filching what fortune, harsh, yet less harsh than humanity, might have left. In the melancholy depth of humour that steeps both our fancy and our heart in the immortal Romance of Cervantes (for, how profoundly melancholy is it to be compelled by one gallant folly to laugh at all that is gentle, and brave, and wise, and generous!) nothing grates on us more than when—last scene of all, the poor Knight lies dead—his exploits for ever over—for ever dumb his eloquent discourses: than when, I say, we are told that, despite of his grief, even little Sancho did not eat or drink the less:—these touches open to us the real world, it is true; but it is not the best part of it. What a pensive thing is true humour! Certain it was, that when Walter, full of contending emotions at all he had witnessed,—harassed, tortured, yet also elevated, by his feelings, stopped opposite the cottage door, and saw there the Corporal sitting comfortably in the porch,—his vile modicum Sabini before him—his pipe in his mouth, and a complacent expression of satisfaction diffusing itself over features which shrewdness and selfishness had marked for their own;—certain it was, that, at this sight Walter experienced a more displeasing revulsion of feeling—a more entire conviction of sadness—a more consummate disgust of this weary world and the motley masquers that walk thereon, than all the tragic scenes he had just witnessed had excited within him.

"And well, Sir," said the Corporal, slowly rising, "how did it go off?—Wasn't the villain bash'd to the dust?—You've nabbed him safe, I hope?"

"Silence," said Walter, sternly, "prepare for our departure. The chaise will be here forthwith; we return to Yorkshire this day. Ask me no more now."

"A—well—baugh!" said the Corporal.

There was a long silence. Walter walked to and fro the road before the cottage. The chaise arrived; the luggage was put in. Walter's foot was on the step; but before the Corporal mounted the rumbling dickey, that invaluable domestic hemmed thrice.

"And had you time, Sir, to think of poor Jacob, and look at the cottage, and slip in a word to your uncle about the bit tato ground?"

We pass over the space of time, short in fact, long in suffering, that elapsed, till the prisoner and his companions reached Knaresbro'. Aram's conduct during this time was not only calm but cheerful. The stoical doctrines he had affected through life, he on this trying interval called into remarkable exertion. He it was who now supported the spirits of his mistress and his friend; and though he no longer pretended to be sanguine of acquittal—though again and again he urged upon them the gloomy fact—first, how improbable it was that this course had been entered into against him without strong presumption of guilt; and secondly, how little less improbable it was, that at that distance of time he should be able to procure evidence, or remember circumstances, sufficient on the instant to set aside such presumption,—he yet dwelt partly on the hope of ultimate proof of his innocence, and still more strongly on the firmness of his own mind to bear, without shrinking, even the hardest fate.

"Do not," he said to Lester, "do not look on these trials of life only with the eyes of the world. Reflect how poor and minute a segment in the vast circle of eternity existence is at the best. Its sorrow and its shame are but moments. Always in my brightest and youngest hours I have wrapt my heart in the contemplation of an august futurity.

　　　　"'The soul, secure in its existence, smiles

>   At the drawn dagger, and defies its point.'

"If I die even the death of the felon, it is beyond the power of fate to separate us for long. It is but a pang, and we are united again for ever; for ever in that far and shadowy clime, where the wicked cease from troubling, and the weary are at rest.' Were it not for Madeline's dear sake, I should long since have been over weary of the world. As it is, the sooner, even by a violent and unjust fate, we leave a path begirt with snares below and tempests above, the happier for that soul which looks to its lot in this earth as the least part of its appointed doom."

In discourses like this, which the nature of his eloquence was peculiarly calculated to render solemn and impressive, Aram strove to prepare his friends for the worst, and perhaps to cheat, or to steel, himself. Ever as he spoke thus, Lester or Ellinor broke on him with impatient remonstrance; but Madeline, as if imbued with a deeper and more mournful penetration into the future, listened in tearless and breathless attention. She gazed upon him with a look that shared the thought he expressed, though it read not (yet she dreamed so) the heart from which it came. In the words of that beautiful poet, to whose true nature, so full of unuttered tenderness—so fraught with the rich nobility of love—we have begun slowly to awaken,

>   "Her lip was silent, scarcely beat her heart.
>   Her eye alone proclaimed 'we will not part!'
>   Thy 'hope' may perish, or thy friends may flee.
>   Farewell to life—but not adieu to thee!"
>   —[Lara]

They arrived at noon at the house of Mr. Thornton, and Aram underwent his examination. Though he denied most of the particulars in Houseman's evidence, and expressly the charge of murder, his commitment was made out; and that day he was removed by the officers, (Barker and Moor, who had arrested him at Grassdale,) to York Castle, to await his trial at the assizes.

The sensation which this extraordinary event created throughout the country, was wholly unequalled. Not only in Yorkshire, and the county in which he had of late resided, where his personal habits were known, but even in the Metropolis, and amongst men of all classes in England, it appears to have caused one mingled feeling of astonishment, horror, and incredulity, which in our times has had no parallel in any criminal prosecution. The peculiar turn of the prisoner—his genius—his learning—his moral life—the interest that by students had been for years attached to his name—his approaching marriage—the length of time that had elapsed since the crime had been committed—the singular and abrupt manner, the wild and legendary spot, in which the skeleton of the lost man had been discovered—the imperfect rumours—the dark and suspicious evidence—all combined to make a tale of such marvellous incident, and breeding such endless conjecture, that we cannot wonder to find it afterwards received a place, not only in the temporary chronicles, but even the most important and permanent histories of the period.

Previous to Walter's departure from Knaresbro' to Grassdale, and immediately subsequent to the discovery at St. Robert's Cave, the coroner's inquest had been held upon the bones so mysteriously and suddenly brought to light. Upon the witness of the old woman at whose house Aram had lodged, and upon that of Houseman, aided by some circumstantial and less weighty evidence, had been issued that warrant on which we have seen the prisoner apprehended.

With most men there was an intimate and indignant persuasion of Aram's innocence; and at this day, in the county where he last resided, there still lingers the same belief. Firm as his gospel faith, that conviction rested in the mind of the worthy Lester; and he sought, by every means he could devise, to soothe and cheer the confinement of his friend. In prison, however (indeed after his examination—after Aram had made himself thoroughly acquainted with all the circumstantial evidence which identified Clarke with Geoffrey Lester, a story that till then he had persuaded himself wholly to disbelieve) a change which, in the presence of Madeline or her father, he vainly attempted wholly to conceal, and to which, when alone, he surrendered himself with a gloomy abstraction—came over his mood, and dashed him from the lofty height of Philosophy, from which he had before looked down on the peril and the ills below.

Sometimes he would gaze on Lester with a strange and glassy eye, and mutter inaudibly to himself, as if unaware of the old man's presence; at others, he would shrink from Lester's proffered hand, and start abruptly from his professions of unaltered, unalterable regard; sometimes he would sit silently, and, with a changeless and stony countenance, look upon Madeline as she now spoke in that exalted tone of consolation which had passed away from himself; and when she had done, instead of replying to her speech, he would say abruptly, "Ay, at the worst you love me, then—love me better than any one on earth—say that, Madeline, again say that!"

And Madeline's trembling lips obeyed the demand.

"Yes," he would renew, "this man, whom they accuse me of murdering, this,—your uncle,—him you never saw since you were an infant, a mere infant; him you could not love! What was he to you?—yet it is dreadful to think of—dreadful, dreadful;" and then again his voice ceased; but his lips moved convulsively, and his eyes seemed to speak meanings that defied words. These alterations in his bearing, which belied his steady and resolute character, astonished and dejected both Madeline and her father. Sometimes they thought that his situation had shaken his reason, or that the horrible suspicion of having murdered the uncle of his intended wife, made him look upon themselves with a secret shudder, and that they were mingled up in his mind by no unnatural, though unjust confusion, with the causes of his present awful and uncertain state. With the generality of the world, these two tender friends believed Houseman the sole and real murderer, and fancied his charge against Aram was but the last expedient of a villain to ward punishment from himself, by imputing crime to another. Naturally, then, they frequently sought to turn the conversation upon Houseman, and on the different circumstances that had brought him acquainted with Aram; but on this ground the prisoner seemed morbidly sensitive, and averse to detailed discussion. His narration, however, such as it was, threw much light upon certain matters on which Madeline and Lester were before anxious and inquisitive.

"Houseman is, in all ways," said he, with great and bitter vehemence, "unredeemed, and beyond the calculations of an ordinary wickedness; we knew each other from our relationship, but seldom met, and still more rarely held long intercourse together. After we separated, when I left Knaresbro', we did not meet for years. He sought me at Grassdale; he was poor, and implored assistance; I gave him all within my power; he sought me again, nay, more than once again, and finding me justly averse to yielding to his extortionate demands, he then broached the purpose he has now effected; he threatened—you hear me—you understand—he threatened me with this charge—the murder of Daniel Clarke, by that name alone I knew the deceased. The menace, and the known villainy of the man, agitated me beyond expression. What was I? a being who lived without the world—who knew not its ways—who desired only rest! The menace haunted me—almost maddened! Your nephew has told you, you say, of broken words, of escaping emotions, which he has noted, even to suspicion, in me; you now behold the cause! Was it not sufficient? My life, nay more, my fame, my marriage, Madeline's peace of mind, all depended on the uncertain fury or craft of a wretch like this! The idea was with me night and day; to avoid it, I resolved on a sacrifice; you may blame me, I was weak, yet I thought then not unwise; to avoid it, I say I offered to bribe this man to leave the country. I sold my pittance to oblige him to it. I bound him thereto by the strongest ties. Nay, so disinterestedly, so truly did I love Madeline, that I would not wed while I thought this danger could burst upon me. I believed that, before my marriage day, Houseman had left the country. It was not so, Fate ordered otherwise. It seems that Houseman came to Knaresbro' to see his daughter; that suspicion, by a sudden train of events, fell on him, perhaps justly; to skreen himself he has sacrificed me. The tale seems plausible; perhaps the accuser may triumph. But, Madeline, you now may account for much that may have perplexed you before. Let me remember—ay—ay—I have dropped mysterious words—have I not? have I not?—owning that danger was around me—owning that a wild and terrific secret was heavy at my breast; nay, once, walking with you the evening before, before the fatal day, I said that we must prepare to seek some yet more secluded spot, some deeper retirement; for, despite my precautions, despite the supposed absence of Houseman from the country itself, a fevered and restless presentiment would at some times intrude itself on me. All this is now accounted for, is it not, Madeline? Speak, speak!"

"All, love all! Why do you look on me with that searching eye, that frowning brow?"

"Did I? no, no, I have no frown for you; but peace, I am not what I ought to be through this ordeal."

The above narration of Aram's did indeed account to Madeline for much that had till then remained unexplained; the appearance of Houseman at Grassdale,—the meeting between him and Aram on the evening she walked with the latter, and questioned him of his ill-boding visitor; the frequent abstraction and muttered hints of her lover; and as he had said, his last declaration of the possible necessity of leaving Grassdale. Nor was there any thing improbable, though it was rather in accordance with the unworldly habits, than with the haughty character of Aram, that he should seek, circumstanced as he was, to silence even the false accuser of a plausible tale, that might well strike horror and bewilderment into a man much more, to all seeming, fitted to grapple with the hard and coarse realities of life, than the moody and secluded scholar. Be that as it may, though Lester deplored, he did not blame this circumstance, which after all had not transpired, nor seemed likely to transpire; and he attributed the prisoner's aversion to enter farther on the matter, to the natural dislike of so proud a man to refer to his own weakness, and to dwell upon the manner in which, despite of that weakness, he had been duped. This story Lester retailed to Walter, and it contributed to throw a damp and uncertainty over those mixed and unquiet feelings with which the latter waited for the coming trial. There were many moments when the young man was tempted to regret that Aram had not escaped a trial which, if he were proved guilty, would for ever blast the happiness of his family; and which might, notwithstanding such a verdict, leave on Walter's own mind an impression of the prisoner's innocence; and an uneasy consciousness that he, through his investigations, had brought him to that doom.

Walter remained in Yorkshire, seeing little of his family, of none indeed but Lester; it was not to be expected that Madeline would see him, and once only he caught the tearful eyes of Ellinor as she retreated from the room he entered, and those eyes beamed kindness and pity, but something also of reproach.

Time passed slowly and witheringly on: a man of the name of Terry having been included in the suspicion, and indeed committed, it appeared that the prosecutor could not procure witnesses by the customary time, and the trial was postponed till the next assizes. As this man was however, never brought up to trial, and appears no more, we have said nothing of him in our narrative, until he thus became the instrument of a delay in the fate of Eugene Aram. Time passed on, Winter, Spring, were gone, and the glory and gloss of Summer were now lavished over the happy earth. In some measure the usual calmness of his demeanour had returned to Aram; he had mastered those moody fits we have referred to, which had so afflicted his affectionate visitors; and he now seemed to prepare and buoy himself up against that awful ordeal of life and death, which he was about so soon to pass. Yet he,—the hermit of Nature, who—

```
      "Each little herb
That grows on mountain bleak, or tangled forest,
Had learnt to name;"
      —Remorse, by S. T. Coleridge
```

he could not feel, even through the bars and checks of a prison, the soft summer air, 'the witchery of the soft blue sky;' he could not see the leaves bud forth, and mellow into their darker verdure; he could not hear the songs of the many-voiced birds; or listen to the dancing rain, calling up beauty where it fell; or mark at night, through his high and narrow casement, the stars aloof, and the sweet moon pouring in her light, like God's pardon, even through the dungeon-gloom and the desolate scenes where Mortality struggles with Despair; he could not catch, obstructed as they were, these, the benigner influences of earth, and not sicken and pant for his old and full communion with their ministry and presence. Sometimes all around him was forgotten, the harsh cell, the cheerless solitude, the approaching trial, the boding fear, the darkened hope, even the spectre of a troubled and fierce remembrance,—all was forgotten, and his spirit was abroad, and his step upon the mountain-top once more.

In our estimate of the ills of life, we never sufficiently take into our consideration the wonderful elasticity of our moral frame, the unlooked for, the startling facility with which the human mind accommodates itself to all change of circumstance, making an object and even a joy from the hardest and seemingly the least redeemed conditions of fate. The man who watched the spider in his cell, may have taken, at least, as much interest in the watch, as when engaged in the most ardent and ambitious objects of his former life; and he was but a type of his brethren; all in similar circumstances would have found some similar occupation. Let any man look over his past life, let him recall not moments, not hours of agony, for to them Custom lends not her blessed magic; but let him single out some lengthened period of physical or moral endurance; in hastily reverting to it, it may seem at first, I grant, altogether wretched; a series of days marked with the black stone,—the clouds without a star;—but let him look more closely, it was not so during the time of suffering; a thousand little things, in the bustle of life dormant and unheeded, then started froth into notice, and became to him objects of interest or diversion; the dreary present, once made familiar, glided away from him, not less than if it had been all happiness; his mind dwelt not on the dull intervals, but the stepping-stone it had created and placed at each; and, by that moral dreaming which for ever goes on within man's secret heart, he lived as little in the immediate world before him, as in the most sanguine period of his youth, or the most scheming of his maturity.

So wonderful in equalizing all states and all times in the varying tide of life, are these two rulers yet levellers of mankind, Hope and Custom, that the very idea of an eternal punishment includes that of an utter alteration of the whole mechanism of the soul in its human state, and no effort of an imagination, assisted by past experience, can conceive a state of torture which custom can never blunt, and from which the chainless and immaterial spirit can never be beguiled into even a momentary escape.

Among the very few persons admitted to Aram's solitude, was Lord—That nobleman was staying, on a visit, with a relation of his in the neighbourhood, and he seized with an excited and mournful avidity, the opportunity thus afforded him of seeing, once more, a character that had so often forced itself on his speculation and surprise. He came to offer not condolence, but respect; services, at such a moment, no individual could render,—he gave however, what was within his power—advice,—and pointed out to Aram the best counsel to engage, and the best method of previous inquiry into particulars yet unexplored. He was astonished to find Aram indifferent on these points, so important. The prisoner, it would seem, had even then resolved on being his own counsel, and conducting his own cause; the event proved that he did not rely in vain on the power of his own eloquence and sagacity, though he might on their result. As to the rest, he spoke with impatience, and the petulance of a wronged man. "For the idle rumours of the world, I do not care," said he, "let them condemn or acquit me as they will;—for my life, I might be willing indeed, that it were spared,—I trust it may be, if not, I can stand face to face with Death. I have now looked on him within these walls long enough to have grown familiar with his terrors. But enough of me; tell me, my Lord, something of the world without, I have grown eager about it at last. I have been now so condemned to feed upon myself, that I have become surfeited with the diet;"—and it was with great difficulty that the Earl drew Aram back to speak of himself: he did so, even when compelled to it, with so much qualification and reserve, mixed with some evident anger at the thought of being sifted and examined—that his visitor was forced finally to drop the subject, and not liking, nor indeed able, at such a time, to converse on more indifferent themes, the last interview he ever had with Aram terminated much more abruptly than he had meant it. His opinion of the prisoner was not, however, shaken in the least. I have seen a letter of his to a celebrated personage of the day, in which, mentioning this interview, he concludes with saying,—"In short, there is so much real dignity about the man, that adverse circumstances increase it tenfold. Of his innocence I have not the remotest doubt; but if he persist in being his own counsel, I tremble for the result,—you know in such cases how much more valuable is practice than genius. But the judge you will say is, in criminal causes, the prisoner's counsel,—God grant he may here prove a successful one! I repeat, were Aram condemned by five hundred juries, I could not believe him guilty. No, the very essence of all human probabilities is against it."

The Earl afterwards saw and conversed with Walter. He was much struck with the conduct of the young Lester, and much impressed with a feeling for a situation, so harassing and unhappy.

"Whatever be the result of the trial," said Walter, "I shall leave the country the moment it is finally over. If the prisoner be condemned, there is no hearth for me in my uncle's home; if not, my suspicions may still remain, and the sight of each other be an equal bane to the accused and to myself. A voluntary exile, and a life that may lead to forgetfulness, are all that I covet.—I now find in my own person," he added, with a faint smile, "how deeply Shakspeare had read the mysteries of men's conduct. Hamlet, we are told, was naturally full of fire and action. One dark discovery quells his spirit, unstrings his heart, and stales to him for ever the uses of the world. I now comprehend the change. It is bodied forth even in the humblest individual, who is met by a similar fate—even in myself."

"Ay," said the Earl, "I do indeed remember you a wild, impetuous, headstrong youth. I scarcely recognize your very appearance. The elastic spring has left your step—there seems a fixed furrow in your brow. These clouds of life are indeed no summer vapour, darkening one moment and gone the next. But my young friend, let us hope the best. I firmly believe in Aram's innocence—firmly!—more rootedly than I can express. The real criminal will appear on the trial. All bitterness between you and Aram must cease at his acquittal; you will be anxious to repair to him the injustice of a natural suspicion: and he seems not one who could long retain malice. All will be well, believe me."

"God send it!" said Walter, sighing deeply.

"But at the worst," continued the Earl, pressing his hand in parting, "if you should persist in your resolution to leave the country, write to me, and I can furnish you with an honourable and stirring occasion for doing so.—Farewell."

While Time was thus advancing towards the fatal day, it was graving deep ravages within the pure breast of Madeline Lester. She had borne up, as we have seen, for some time, against the sudden blow that had shivered her young hopes, and separated her by so awful a chasm from the side of Aram; but as week after week, month after month rolled on, and he still lay in prison, and the horrible suspense of ignominy and death still hung over her, then gradually her courage began to fail, and her heart to sink. Of all the conditions to which the heart is subject, suspense is the one that most gnaws, and cankers into, the frame. One little month of that suspense, when it involves death, we are told, in a very remarkable work lately published by an eye-witness. [Note: See Mr. Wakefield's work on 'The Punishment of Death.'] is sufficient to plough fixed lines and furrows in the face of a convict of five-and-twenty—sufficient to dash the brown hair with grey, and to bleach the grey to white. And this suspense—suspense of this nature, for more than eight whole months, had Madeline to endure!

About the end of the second month the effect upon her health grew visible. Her colour, naturally delicate as the hues of the pink shell or the youngest rose, faded into one marble whiteness, which again, as time proceeded, flushed into that red and preternatural hectic, which once settled, rarely yields its place but to the colours of the grave. Her flesh shrank from its rounded and noble proportions. Deep hollows traced themselves beneath eyes which yet grew even more lovely as they grew less serenely bright. The blessed Sleep sunk not upon her brain with its wonted and healing dews. Perturbed dreams, that towards dawn succeeded the long and weary vigil of the night, shook her frame even more than the anguish of the day in these dreams one frightful vision—a crowd—a scaffold—and the pale majestic face of her lover, darkened by unutterable pangs of pride and sorrow, were for ever present before her. Till now, she and Ellinor had always shared the same bed: this Madeline would not now suffer. In vain Ellinor wept and pleaded. "No," said Madeline, with a hollow voice; "at night I see him. My soul is alone with his; but—but,"—and she burst into an agony of tears—"the most dreadful thought is this, I cannot master my dreams. And sometimes I start and wake, and find that in sleep I have believed him guilty. Nay, O God! that his lips have proclaimed the guilt! And shall any living being—shall any but God, who reads not words but hearts, hear this hideous falsehood—this ghastly mockery of the lying sleep? No, I must be alone! The very stars should not hear what is forced from me in the madness of my dreams."

But not in vain, or not excluded from her, was that elastic and consoling spirit of which I have before spoken. As Aram recovered the tenor of his self-possession, a more quiet and peaceful calm diffused itself over the mind of Madeline. Her high and starry nature could comprehend those sublime inspirations of comfort, which lift us from the lowest abyss of this world to the contemplation of all that the yearning visions of mankind have painted in another. She would sit, rapt and absorbed for hours together, till these contemplations assumed the colour of a gentle and soft insanity. "Come, dearest Madeline," Ellinor would say,—"Come, you have thought enough; my poor father asks to see you."

"Hush!" Madeline answered. "Hush, I have been walking with Eugene in heaven; and oh! there are green woods, and lulling waters above, as there are on earth, and we see the stars quite near, and I cannot tell you how happy their smile makes those who look upon them. And Eugene never starts there, nor frowns, nor walks aside, nor looks on me with an estranged and chilling look; but his face is as calm and bright as the face of an angel;—and his voice!—it thrills amidst all the music which plays there night and day—softer than their softest note. And we are married, Ellinor, at last. We were married in heaven, and all the angels came to the marriage! I am now so happy that we were not wed before! What! are you weeping, Ellinor? Ah, we never weep in heaven! but we will all go there again—all of us, hand in hand!"

These affecting hallucinations terrified them, lest they should settle into a confirmed loss of reason; but perhaps without cause. They never lasted long, and never occurred but after moods of abstraction of unusual duration. To her they probably supplied what sleep does to others—a relaxation and refreshment—an escape from the consciousness of life. And indeed it might always be noted, that after such harmless aberrations of the mind, Madeline seemed more collected and patient in thought, and for the moment, even stronger in frame than before. Yet the body evidently pined and languished, and each week made palpable decay in her vital powers.

Every time Aram saw her, he was startled at the alteration; and kissing her cheek, her lips, her temples, in an agony of grief, wondered that to him alone it was forbidden to weep. Yet after all, when she was gone, and he again alone, he could not but think death likely to prove to her the most happy of earthly boons. He was not sanguine of acquittal, and even in acquittal, a voice at his heart suggested insuperable barriers to their union, which had not existed when it was first anticipated.

"Yes, let her die," he would say, "let her die; she at least is certain of Heaven!" But the human infirmity clung around him, and notwithstanding this seeming resolution in her absence, he did not mourn the less, he was not stung the less, when he saw her again, and beheld a new character from the hand of death graven upon her form. No; we may triumph over all weakness, but that of the affections. Perhaps in this dreary and haggard interval of time, these two persons loved each other more purely, more strongly, more enthusiastically, than they had ever done at any former period of their eventful history. Over the hardest stone, as over the softest turf, the green moss will force its verdure and sustain its life!

CHAPTER IV.

THE EVENING BEFORE THE TRIAL.—THE COUSINS.—THE CHANGE IN
MADELINE.—THE FAMILY OF GRASSDALE MEET ONCE MORE BENEATH ONE
ROOF.

```
Each substance of a grief hath twenty shadows,
For Sorrow's eye, glazed with blinding tears,
Divides one thing entire to many objects.
       . . . . . . . . . . . .
      [Hope] is a flatterer,
A parasite, a keeper back of death;
Who gently would dissolve the bands of death
Which false Hope lingers in extremity?
      —Richard II.
```

It was the evening before the trial. Lester and his daughters lodged at a retired and solitary house in the suburbs of the town of York; and thither, from the village some miles distant, in which he had chosen his own retreat, Walter now proceeded across fields laden with the ripening corn. The last and the richest month of summer had commenced, but the harvest was not yet begun, and deep and golden showed the vegetation of life, bedded among the dark verdure of the hedge-rows, and "the merrie woods!" The evening was serene and lulled; at a distance arose the spires and chimneys of the town, but no sound from the busy hum of men reached the ear. Nothing perhaps gives a more entire idea of stillness than the sight of those abodes where "noise dwelleth," but where you cannot now hear even its murmurs. The stillness of a city is far more impressive than that of Nature; for the mind instantly compares the present silence with the wonted uproar. The harvest-moon rose slowly from a copse of gloomy firs, and diffused its own unspeakable magic into the hush and transparency of the night. As Walter walked slowly on, the sound of voices from some rustic party going homeward, broke jocundly on the silence, and when he paused for a moment at the stile, from which he first caught a glimpse of Lester's house, he saw, winding along the green hedgerow, some village pair, the "lover and the maid," who could meet only at such hours, and to whom such hours were therefore especially dear. It was altogether a scene of pure and true pastoral character, and there was all around a semblance of tranquillity, of happiness, which suits with the poetical and the scriptural paintings of a pastoral life; and which perhaps, in a new and fertile country, may still find a realization. From this scene, from these thoughts, the young loiterer turned with a sigh towards the solitary house in which this night could awaken none but the most anxious feelings, and that moon could beam only on the most troubled hearts.

"Terra salutiferas herbas, eademque nocentes
Nutrit; et urticae proxima saepe rosa est."

He now walked more quickly on, as if stung by his reflections, and avoiding the path which led to the front of the house, gained a little garden at the rear, and opening a gate that admitted to a narrow and shaded walk, over which the linden and nut trees made a sort of continuous and natural arbour, the moon, piercing at broken intervals through the boughs, rested on the form of Ellinor Lester.

"This is most kind, most like my own sweet cousin," said Walter approaching; "I cannot say how fearful I was, lest you should not meet me after all."

"Indeed, Walter," replied Ellinor, "I found some difficulty in concealing your note, which was given me in Madeline's presence; and still more, in stealing out unobserved by her, for she has been, as you may well conceive, unusually restless the whole of this agonizing day. Ah, Walter, would to God you had never left us!"

"Rather say," rejoined Walter—"that this unhappy man, against whom my father's ashes still seem to me to cry aloud, had never come into our peaceful and happy valley! Then you would not have reproached me, that I have sought justice on a suspected murderer; nor I have longed for death rather than, in that justice, have inflicted such distress and horror on those whom I love the best!"

"What! Walter, you yet believe—you are yet convinced that Eugene Aram is the real criminal?"

"Let to-morrow shew," answered Walter. "But poor, poor Madeline! How does she bear up against this long suspense? You know I have not seen her for months."

"Oh! Walter," said Ellinor, weeping bitterly, "you would not know her, so dreadfully is she altered. I fear—" (here sobs choked the sister's voice, so as to leave it scarcely audible)—"that she is not many weeks for this world!"

"Great God! is it so?" exclaimed Walter, so shocked, that the tree against which he leant scarcely preserved him from falling to the ground, as the thousand remembrances of his first love rushed upon his heart. "And Providence singled me out of the whole world, to strike this blow!"

Despite her own grief, Ellinor was touched and smitten by the violent emotion of her cousin; and the two young persons, lovers—though love was at this time the least perceptible feeling of their breasts—mingled their emotions, and sought, at least to console and cheer each other.

"It may yet be better than our fears," said Ellinor, soothingly. "Eugene may be found guiltless, and in that joy we may forget all the past."

Walter shook his head despondingly. "Your heart, Ellinor, was always kind to me. You now are the only one to do me justice, and to see how utterly reproachless I am for all the misery the crime of another occasions. But my uncle—him, too, I have not seen for some time: is he well?"

"Yes, Walter, yes," said Ellinor, kindly disguising the real truth, how much her father's vigorous frame had been bowed by his state of mind. "And I, you see," added she, with a faint attempt to smile,—"I am, in health at least, the same as when, this time last year, we were all happy and full of hope."

Walter looked hard upon that face, once so vivid with the rich colour and the buoyant and arch expression of liveliness and youth, now pale, subdued, and worn by the traces of constant tears; and, pressing his hand convulsively on his heart, turned away.

"But can I not see my uncle?" said he, after a pause.

"He is not at home: he has gone to the Castle," replied Ellinor.

"I shall meet him, then, on his way home," returned Walter. "But, Ellinor, there is surely no truth in a vague rumour which I heard in the town, that Madeline intends to be present at the trial to-morrow."

"Indeed, I fear that she will. Both my father and myself have sought strongly and urgently to dissuade her; but in vain. You know, with all that gentleness, how resolute she is when her mind is once determined on any object."

"But if the verdict should be against the prisoner, in her state of health consider how terrible would be the shock!—Nay, even the joy of acquittal might be equally dangerous—for Heaven's sake! do not suffer her."

"What is to be done, Walter?" said Ellinor, wringing her hands. "We cannot help it. My father has, at last, forbid me to contradict the wish. Contradiction, the physician himself says, might be as fatal as concession can be. And my father adds, in a stern, calm voice, which it breaks my heart to hear, 'Be still, Ellinor. If the innocent is to perish, the sooner she joins him the better: I would then have all my ties on the other side the grave!'"

"How that strange man seems to have fascinated you all!" said Walter, bitterly.

Ellinor did not answer: over her the fascination had never been to an equal degree with the rest of her family.

"Ellinor!" said Walter, who had been walking for the last few moments to and fro with the rapid strides of a man debating with himself, and who now suddenly paused, and laid his hand on his cousin's arm—"Ellinor! I am resolved. I must, for the quiet of my soul, I must see Madeline this night, and win her forgiveness for all I have been made the unintentional agent of Providence to bring upon her. The peace of my future life may depend on this single interview. What if Aram be condemned—and—and—in short, it is no matter—I must see her."

"She would not hear of it, I fear," said Ellinor, in alarm. "Indeed, you cannot—you do not know her state of mind."

"Ellinor!" said Walter, doggedly, "I am resolved." And so saying, he moved towards the house.

"Well, then," said Ellinor, whose nerves had been greatly shattered by the scenes and sorrow of the last several months, "if it must be so, wait at least till I have gone in, and consulted or prepared her."

"As you will, my gentlest, kindest cousin; I know your prudence and affection. I leave you to obtain me this interview; you can, and will, I am convinced."

"Do not be sanguine, Walter. I can only promise to use my best endeavours," answered Ellinor, blushing as he kissed her hand; and, hurrying up the walk, she disappeared within the house.

Walter walked for some moments about the alley in which Ellinor had left him, but growing impatient, he at length wound through the overhanging trees, and the house stood immediately before him,—the moonlight shining full on the window-panes, and sleeping in quiet shadow over the green turf in front. He approached yet nearer, and through one of the windows, by a single light in the room, he saw Ellinor leaning over a couch, on which a form reclined, that his heart, rather than his sight, told him was his once-adored Madeline. He stopped, and his breath heaved thick;—he thought of their common home at Grassdale—of the old Manor-house—of the little parlour with the woodbine at its casement—of the group within, once so happy and light-hearted, of which he had formerly made the one most buoyant, and not least-loved. And now this strange—this desolate house—himself estranged from all once regarding him,—(and those broken-hearted,)—this night ushering what a morrow!—he groaned almost aloud, and retreated once more into the shadow of the trees. In a few minutes the door at the right of the building opened, and Ellinor came forth with a quick step.

"Come in, dear Walter," said she; "Madeline has consented to see you—nay, when I told her you were here, and desired an interview, she paused but for one instant, and then begged me to admit you."

"God bless her!" said poor Walter, drawing his hand across his eyes, and following Ellinor to the door.

"You will find her greatly changed!" whispered Ellinor, as they gained the outer hall; "be prepared!"

Walter did not reply, save by an expressive gesture; and Ellinor led him into a room, which communicated, by one of those glass doors often to be seen in the old-fashioned houses of country towns, with the one in which he had previously seen Madeline. With a noiseless step, and almost holding his breath, he followed his fair guide through this apartment, and he now stood by the couch on which Madeline still reclined. She held out her hand to him—he pressed it to his lips, without daring to look her in the face; and after a moment's pause, she said—

"So, you wished to see me, Walter! It is an anxious night this for all of us!"

"For all!" repeated Walter, emphatically; "and for me not the least!"

"We have known some sad days since we last met!" renewed Madeline; and there was another, and an embarrassed pause.

"Madeline—dearest Madeline!" said Walter, at length dropping on his knee; "you, whom while I was yet a boy, I so fondly, passionately loved;—you, who yet are—who, while I live, ever will be, so inexpressibly dear to me—say but one word to me on this uncertain and dreadful epoch of our fate—say but one word to me—say you feel you are conscious that throughout these terrible events I have not been to blame—I have not willingly brought this affliction upon our house—least of all upon that heart which my own would have forfeited its best blood to preserve from the slightest evil;—or, if you will not do me this justice, say at least that you forgive me!"

"I forgive you, Walter! I do you justice, my cousin!" replied Madeline, with energy; and raising herself on her arm. "It is long since I have felt how unreasonable it was to throw any blame upon you—the mere and passive instrument of fate. If I have forborne to see you, it was not from an angry feeling, but from a reluctant weakness. God bless and preserve you, my dear cousin! I know that your own heart has bled as profusely as ours; and it was but this day that I told my father, if we never met again, to express to you some kind message as a last memorial from me. Don't weep, Walter! It is a fearful thing to see men weep! It is only once that I have seen him weep,—that was long, long ago! He has no tears in the hour of dread and danger. But no matter, this is a bad world, Walter, and I am tired of it. Are not you? Why do you look so at me, Ellinor? I am not mad! Has she told you that I am, Walter? Don't believe her! Look at me! I am calm and collected! Yet to-morrow is—O God! O God!—if!—if!—"

Madeline covered her face with her hands, and became suddenly silent, though only for a short time; when she again lifted up her eyes, they encountered those of Walter; as through those blinding and agonised tears, which are only wrung from the grief of manhood, he gazed upon that face on which nothing of herself, save the divine and unearthly expression which had always characterised her loveliness, was left.

"Yes, Walter, I am wearing fast away—fast beyond the power of chance! Thank God, who tempers the wind to the shorn lamb, if the worst happen, we cannot be divided long. Ere another Sabbath has passed, I may be with him in Paradise! What cause shall we then have for regret?"

Ellinor flung herself on her sister's neck, sobbing violently.—"Yes, we shall regret you are not with us, Ellinor; but you will also soon grow tired of the world; it is a sad place—it is a wicked place—it is full of snares and pitfalls. In our walk to-day lies our destruction for to-morrow! You will find this soon, Ellinor! And you, and my father, and Walter, too, shall join us! Hark! the clock strikes! By this time to-morrow night, what triumph!—or to me at least (sinking her voice into a whisper, that thrilled through the very bones of her listeners) what peace!"

Happily for all parties, this distressing scene was here interrupted. Lester entered the room with the heavy step into which his once elastic and cheerful tread had subsided.

"Ha, Walter!" said he, irresolutely glancing over the group; but Madeline had already sprang from her seat.

"You have seen him!—you have seen him! And how does he—how does he look? But that I know; I know his brave heart does not sink. And what message does he send to me? And—and—tell me all, my father: quick, quick!"

"Dear, miserable child!—and miserable old man!" muttered Lester, folding her in his arms; "but we ought to take courage and comfort from him, Madeline. A hero, on the eve of battle, could not be more firm—even more cheerful. He smiled often—his old smile; and he only left tears and anxiety to us. But of you, Madeline, we spoke mostly: he would scarcely let me say a word on any thing else. Oh, what a kind heart!—what a noble spirit! And perhaps a chance tomorrow may quench both. But, God! be just, and let the avenging lightning fall on the real criminal, and not blast the innocent man!"

"Amen!" said Madeline deeply.

"Amen!" repeated Walter, laying his hand on his heart.

"Let us pray!" exclaimed Lester, animated by a sudden impulse, and falling on his knees. The whole group followed his example; and Lester, in a trembling and impassioned voice, poured forth an extempore prayer, that Justice might fall only where it was due. Never did that majestic and pausing Moon, which filled that lowly room as with the presence of a spirit, witness a more impressive adjuration, or an audience more absorbed and rapt. Full streamed its holy rays upon the now snowy locks and upward countenance of Lester, making his venerable person more striking from the contrast it afforded to the dark and sunburnt cheek—the energetic features, and chivalric and earnest head of the young man beside him. Just in the shadow, the raven locks of Ellinor were bowed over her clasped hands,—nothing of her face visible; the graceful neck and heaving breast alone distinguished from the shadow;—and, hushed in a death-like and solemn repose, the parted lips moving inaudibly; the eye fixed on vacancy; the wan transparent hands, crossed upon her bosom; the light shone with a more softened and tender ray upon the faded but all-angelic form and countenance of her, for whom Heaven was already preparing its eternal recompense for the ills of Earth!

CHAPTER V.

THE TRIAL.
"Equal to either fortune."—Speech of Eugene Aram.

A thought comes over us, sometimes, in our career of pleasure, or the troublous exultation of our ambitious pursuits; a thought come over us, like a cloud, that around us and about us Death—Shame—Crime—Despair, are busy at their work. I have read somewhere of an enchanted land, where the inmates walked along voluptuous gardens, and built palaces, and heard music, and made merry; while around, and within, the land, were deep caverns, where the gnomes and the fiends dwelt: and ever and anon their groans and laughter, and the sounds of their unutterable toils, or ghastly revels, travelled to the upper air, mixing in an awful strangeness with the summer festivity and buoyant occupation of those above. And this is the picture of human life! These reflections of the maddening disparities of the world are dark, but salutary:—

"They wrap our thoughts at banquets in the shroud;" [Young.]

but we are seldom sadder without being also wiser men!

The third of August 1759 rose bright, calm, and clear: it was the morning of the trial; and when Ellinor stole into her sister's room, she found Madeline sitting before the glass, and braiding her rich locks with an evident attention and care.

"I wish," said she, "that you had pleased me by dressing as for a holiday. See, I am going to wear the dress I was to have been married in."

Ellinor shuddered; for what is more appalling than to find the signs of gaiety accompanying the reality of anguish!

"Yes," continued Madeline, with a smile of inexpressible sweetness, "a little reflection will convince you that this day ought not to be one of mourning. It was the suspense that has so worn out our hearts. If he is acquitted, as we all believe and trust, think how appropriate will be the outward seeming of our joy! If not, why I shall go before him to our marriage home, and in marriage garments. Ay," she added after a moment's pause, and with a much more grave, settled, and intense expression of voice and countenance—"ay; do you remember how Eugene once told us, that if we went at noonday to the bottom of a deep pit, [Note: The remark is in Aristotle. Buffon quotes it, with his usual adroit felicity, in, I think, the first volume of his great work.] we should be able to see the stars, which on the level ground are invisible. Even so, from the depths of grief—worn, wretched, seared, and dying—the blessed apparitions and tokens of Heaven make themselves visible to our eyes. And I know—I have seen—I feel here," pressing her hand on her heart, "that my course is run; a few sands only are left in the glass. Let us waste them bravely. Stay, Ellinor! You see these poor withered rose-leaves: Eugene gave them to me the day before—before that fixed for our marriage. I shall wear them to-day, as I would have worn them on the wedding-day. When he gathered the poor flower, how fresh it was; and I kissed off the dew: now see it! But, come, come; this is trifling: we must not be late. Help me, Nell, help me: come, bustle, quick, quick! Nay, be not so slovenly; I told you I would be dressed with care to-day."

And when Madeline was dressed, though the robe sat loose and in large folds over her shrunken form, yet, as she stood erect, and looked with a smile that saddened Ellinor more than tears at her image in the glass, perhaps her beauty never seemed of a more striking and lofty character,—she looked indeed, a bride, but the bride of no earthly nuptials. Presently they heard an irresolute and trembling step at the door, and Lester knocking, asked if they were prepared.

"Come in, father," said Madeline, in a calm and even cheerful voice; and the old man entered.

He cast a silent glance over Madeline's white dress, and then at his own, which was deep mourning: the glance said volumes, and its meaning was not marred by words from any one of the three.

"Yes, father," said Madeline, breaking the pause,—"We are all ready. Is the carriage here?"

"It is at the door, my child."

"Come then, Ellinor, come!"—and leaning on her arm, Madeline walked towards the door. When she got to the threshold, she paused, and looked round the room.

"What is it you want?" asked Ellinor.

"I was but bidding all here farewell," replied Madeline, in a soft and touching voice: "And now before we leave the house, Father,—Sister, one word with you;—you have ever been very, very kind to me, and most of all in this bitter trial, when I must have taxed your patience sadly—for I know all is not right here, (touching her forehead)—I cannot go forth this day without thanking you. Ellinor, my dearest friend—my fondest sister—my playmate in gladness—my comforter in grief—my nurse in sickness;—since we were little children, we have talked together, and laughed together, and wept together, and though we knew all the thoughts of each other, we have never known one thoughts that we would have concealed from God;—and now we are going to part?—do not stop me, it must be so, I know it. But, after a little while may you be happy again, not so buoyant as you have been, that can never be, but still happy!—You are formed for love and home, and for those ties you once thought would be mine. God grant that I may have suffered for us both, and that when we meet hereafter, you may tell me you have been happy here!"

"But you, father," added Madeline, tearing herself from the neck of her weeping sister, and sinking on her knees before Lester, who leaned against the wall convulsed with his emotions, and covering his face with his hands—"but you,—what can I say to you?—You, who have never,—no, not in my first childhood, said one harsh word to me—who have sunk all a father's authority in a father's love,—how can I say all that I feel for you?—the grateful overflowing, (paining, yet—oh, how sweet!) remembrances which crowd around and suffocate me now?—The time will come when Ellinor and Ellinor's children must be all in all to you—when of your poor Madeline nothing will be left but a memory; but they, they will watch on you and tend you, and protect your grey hairs from sorrow, as I might once have hoped I also was fated to do."

"My child! my child! you break my heart!" faltered forth at last the poor old man, who till now had in vain endeavoured to speak.

"Give me your blessing, dear father," said Madeline, herself overcome by her feelings;—"Put your hand on my head and bless me—and say, that if I have ever unconsciously given you a moment's pain—I am forgiven!"

"Forgiven!" repeated Lester, raising his daughter with weak and trembling arms as his tears fell fast upon her cheek,—"Never did I feel what an angel had sate beside my hearth till now!—But be comforted—be cheered. What, if Heaven had reserved its crowning mercy till this day, and Eugene be amongst us, free, acquitted, triumphant before the night!"

"Ha!" said Madeline, as if suddenly roused by the thought into new life:—"Ha! let us hasten to find your words true. Yes! yes!—if it should be so—if it should. And," added she, in a hollow voice, (the enthusiasm checked,) "if it were not for my dreams, I might believe it would be so:—But—come—I am ready now!"

The carriage went slowly through the crowd that the fame of the approaching trial had gathered along the streets, but the blinds were drawn down, and the father and daughter escaped that worst of tortures, the curious gaze of strangers on distress. Places had been kept for them in court, and as they left the carriage and entered the fatal spot, the venerable figure of Lester, and the trembling and veiled forms that clung to him, arrested all eyes. They at length gained their seats, and it was not long before a bustle in the court drew off attention from them. A buzz, a murmur, a movement, a dread pause! Houseman was first arraigned on his former indictment, acquitted, and admitted evidence against Aram, who was thereupon arraigned. The prisoner stood at the bar! Madeline gasped for breath, and clung, with a convulsive motion, to her sister's arm. But presently, with a long sigh she recovered her self-possession, and sat quiet and silent, fixing her eyes upon Aram's countenance; and the aspect of that countenance was well calculated to sustain her courage, and to mingle a sort of exulting pride, with all the strained and fearful acuteness of her sympathy. Something, indeed, of what he had suffered, was visible in the prisoner's features; the lines around the mouth in which mental anxiety generally the most deeply writes its traces, were grown marked and furrowed; grey hairs were here and there scattered amongst the rich and long luxuriance of the dark brown locks, and as, before his imprisonment, he had seemed considerably younger than he was, so now time had atoned for its past delay, and he might have appeared to have told more years than had really gone over his head; but the remarkable light and beauty of his eye was undimmed as ever, and still the broad expanse of his forehead retained its unwrinkled surface and striking expression of calmness and majesty. High, self-collected, serene, and undaunted, he looked upon the crowd, the scene, the judge, before and around him; and, even among those who believed him guilty, that involuntary and irresistible respect which moral firmness always produces on the mind, forced an unwilling interest in his fate, and even a reluctant hope of his acquittal.

Houseman was called upon. No one could regard his face without a certain mistrust and inward shudder. In men prone to cruelty, it has generally been remarked, that there is an animal expression strongly prevalent in the countenance. The murderer and the lustful man are often alike in the physical structure. The bull-throat—the thick lips—the receding forehead—the fierce restless eye—which some one or other says reminds you of the buffalo in the instant before he becomes dangerous, are the outward tokens of the natural animal unsoftened—unenlightened—unredeemed—consulting only the immediate desires of his nature, whatever be the passion (lust or revenge) to which they prompt. And this animal expression, the witness of his character, was especially wrought, if we may use the word, in Houseman's rugged and harsh features; rendered, if possible, still more remarkable at that time by a mixture of sullenness and timidity. The conviction that his own life was saved, could not prevent remorse at his treachery in accusing his comrade—a sort of confused principle of which villains are the most susceptible, when every other honest sentiment has deserted them.

With a low, choked, and sometimes a faltering tone, Houseman deposed, that, in the night between the 7th and 8th of January 1744-5, sometime before 11 o'clock, he went to Aram's house—that they conversed on different matters—that he stayed there about an hour—that some three hours afterwards he passed, in company with Clarke, by Aram's house, and Aram was outside the door, as if he were about to return home—that Aram invited them both to come in—that they did so—that Clarke, who intended to leave the town before day-break, in order, it was acknowledged, to make secretly away with certain property in his possession, was about to quit the house, when Aram proposed to accompany him out of the town—that he (Aram) and Houseman then went forth with Clarke—that when they came into the field where St. Robert's Cave is, Aram and Clarke went into it, over the hedge, and when they came within six or eight yards off the Cave, he saw them quarrelling—that he saw Aram strike Clarke several times, upon which Clarke fell, and he never saw him rise again—that he saw no instrument Aram had, and knew not that he had any—that upon this, without any interposition or alarm, he left them and returned home—that the next morning he went to Aram's house, and asked what business he had with Clarke last night, and what he had done with him? Aram replied not to this question; but threatened him, if he spoke of his being in Clarke's company that night; vowing revenge either by himself or some other person if he mentioned any thing relating to the affair. This was the sum of Houseman's evidence.

A Mr. Beckwith was next called, who deposed that Aram's garden had been searched, owing to a vague suspicion that he might have been an accomplice in the frauds of Clarke—that some parts of clothing, and also some pieces of cambric which he had sold to Clarke a little while before, were found there.

The third witness was the watchman, Thomas Barnet, who deposed, that before midnight (it might be a little after eleven) he saw a person come out from Aram's house, who had a wide coat on, with the cape about his head, and seemed to shun him; whereupon he went up to him, and put by the cape of his great coat, and perceived it to be Richard Houseman. He contented himself with wishing him good night.

The officers who executed the warrant then gave their evidence as to the arrest, and dwelt on some expressions dropped by Aram before he arrived at Knaresbro', which, however, were felt to be wholly unimportant.

After this evidence there was a short pause;—and then a shiver, that recoil and tremor which men feel at any exposition of the relics of the dead, ran through the court; for the next witness was mute—it was the skull of the Deceased! On the left side there was a fracture, that from the nature of it seemed as it could only have been made by the stroke of some blunt instrument. The piece was broken, and could not be replaced but from within.

The surgeon, Mr. Locock, who produced it, gave it as his opinion that no such breach could proceed from natural decay—that it was not a recent fracture by the instrument with which it was dug up, but seemed to be of many years' standing.

This made the chief part of the evidence against Aram; the minor points we have omitted, and also such as, like that of Aram's hostess, would merely have repeated what the reader knew before.

And now closed the criminatory evidence—and now the prisoner was asked, in that peculiarly thrilling and awful question—What he had to say in his own behalf? Till now, Aram had not changed his posture or his countenance—his dark and piercing eye had for one instant fixed on each witness that appeared against him, and then dropped its gaze upon the ground. But at this moment a faint hectic flushed his cheek, and he seemed to gather and knit himself up for defence. He glanced round the court, as if to see what had been the impression created against him. His eye rested on the grey locks of Rowland Lester, who, looking down, had covered his face with his hands. But beside that venerable form was the still and marble face of Madeline; and even at that distance from him, Aram perceived how intent was the hush and suspense of her emotions. But when she caught his eye—that eye which even at such a moment beamed unutterable love, pity, regret for her—a wild, a convulsive smile of encouragement, of anticipated triumph, broke the repose of her colourless features, and suddenly dying away, left her lips apart, in that expression which the great masters of old, faithful to Nature, give alike to the struggle of hope and the pause of terror.

"My Lord," began Aram, in that remarkable defence still extant, and still considered as wholly unequalled from the lips of one defending his own, and such a, cause;—"My Lord, I know not whether it is of right, or through some indulgence of your Lordship, that I am allowed the liberty at this bar, and at this time, to attempt a defence; incapable and uninstructed as I am to speak. Since, while I see so many eyes upon me, so numerous and awful a concourse, fixed with attention, and filled with I know not what expectancy, I labour, not with guilt, my Lord, but with perplexity. For, having never seen a court but this, being wholly unacquainted with law, the customs of the bar, and all judiciary proceedings, I fear I shall be so little capable of speaking with propriety, that it might reasonably be expected to exceed my hope, should I be able to speak at all.

"I have heard, my Lord, the indictment read, wherein I find myself charged with the highest of human crimes. You will grant me then your patience, if I, single and unskilful, destitute of friends, and unassisted by counsel, attempt something perhaps like argument in my defence. What I have to say will be but short, and that brevity may be the best part of it.

"My Lord, the tenor of my life contradicts this indictment. Who can look back over what is known of my former years, and charge me with one vice—one offence? No! I concerted not schemes of fraud—projected no violence—injured no man's property or person. My days were honestly laborious—my nights intensely studious. This egotism is not presumptuous—is not unreasonable. What man, after a temperate use of life, a series of thinking and acting regularly, without one single deviation from a sober and even tenor of conduct, ever plunged into the depth of crime precipitately, and at once? Mankind are not instantaneously corrupted. Villainy is always progressive. We decline from right—not suddenly, but step after step.

"If my life in general contradicts the indictment, my health at that time in particular contradicts it yet more. A little time before, I had been confined to my bed, I had suffered under a long and severe disorder. The distemper left me but slowly, and in part. So far from being well at the time I am charged with this fact, I never, to this day, perfectly recovered. Could a person in this condition execute violence against another?—I, feeble and valetudinary, with no inducement to engage—no ability to accomplish—no weapon wherewith to perpetrate such a fact;—without interest, without power, without motives, without means!

"My Lord, Clarke disappeared: true; but is that a proof of his death? The fallibility of all conclusions of such a sort, from such a circumstance, is too obvious to require instances. One instance is before you: this very castle affords it.

"In June 1757, William Thompson, amidst all the vigilance of this place, in open daylight, and double-ironed, made his escape; notwithstanding an immediate inquiry set on foot, notwithstanding all advertisements, all search, he was never seen or heard of since. If this man escaped unseen through all these difficulties, how easy for Clarke, whom no difficulties opposed. Yet what would be thought of a prosecution commenced against any one seen last with Thompson?

"These bones are discovered! Where? Of all places in the world, can we think of any one, except indeed the church-yard, where there is so great a certainty of finding human bones, as a hermitage? In times past, the hermitage was a place, not only of religious retirement, but of burial. And it has scarce, or never been heard of, but that every cell now known, contains, or contained these relics of humanity; some mutilated—some entire! Give me leave to remind your Lordship, that here sat SOLITARY SANCTITY, and here the hermit and the anchorite hoped that repose for their bones when dead, they here enjoyed when living. I glance over a few of the many evidences that these cells were used as repositories of the dead, and enumerate a few of the many caves similar in origin to St. Robert's, in which human bones have been found." Here the prisoner instanced, with remarkable felicity, several places, in which bones had been found, under circumstances, and in spots analogous to those in point. [Note: See his published defence.] And the reader, who will remember that it is the great principle of the law, that no man can be condemned for murder unless the body of the deceased be found, will perceive at once how important this point was to the prisoner's defence. After concluding his instances with two facts of skeletons found in fields in the vicinity of Knaresbro', he burst forth—"Is then the invention of those bones forgotten or industriously concealed, that the discovery of these in question may appear the more extraordinary? Extraordinary—yet how common an event! Every place conceals such remains. In fields—in hills—in high-way sides—on wastes—on commons, lie frequent and unsuspected bones. And mark,—no example perhaps occurs of more than one skeleton being found in one cell. Here you find but one, agreeable to the peculiarity of every known cell in Britain. Had two skeletons been discovered, then alone might the fact have seemed suspicious and uncommon. What! Have we forgotten how difficult, as in the case of Perkin Warbeck and Lambert Symnell, it has been sometimes to identify the living; and shall we now assign personality to bones—bones which may belong to either sex? How know you that this is even the skeleton of a man? But another skeleton was discovered by some labourer! Was not that skeleton averred to be Clarke's full as confidently as this?

"My Lord, my Lord—must some of the living be made answerable for all the bones that earth has concealed and chance exposed? The skull that has been produced, has been declared fractured. But who can surely tell whether it was the cause or the consequence of death. In May, 1732 the remains of William Lord Archbishop of this province were taken up by permission in their cathedral, the bones of the skull were found broken as these are. Yet he died by no violence! by no blow that could have caused that fracture. Let it be considered how easily the fracture on the skull produced is accounted for. At the dissolution of religious houses, the ravages of the times affected both the living and the dead. In search after imaginary treasures, coffins were broken, graves and vaults dug open, monuments ransacked, shrines demolished, Parliament itself was called in to restrain these violations. And now are the depredations, the iniquities of those times, to be visited on this? But here, above all, was a castle vigorously besieged; every spot around was the scene of a sally, a conflict, a flight, a pursuit. Where the slaughtered fell, there were they buried. What place is not burial earth in war? How many bones must still remain in the vicinity of that siege, for futurity to discover! Can you, then, with so many probable circumstances, choose the one least probable? Can you impute to the living what Zeal in its fury may have done; what Nature may have taken off and Piety interred, or what War alone may have destroyed, alone deposited?

"And now, glance over the circumstantial evidence, how weak, how frail! I almost scorn to allude to it. I will not condescend to dwell upon it. The witness of one man, arraigned himself! Is there no chance that to save his own life he might conspire against mine?—no chance that he might have committed this murder, if murder hath indeed been done? that conscience betrayed to his first exclamation? that craft suggested his throwing that guilt on me, to the knowledge of which he had unwittingly confessed? He declares that he saw me strike Clarke, that he saw him fall; yet he utters no cry, no reproof. He calls for no aid; he returns quietly home; he declares that he knows not what became of the body, yet he tells where the body is laid. He declares that he went straight home, and alone; yet the woman with whom I lodged declares that Houseman and I returned to my house in company together;—what evidence is this? and from whom does it come?—ask yourselves. As for the rest of the evidence, what does it amount to? The watchman sees Houseman leave my house at night. What more probable, but what less connected with the murder, real or supposed, of Clarke? Some pieces of clothing are found buried in my garden. But how can it be shewn that they belonged to Clarke? Who can swear to, who can prove any thing so vague? And if found there, even if belonging to Clarke, what proof that they were there deposited by me? How likely that the real criminal may in the dead of night have preferred any spot, rather than that round his own home, to conceal the evidence of his crime!

"How impotent such evidence as this! and how poor, how precarious, even the strongest of mere circumstantial evidence invariably is! Let it rise to probability, to the strongest degree of probability; it is but probability still. Recollect the case of the two Harrisons, recorded by Dr. Howell; both suffered on circumstantial evidence on account of the disappearance of a man, who, like Clarke, contracted debts, borrowed money, and went off unseen. And this man returned several years after their execution. Why remind you of Jaques du Moulin, in the reign of Charles the Second?—why of the unhappy Coleman, convicted, though afterwards found innocent, and whose children perished for want, because the world believed the father guilty? Why should I mention the perjury of Smith, who, admitted king's-evidence, screened himself by accusing Fainloth and Loveday of the murder of Dunn? the first was executed, the second was about to share the same fate, when the perjury of Smith was incontrovertibly proved.

"And now, my Lord, having endeavoured to shew that the whole of this charge is altogether repugnant to every part of my life; that it is inconsistent with my condition of health about that time; that no rational inference of the death of a person can be drawn from his disappearance; that hermitages were the constant repositories of the bones of the recluse; that the proofs of these are well authenticated; that the revolutions in religion, or the fortune of war, have mangled or buried the dead; that the strongest circumstantial evidence is often lamentably fallacious, that in my case, that evidence, so far from being strong, is weak, disconnected, contradictory; what remains? A conclusion, perhaps, no less reasonably than impatiently wished for. I, at last, after nearly a year's confinement, equal to either fortune, entrust myself to the candour, the justice, the humanity of your Lordship, and to yours, my countrymen, gentlemen of the jury."

The prisoner ceased: and the painful and choking sensations of sympathy, compassion, regret, admiration, all uniting, all mellowing into one fearful hope for his acquittal, made themselves felt through the crowded court.

In two persons only, an uneasy sentiment remained—a sentiment that the prisoner had not completed that which they would have asked from him. The one was Lester;—he had expected a more warm, a more earnest, though, perhaps, a less ingenious and artful defence. He had expected Aram to dwell far more on the improbable and contradictory evidence of Houseman, and above all, to have explained away, all that was still left unaccounted for in his acquaintance with Clarke (as we will still call the deceased), and the allegation that he had gone out with him on the fatal night of the disappearance of the latter. At every word of the prisoner's defence, he had waited almost breathlessly, in the hope that the next sentence would begin an explanation or a denial on this point: and when Aram ceased, a chill, a depression, a disappointment, remained vaguely on his mind. Yet so lightly and so haughtily had Aram approached and glanced over the immediate evidence of the witnesses against him, that his silence her might have been but the natural result of a disdain, that belonged essentially to his calm and proud character. The other person we referred to, and whom his defence had not impressed with a belief in its truth, equal to an admiration for its skill, was one far more important in deciding the prisoner's fate—it was the Judge!

But Madeline—Great God! how sanguine is a woman's heart, when the innocence, the fate of the one she loves is concerned!—a radiant flush broke over a face so colourless before; and with a joyous look, a kindled eye, a lofty brow, she turned to Ellinor, pressed her hand in silence, and once more gave up her whole soul to the dread procedure of the court.

The Judge now began.—It is greatly to be regretted, that we have no minute and detailed memorial of the trial, except only the prisoner's defence. The summing up of the Judge was considered at that time scarce less remarkable than the speech of the prisoner. He stated the evidence with peculiar care and at great length to the jury. He observed how the testimony of the other deponents confirmed that of Houseman; and then, touching on the contradictory parts of the latter, he made them understand, how natural, how inevitable was some such contradiction in a witness who had not only to give evidence against another, but to refrain from criminating himself. There could be no doubt but that Houseman was an accomplice in the crime; and all therefore that seemed improbable in his giving no alarm when the deed was done, was easily rendered natural, and reconcileable with the other parts of his evidence. Commenting then on the defence of the prisoner (who, as if disdaining to rely on aught save his own genius or his own innocence, had called no witnesses, as he had employed no counsel), and eulogizing its eloquence and art, till he destroyed their effect by guarding the jury against that impression which eloquence and art produce in defiance of simple fact, he contended that Aram had yet alleged nothing to invalidate the positive evidence against him.

I have often heard, from men accustomed to courts of law, that nothing is more marvellous, than the sudden change in a jury's mind, which the summing up of the Judge can produce; and in the present instance it was like magic. That fatal look of a common intelligence, of a common assent, was exchanged among the doomers of the prisoner's life and death as the Judge concluded.

They found the prisoner guilty.

The Judge drew on the black cap.

CHAPTER VI.

THE DEATH.—THE PRISON.—AN INTERVIEW.—ITS RESULT.

> "Lay her i' the earth,
> And from her fair and unpolluted flesh
> May violets spring."
> ....
> "See in my heart there was a kind of fighting
>
> That would not let me sleep."
> —Hamlet.

"Bear with me a little longer," said Madeline. "I shall be well, quite well presently."

Ellinor let down the carriage window, to admit the air; and she took the occasion to tell the coachman to drive faster. There was that change in Madeline's voice which alarmed her.

"How noble was his look! you saw him smile!" continued Madeline, talking to herself: "And they will murder him after all. Let me see, this day week, ay, ere this day week we shall meet again."

"Faster; for God's sake, Ellinor, tell them to drive faster!" cried Lester, as he felt the form that leant on his bosom wax heavier and heavier. They sped on; the house was in sight; that lonely and cheerless house; not their sweet home at Grassdale, with the ivy round its porch, and the quiet church behind. The sun was setting slowly, and Ellinor drew the blind to shade the glare from her sister's eyes.

Madeline felt the kindness, and smiled. Ellinor wiped her eyes, and tried to smile again. The carriage stopped, and Madeline was lifted out; she stood, supported by her father and Ellinor, for a moment on the threshold. She looked on the golden sun, and the gentle earth, and the little motes dancing in the western ray—all was steeped in quiet, and full of the peace and tranquillity of the pastoral life! "No, no," she muttered, grasping her father's hand. "How is this? this is not his hand! Ah, no, no; I am not with him! Father," she added in a louder and deeper voice, rising from his breast, and standing alone and unaided. "Father, bury this little packet with me, they are his letters; do not break the seal, and—and tell him that I never felt how deeply I—I—loved him—till all—the world—had—deserted him!"—

She uttered a faint cry of pain, and fell at once to the ground; she lived a few hours longer, but never made speech or sign, or evinced token of life but its breath, which died at last gradually,—imperceptibly—away.

On the following evening Walter obtained entrance to Aram's cell: that morning the prisoner had seen Lester; that morning he had heard of Madeline's death. He had shed no tear; he had, in the affecting language of Scripture, "turned his face to the wall;" none had seen his emotions; yet Lester felt in that bitter interview, that his daughter was duly mourned.

He did not lift his eyes, when Walter was admitted, and the young man stood almost at his knee before he perceived him. He then looked up and they gazed on each other for a moment, but without speaking, till Walter said in a hollow voice: "Eugene Aram!"

"Ay!"

"Madeline Lester is no more."

"I have heard it! I am reconciled. Better now than later."

"Aram!" said Walter, in a tone trembling with emotion, and passionately clasping his hands, "I entreat, I implore you, at this awful time, if it be within your power, to lift from my heart a load that weighs it to the dust, that if left there, will make me through life a crushed and miserable man;—I implore you, in the name of common humanity, by your hopes of Heaven, to remove it! The time now has irrevocably passed when your denial or your confession could alter your doom; your days are numbered, there is no hope of reprieve; I implore you then, if you were led, I will not ask how or wherefore, to the execution of the crime for the charge of which you die, to say, to whisper to me but one word of confession, and I, the sole child of the murdered man, will forgive you from the bottom of my soul."

Walter paused, unable to proceed.

Aram's brow worked; he turned aside; he made no answer; his head dropped on his bosom, and his eyes were unmovedly fixed on the earth.

"Reflect," continued Walter, recovering himself, "Reflect! I have been the mute instrument in bringing you to this awful fate, in destroying the happiness of my own house—in—in—in breaking the heart of the woman whom I adored even as a boy. If you be innocent, what a dreadful memory is left to me! Be merciful, Aram! be merciful. And if this deed was done by your hand, say to me but one word to remove the terrible uncertainty that now harrows up my being. What now is earth, is man, is opinion, to you? God only now can judge you. The eye of God reads your heart while I speak, and in the awful hour when Eternity opens to you, if the guilt has been indeed committed, think, oh think, how much lighter will be your offence, if, by vanquishing the stubborn heart, you can relieve a human being from a doubt that otherwise will make the curse—the horror of an existence. Aram, Aram, if the father's death came from you, shall the life of the son be made a burthen to him, through you also?"

"What would you have of me? speak!" said Aram, but without lifting his face from his breast.

"Much of your nature belies this crime.—You are wise, calm, beneficent to the distressed. Revenge, passion,—nay, the sharp pangs of hunger, may have urged to one deed; but your soul is not wholly hardened: nay, I think I would so far trust you, that, if at this dread moment—the clay of Madeline Lester scarce yet cold, woe busy and softening at your breast, and the son of the murdered dead before you;—if at this moment you can lay your hand on your heart, and say: 'Before God, and at peril of my soul, I am innocent of this deed,' I will depart—I will believe you, and bear, as bear I may, the reflection, that, in any way I have been one of the unconscious agents of condemning to a fearful death an innocent man! If innocent in this—how good! how perfect in all else! But, if you cannot at so dark a crisis take that oath,—then! oh then! be just—be generous, even in guilt, and let me not be haunted throughout life by the spectre of a ghastly and restless doubt! Speak! oh! speak!"

Well, well may we judge how crushing must have been that doubt in the breast of one naturally bold and fiery, when it thus humbled the very son of the murdered man to forget wrath and vengeance, and descend to prayer! But Walter had heard the defence of Aram; he had marked his mien: not once in that trial had he taken his eyes from the prisoner, and he had felt, like a bolt of ice through his heart, that the sentence passed on the accused, his judgment could not have passed! How dreadful must then have been the state of his mind when, repairing to Lester's house he found it the house of death—the pure, the beautiful spirit gone—the father mourning for his child, and not to be comforted—and Ellinor!—No! scenes like these, thoughts like these, pluck the pride from a man's heart.

"Walter Lester!" said Aram, after a pause; but raising his head with dignity, though on the features there was but one expression—woe, unutterable woe. "Walter Lester! I had thought to quit life with my tale untold: but you have not appealed to me in vain! I tear the self from my heart!—I renounce the last haughty dream, in which I wrapt myself from the ills around me. You shall learn all, and judge accordingly. But to your ear the tale can scarce be told:—the son cannot hear in silence that which, unless I too unjustly, too wholly condemn myself, I must say of the dead! But Time," continued Aram, mutteringly, and with his eyes on vacancy, "Time does not press too fast. Better let the hand speak than the tongue:—yes; the day of execution is—ay, ay—two days yet to it—to-morrow? no! Young man," he said abruptly, turning to Walter, "on the day after to-morrow, about seven in the evening, the eve before that morn fated to be my last—come to me. At that time I will place in your hands a paper containing the whole history that connects myself with your father. On the word of a man on the brink of another world, no truth that imparts your interest therein shall be omitted. But read it not till I am no more; and when read, confide the tale to none, till Lester's grey hairs have gone to the grave. This swear! 'tis an oath difficult perhaps to keep, but—" "As my Redeemer lives, I will swear to both conditions!" cried Walter, with a solemn fervour.

"But tell me now at least"—"Ask me no more!" interrupted Aram, in his turn. "The time is near, when you will know all! Tarry that time, and leave me! Yes, leave me now—at once—leave me!"

To dwell lingeringly over those passages which excite pain without satisfying curiosity, is scarcely the duty of the drama, or of that province even nobler than the drama; for it requires minuter care—indulges in more complete description—yields to more elaborate investigation of motives—commands a greater variety of chords in the human heart—to which, with poor and feeble power for so high, yet so ill-appreciated a task we now, not irreverently if rashly, aspire!

We pass at once—we glance not around us at the chamber of death—at the broken heart of Lester—at the two-fold agony of his surviving child—the agony which mourns and yet seeks to console another—the mixed emotions of Walter, in which, an unsleeping eagerness to learn the fearful all formed the main part—the solitary cell and solitary heart of the convicted—we glance not at these;—we pass at once to the evening in which Aram again saw Walter Lester, and for the last time.

"You are come, punctual to the hour," said he, in a low clear voice: "I have not forgotten my word; the fulfilment of that promise has been a victory over myself which no man can appreciate: but I owed it to you. I have discharged the debt. Enough!—I have done more than I at first purposed. I have extended my narration, but, superficially in some parts, over my life: that prolixity, perhaps I owed to myself. Remember your promise: this seal is not broken till the pulse is stilled in the hand which now gives you these papers!"

Walter renewed his oath, and Aram, pausing for a moment, continued in an altered and softening voice:

"Be kind to Lester: soothe, console him—never by a hint let him think otherwise of me than he does. For his sake more than mine I ask this. Venerable, kind old man! the warmth of human affection has rarely glowed for me. To the few who loved me, how deeply I have repaid the love! But these are not words to pass between you and me. Farewell! Yet, before we part, say this much: whatever I have revealed in this confession—whatever has been my wrong to you, or whatever (a less offence) the language I have now, justifying myself, used to—to your father—say, that you grant me that pardon which one man may grant another."

"Fully, cordially," said Walter.

"In the day that for you brings the death that to-morrow awaits me," said Aram, in a deep tone, "be that forgiveness accorded to yourself! Farewell. In that untried variety of Being which spreads beyond us, who knows, but progressing from grade to grade, and world to world, our souls, though in far distant ages, may meet again!—one dim and shadowy memory of this hour the link between us, farewell—farewell!"

For the reader's interest we think it better (and certainly it is more immediately in the due course of narrative, if not of actual events) to lay at once before him the Confession that Aram placed in Walter's hands, without waiting till that time when Walter himself broke the seal of a confession, not of deeds alone, but of thoughts how wild and entangled—of feelings how strange and dark—of a starred soul that had wandered from, how proud an orbit, to what perturbed and unholy regions of night and chaos! For me, I have not sought to derive the reader's interest from the vulgar sources, that such a tale might have afforded; I have suffered him, almost from the beginning, to pierce into Aram's secret; and I have prepared him for that guilt, with which other narrators of this story might have only sought to surprise.

CHAPTER VII.

THE CONFESSION.—AND THE FATE.

```
"In winter's tedious nights, sit by the fire
With good old folks, and let them tell thee tales
Of woful ages long ago betid:
And ere thou bid good night, to quit their grief,
Tell them the lamentable fall of me."
             —Richard II.
```

"I was born at Ramsgill, a little village in Netherdale. My family had originally been of some rank; they were formerly lords of the town of Aram, on the southern banks of the Tees. But time had humbled these pretensions to consideration; though they were still fondly cherished by the heritors of an ancient name, and idle but haughty recollections. My father resided on a small farm, and was especially skilful in horticulture, a taste I derived from him. When I was about thirteen, the deep and intense Passion that has made the Demon of my life, first stirred palpably within me. I had always been, from my cradle, of a solitary disposition, and inclined to reverie and musing; these traits of character heralded the love that now seized me—the love of knowledge. Opportunity or accident first directed my attention to the abstruser sciences. I poured my soul over that noble study, which is the best foundation of all true discovery; and the success I met with soon turned my pursuits into more alluring channels. History, poetry, the mastery of the past, the spell that admits us into the visionary world, took the place which lines and numbers had done before. I became gradually more and more rapt and solitary in my habits; knowledge assumed a yet more lovely and bewitching character, and every day the passion to attain it increased upon me; I do not, I have not now the heart to do it—enlarge upon what I acquired without assistance, and with labour sweet in proportion to its intensity.

```
[We learn from a letter of Eugene Aram's, now extant, that his
  method of acquiring the learned languages, was, to linger over five
  lines at a time, and never to quit a passage till he thought he had
  comprehended its meaning.]
```

The world, the creation, all things that lived, moved, and were, became to me objects contributing to one passionate, and, I fancied, one exalted end. I suffered the lowlier pleasures of life, and the charms of its more common ties, to glide away from me untasted and unfelt. As you read, in the East, of men remaining motionless for days together, with their eyes fixed upon the heavens, my mind, absorbed in the contemplation of the things above its reach, had no sight of what passed around. My parents died, and I was an orphan. I had no home, and no wealth; but wherever the field contained a flower, or the heavens a star, there was matter of thought and food for delight to me. I wandered alone for months together, seldom sleeping but in the open air, and shunning the human form as that part of God's works from which I could learn the least. I came to Knaresbro': the beauty of the country, a facility in acquiring books from a neighbouring library that was open to me, made me resolve to settle there. And now, new desires opened upon me with new stores: I became seized, possessed, haunted with the ambition of enlightening my race. At first, I had loved knowledge solely for itself: I now saw afar an object grander than knowledge. To what end, said I, are these labours? Why do I feed a lamp which consumes itself in a desert place? Why do I heap up riches, without asking who shall gather them? I was restless and discontented. What could I do? I was friendless; I was strange to my kind; I was shut out from all uses by the wall of my own poverty. I saw my desires checked when their aim was at the highest: all that was proud, and aspiring, and ardent in my nature, was cramped and chilled. I exhausted the learning within my reach. Where, with my appetite excited not slaked, was I, destitute and penniless, to search for more? My abilities, by bowing them to the lowliest tasks, but kept me from famine:—

was this to be my lot for ever? And all the while, I was thus grinding down my soul in order to satisfy the vile physical wants, what golden hours, what glorious advantages, what openings into new heavens of science, what chances of illumining mankind were for ever lost to me! Sometimes when the young, whom I taught some elementary, all-unheeded, initiations into knowledge, came around me; when they looked me in the face with their laughing eyes; when, for they all loved me, they told me their little pleasures and their petty sorrows, I have wished that I could have gone back again into childhood, and becoming as one of them, enter into that heaven of quiet which was denied me now. Yet more often it was with an indignant and chafed rather than a sorrowful spirit that I looked upon my lot; and if I looked beyond it, what could I see of hope? Dig I could; but was all that thirsted and swelled within to be dried up and stifled, in order that I might gain the sustenance of life? Was I to turn menial to the soil, and forget that knowledge was abroad? Was I to starve my mind, that I might keep alive my body? Beg I could not. Where ever lived the real student, the true minister and priest of knowledge, who was not filled with the lofty sense of the dignity of his calling? Was I to shew the sores of my pride, and strip my heart from its clothing, and ask the dull fools of wealth not to let a scholar starve? Pah!—He whom the vilest poverty ever stooped to this, may be the quack, but never the true disciple, of Learning. Steal, rob—worse—ay, all those I or any of my brethren might do:—beg? never! What did I then? I devoted the lowliest part of my knowledge to the procuring the bare means of life, and the grandest,—the knowledge that pierced to the depths of earth, and numbered the stars of heaven—why, that was valueless, save to the possessor.

"In Knaresbro', at this time, I met a distant relation, Richard Houseman. Sometimes in our walks we encountered each other; for he sought me, and I could not always avoid him. He was a man like myself, born to poverty, yet he had always enjoyed what to him was wealth. This seemed a mystery to me; and when we met, we sometimes conversed upon it. 'You are poor, with all your wisdom,' said he. 'I know nothing; but I am never poor. Why is this? The world is my treasury.—I live upon my kind.—Society is my foe.—Laws order me to starve; but self-preservation is an instinct more sacred than society, and more imperious then laws.'

"The undisguised and bold manner of his discourse impressed while it revolted me. I looked upon him as a study, and I combated, in order to learn, him. He had been a soldier—he had seen the greatest part of Europe—he possessed a strong shrewd sense—he was a villain—but a villain bold—adroit—and not then thoroughly unredeemed. His conversation created dark and perturbed reflections. What was that state of society—was it not at war with its own elements—in which vice prospered more than virtue? Knowledge was my dream, that dream I might realize, not by patient suffering, but by active daring. I might wrest from society, to which I owed nothing, the means to be wise and great. Was it not better and nobler to do this, even at my life's hazard, than lie down in a ditch and die the dog's death? Was it not better than such a doom—ay better for mankind—that I should commit one bold wrong, and by that wrong purchase the power of good? I asked myself that question. It is a fearful question; it opens a labyrinth of reasonings, in which the soul may walk and lose itself for ever.

"One day Houseman met me, accompanied by a stranger who had just visited our town, for what purpose you know already. His name—supposed name—was Clarke. Man, I am about to speak plainly of that stranger—his character and his fate. And yet—yet you are his son! I would fain soften the colouring; but I speak truth of myself, and I must not, unless I would blacken my name yet deeper than it deserves, varnish truth when I speak of others. Houseman joined, and presented to me this person. From the first I felt a dislike creep through me at the stranger, which indeed it was easy to account for. He was of a careless and somewhat insolent manner. His countenance was impressed with the lines and character of a thousand vices: you read in the brow and eye the history of a sordid yet reckless life. His conversation was repellent to me beyond expression. He uttered the meanest sentiments, and he chuckled over them as the maxims of a superior sagacity; he avowed himself a knave upon system, and upon the lowest scale. To overreach, to deceive, to elude, to shuffle, to fawn, and to lie, were the arts that he confessed to with so naked and cold a grossness, that one perceived that in the long habits of debasement he was unconscious of what was not debased. Houseman seemed to draw him out: he told us anecdotes of his rascality, and the distresses to which it had brought him; and he finished by saying: 'Yet you see me now almost rich, and wholly contented. I have always been the luckiest of human beings; no matter what ill-chances to-day, good turns up to-morrow. I confess that I bring on myself the ill, and Providence sends me the good.' We met accidentally more than once, and his conversation was always of the same strain—his luck and his rascality: he had no other theme, and no other boast. And did not this stir into gloomy speculation the depths of my mind? Was it not an ordination that called upon men to take fortune in their own hands, when Fate lavished her rewards on this low and creeping thing, that could only enter even Vice by its sewers and alleys? Was it worth while to be virtuous, and look on, while the bad seized upon the feast of life? This man was instinct with the basest passions, the pettiest desires: he gratified them, and Fate smiled upon his daring. I, who had shut out from my heart the poor temptations of sense—I, who fed only the most glorious visions, the most august desires—I, denied myself their fruition, trembling and spell-bound in the cerements of human laws, without hope, without reward,—losing the very powers of virtue because I would not stray into crime.

"These thoughts fell on me darkly and rapidly; but they led to no result. I saw nothing beyond them. I suffered my indignation to gnaw my heart; and preserved the same calm and serene demeanour which had grown with my growth of mind. Nay, while I upbraided Fate, I did not cease to love mankind. I envied—what? the power to serve them! I had been kind and loving to all things from a boy; there was not a dumb animal that would not single me from a crowd as its protector, [Note: All the authentic anecdotes of Aram corroborate the fact of his natural gentleness to all things. A clergyman (the Rev. Mr. Hinton) said that he used frequently to observe Aram, when walking in the garden, stoop down to remove a snail or worm from the path, to prevent its being destroyed. Mr. Hinton ingeniously conjectured that Aram wished to atone for his crime by shewing mercy to every animal and insect: but the fact is, that there are several anecdotes to shew that he was equally humane before the crime was committed. Such are the strange contradictions of the human heart!] and yet I was doomed—but I must not premeditate my tale. In returning, at night, to my own home, from my long and solitary walks, I often passed the house in which Clarke lodged; and sometimes I met him reeling by the door, insulting all who passed; and yet their resentment was absorbed in their disgust. 'And this loathsome, and grovelling thing,' said I, inly, 'squanders on low excesses, wastes upon outrages to society, that with which I could make my soul as a burning lamp, that should shed a light over the world!'"

"There was that in this man's vices which revolted me far more than the villainy of Houseman. The latter had possessed no advantages of education; he descended to no minutiae of sin, he was a plain, blunt, coarse wretch, and his sense threw something respectable around his vices. But in Clarke you saw the traces of happier opportunities of better education; it was in him not the coarseness of manner so much as the sickening, universal canker of vulgarity of mind. Had Houseman money in his purse, he would have paid a debt and relieved a friend from mere indifference; not so the other. Had he been overflowing with wealth, he would have slipped from a creditor, and duped a friend; there was a pitiful and debasing weakness in his nature, which made him regard the lowest meanness as the subtlest wit. His mind too was not only degraded, but broken by his habits of life; a strange, idiotic folly, that made him love laughing at his own littleness, ran through his character. Houseman was young; he might amend; but Clarke had grey hairs and dim eyes; was old in constitution, if not years; and every thing in him was hopeless and confirmed; the leprosy was in the system. Time, in this, has made Houseman what Clarke was then.

"One day, in passing through the street, though it was broad noon, I encountered Clarke in a state of intoxication, and talking to a crowd he had collected around him. I sought to pass in an opposite direction; he would not suffer me; he, whom I sickened to touch, to see, threw himself in my way, and affected gibe and insult, nay even threat. But when he came near, he shrank before the mere glance of my eye, and I passed on unheeding him. The insult galled me; he had taunted my poverty, poverty was a favourite jest with him; it galled me; anger, revenge, no! those passions I had never felt for any man. I could not rouse them for the first time for such a cause; yet I was lowered in my own eyes, I was stung. Poverty! he taunt me! He dream himself, on account of a little yellow dust, my superior! I wandered from the town, and paused by the winding and shagged banks of the river. It was a gloomy winter's day, the waters rolled on black and sullen, and the dry leaves rustled desolately beneath my feet. Who shall tell us that outward nature has no effect upon our mood? All around seemed to frown upon my lot. I read in the face of heaven and earth a confirmation of the curse which man hath set upon poverty. I leant against a tree that overhung the waters, and suffered my thoughts to glide on in the bitter silence of their course. I heard my name uttered—I felt a hand on my arm, I turned, and Houseman was by my side.

"'What, moralizing?' said he, with his rude smile.

"I did not answer him.

"'Look,' said he, pointing to the waters, 'where yonder fish lies waiting his prey, that prey his kind. Come, you have read Nature, is it not so universally?'

"I did not answer him.

"'They who do not as the rest,' he renewed, 'fulfil not the object of their existence; they seek to be wiser than their tribe, and are fools for their pains. Is it not so? I am a plain man, and would learn.'

"Still I did not answer.

"'You are silent,' said he; 'do I offend you?'

"'No!'

"'Now, then,' he continued, 'strange as it may seem, we, so different in mind, are at this moment alike in fortunes. I have not a guinea in the wide world; you, perhaps, are equally destitute. But mark the difference, I, the ignorant man, ere three days have passed, will have filled my purse; you, the wise man, will be still as poor. Come, cast away your wisdom, and do as I do.'

"'How?'

"'Take from the superfluities of others what your necessities crave. My horse, my pistol, a ready hand, a stout heart, these are to me, what coffers are to others. There is the chance of detection and of death; I allow it. But is not this chance better than some certainties?'

"I turned away my face. In the silence of my chamber, and in the solitude of my heart, I had thought, as the robber spoke—there was a strife within me.

"'Will you share the danger and the booty?' renewed Houseman, in a low voice.

"I turned my eyes upon him. 'Speak out,' said I; 'explain your purpose!'

"Houseman's looks brightened.

"'Listen!' said he; 'Clarke, despite his present wealth lawfully gained, is about to purloin more; he has converted his legacy into jewels; he has borrowed other jewels on false pretences; he purposes to make these also his own, and to leave the town in the dead of night; he has confided to me his intention, and asked my aid. He and I, be it known to you, were friends of old; we have shared together other dangers, and other spoils; he has asked my assistance in his flight. Now do you learn my purpose? Let us ease him of his burthen! I offer to you the half; share the enterprise and its fruits.'

"I rose, I walked away, I pressed my hands on my heart; I wished to silence the voice that whispered me within. Houseman saw the conflict; he followed me; he named the value of the prize he proposed to gain; that which he called my share placed all my wished within my reach!—the means of gratifying the one passion of my soul, the food for knowledge, the power of a lone blessed independence upon myself,—and all were in my grasp; no repeated acts of fraud; no continuation of sin, one single act sufficed! I breathed heavily, but I threw not off the emotion that seized my soul; I shut my eyes and shuddered, but the vision still rose before me.

"'Give me your hand,' said Houseman. [Note: Though, in the above part of Aram's confession, it would seem as if Houseman did not allude to more than the robbery of Clarke; it is evident from what follows, that the more heinous crime also was then at least hinted at by Houseman.]

"'No, no,' I said, breaking away from him. 'I must pause—I must consider—I do not yet refuse, but I will not now decide.'—

"Houseman pressed, but I persevered in my determination;—he would have threatened me, but my nature was haughtier than his, and I subdued him. It was agreed that he should seek me that night and learn my choice—the next night was the one on which the deed was to be done. We parted—I returned an altered man to my home. Fate had woven her mesh around me—a new incident had occurred which strengthened the web: there was a poor girl whom I had been accustomed to see in my walks. She supported her family by her dexterity in making lace,—a quiet, patient-looking, gentle creature. Clarke had, a few days since, under pretence of purchasing lace, decoyed her to his house (when all but himself were from home), where he used the most brutal violence towards her. The extreme poverty of the parents had enabled him easily to persuade them to hush up the matter, but something of the story got abroad; the poor girl was marked out for that gossip and scandal, which among the very lowest classes are as coarse in the expression as malignant in the sentiment; and in the paroxysm of shame and despair, the unfortunate girl had that day destroyed herself. This melancholy event wrung forth from the parents the real story: the event and the story reached my ears in the very hour in which my mind was wavering to and fro. Can you wonder that they fixed it at once, and to a dread end? What was this wretch? aged with vice—forestalling time—tottering on to a dishonoured grave—soiling all that he touched on his way—with grey hairs and filthy lewdness, the rottenness of the heart, not its passion, a nuisance and a curse to the world. What was the deed—that I should rid the earth of a thing at once base and venomous? Was it crime? Was it justice? Within myself I felt the will—the spirit that might bless mankind. I lacked the means to accomplish the will and wing the spirit. One deed supplied me with the means. Had the victim of that deed been a man moderately good—pursuing with even steps the narrow line between vice and virtue—blessing none but offending none,—it might have been yet a question whether mankind would not gain more by the deed than lose. But here was one whose steps stumbled on no good act—whose heart beat to no generous emotion;—there was a blot—a foulness on creation,—nothing but death could wash it out and leave the world fair. The soldier receives his pay, and murthers, and sleeps sound, and men applaud. But you say he smites not for pay, but glory. Granted—though a sophism. But was there no glory to be gained in fields more magnificent than those of war—no glory to be gained in the knowledge which saves and not destroys? Was I not about to strike for that glory, for the means of earning it? Nay, suppose the soldier struck for patriotism, a better feeling than glory, would not my motive be yet larger than patriotism? Did it not body forth a broader circle? Could the world stop the bound of its utilities? Was there a corner of the earth—was there a period in time, which an ardent soul, freed from, not chained as now, by the cares of the body, and given wholly up to wisdom, might not pierce, vivify, illumine? Such were the questions which I asked:—time only answered them.

"Houseman came, punctual to our dark appointment. I gave him my hand in silence. We understood each other. We said no more of the deed itself, but of the manner in which it should be done. The melancholy incident I have described made Clarke yet more eager to leave the town. He had settled with Houseman that he would abscond that very night, not wait for the next, as at first he had intended. His jewels and property were put in a small compass. He had arranged that he would, towards midnight or later, quit his lodging; and about a mile from the town, Houseman had engaged to have a chaise in readiness. For this service Clarke had promised Houseman a reward, with which the latter appeared contented. It was arranged that I should meet Houseman and Clarke at a certain spot in their way from the town, and there—! Houseman appeared at first fearful, lest I should relent and waver in my purpose. It is never so with men whose thoughts are deep and strong. To resolve was the arduous step—once resolved, and I cast not a look behind. Houseman left me for the present. I could not rest in my chamber. I went forth and walked about the town; the night deepened—I saw the lights in each house withdrawn, one by one, and at length all was hushed—Silence and Sleep kept court over the abodes of men. That stillness—that quiet—that sabbath from care and toil—how deeply it sank into my heart! Nature never seemed to me to make so dread a pause. I felt as if I and my intended victim had been left alone in the world. I had wrapped myself above fear into a high and preternatural madness of mind. I looked on the deed I was about to commit as a great and solemn sacrifice to Knowledge, whose Priest I was. The very silence breathed to me of a stern and awful sanctity—the repose, not of the charnel-house, but the altar. I heard the clock strike hour after hour, but I neither faltered nor grew impatient. My mind lay hushed in its design.

"The Moon came out, but with a pale and sickly countenance. Winter was around the earth; the snow, which had been falling towards eve, lay deep upon the ground; and the Frost seemed to lock the Universal Nature into the same calm and deadness which had taken possession of my soul.

"Houseman was to have come to me at midnight, just before Clarke left his house, but it was nearly two hours after that time ere he arrived. I was then walking to and fro before my own door; I saw that he was not alone, but with Clarke. 'Ha!' said he, 'this is fortunate, I see you are just going home. You were engaged, I recollect, at some distance from the town, and have, I suppose, just returned. Will you admit Mr. Clarke and myself for a short time—for to tell you the truth,' said he, in a lower voice—'The watchman is about, and we must not be seen by him! I have told Clarke that he may trust you, we are relatives!'

"Clarke, who seemed strangely credulous and indifferent, considering the character of his associate,—but those whom fate destroys she first blinds, made the same request in a careless tone, assigning the same cause. Unwillingly, I opened the door and admitted them. We went up to my chamber. Clarke spoke with the utmost unconcern of the fraud he purposed, and with a heartlessness that made my veins boil, of the poor victim his brutality had destroyed. All this was as iron bands round my purpose. They stayed for nearly an hour, for the watchman remained some time in that beat—and then Houseman asked me to accompany them a little way out of the town. Clarke seconded the request. We walked forth; the rest—why need I repeat? Houseman lied in the court; my hand struck—but not the death-blow: yet, from that hour, I have never given that right hand in pledge of love or friendship—the curse of memory has clung to it.

"We shared our booty; mine I buried, for the present. Houseman had dealings with a gipsy hag, and through her aid removed his share, at once, to London. And now, mark what poor strugglers we are in the eternal web of destiny! Three days after that deed, a relation who neglected me in life, died, and left me wealth!—wealth at least to me!—Wealth, greater than that for which I had...! The news fell on me as a thunderbolt. Had I waited but three little days! Great God! when they told me,—I thought I heard the devils laugh out at the fool who had boasted wisdom! Tell me not now of our free will—we are but the things of a never-swerving, an everlasting Necessity!—pre-ordered to our doom—bound to a wheel that whirls us on till it touches the point at which we are crushed! Had I waited but three days, three little days!—Had but a dream been sent me, had but my heart cried within me,—'Thou hast suffered long, tarry yet!' [Note: Aram has hitherto been suffered to tell his own tale without comment or interruption. The chain of reasonings, the metaphysical labyrinth of defence and motive, which he wrought around his act, it was, in justice to him, necessary to give at length, in order to throw a clearer light on his character—and lighten, perhaps, in some measure the heinousness of his crime. No moral can be more impressive than that which teaches how man can entangle himself in his own sophisms—that moral is better, viewed aright, than volumes of homilies. But here I must pause for one moment, to bid the reader mark, that that event which confirmed Aram in the bewildering doctrines of his fatalism, ought rather to inculcate the Divine virtue—the foundation of all virtues, Heathen or Christian—that which Epictetus made clear, and Christ sacred—FORTITUDE. The reader will note, that the answer to the reasonings that probably convinced the mind of Aram, and blinded him to his crime, may be found in the change of feelings by which the crime was followed. I must apologize for this interruption—it seemed to me advisable in this place;—though, in general, the moment we begin to inculcate morality as a science, we ought to discard moralizing as a method.] No, it was for this, for the guilt and its penance, for the wasted life and the shameful death—with all my thirst for good, my dreams of glory—that I was born, that I was marked from my first sleep in the cradle!

"The disappearance of Clarke of course created great excitement;—those whom he had over-reached had naturally an interest in discovering him. Some vague surmises that he might have been made away with, were rumoured abroad. Houseman and I, owing to some concurrence of circumstance, were examined,—not that suspicion attached to me before or after the examination. That ceremony ended in nothing. Houseman did not betray himself; and I, who from a boy had mastered my passions, could master also the nerves, which are the passions' puppets: but I read in the face of the woman with whom I lodged, that I was suspected. Houseman told me that she had openly expressed her suspicion to him; nay, he entertained some design against her life, which he naturally abandoned on quitting the town. This he did soon afterwards. I did not linger long behind him. I dug up my jewels,—I concealed them about me, and departed on foot to Scotland. There I converted my booty into money. And now I was above want—was I at rest? Not yet. I felt urged on to wander—Cain's curse descends to Cain's children. I travelled for some considerable time,—I saw men and cities, and I opened a new volume in my kind. It was strange; but before the deed, I was as a child in the ways of the world, and a child, despite my knowledge, might have duped me. The moment after it, a light broke upon me,—it seemed as if my eyes were touched with a charm, and rendered capable of piercing the hearts of men! Yes, it was a charm—a new charm—it was Suspicion! I now practised myself in the use of arms,—they made my sole companions. Peaceful, as I seemed to the world, I felt there was that eternally within me with which the world was at war.

"I do not deceive you. I did not feel what men call remorse! Having once convinced myself that I had removed from the earth a thing that injured and soiled its tribes,—that I had in crushing one worthless life, but without crushing one virtue—one feeling—one thought that could benefit others, strode to a glorious end;—having once convinced myself of this, I was not weak enough to feel a vague remorse for a deed I would not allow, in my case, to be a crime. I did not feel remorse, but I felt regret. The thought that had I waited three days I might have been saved, not from guilt, but from the chance of shame,—from the degradation of sinking to Houseman's equal—of feeling that man had the power to hurt me—that I was no longer above the reach of human malice, or human curiosity—that I was made a slave to my own secret—that I was no longer lord of my heart, to shew or to conceal it—that at any hour, in the possession of honours, by the hearth of love, I might be dragged forth and proclaimed a murderer—that I held my life, my reputation, at the breath of accident—that in the moment I least dreamed of, the earth might yield its dead, and the gibbet demand its victim;—this could I feel—all this—and not make a spectre of the past:—a spectre that walked by my side—that slept at my bed—that rose from my books—that glided between me and the stars of heaven, that stole along the flowers, and withered their sweet breath—that whispered in my ear, 'Toil, fool, and be wise; the gift of wisdom is to place us above the reach of fortune, but thou art her veriest minion!' Yes; I paused at last from my wanderings, and surrounded myself with books, and knowledge became once more to me what it had been, a thirst; but not what it had been, a reward. I occupied my thoughts—I laid up new hoards within my mind—I looked around, and I saw few whose stores were like my own,—but where, with the passion for wisdom still alive within me—where was that once more ardent desire which had cheated me across so dark a chasm between youth and manhood—between past and present life—the desire of applying that wisdom to the service of mankind? Gone—dead—buried for ever in my bosom, with the thousand dreams that had perished before it! When the deed was done, mankind seemed suddenly to have grown my foes. I looked upon them with other eyes. I knew that I carried within, that secret which, if bared to-day, would make them loath and hate me,—yea, though I coined my future life into one series of benefits on them and their posterity! Was not this thought enough to quell my ardour—to chill activity into rest? The more I might toil, the brighter honours I might win—the greater services I might bestow on the world, the more dread and fearful might be my fall at last! I might be but piling up the scaffold from which I was to be hurled! Possessed by these thoughts, a new view of human affairs succeeded to my old aspirings;—the moment a man feels that an object has ceased to charm, he reconciles himself by reasonings to his loss. 'Why,' said I; 'why flatter myself that I can serve—that I can enlighten mankind? Are we fully sure that individual wisdom has ever, in reality, done so? Are we really better because Newton lived, and happier because Bacon thought?' This dampening and frozen line of reflection pleased the present state of my mind more than the warm and yearning enthusiasm it had formerly nourished. Mere worldly ambition from a boy I had disdained;—the true worth of sceptres and crowns—the inquietude of power—the humiliations of vanity—had never been disguised from my sight. Intellectual ambition had inspired me. I now regarded it equally as a delusion. I coveted light solely for my own soul to bathe in. I would have drawn down the Promethean fire; but I would no longer have given to man what it was in the power of circumstance alone (which I could control not) to make his enlightener or his ruin—his blessing or his curse. Yes, I loved—I love still;—could I live for ever, I should for ever love knowledge! It is a companion—a solace—a pursuit—a Lethe. But, no more!—oh! never more for me was the bright ambition that makes knowledge a means, not end. As, contrary to the vulgar notion, the bee is said to gather her honey unprescient of the winter, labouring without a motive, save the labour, I went on, year after year, hiving all that the earth presented to my toils, and asking not to what use. I had rushed into a dread world, that I might indulge a dream. Lo! the dream was fled; but I could not retrace my steps.

"Rest now became to me the sole to kalon—the sole charm of existence. I grew enamoured of the doctrine of those old mystics, who have placed happiness only in an even and balanced quietude. And where but in utter loneliness was that quietude to be enjoyed? I no longer wondered that men in former times, when consumed by the recollection of some haunting guilt, fled to the desert and became hermits. Tranquillity and Solitude are the only soothers of a memory deeply troubled—light griefs fly to the crowd—fierce thoughts must battle themselves to rest. Many years had flown, and I had made my home in many places. All that was turbulent, if not all that was unquiet, in my recollections, had died away. Time had lulled me into a sense of security. I breathed more freely. I sometimes stole from the past. Since I had quitted Knaresbro' chance had thrown it in my power frequently to serve my brethren—not by wisdom, but by charity or courage—by individual acts that it soothed me to remember. If the grand aim of enlightening a world was gone—if to so enlarged a benevolence had succeeded apathy or despair, still the man, the human man, clung to my heart—still was I as prone to pity—as prompt to defend—as glad to cheer, whenever the vicissitudes of life afforded me the occasion; and to poverty, most of all, my hand never closed. For oh! what a terrible devil creeps into that man's soul, who sees famine at his door! One tender act and how many black designs, struggling into life within, you may crush for ever! He who deems the world his foe, convince him that he has one friend, and it is like snatching a dagger from his hand!

"I came to a beautiful and remote part of the country. Walter Lester, I came to Grassdale!—the enchanting scenery around—the sequestered and deep retirement of the place arrested me at once. 'And among these valleys,' I said, 'will I linger out the rest of my life, and among these quiet graves shall mine be dug, and my secret shall die with me!'

"I rented the lonely house in which I dwelt when you first knew me—thither I transported my books and instruments of science. I formed new projects in the vast empire of wisdom, and a deep quiet, almost amounting to content, fell like a sweet sleep upon my soul!

"In this state of mind, the most free from memory and from the desire to pierce the future that I had known for twelve years, I first saw Madeline Lester. Even with that first time a sudden and heavenly light seemed to dawn upon me. Her face—its still—its serene—its touching beauty, shone upon me like a vision. My heart warmed as I saw it—my pulse seemed to wake from its even slowness. I was young once more. Young! the youth, the freshness, the ardour—not of the frame only, but of the soul. But I then only saw, or spoke to her—scarce knew her—not loved her—nor was it often that we met. When we did so, I felt haunted, as by a holy spirit, for the rest of the day—an unquiet yet delicious emotion agitated all within—the south wind stirred the dark waters of my mind, but it passed, and all became hushed again. It was not for two years from the time we first saw each other, that accident brought us closely together. I pass over the rest. We loved! Yet oh what struggles were mine during the progress of that love! How unnatural did it seem to me to yield to a passion that united me with my kind; and as I loved her more, how far more urgent grew my fear of the future! That which had almost slept before awoke again to terrible life. The soil that covered the past might be riven, the dead awake, and that ghastly chasm separate me for ever from HER! What a doom, too, might I bring upon that breast which had begun so confidingly to love me! Often—often I resolved to fly—to forsake her—to seek some desert spot in the distant parts of the world, and never to be betrayed again into human emotions! But as the bird flutters in the net, as the hare doubles from its pursuers, I did but wrestle—I did but trifle—with an irresistible doom. Mark how strange are the coincidences of fate—fate that gives us warnings and takes away the power to obey them—the idle prophetess—the juggling fiend! On the same evening that brought me acquainted with Madeline Lester, Houseman, led by schemes of fraud and violence into that part of the country, discovered and sought me! Imagine my feelings, when in the hush of night I opened the door of my lonely home to his summons, and by the light of that moon which had witnessed so never-to-be-forgotten a companionship between us, beheld my accomplice in murder after the lapse of so many years. Time and a course of vice had changed and hardened, and lowered his nature; and in the power, at the will of that nature, I beheld myself abruptly placed. He passed that night under my roof. He was poor. I gave him what was in my hands. He promised to leave that part of England—to seek me no more.

"The next day I could not bear my own thoughts, the revulsion was too sudden, too full of turbulent, fierce, torturing emotions; I fled for a short relief to the house to which Madeline's father had invited me. But in vain I sought, by wine, by converse, by human voices, human kindness, to fly the ghost that had been raised from the grave of time. I soon returned to my own thoughts. I resolved to wrap myself once more in the solitude of my heart. But let me not repeat what I have said before, somewhat prematurely, in my narrative. I resolved—I struggled in vain, Fate had ordained, that the sweet life of Madeline Lester should wither beneath the poison tree of mine. Houseman sought me again, and now came on the humbling part of crime, its low calculations, its poor defence, its paltry trickery, its mean hypocrisy! They made my chiefest penance! I was to evade, to beguile, to buy into silence, this rude and despised ruffian. No matter now to repeat how this task was fulfilled; I surrendered nearly my all, on the condition of his leaving England for ever: not till I thought that condition already fulfilled, till the day had passed on which he should have left England, did I consent to allow Madeline's fate to be irrevocably woven with mine. Fool that I was, as if laws could bind us closer than love had done already.

"How often, when the soul sins, are her loftiest feelings punished through her lowest! To me, lone, rapt, for ever on the wing to unearthly speculation, galling and humbling was it indeed, to be suddenly called from the eminence of thought, to barter, in pounds and pence, for life, and with one like Houseman. These are the curses that deepen the tragedy of life, by grinding down our pride. But I wander back to what I have before said. I was to marry Madeline,—I was once more poor, but want did not rise before me; I had succeeded in obtaining the promise of a competence from one whom you know. For that I had once forced from my kind, I asked now, but not with the spirit of the beggar, but of the just claimant, and in that spirit it was granted. And now I was really happy; Houseman I believed removed for ever from my path; Madeline was about to be mine: I surrendered myself to love, and blind and deluded, I wandered on, and awoke on the brink of that precipice into which I am about to plunge. You know the rest. But oh! what now was my horror! It had not been a mere worthless, isolated unit in creation that I had blotted out of the sum of life. I had shed the blood of his brother whose child was my betrothed! Mysterious avenger—weird and relentless fate! How, when I deemed myself the farthest from her, had I been sinking into her grasp! Mark, young man, there is a moral here that few preachers can teach thee! Mark. Men rarely violate the individual rule in comparison to their violation of general rules. It is in the latter that we deceive by sophisms which seem truths. In the individual instance it was easy for me to deem that I had committed no crime. I had destroyed a man, noxious to the world; with the wealth by which he afflicted society I had been the means of blessing many; in the individual consequences mankind had really gained by my deed; the general consequence I had overlooked till now, and now it flashed upon me. The scales fell from my eyes, and I knew myself for what I was! All my calculations were dashed to the ground at once, for what had been all the good I had proposed to do—the good I had done—compared to the anguish I now inflicted on your house? Was your father my only victim? Madeline, have I not murdered her also? Lester, have I not shaken the sands in his glass? You, too, have I not blasted the prime and glory of your years? How incalculable—how measureless—how viewless the consequences of one crime, even when we think we have weighed them all with scales that would have turned with a hair's weight! Yes; before I had felt no remorse. I felt it now. I had acknowledged no crime, and now crime seemed the essence itself of my soul. The Theban's fate, which had seemed to the men of old the most terrible of human destinies, was mine. The crime—the discovery—the irremediable despair—hear me, as the voice of a man who is on the brink of a world, the awful nature of which Reason cannot pierce—hear me! when your heart tempts to some wandering from the line allotted to the rest of men, and whispers 'This may be crime in others, but is not so in thee'—tremble; cling fast, fast to the path you are lured to leave. Remember me!

"But in this state of mind I was yet forced to play the hypocrite. Had I been alone in the world—had Madeline and Lester not been to me what they were, I might have avowed my deed and my motives—I might have spoken out to the hearts of men—I might have poured forth the gloomy tale of reasonings and of temptings, in which we lose sense, and become the archfiend's tools! But while their eyes were on me; while their lives and hearts were set on my acquittal, my struggle against truth was less for myself than them. For them I girded up my soul, a villain I was; and for them, a bold, a crafty, a dexterous, villain I became! My defence fulfilled its end: Madeline died without distrusting the innocence of him she loved. Lester, unless you betray me, will die in the same belief. In truth, since the arts of hypocrisy have been commenced, the pride of consistency would have made it sweet to me to leave the world in a like error, or at least in doubt. For you I conquer that desire, the proud man's last frailty. And now my tale is done. From what passes at this instant within my heart, I lift not the veil! Whether beneath, be despair, or hope, or fiery emotions, or one settled and ominous calm, matters not. My last hours shall not belie my life: on the verge of death I will not play the dastard, and tremble at the Dim Unknown. The thirst, the dream, the passion of my youth, yet lives; and burns to learn the sublime and shaded mysteries that are banned Mortality. Perhaps I am not without a hope that the Great and Unseen Spirit, whose emanation within me I have nursed and worshipped, though erringly and in vain, may see in his fallen creature one bewildered by his reason rather than yielding to his vices. The guide I received from Heaven betrayed me, and I was lost; but I have not plunged wittingly from crime to crime. Against one guilty deed, some good, and much suffering may be set: and, dim and afar off from my allotted bourne, I may behold in her glorious home the starred face of her who taught me to love, and who, even there, could scarce be blessed without shedding the light of her divine forgiveness upon me. Enough! ere you break this seal, my doom rests not with man nor earth. The burning desires I have known—the resplendent visions I have nursed—the sublime aspirings that have lifted me so often from sense and clay—these tell me, that, whether for good or ill—I am the thing of an Immortality, and the creature of a God! As men of the old wisdom drew their garments around their face, and sat down collectedly to die, I wrap myself in the settled resignation of a soul firm to the last, and taking not from man's vengeance even the method of its dismissal. The courses of my life I swayed with my own hand: from my own hand shall come the manner and moment of my death!

"Eugene Aram."

On the day after that evening in which Aram had given the above confession to Walter Lester;—on the day of execution, when they entered the condemned cell, they found the prisoner lying on the bed; and when they approached to take off the irons, they found, that he neither stirred nor answered to their call. They attempted to raise him, and he then uttered some words in a faint voice. They perceived that he was covered with blood. He had opened his veins in two places in the arm with a sharp instrument he had some time since concealed. A surgeon was instantly sent for, and by the customary applications the prisoner in some measure was brought to himself. Resolved not to defraud the law of its victim, they bore him, though he appeared unconscious of all around, to the fatal spot. But when he arrived at that dread place, his sense suddenly seemed to return. He looked hastily round the throng that swayed and murmured below, and a faint flush rose to his cheek: he cast his eyes impatiently above, and breathed hard and convulsively. The dire preparations were made, completed; but the prisoner drew back for an instant—was it from mortal fear? He motioned to the Clergyman to approach, as if about to whisper some last request in his ear. The clergyman bowed his head,—there was a minute's awful pause—Aram seemed to struggle as for words, when, suddenly throwing himself back, a bright triumphant smile flashed over his whole face. With that smile, the haughty Spirit passed away, and the law's last indignity was wreaked upon a breathless corpse!

CHAPTER VIII.

AND LAST. THE TRAVELLER'S RETURN.—THE COUNTRY VILLAGE ONCE MORE VISITED;—ITS INHABITANTS.—THE REMEMBERED BROOK.—THE DESERTED MANOR-HOUSE.—THE CHURCHYARD.—THE TRAVELLER RESUMES HIS JOURNEY.—THE COUNTRY TOWN.—A MEETING OF TWO LOVERS AFTER LONG ABSENCE AND MUCH SORROW.—CONCLUSION.

"The lopped tree in time may grow again,
Most naked plants renew both fruit and flower;
The sorriest wight may find release from pain,
The driest soil suck in some moistening shower:
Time goes by turns, and chances change by course
From foul to fair."
—Robert Southwell, the Jesuit.

Sometimes towards the end of a gloomy day, the sun before but dimly visible, breaks suddenly out, and clothes the landscape with a smile; then beneath your eye, which during the clouds and sadness of day, had sought only the chief features of the prospect around, (some grey hill, or rising spire, or sweeping wood,) the less prominent, yet not less lovely features of the scene, mellow forth into view; over them, perhaps, the sun sets with a happier and richer glow than over the rest of Nature; and thus they leave upon your mind its last grateful impression, and console you for the gloom and sadness which the parting light they catch and reflect, dispels.

Just so in our tale; it continues not in cloud and sorrow to the last; some little ray breaks forth at the close; in that ray, characters which before received but a slight portion of the interest that prouder and darker ones engrossed, are thrown into light, and cheer from the mind of him who hath watched and tarried with us till now,—we will not say all the sadness that may perhaps linger on his memory,—and yet something of the gloom.

It was some years after the date of the last event we have recorded, and it was a fine warm noon in the happy month of May, when a horseman was slowly riding through the long—straggling—village of Grassdale. He was a man, though in the prime of youth, (for he might yet want some two years of thirty,) that bore the steady and earnest air of one who has seen not sparingly of the world; his eye keen but tranquil, his sunburnt though handsome features, which either exertion or thought, or care, had despoiled of the roundness of their early contour, leaving the cheek somewhat sunken, and the lines somewhat marked, were impressed with a grave, and at that moment with a melancholy and soft expression; and now, as his horse proceeded slowly through the green lane, which in every vista gave glimpses of rich verdant valleys, the sparkling river, or the orchard ripe with the fragrant blossoms of spring; his gaze lost the calm expression it habitually wore, and betrayed how busily Remembrance was at work. The dress of the horseman was of foreign fashion, and at that day, when the garb still denoted the calling, sufficiently military to show the profession he had belonged to. And well did the garb become the short dark moustache, the sinewy chest and length of limb of the young horseman: recommendations, the two latter, not despised in the court of the great Frederic of Prussia, in whose service he had borne arms. He had commenced his career in that battle terminating in the signal defeat of the bold Daun, when the fortunes of that gallant general paled at last before the star of the greatest of modern kings. The peace of 1763 had left Prussia in the quiet enjoyment of the glory she had obtained, and the young Englishman took the advantage it afforded him of seeing as a traveller, not despoiler, the rest of Europe.

The adventure and the excitement of travel pleased and left him even now uncertain whether or not his present return to England would be for long. He had not been a week returned, and to this part of his native country he had hastened at once.

He checked his horse as he now past the memorable sign, that yet swung before the door of Peter Dealtry; and there, under the shade of the broad tree, now budding into all its tenderest verdure, a pedestrian wayfarer sate enjoying the rest and coolness of his shelter. Our horseman cast a look at the open door, across which, in the bustle of housewifery, female forms now and then glanced and vanished, and presently he saw Peter himself saunter forth to chat with the traveller beneath his tree. And Peter Dealtry was the same as ever, only he seemed perhaps shorter and thinner than of old, as if Time did not so much break as wear mine host's slender person gradually away.

The horseman gazed for a moment, but observing Peter return the gaze, he turned aside his head, and putting his horse into a canter, soon passed out of cognizance of the Spotted Dog.

He now came in sight of the neat white cottage of the old Corporal, and there, leaning over the pale, a crutch under one arm, and his friendly pipe in one corner of his shrewd mouth, was the Corporal himself. Perched upon the railing in a semi-doze, the ears down, the eyes closed, sat a large brown cat: poor Jacobina, it was not thyself! death spares neither cat nor king; but thy virtues lived in thy grandchild; and thy grandchild, (as age brings dotage,) was loved even more than thee by the worthy Corporal. Long may thy race flourish, for at this day it is not extinct. Nature rarely inflicts barrenness on the feline tribe; they are essentially made for love, and love's soft cares, and a cat's lineage outlives the lineage of kaisars.

At the sound of hoofs the Corporal turned his head, and he looked long and wistfully at the horseman, as, relaxing his horse's pace into a walk, our traveller rode slowly on.

"'Fore George," muttered the Corporal, "a fine man—a very fine man; 'bout my inches—augh!"

A smile, but a very faint smile, crossed the lip of the horseman, as he gazed on the figure of the stalwart Corporal.

"He eyes me hard," thought he; "yet he does not seem to remember me. I must be greatly changed. 'Tis fortunate, however, that I am not recognised: fain, indeed, at this time, would I come and go unnoticed and alone."

The horseman fell into a reverie, which was broken by the murmur of the sunny rivulet, fretting over each little obstacle it met, the happy and spoiled child of Nature! That murmur rang on the horseman's ear like a voice from his boyhood, how familiar was it, how dear! No tone of music—no haunting air, ever recalled so rushing a host of memories and associations as that simple, restless, everlasting sound! Everlasting!—all had changed,—the trees had sprung up or decayed,—some cottages around were ruins,—some new and unfamiliar ones supplied their place, and on the stranger himself—on all those whom the sound recalled to his heart, Time had been, indeed, at work, but with the same exulting bound and happy voice that little brook leaped along its way. Ages hence, may the course be as glad, and the murmur as full of mirth! They are blessed things, those remote and unchanging streams!—they fill us with the same love as if they were living creatures!—and in a green corner of the world there is one that, for my part, I never see without forgetting myself to tears—tears that I would not lose for a king's ransom; tears that no other sight or sound could call from their source; tears of what affection, what soft regret; tears that leave me for days afterwards, a better and a kinder man!

The traveller, after a brief pause, continued his road; and now he came full upon the old Manorhouse. The weeds were grown up in the garden, the mossed paling was broken in many places, the house itself was shut up, and the sun glanced on the deep-sunk casements without finding its way into the desolate interior. High above the old hospitable gate hung a board, announcing that the house was for sale, and referring the curious, or the speculating, to the attorney of the neighbouring town. The horseman sighed heavily, and muttered to himself; then turning up the road that led to the back entrance, he came into the court-yard, and leading his horse into an empty stable, he proceeded on foot through the dismantled premises, pausing with every moment, and holding a sad and ever-changing commune with himself. An old woman, a stranger to him, was the sole inmate of the house, and imagining he came to buy, or at least, examine, she conducted him through the house, pointing out its advantages, and lamenting its dilapidated state. Our traveller scarcely heard her,—but when he came to one room which he would not enter till the last, (it was the little parlour in which the once happy family had been wont to sit,) he sank down in the chair that had been Lester's honoured seat, and covering his face with his hands, did not move or look up for several moments. The old woman gazed at him with surprise.—"Perhaps, Sir, you knew the family, they were greatly beloved."

The traveller did not answer; but when he rose, he muttered to himself,—"No, the experiment is made in vain! Never, never could I live here again—it must be so—my forefathers' house must pass into a stranger's hands." With this reflection he hurried from the house, and re-entering the garden, turned through a little gate that swung half open on its shattered hinges, and led into the green and quiet sanctuaries of the dead. The same touching character of deep and undisturbed repose that hallows the country church-yard,—and that more than most— yet brooded there as when, years ago, it woke his young mind to reflection then unmingled with regret.

He passed over the rude mounds of earth that covered the deceased poor, and paused at a tomb of higher, though but of simple pretensions; it was not yet discoloured by the dews and seasons, and the short inscription traced upon it was strikingly legible, in comparison with those around.

```
            Rowland Lester,
         Obiit 1760, aet. 64.
Blessed are they that mourn, for they shall be comforted.
```

By that tomb the traveller remained in undisturbed contemplation for some time, and when he turned, all the swarthy colour had died from his cheek, his eyes were dim, and the wonted pride of a young man's step and a soldier's bearing, was gone from his mien.

As he looked up, his eye caught afar, embedded among the soft verdure of the spring, one lone and grey house, from whose chimney there rose no smoke—sad, inhospitable, dismantled as that beside which he now stood;—as if the curse which had fallen on the inmates of either mansion, still clung to either roof. One hasty glance only, the traveller gave to the solitary and distant abode,—and then started and quickened his pace.

On re-entering the stables, the traveller found the Corporal examining his horse from head to foot with great care and scrupulosity.

"Good hoofs too, humph!" quoth the Corporal, as he released the front leg; and, turning round, saw, with some little confusion, the owner of the steed he had been honouring with so minute a survey. "Oh,—augh! looking at the beastie, Sir, lest it might have cast a shoe. Thought your honour might want some intelligent person to shew you the premises, if so be you have come to buy; nothing but an old 'oman there; dare say your honour does not like old 'omen—augh!"

"The owner is not in these parts?" said the horseman.

"No, over seas, Sir; a fine young gentleman, but hasty; and—and—but Lord bless me! sure—no, it can't be—yes, now you turn—it is—it is my young master!" So saying, the old Corporal, roused into affection, hobbled up to the wanderer, and seized and kissed his hand. "Ah, Sir, we shall be glad, indeed, to see you back after such doings. But's all forgotten now, and gone by—augh! Poor Miss Ellinor, how happy she'll be to see your honour. Ah! how she be changed, surely!"

"Changed; ay, I make no doubt! What! does she look in weak health?"

"No; as to that, your honour, she be winsome enough still," quoth the Corporal, smacking his lips; "I seed her the week afore last, when I went over to—, for I suppose you knows as she lives there, all alone like, in a small house, with a green rail afore it, and a brass knocker on the door, at top of the town, with a fine view of the—hills in front? Well, Sir, I seed her, and mighty handsome she looked, though a little thinner than she was; but, for all that, she be greatly changed."

"How! for the worse?"

"For the worse, indeed," answered the Corporal, assuming an air of melancholy and grave significance; "she be grown religious, Sir, think of that—augh—bother—whaugh!"

"Is that all?" said Walter, relieved, and with a slight smile. "And she lives alone?"

"Quite, poor young lady, as if she had made up her mind to be an old maid; though I know as how she refused Squire Knyvett of the Grange waiting for your honour's return, mayhap!"

"Lead out the horse, Bunting; but stay, I am sorry to see you with a crutch; what's the cause? no accident, I trust?"

"Merely rheumatics—will attack the youngest of us; never been quite myself since I went a travelling with your honour—augh!—without going to Lunnon arter all. But I shall be stronger next year, I dare to say—!"

"I hope you will, Bunting. And Miss Lester lives alone, you say?"

"Ay; and for all she be so religious, the poor about do bless her very footsteps. She does a power of good; she gave me half-a-guinea, your honour; an excellent young lady, so sensible like!"

"Thank you; I can tighten the girths!—so!—there, Bunting, there's something for old companion's sake."

"Thank your honour; you be too good, always was—baugh! But I hopes your honour be a coming to live here now; 'twill make things smile agin!"

"No, Bunting, I fear not," said Walter, spurring through the gates of the yard; "Good day."

"Augh, then," cried the Corporal, hobbling breathlessly after him, "if so be as I shan't see your honour agin, at which I am extramely consarned, will your honour recollect your promise, touching the 'tato ground? The steward, Master Bailey, 'od rot him, has clean forgot it—augh!"

"The same old man, Bunting, eh? Well, make your mind easy, it shall be done."

"Lord bless your honour's good heart; thankye; and—and"—laying his hand on the bridle—"your honour did say, the bit cot should be rent-free. You see, your honour," quoth the Corporal, drawing up with a grave smile, "I may marry some day or other, and have a large family; and the rent won't sit so easy then—augh!"

"Let go the rein, Bunting—and consider your house rent-free."

"And, your honour—and—"

But Walter was already in a brisk trot; and the remaining petitions of the Corporal died in empty air.

"A good day's work, too," muttered Jacob, hobbling homeward. "What a green un 'tis still! Never be a man of the world—augh!"

For two hours Walter did not relax the rapidity of his pace; and when he did so at the descent of a steep hill, a small country town lay before him, the sun glittering on its single spire, and lighting up the long, clean, centre street, with the good old-fashioned garden stretching behind each house, and detached cottages around, peeping forth here and there from the blossoms and verdure of the young may. He rode into the yard of the principal inn, and putting up his horse, inquired in a tone that he persuaded himself was the tone of indifference, for Miss Lester's house.

"John," said the landlady, (landlord there was none,) summoning a little boy of about ten years old—"run on, and shew this gentleman the good lady's house: and—stay—his honour will excuse you a moment—just take up the nosegay you cut for her this morning: she loves flowers. Ah! Sir, an excellent young lady is Miss Lester," continued the hostess, as the boy ran back for the nosegay; "so charitable, so kind, so meek to all. Adversity, they say, softens some characters; but she must always have been good. And so religious, Sir, though so young! Well, God bless her! and that every one must say. My boy John, Sir, he is not eleven yet, come next August—a 'cute boy, calls her the good lady: we now always call her so here. Come, John, that's right. You stay to dine here, Sir? Shall I put down a chicken?"

At the farther extremity of the town stood Miss Lester's dwelling. It was the house in which her father had spent his last days; and there she had continued to reside, when left by his death to a small competence, which Walter, then abroad, had persuaded her, (for her pride was of the right kind,) to suffer him, though but slightly, to increase. It was a detached and small building, standing a little from the road; and Walter paused for some moments at the garden-gate, and gazed round him before he followed his young guide, who, tripping lightly up the gravel-walk to the door, rang the bell, and inquired if Miss Lester was within?

Walter was left for some moments alone in a little parlour:—he required those moments to recover himself from the past that rushed sweepingly over him. And was it—yes, it was Ellinor that now stood before him! Changed she was, indeed; the slight girl had budded into woman; changed she was, indeed; the bound had for ever left that step, once so elastic with hope; the vivacity of the quick, dark eye was soft and quiet; the rich colour had given place to a hue fainter, though not less lovely. But to repeat in verse what is poorly bodied forth in prose—

```
"And years had past, and thus they met again;
The wind had swept along the flower since then,
O'er her fair cheek a paler lustre spread,
As if the white rose triumphed o'er the red.
No more she walk'd exulting on the air;
Light though her step, there was a languour there;
No more—her spirit bursting from its bound,—
She stood, like Hebe, scattering smiles around."
```

"Ellinor!" said Walter mournfully, "thank God! we meet at last."

"That voice—that face—my cousin—my dear, dear Walter!"

All reserve—all consciousness fled in the delight of that moment; and Ellinor leant her head upon his shoulder, and scarcely felt the kiss that he pressed upon her lips.

"And so long absent!" said Ellinor, reproachfully.

"But did you not tell me that the blow that had fallen on our house had stricken from you all thoughts of love—had divided us for ever? And what, Ellinor, was England or home without you?"

"Ah!" said Ellinor, recovering herself, and a deep paleness succeeding to the warm and delighted flush that had been conjured to her cheek, "Do not revive the past—I have sought for years—long, solitary, desolate years, to escape from its dark recollections!"

"You speak wisely, dearest Ellinor; let us assist each other in doing so. We are alone in the world—let us unite our lot. Never, through all I have seen and felt,—in the starry nightwatch of camps—in the blaze of courts—by the sunny groves of Italy—in the deep forests of the Hartz—never have I forgotten you, my sweet and dear cousin. Your image has linked itself indissolubly with all I conceived of home and happiness, and a tranquil and peaceful future; and now I return, and see you, and find you changed, but, oh, how lovely! Ah, let us not part again! A consoler, a guide, a soother, father, brother, husband,—all this my heart whispers I could be to you!"

Ellinor turned away her face, but her heart was very full. The solitary years that had passed over her since they last met, rose up before her. The only living image that had mingled through those years with the dreams of the departed, was his who now knelt at her feet;—her sole friend—her sole relative—her first—her last love! Of all the world, he was the only one with whom she could recur to the past; on whom she might repose her bruised, but still unconquered affections.

And Walter knew by that blush—that sigh—that tear, that he was remembered—that he was beloved—that his cousin was his own at last!

"But before you end," said my friend, to whom I shewed the above pages, originally concluding my tale with the last sentence, "you must, it is a comfortable and orthodox old fashion, tell us a little about the fate of the other persons, to whom you have introduced us;—the wretch Houseman?"—

"True; in the mysterious course of mortal affairs, the greater villain had escaped, the more generous and redeemed one fallen. But though Houseman died without violence, died in his bed, as honest men die, we can scarcely believe that his life was not punishment enough. He lived in strict seclusion—the seclusion of poverty, and maintained himself by dressing flax. His life was several times attempted by the mob, for he was an object of universal execration and horror; and even ten years afterwards, when he died, his body was buried in secret at the dead of night, for the hatred of the world survived him!"

"And the Corporal, did he marry in his old age?"

"History telleth of one Jacob Bunting, whose wife, several years younger than himself, played him certain sorry pranks with the young curate of the parish: the said Jacob, knowing nothing thereof, but furnishing great objectation unto his neighbours, by boasting that he turned an excellent penny by selling poultry to his reverence above market prices,—'For Bessy, my girl, I'm a man of the world—augh!'"

"Contented! a suitable fate for the old dog—But Peter Dealtry?"

"Of Peter Dealtry know we nothing more, save that we have seen at Grassdale church-yard, a small tombstone inscribed to his memory, with the following sacred poesy thereto appended,—

```
"'We flourish, saith the holy text
One hour, and are cut down the next:
I was like grass but yesterday,
But Death has mowed me into hay.'"
```

"And his namesake, Sir Peter Grindlescrew Hales?"

"Went through a long life, honoured and respected, but met with domestic misfortunes in old age. His eldest son married a maid servant, and his youngest daughter—"

"Eloped with the groom?"

"By no means,—with a young spendthrift;—the very picture of what Sir Peter was in his youth: they were both disinherited, and Sir Peter died in the arms of his eight remaining children, seven of whom never forgave his memory for not being the eighth, viz. chief heir."

"And his cotemporary, John Courtland, the non-hypochondriac?"

"Died of sudden suffocation, as he was crossing Hounslow Heath."

"But Lord—?"

"Lived to a great age; his last days, owing to growing infirmities, were spent out of the world; every one pitied him,—it was the happiest time of his life!"

"Dame Darkmans?"

"Was found dead in her bed, from over fatigue, it was supposed, in making merry at the funeral of a young girl on the previous day."

"Well!—hem,—and so Walter and his cousin were really married; and did they never return to the old Manor-house?"

"No; the memory that is allied only to melancholy, grows sweet with years, and hallows the spot which it haunts; not so the memory allied to dread, terror, and something too of shame. Walter sold the property with some pangs of natural regret; after his marriage with Ellinor he returned abroad for some time, but finally settling in England, engaged in active life, and left to his posterity a name they still honour; and to his country, the memory of some services that will not lightly pass away."

But one dread and gloomy remembrance never forsook his mind, and exercised the most powerful influence over the actions and motives of his life. In every emergency, in every temptation, there rose to his eyes the fate of him so gifted, so noble in much, so formed for greatness in all things, blasted by one crime—self-sought, but self-denied; a crime, the offspring of bewildered reasonings—all the while speculating upon virtue. And that fate revealing the darker secrets of our kind, in which the true science of morals in chiefly found, taught him the twofold lesson, caution for himself, and charity for others. He knew henceforth that even the criminal is not all evil; the angel within us is not easily expelled; it survives sin, ay, and many sins, and leaves us sometimes in amaze and marvel, at the good that lingers round the heart even of the hardiest offender.

And Ellinor clung with more than revived affection to one with whose lot she was now allied. Walter was her last tie upon earth, and in him she learnt, day by day, more lavishly to treasure up her heart. Adversity and trial had ennobled the character of both; and she who had so long seen in her cousin all she could love, beheld now in her husband that greater and more enduring spell—all that she could venerate and admire. A certain religious fervour, in which, after the calamities of her family, she had indulged, continued with her to the last; but, (softened by human ties, and the reciprocation of earthly duties and affections,) it was fortunately preserved either from the undue enthusiasm or the undue austerity into which it would otherwise, in all likelihood, have merged. What remained, however, uniting her most cheerful thoughts with something serious, and the happiest moments of the present with the dim and solemn forecast of the future, elevated her nature, not depressed, and made itself visible rather in tender than in sombre, hues. And it was sweet when the thought of Madeline and her father came across her, to recur at once for consolation to that Heaven in which she believed their tears were dried, and their past sorrows but a forgotten dream! There is, indeed, a time of life when these reflections make our chief, though a melancholy, pleasure. As we grow older, and sometimes a hope, sometimes a friend, is shivered from our path, the thought of an immortality will press itself forcibly upon us! and there, by little and little, as the ant piles grain after grain, the garners of a future sustenance, we learn to carry our hopes, and harvest, as it were, our wishes.

Our cousins then were happy. Happy, for they loved one another entirely; and on those who do so love, I sometimes think, that, barring physical pain and extreme poverty, the ills of life fall with but idle malice. Yes, they were happy in spite of the past, and in defiance of the future.

"I am satisfied then," said my friend,—"and your tale is fairly done!"

And now, Reader, farewell! If, sometimes as thou hast gone with me to this our parting spot, thou hast suffered thy companion to win the mastery over thine interest, to flash now on thy convictions, to touch now thy heart, to guide thy hope, to excite thy anxiety, to gain even almost to the sources of thy tears—then is there a tie between thee and me which cannot readily be broken! And when thou hearest the malice that wrongs affect the candour which should judge, thou wilt be surprised to feel how unconsciously He who has, even in a tale, once wound himself around those feelings not daily excited, can find in thy sympathies the defence, or, in thy charity the indulgence,—of a friend!

Printed in Great Britain
by Amazon